MW01491465

Christmas Revels

FOUR REGENCY NOVELLAS

Kate Parker

Louisa Cornell

Anna D. Allen

Hannah Meredith

SPS

Singing Spring Press

This is a work of fiction. All names, characters, and incidents are the product of the author's imagination. Any resemblance to actual occurrences or persons, living or dead, is coincidental. Historical events and personages are fictionalized.

CHRISTMAS REVELS : FOUR REGENCY NOVELLAS

ISBN: 978-0-9895641-8-2 (Print)
ISBN: 978-0-9895641-9-9 (E-book)

Published by Singing Spring Press

Table of Contents

A Light in Winter
or
The Wicked Will

by

Anna D Allen

Part One

WITH OCTOBER SUNLIGHT POURING through the lead-paned window, Connor Grayson, the new Viscount Roxbury, sat in the dusty, paper-filled office of a country solicitor. The journey from Cornwall to the village of Roxbury in Derbyshire—by the wretched means of stage coach, no less—had exhausted him. But he had been patient and spent the night at the inn before calling upon the solicitor.

Connor had never expected any inheritance, let alone the title, but with the arrival of a single letter, he had instantly transformed from a deeply-in-debt estate manager to a peer of the realm. He felt no joy at his uncle's death—neither had he shed a tear—but the news brought a welcomed sigh of relief; a lifetime of difficulties solved as if by divine providence. A few more minutes were inconsequential.

"I now see why your uncle called you the red sheep of the family," said the short, elderly solicitor with silver-rimmed spectacles perched on the tip of his nose. He rummaged through the papers on his desk in search of the late viscount's will.

Self-conscious, Connor ran his fingers through his rust-colored hair, an inheritance from his late, and still lamented, mother. He sometimes thought if it were long and paired with a beard, he would look like some crazed Viking come to pillage fair England. This was probably exactly how his uncle had viewed Connor's Irish mother—just some wench from beyond the pale come to ensnare his younger brother with her silver tongue and long red tresses. Her pedigree as an earl's granddaughter failed to impress her husband's family. Her lack of fortune distressed them even more. Connor had the audacity—in his uncle's eyes—to be her very image, and the viscount had rejected the son as he had the mother, the father banished with them for the sin of poor judgment. All contact ceased from that moment.

"He didn't think much of you, did he?" the solicitor continued in a matter-of-fact but not unfriendly tone as his fingers flicked through stacks of paper. Without raising his head, he peered up over the rim of his spectacles at Connor. "You must excuse my bluntness. I'm paid to be honest."

The comment did not elicit any offense from Connor; it merely surprised him, and he wondered how much the solicitor knew about his relationship with his paternal family.

"No, he didn't," Connor quietly replied.

"Well. That, then, is in your favor. Couldn't abide the gentleman." He lowered his eyes and continued the search, all the while chatting. "Reeking of toilet water—

ghastly—and always jabbing people with his walking-stick to emphasize some point he was making. Every little thing displeased him—I could do no right in his eyes, nor could anyone else—and he forever looked as if he smelled something...." He glanced up and raised his eyebrows. "...*Disagreeable*. And that disagreeable thing being whomever had the misfortune to speak to him." He stood upright and addressed Connor directly. "And the way he treated my missus...."

A shout went up in the outer room.

"Found it, Mr. Thornhurst." The thin office clerk, waving a paper in the air, came bounding into the room.

"Ah, good," Mr. Thornhurst said taking the paper from him, "Thank you, Eaves."

All arms and legs, Eaves stood there smiling.

"Are you warm enough in here, my lord?" he asked Connor. "I could put some more coal on the fire."

My lord. There it was. Mr. Thornhurst had called Connor that when he had arrived moments earlier—the first person to do so, as Connor had informed no one of his real reason for leaving his employment and travelling to Roxbury. It was a shock to hear the words and then realize they referred to him and would for the rest of his life. Never one to tug his forelock—education and his father's name saved him from that ignominy—Connor had always worked in that twilight realm between gentleman and servant.

He was always treated respectably, as clearly he did not belong to the great unwashed, but his position caused some confusion, he knew, when the time came to compile guest lists. He had often imagined the discussions in the great houses of Cornwall: *Mr. Grayson? What next? Should we invite the governess, too? Cook, maybe? At that rate, we'll end up like France. Or even worse, like America, with no one knowing their place.*

Connor had known his place quite well. He oversaw everything, with the primary responsibility of producing revenue off the land for his employer... only without any of the privileges that came with that responsibility. Nor any of the pleasures, either. But now, he was a viscount, and while he would have many of the same responsibilities he was accustomed to, he would also have the privileges. He now owned the land. The income now belonged to him. And if he did not want to deal with those responsibilities, he could simply foist them off on his own estate manager.

But Connor knew he was not the kind of man to do that. His mind would not rest well if he did. He could never be the indolent country gentleman concerned with nothing but the quality of the hunting and the dishes at his table. He needed work.

"Thank you, Mr. Eaves," Connor said with a polite smile, "I am quite all right." But still Eaves hovered.

"I didn't think we'd ever find you," Eaves continued, "but Mr. Thornhurst never doubted, although finding you in Cornwall—an estate manager, no less— surprised him as much as it did me. We didn't even know you existed until his late lordship dictated the will...."

Connor felt uncertain and could not discern if the man merely behaved in a normal, friendly manner or if he were fawning all over him because of the title—as if now, somehow, Connor could secure him a place in Heaven. He supposed he would have to get used to it, as well as to the reverse, with people misjudging him and thinking ill of him simply because he held a title. Few would ever again judge him for himself. They'd know nothing of the loss of his mother, of his father's drinking and gambling, of the lack of prospects that had forced Connor to work as an estate manager on an elderly duke's remote and never-visited Cornwall estate. All that anyone would ever see now was a viscount.

With a wave of his hand, Mr. Thornhurst finally motioned the rambling Eaves from the room and sat down opposite Connor at the desk.

"Now, as I said in my letter," Mr. Thornhurst began, his eyes glancing down at the still-folded document, "the only thing entailed is Roxbury Hall. Have you been out to see it yet?" He looked up at Connor.

"No," Connor replied, "It was dark when I arrived last night, and I came straight here this morning." He had wanted to visit Roxbury Hall first. Any villager could have pointed the way. He could have stood there now, before his own house, on his own land, to manage and maintain and develop as he saw fit. *His.* He had wanted something of his own for so long, and now, he was almost afraid... afraid to hope... afraid it was not real... afraid there was some mistake soon corrected. Mr. Thornhurst's original letter to Connor had indicated a financial problem with the estate. So Connor had resisted the urge to visit the estate first in favor of confirmation and clarification of the inheritance.

"A crumbling wreck." Mr. Thornhurst referred to Roxbury Hall. "Knowing the late viscount, I'm surprised he didn't start pulling down the walls, given that he knew you were to inherit it. But the land is good, and with money and a good estate manager, it could be quite productive."

There it was. Money. Connor's constant problem. Ever since his father's death. Before his death, even.

"So it's true." He tried to sound straightforward and practical about the matter, even indifferent, so as not to reveal his disappointment. "The estate is insolvent."

"I'm afraid so. There's no money. Just the hall and the land."

Connor shrugged, trying to appear nonchalant, despite slowly realizing nothing had changed in his life. He was still responsible for everything. And still without money. "I didn't expect any of my uncle's money. Or his title, for that matter."

"The loss of his son was a shock. Only twenty-five." Mr. Thornhurst shook his head. "Such a shame. Still, I suppose some of the blame goes to Lord Roxbury, marrying as late as he did. Had only 'the heir,' and never the requisite 'spare.'"

Connor barely heard the man as the full implications settled down on him. He was a viscount—with responsibilities to tenants, neighbors, and the entire district—but without any money. Worse, with a mountain of debt. A growing nausea filled his stomach, and he spoke without thinking.

"This new inheritance has simply compounded my problems." And he began to confess the disgraceful details to Mr. Thornhurst. The solicitor took it all in without betraying the slightest hint of emotion—or judgment—but simply nodded his head from time to time while Connor explained his father's penchant for gambling. Had it been for trivial amounts, as Connor and his mother had always assumed, it would have been bearable. Instead, the figures exceeded anything the family could ever repay, and upon his father's death, Connor had inherited the whole mess. To date, he had managed to pay the ever-growing interest, but never did the payments touch the principle, which remained the same as the day his father died. At least the debt was owed to honorable men.

Mr. Thornhurst nodded his head and said, "As a viscount, of course, you cannot be thrown in debtors' prison. So there is that one consolation."

To Connor's surprise, that one consolation—a privilege of his newfound rank—afforded some minuscule sense of relief. At least he need not fear rotting away in some moldering cell with no way to earn a living while creditors demanded their money. That, he supposed, was something.

"And in regard to money, there may be a solution." Mr. Thornhurst held up the piece of paper and then began to unfold it. "Your uncle's will." He spread it out on the desk before him and peered down at the page. "There is a condition here where you might obtain your uncle's money: 'Marry Miss Katherine Woodbridge of Lilac Cottage in the village of Roxbury.... Should Miss Woodbridge die without issue or if my heir marries another lady, the money will pass to George Meynell and his heirs.'" Thornhurst looked up and said, "The late viscountess was a Meynell. This money was hers, to do with as her husband saw fit, of course. So it appears, the late Lord Roxbury intended for this money to return to his wife's family, unless you married Miss Katherine Woodbridge."

Connor thought he should be shocked, appalled by the idea of marrying a total stranger—at the command of his uncle, no less—all to gain money. But he wasn't. Whether it was because he had reached such a level of desperation or because he recognized the nobility often arranged marriages on mercenary grounds, he did not know. More likely, he thought, it was because he now at least had a solution to his problem. Provided, of course, the amount covered his needs.

Connor sat back and asked, "How much money are we talking about?"

Mr. Thornhurst read the figure—more than Connor could hope for, enough to cover the debts with plenty remaining to run Roxbury Hall and still live a life of leisure. The matter, it appeared, was decided.

"Then it seems clear that I simply have to marry this lady," Connor said with a deep breath and a sense of resolution, "assuming she is willing, and I will receive the money."

"Your uncle was not being generous with this clause," Thornhurst pointed out, handing Connor the will to look over. "Quite cruel, if you ask me."

"What is the problem?" Connor asked, reading the provision.

"Miss Woodbridge is eighty if she is a day," Thornhurst said, "a horrid woman who is only alive because neither God nor the Devil wish to deal with her."

Now, Connor understood completely. This was his uncle's last chance to cause further misery, his one last jab at the unwanted relation, and Connor felt all hope for a solution fading, anger quickly replacing it.

"Then you have brought me here for nothing," he stated.

"No, not quite." Mr. Thornhurst looked quite pensive for a moment and then raised his forefinger. "I propose that you marry the lady."

"What?!"

Mr. Thornhurst waved aside Connor's objection. "She will be willing, as she is vain and poor and would be thrilled at the prospect of being Lady Roxbury. Take the money, pay your debts, and make Roxbury Hall what you can of it while the lady lives."

"You cannot be serious."

"You are the one in debt," Thornhurst shrugged and pointed at the will in Connor's hands, "This is the way out. And with some hard work, you might end up with a nice little estate with abundant revenues."

Connor sat stunned at the idea—an eighty-year-old bride—and cringed. Of all the things he was prepared to do, this was not one of them. He always imagined working off the debt, and the idea of marrying for money did not offend his pride. But to marry a lady old enough to be his grandmother for financial gain was morally repugnant to him.

Thornhurst stood up and took down his scarf from a hook on the wall. Wrapping it around his neck, he said with a smile, "Shall we call upon the lady and see what she thinks of the idea?"

It was not really a question, and after a short walk through Roxbury village—past the church, across the green, and down a little lane—Connor found himself standing next to Mr. Thornhurst outside the closed door of a small grey stone cottage as the solicitor rang the bell.

"Mary? Kitty?" a female voice screeched inside, "The bell. The bell. Mary, answer the bell."

It was a few moments before the door opened, a wide-eyed blonde servant girl of about twelve standing there, flour smudged on her face and apron, the smell of warm confections wafting out to the two gentlemen. Just beyond the girl, Connor saw a flight of stairs, a pair of feet descending quickly but stopping and then retreating back up the steps. Whoever she was, Connor mused, she had lovely ankles.

"Mr. Edward Thornhurst." The solicitor presented his card to the girl standing before them. "We have business with Miss Woodbridge." Without a curtsey or a word, the girl dashed away, leaving the door wide open and the two men standing there on the doorstep. Thornhurst motioned to Connor, and they entered, closing the door behind them. Connor again glanced up at the top of the stairs, and this time glimpsed a pretty face framed by wisps of loose brown hair peering around a corner and down at him. As he looked up, the face quickly disappeared back around the corner.

A door opened to their left, the girl standing there and motioning them in. Connor had to duck as he entered the room so as not to smash his head on the plastered stone, the doorway being so low. As he straightened to his full height in the cold, damp, low-ceilinged parlor, he saw his potential bride sitting beside the dwindling flames in the grate.

Thornhurst had been generous in his description. A gnarled old creature, her tightlipped mouth formed a perpetual frown. Ice blue eyes stared with disapproval at the two men. Her dress was two decades out of fashion, and a mobcap covered her white head. She held out a bony blue-veined hand to Thornhurst, who quickly bowed over it.

"Mr. Thornhurst," she said, withdrawing her hand and putting it under the blanket tucked about her, "what brings you out of that dusty hovel of an office on such a chilled day as this?"

"I thought you might wish to make the acquaintance of the new Viscount Roxbury." Thornhurst motioned to Connor, who in turn bowed before the lady. She seemed to sit up taller, and while her eyes brightened and she appeared pleased, she did not smile.

"I knew your uncle," she said, "No kinder gentleman ever lived. He shall be greatly missed by all in Roxbury. My condolences on your loss."

Connor was not sure if she were trying to be polite or truly believed the words. Whatever the case, he sensed no sincerity in the sentiments.

"Thank you, ma'am," Connor replied with the same lack of sincerity.

"Please sit down." Miss Woodbridge indicated the threadbare settee. "I understand from Mary that you have some *business* with me."

As soon as the men sat, Thornhurst opened his mouth to reply, but before a word came out, a younger woman entered the room. She carried a tray arrayed with tea and accompaniments, and while she appeared nothing more than a servant, Connor immediately stood, Thornhurst quickly following his lead.

"I brought some tea, Aunt," she said without looking at either man as she set the tea on the side table, "I thought your callers might like something warm to chase away the chill in the air."

For the first time, she looked up at them, and Connor saw the same face he'd seen at the top of the stairs, the wisps of hair now pulled neatly back. It was not a young face as he'd originally thought, although she was hardly old either, and Connor noticed traces of grey in her brown hair. She was short, and if not for the apron tied about her waist, Connor might have thought her a little on the plump side. Current fashion so easily hid the curves of a woman's body and could have made her appear voluminous rather than curvaceous. Instead, the apron highlighted her narrow waist and suggested ample hips, and for the briefest moment—he hoped she failed to notice—his eyes swept over the swell of her breasts. She smiled at him, creases forming around her sparkling blue eyes.

"By happy coincidence," she said to him, "some tarts have just come from the oven."

Miss Woodbridge glared at the woman.

"If I required tea," Miss Woodbridge scolded, "I would call for it."

The younger woman's smile disappeared, the sparkle fading from her eyes. She seemed to hesitate over the tray, as if trying to decide if she should serve the guests or just pick it up and retreat. Then Connor realized she did not appear the least bit chastened. She appeared annoyed and even a touch angry, although she hid it well.

"Please," Connor asked Miss Woodbridge in an attempt to defuse the situation, "Whom do we have the pleasure of meeting?"

Miss Woodbridge rolled her eyes and with obvious reluctance motioned to the woman, "My grandniece, Miss Katherine Woodbridge. Katherine with a K, not the more elegant Catherine with a C as with my own name. Her mother's doing, no doubt."

The two men looked at each other, and Connor could see Thornhurst thought the same thing.

"Miss *Katherine* Woodbridge?" Thornhurst asked the younger lady.

"Yes," she replied, a faint smile returning to her face.

"You reside in this house?" Connor asked.

She nodded, "I arrived five months ago."

Before his uncle's death four months earlier but after the will was made, Connor quickly calculated, an unexpected hope growing in him.

"My apologies, Miss Woodbridge," Thornhurst said to the elder lady, "but it seems our business is with the younger Miss Woodbridge."

"With Kitty?" Miss Woodbridge screeched, "What business could you have with her?" She turned and again glared at her niece. "Is there something I should be made aware of, Kitty? Is there some reason your brother sent you to live here with me other than that which he stated? Some ill-doings on your part...?"

"Miss Woodbridge," Connor interrupted, "To suggest such a thing is inappropriate and ill becomes a lady such as yourself. My business with your niece is not your concern." With the old woman's mouth gaping, he turned to Katherine and quickly asked, "Miss Woodbridge, would you care for a walk? Just down the lane a bit."

She appeared startled by the question, as did the elder Miss Woodbridge, but Katherine quickly recovered from the surprise.

"I'd be delighted," she smiled, "but I need to know with whom I shall be walking, sir." He again noticed the sparkle in her eyes, this time with a playful glint to it.

"Oh. Connor Grayson, at your service." And he bowed slightly from the waist.

As the younger Miss Woodbridge hurried off to find a wrap, Connor and Thornhurst said their goodbyes to the elder Miss Woodbridge and slipped outside to wait.

"The will said Katherine with a K, didn't it?" Connor asked as soon as the door closed behind them.

"Yes, it did," Thornhurst smiled.

"Not a C?"

"Not a C." After a silent moment, Thornhurst added, "Eaves's wife is Katherine with a K. I suppose it's only natural he'd spell it that way when he wrote up the will for Lord Roxbury. Lucky for you."

"Assuming the lady agrees," Connor pointed out.

"Letter of the law versus the spirit of the law," Thornhurst said with a mischievous spark in his eye.

"I beg your pardon?"

"Well, in this case, the letter of the will versus the spirit of the will. I won't tell if you don't tell."

Katherine could not imagine what business Mr. Thornhurst and his companion had to discuss with her, but Aunt Catherine had behaved abominably, and Katherine needed some fresh air, especially after the lies her aunt had told about Lord Roxbury. As far as Katherine could tell, Aunt Catherine never associated with the viscount in any capacity, as friend, neighbor, or otherwise.

Putting on her bonnet, Katherine glanced out the window at the young gentleman speaking with Mr. Thornhurst. He was handsome, this Mr. Grayson, with his ginger hair—a tad too long for fashion—and it curled there, just at the nape of his neck. The color went well with his eyes, green, like the eyes of the vicar's cat, Theobald. A scattering of freckles spread out over his nose and across his high cheekbones, only slightly darker against the light tan of his skin. She imagined him working out of doors or spending long hours in the saddle. His wide, expressive mouth with its pale pink lips particularly appealed to her as he spoke. She noticed he was quick to smile, and that smile contained a certain, irresistible sweetness.

When Katherine was a miss just out of the schoolroom, his mere presence would have quite unnerved her. As it was, his direct gaze upon their introduction had filled her with an unexpected flush, and inwardly, she laughed at herself. He was practically a boy, while she was... well, much too old at thirty-eight to be thinking such foolish thoughts of such impossible things.

With the sound of her aunt fussing to Mary about cold tea and undercooked tarts, Katherine quietly slipped out of the cottage and joined the two waiting gentlemen.

"I really must apologize for my aunt," she said, pulling on her knit gloves, "She is in a frightful mood today. Quite out of the ordinary." Although, in truth, she had become unusually petulant of late.

"We should be the ones to apologize," the younger gentleman said, "coming unannounced as we did. A complete stranger accompanied by a solicitor. It was probably most disturbing for her. The presence of a solicitor rarely bodes well." Katherine saw genuine compassion and sympathy in his eyes, along with something else, a kind of worry mixed with unease. And it bothered her. She turned to Mr. Thornhurst.

"What did you wish to discuss with me?" she asked.

The solicitor opened his mouth to speak, but his companion interrupted.

"*I* wish to discuss a matter with you," he said. He looked around, as if fearing someone might overhear, and quietly added, "Of a personal nature."

"I don't understand." Katherine looked from him to Mr. Thornhurst. Both men appeared uncomfortable with furtive glances passing between them.

"Let us walk a while," Mr. Thornhurst suggested, motioning toward the lane. "It will afford us some degree of privacy, and the air will do us good."

Silently, Katherine and the younger gentleman strolled side by side down the lane leading out of the village and toward the parklands of Roxbury Hall. Mr. Thornhurst trailed behind them like a Spanish *duenna*, while the light breeze sent down gentle showers of red and gold leaves from the trees.

The day had turned out warmer than Katherine expected. That morning, when she had hung out a bit of Aunt Catherine's laundry, it had been chilly, with a silvery frost lingering in the shadows. But now, near noon, it was one of those days when autumn forgot its age and thought itself young again, remembering halcyon days of warmth and green when bees buzzed among the flowers. Soon enough, though, Katherine knew, the wind would shift, ending all illusion of warmth, and autumn would shudder with thoughts of the cold days and darkness to come.

For now, Katherine would not think of such things. Instead, she enjoyed the sun's warmth, broken only by brief moments in cold shade, as she walked alongside this handsome, young gentleman. She glanced back to see if Mr. Thornhurst kept pace with them. He followed along behind them at some distance, she saw, and it occurred to her that he appeared to be acting as chaperone. An absurd idea, Katherine thought, amused by the workings of her mind, as if she were some schoolgirl walking out with a suitor. She stopped walking, her companion doing likewise, and allowed Mr. Thornhurst to catch up with them.

"Excuse my bluntness, Mr. Grayson," Katherine finally asked in a light tone, "but if you have business with me, why is Mr. Thornhurst's presence required? A chaperone is hardly necessary at my age." She smiled, knowing perfectly well no one in Roxbury would ever think anything untoward might occur between her and the tall young gentleman.

"The lady is right, my lord," Thornhurst said, "My presence is not needed."

"My lord?" Katherine asked the gentleman she had called *Mr. Grayson*. His mouth twisted at the sound of the words, and he lowered his eyes, giving Katherine the distinct impression he did not like the appellation, as he looked boyishly embarrassed.

"I fear I am the new Lord Roxbury," he said.

"Oh," she said, uncertain how to respond. Given his tone, congratulations seemed inappropriate. This new bit of information, though, just added to her confusion. Clearly, he had come to Roxbury either to assume his duties as viscount or simply to look over his estate before returning to wherever he lived while others in his employment tended to matters here. Perhaps that was it. Perhaps he needed a temporary housekeeper at Roxbury Hall—Mrs. Morris was getting on in years and could use the help—until further, permanent arrangements could be made. Perhaps someone in the village had recommended her, although she could not fathom why. Aunt Catherine needed her.

"I'll just go back to my office," Thornhurst said, stepping away from them, "and draw up those papers we were discussing."

Katherine noticed a look of understanding passed between the two men.

"Very well, then, Mr. Thornhurst," Lord Roxbury said, and they continued on their walk as the solicitor headed back toward the village. They followed the hard dirt road past the stone wall enclosing the orchard where Mr. Rowse kept pigs, before venturing on across still green fields with pillows of grazing sheep.

"So what is this business you wish to discuss with me, my lord?" Katherine asked. He opened his mouth to speak, only to close it and look away from her. He seemed nervous, again recalling to Katherine's mind the silly idea of a young swain courting his ladylove.

"I think I preferred it when you called me Mr. Grayson." He smiled with his attempt at joviality, but when Katherine failed to respond in kind, he grew serious. "Forgive my asking, but why do you live with your aunt?"

Katherine was unsure how to answer. There was the simple reason, easily and quickly told. She had no one. Aunt Catherine had no one. And the family simply decided they deserved one another. At least this way, none of the family would have to deal with either old maid.

The complicated reason, though, in hindsight, lacked its former, painful bite. The events once mirrored a tragedy with its outrage and injustice, or at least it had to the seventeen-year-old girl she had been all those years ago. Katherine had thought it love—her father called in a childish fancy—and looking back, Katherine still believed it had been love, albeit a misplaced kind. Thomas Cooper had been the newly-arrived gamekeeper to Lord Harrington, whose estate abutted her father's land. It had never occurred to Katherine that a man could be beautiful until the moment she first saw him walking through the forest with Lord Harrington and her father. They became friends—nothing more—and she sometimes joined him as he made his rounds. She thought that he felt something for her—perhaps he did—and fortunately, it never went further, as, it turned out, he had a wife in another county. They were, however, seen together, and it sent tongues wagging. Poor Mr. Cooper barely kept his position with Lord Harrington, while Katherine was sent to live with her grandmother. A crisis averted. An embarrassment forgotten. It, sadly, failed to amount to even a youthful indiscretion, and were she now married, her children would laugh at the tale—*our scandalous mother caught talking to the gamekeeper. She probably even smiled at the butcher. Or dropped her handkerchief for the grocer.*

But that temporary placement had evolved into a twenty-one-year exile. Due to severe rheumatism, her grandmother rarely ventured out, so the little society they enjoyed had to come to them. The few to call mostly included her grandmother's equally elderly friends. While the village abounded with young ladies, it suffered from a dearth of eligible young gentlemen, and on the occasions Katherine attended fêtes and assemblies, nothing ever progressed beyond polite niceties. It was inconsequential, given her lack of dowry; she had nothing to recommend her but herself.

When her grandmother died, Katherine had hoped there might be a small annuity left for her, just something she could live on. But there was nothing. Instead, Katherine returned to her family home. The reunion did not last long, and her brother quickly found another position for her, this time with Great Aunt Catherine. Only then did Katherine realize her life would never be more than this, a mere servant to old ladies, until she herself were an old lady in need of another's care and attention.

The simple answer to Lord Roxbury's question came more readily.

"Someone needed to make sure the servants didn't steal the linens," Katherine said, unable to keep the touch of bitterness from her voice, "I seemed the obvious choice for the position."

"She's not the most amiable person, is she?"

"That is unkind." Katherine did not scold and said it in a matter-of-fact way, but secretly, she acknowledged some truth in the observation. How like caring for a child it really was, she thought—although, not as bad as it had been with her grandmother—constantly watching the elderly lady and making sure she was all right, without ever being able to chastise or discipline out of respect and deference.

"She has been temperamental of late," Katherine admitted. She had known Aunt Catherine all her life. Her namesake used to visit her grandmother for extended stays, and while rather dour and prone to melancholia, Aunt Catherine had always thrived in company and enjoyed gatherings. Mr. Thornhurst's arrival that morning should have lifted her spirits, but instead, she had been uncharacteristically waspish, which seemed more and more to be her natural state.

They walked without a word for some distance, the stillness broken only by the crunch of gravel beneath her companion's booted feet. At times, she thought he wished to say something, and he appeared to be summoning up his courage, only to change his mind and remain silent. When at last he spoke, his quiet comment startled her.

"I don't think she appreciates your presence in her house."

The direction of this conversation disturbed her, and she decided to end it before it went any further. Even if she agreed with his observations, he spoke of her family, making Katherine duty-bound to defend her aunt. Katherine stopped walking and turned to face him.

"Mr. Grayson... I mean, my lord. You are too familiar." Katherine hoped she didn't sound too harsh, but he looked almost frightened. She doubted she was the cause. "Please tell me what business you wish to discuss."

He glanced around and then took a deep breath.

"One question first," he said.

"Go on."

"How... old... are you?" He spoke slowly, grimacing a touch when he articulated the word *old*, as if testing the waters and fearing offense. Rightly so. She was taken aback by the impertinent question but hesitated for a moment before answering—preparing, as she did, to put him in his place. Lord or not, no gentleman had any business asking a lady for such a personal detail. Then, as she wondered what prompted him to dare the displeasure of any female over such a matter, curiosity got the better of her.

"Thirty-eight," she said.

He exhaled, as if he had been holding his breath, and smiled. "That's good." He sounded pleased with her answer.

"My lord?" she asked, momentarily confused, but he seemed not to hear her.

"Eight years difference," he continued. "I'm just thirty, you see."

No. She did not see. He made no sense, as if he were quite addle-brained. Her age had nothing to do with anything. And while she tried to comprehend this, another, nagging thought tugged at her mind. *Thirty?* He was *thirty years old?* Surely not. He seemed still a boy, or at least, as if he had only just come of age. However, he possessed none of that gangliness of youth when boys seemed overgrown, all arms and legs, nor had he foundered in that equally awkward underdeveloped stage, when boys get lost in clothes they've yet to fill.

Tall and slender, solid and sturdy, nothing about Lord Roxbury, on further reflection, suggested immaturity in the slightest. *Yes*, Katherine had to admit, Lord Roxbury appeared very much a man. In truth, she spent far too much time among the elderly and had forgotten how young—and how old—youth really was.

He seemed to relax somewhat, although Katherine still sensed a nervousness in him as he glanced around at their surroundings. They stood along the edge of the fields near a footpath leading into the forest ablaze in golden red and orange.

"Which way do you recommend?" he asked.

Katherine pointed toward the footpath; it eventually branched off and circled back to the village. So they began to walk again, this time heading into the forest. Katherine immediately noticed a change in the temperature, the air edged with a chill as they left the warmth of the sun and passed into the shade.

"My business, then," Lord Roxbury began with a deep breath. "As you are undoubtedly well-aware, I inherited my uncle's title and Roxbury Hall—part of the entailment. But what I tell you now is in the strictest confidence."

"I am not one to gossip, my lord. You may put your trust in me."

"Knowing village life as I do, everyone will know every detail soon enough without a word from you or me, but I do appreciate your discretion."

They ventured deeper in the wood, the path skirting massive green, moss-covered rocks, while a golden canopy spread high above them and defused the light. The already-fallen leaves lay scattered on the forest floor, like a carpet of red. All was hush and still as Lord Roxbury explained.

"Unfortunately, the entailment did not include his money."

"The estate is insolvent?"

"Quite. Or so Mr. Thornhurst has told me. I have no reason to doubt him."

"That would explain a few things," Katherine said.

"Such as?"

"I am told by several people that after the late Lord Roxbury's son died, he stopped maintaining the estate. All upkeep on his tenants' cottages ceased, and when some of them moved on, he just left the cottages to decay. He even allowed his fields to lay fallow." Katherine glanced up at her companion. He looked pensive, his brows knitted together.

"I suspect a lack of funds had nothing to do with that," he said, "More likely, he wished to make life difficult for me."

"My lord?" His words caused, not confusion, but a strange kind of pain. She could not fathom why anyone would wish to make another person's life more difficult. He did not respond, though, waving aside her query as if it were nothing. But Katherine knew there was something more that he simply did not wish to discuss.

"No. You see, there is plenty of money," he continued, "He just did not leave it to me."

"Oh."

"This would not be a problem, except four years ago, I inherited my father's debts, which are quite enormous. My uncle's money would easily pay off the debts."

"I am sorry to hear of your difficulties," Katherine said, "and the loss of both your uncle and father." She did not know what else she could say. She sympathized with the gentleman. But the whole conversation baffled her. She could find no reasonable explanation as to why exactly Lord Roxbury was now discussing his finances with her. And yet.... And yet.... Something nagged at her mind, a sense that this was oh so very familiar, despite her complete lack of experience in such matters. And as much as she tried to tamp down these thoughts as utter foolishness—at her age!—with each passing moment, the notion grew stronger, its shape taking form and becoming more and more apparent.

"My uncle, however, made a provision in his will." He stopped walking and turned to face her. When he spoke again, his voice was low and quiet. "If I married one Miss Katherine Woodbridge of Lilac Cottage, the money would come with the estate."

Heaven above! He was *proposing!* It was not her overactive imagination.

"Me?" She managed to stammer like some half-wit, so confused were her thoughts. She looked down at the ground and tried to comprehend. *Why on earth would the late viscount name, of all people...?*

"My uncle referred to your aunt."

She jerked her head up in shock. She had not expected that, and it made no sense whatsoever. "Some cruel joke?" she asked.

"Undoubtedly. God knows why." Lord Roxbury shrugged. "Only... Mr. Thornhurst's clerk made a mistake. He spelled Katherine with a K."

"I see."

"Do you?"

Despite the whirlwind of thoughts rushing through her head, Katherine remained—much to her surprise—calm. "Yes. A thirty-eight-year-old bride is preferable to an eighty-year-old bride."

"Yes. Quite."

The whirlwind in her head seemed to move into her stomach—or maybe her heart—and Katherine glanced around. "I need to sit down."

"Oh, of course." And then he glanced around. "Here. This one looks dry." Before Katherine even realized what was happening, Lord Roxbury had taken her hand, slipped his arm about her with his hand resting on the small of her back, and guided her over to the least mossy rock near them. Only then did she realize it was the most intimate physical gesture she had ever experienced from a man. She had never even waltzed before. And even after he removed his hand, she could still feel its strength just there, lingering in the curve of her back, and the gentle force he had used to lead her.

"I've given you a shock," he said.

"No, no. Not at all." She shook her head, but on further consideration, she admitted, "Well, yes." Despite all her suspicions, she had never expected this, not at her age, not this late in her life. It was the sort of thing that happened to other people, not to her. Handsome, titled gentlemen proposed to ladies of great beauty, or great fortune. They did not propose to penniless old maids living with their elderly spinster aunts.

He sat down beside her on the rock, and his face softened with concern.

"Have I insulted you?" he asked.

"Gracious, no!" While, in truth, Katherine was completely unsure what exactly she felt, she knew she felt no insult by his proposal.

"Do you like the idea?" he asked, his face a mixture of hope and worry.

Much to her dismay—she'd only just met the man—Katherine wanted to say yes. And her reasons were just as mercenary as his. And less noble.

She was afraid.

Aunt Catherine had outlived her usefulness, and look what had become of her. And she possessed an income—albeit frustratingly small. Katherine didn't even have that. For the time, she served a purpose and was useful. She could look after things, make sure no one pinched the silver, manage accounts and see to it that the butcher didn't overcharge for beef. In that meager capacity, she had value to her family. But one day, she would outlive that usefulness, lose all value, and become a burden. *And what then?* With no one to look after her.

The world abounded with females like her, unmarried, childless, who could be relied upon to care for others and then easily discarded once they outlived their usefulness. Katherine knew what became of such women. She remembered the Misses Eleanor and Jane Doyle, living with and caring for their elderly father, a tenant to Lord Harrington. After their father's death, Miss Eleanor had ended up in the madhouse while her sister married the village simpleton—though, he was strong and had no difficulties doing a day's work, and Miss Jane made certain there was no short shrift for that work. But poor Miss Jane always looked so wrung out and exhausted, caring for a child trapped in a giant's body.

But most ended up like her grandmother and Aunt Catherine, in darkened rooms, forever chilled, waiting... waiting for someone to call, waiting for tea, waiting for supper, waiting for bedtime, waiting for dawn, waiting.

Despite all her fears, Katherine had to be practical. For all she knew, Lord Roxbury might be some drunken blackguard who enjoyed beating children. Or practiced even worse depravities. And even if that were not the case and he was the respectable gentleman he appeared to be, she might very well find herself trading one kind of servitude for another. Or, after marrying, they might discover they could not abide the presence of one another... although, that was a problem many couples faced.

"I do not know you, my lord," she replied with a calm quiet. "And you do not know me."

With an eagerness, he spoke as if he had not heard. "You would be Lady Roxbury. You would have your own home, to run as you please. There would be plenty of money. There would be a generous settlement. We could spend the season in town...."

"I do not care for town."

"Or wherever you wish. Bath. Brighton. Or here. You'd want for nothing. No problems."

"Or I might simply be exchanging one set of problems for another," Katherine pointed out. "And you forget what a viscount most needs in this world: the requisite heir and a spare. It is unlikely I could produce a healthy child." She hated admitting it, but it was the truth. She had always wanted children, and even though it was a remote possibility, this might be her only chance. It was the other reason she wanted to accept his proposal.

"Miss Woodbridge," he said, more somber, "as it appears now, regardless of what I do, everything will eventually go to some distant cousin whom I have never even heard of. An heir is the least of my concerns. Yes, a child would be a very welcomed event, but if I marry, only to die without issue, I will still be better off than I am now." He then quietly added, "I suspect you would be better off as well."

The truth hurt, and he had no right to say it. He had no right to judge her life. But secretly, Katherine agreed with him. Never to worry again about leaking roofs. Never to count pennies again to see if they might purchase sugar. Never to lie again to the butcher about paying the bill next week.

No more turning of sleeves to make a dress last longer. No more dim evenings with one candle. No more low fires in want of coal. No more cold beds.

To sleep in clean sheets she did not have to wash herself. To bathe in a tub and not just a basin. And the possibility of having someone there, someone to share the responsibilities... and the burdens.... It was all so very tempting.

But instead, Katherine said, "My lord, you know nothing of my life."

"I know you deserve your own home." Lord Roxbury continued, unfazed.

"Your home?"

"Yes."

"As your wife?"

"Yes."

"So you can get the money?"

At the words, he suddenly went still and quiet, and then he stood up and slowly turned to face her.

"Well...," he said, "when you put it that way...."

He looked so defeated. She did not mean to hurt him but simply to point out the reality of their situation, as she was being just as mercenary about it as he was.

"May I at least think about it?" Katherine asked with a faint smile.

"Of course," he assured her and then added, "And if you decide against it, I can always ask your aunt."

Katherine couldn't help but laugh, as much at his joke as at the image of the handsome young Lord Roxbury standing before the altar with her ancient and crabby aunt while the Reverend Mr. Tipton performed the ceremony before the entire congregation.

"I'm sure you would be very happy together," she said with a smile.

By God! He liked this woman!

When they had first started walking, it suddenly occurred to him that he could do what so many other titled gentlemen lacking funds did in this very modern world—find a wife in London on the marriage mart. Any rich cit's daughter would do. The season was some time off, but he could manage until then.

Only, he began to imagine it all, the debutants with their mamas, the fawning and flattering ladies, the licentious widows, the bored wives, all paraded before him like cattle for purchase, and he saw himself ending up with some beautiful young creature who professed to love and adore him when, in reality, she loved and adored his title, while he, in return, loved and adored her dowry. He didn't want a marriage based on lies and deception. As for a marriage based on love... well, he knew from his childhood such marriages came with their own set of problems, and he didn't want that. Friendship, mutual understanding... that was enough for him.

And here was Miss Woodbridge. She didn't fawn all over him. She didn't simper or flatter. She did nothing in an effort to make him fall in love with her. Connor sensed nothing false about her. She was honest. She knew her own mind and did not hesitate to disagree with him. He believed she spoke to him without regard for his title and that she would have treated him exactly the same if he'd still been mere Mr. Grayson. Connor sensed that they knew where they stood with each other.

It didn't hurt that he thought her so very pretty. She smiled. She laughed. She scolded—gently, but enough to demonstrate her displeasure. She had endured his onslaught of inappropriate questions with grace, even though he could see the disapproval in her captivating blue eyes. And, through it all, she revealed an unexpected intelligence. And a surprising vulnerability, despite her obvious strength of will. His proposal had shaken her—he saw that immediately— and he feared she might be unwell. Then, when he took her hand and placed his other hand on her lower back— simply as a means to guide her—he felt her trembling ever so slightly, but she held her composure amazingly well.

He worried he had offended her by making the offer—asking the most intimate thing a man could probably ask of a lady, to be his wife, to share his table and his bed, for the rest of their lives, all for money. And he a complete stranger. A lesser woman would have slapped him. Or in the very least, marched off in a huff with a visit from her brother soon to follow. But she was not offended. And the relief he felt when she indicated she was not entirely averse to the idea of marrying him filled Connor with a sense of hope and possibility. Even their age difference—a mere eight years—had been a welcome relief, Connor fearing she might be one of those well-aged fifty-year-olds. But as it stood, there was still a chance—remote as it was—they might have children. *If* she accepted him.

"Do you feel well enough to continue?" Connor asked, motioning toward the footpath.

"Yes," Miss Woodbridge replied, and Connor took her gloved hand as she stood up. But once she was on her feet, he did not release her hand. Instead, as they began to walk again, he tucked her fingers into the crook of his arm. They could have been any courting couple out for a stroll, rather than virtual strangers trying to solve a financial difficulty.

They walked in silence; Connor noticed Miss Woodbridge seemed suddenly shy. She didn't look at him but instead appeared to keep her eyes lowered, as if studying the forest floor. He no longer felt her tremble, and he assumed she was contemplating his offer and what it signified. He was grateful she at least took it seriously.

As they came to where the footpath divided, Connor pointed to the left—his instinct telling him that path led back to the village—and asked, "This way?"

"Yes." She looked up at him, and he saw the faint hint of a polite smile.

And then, in an effort to make conversation, Connor pointed in the opposite direction and asked, "Where does that go?"

Miss Woodbridge broke out in a wide grin that brightened her eyes with amusement. "That's the way to Roxbury Hall."

Connor's heart leapt up. *Roxbury Hall. His* property. *His* land. To do with as he pleased until his dying day.

And no banker, no creditor, no bailiff could ever take it away from him... no one. Except God, or maybe an act of Parliament. The excitement took his breath away. He was suddenly a child again, waiting in anticipation for his mother's Christmas pudding.

"Would you mind if we...?" he asked with a smile and gestured toward the path heading off to the right.

"You mean you haven't been there yet?"

He shook his head. "Is it far?"

"Half a mile. Maybe a mile. I'm not a surveyor." He noticed the mischievous glint in her eye. "Shall we?" Taking a step in the direction of his new home, she gently pulled at his arm. He needed no encouragement, and they were soon heading down the path.

"So where were you before all this?" she asked as they walked.

"Cornwall. I was an estate manager to the Duke of Rutland. A very small, seldom-visited piece of property. I only ever met the man twice in fifteen years."

"You've been an estate manager since you were fifteen?" She sounded doubtful.

"No." Connor laughed. "I began working there with my father. He taught me how to run everything."

"And this is the father who left you with so many debts?"

"Yes." It saddened Connor that this debt was the last legacy of his father, as if that mistake summed up the man's entire life, when it didn't. Beyond loving his father, Connor had liked him, too. He remembered happier days, before the money had run out when they had lived in polite comfort in Bath. But with the cessation of the allowance from the late Lord Roxbury, his father's reserves had gradually dwindled—despite his mother's careful economy—until his father was forced to look for work.

Without realizing it, Connor found himself relating all this to Miss Woodbridge as they walked. He should have stopped himself from revealing such personal details of his life, but he found talking to her came so easily and naturally, as it might with an old friend. Even when Connor told of his father's gambling, she responded with sympathy, not judgment.

"That's how he paid for my education," Connor said, "He had gambled in his youth—as young bucks are prone to do—but neither my mother nor I knew he had returned to that former vice. He was lucky. For a while. Then it all fell apart. And everything became just one more draw of the cards and his luck would change."

"But it didn't." She spoke with quiet understanding.

"No." He looked down at the ground, at the red leaves underfoot, and quietly added, "He died about a year after my mother. Some said he died of a broken heart, but I think he just went looking for her." It *sounded* so romantic. Theirs was a love match, after all, but to him, witnessing their lives together, they always seemed so miserable, forever disappointed with each other. Despite their love, the world tore them apart.

Connor looked up, and before Miss Woodbridge could respond—he knew she would offer some truly sincere condolence for his loss—he abruptly asked, "You will tell me when we cross over onto my land, won't you?"

Miss Woodbridge released his arm and stopped so suddenly that Connor kept walking and had to turn around to face her. She made a sound, part gasp, part laugh, and gave him an incredulous look.

"My lord, we have been on your land almost since the moment we left Lilac Cottage."

"Since we left Lilac Cottage?"

"Most of the village belongs to you. Not Lilac Cottage. Mr. Thornhurst is our landlord."

It was Connor's turn to be incredulous. "This forest, those fields...?"

"The sheep, the orchard, Mr. Rowse's pigs, nearly every building in the village... all yours. Even the parish is yours to give as you please. And there's a stone circle just to the west and they say on the shortest day of the year...."

"Even the parish...?" Connor felt like a complete fool. He had no idea. The enormity of the responsibility weighed down on him now even more. Trying to make light of it, he said, "Well, I'll need to hear the vicar's sermons first before any decisions are made in that matter." Miss Woodbridge did not laugh. At least he now knew she only laughed when she found something funny and not just to please him. He also realized she understood the enormity of it all, as well.

"Are you all right?" she asked.

"Yes, yes. Quite. Thank you." But in truth, he felt overwhelmed, even a little numb. He had gone from nothing to all this. He had spent the last eight years sleeping on a cot in a tiny room just off his office, and now, he was literally lord of all he surveyed. Every leaf on every tree, falling as they were, belonged to him. Every mossy rock, every fluttering bird, every hill and gully, every blade of grass. *His.*

"It's not much farther now." Miss Woodbridge spoke gently. "We can get you a brandy."

"Do I look that bad?" He attempted a smile but only managed to turn up one side of his mouth.

"You've gone rather pale."

Without another word, Miss Woodbridge took his hand and led the way down the path, until at last they rounded a bend and Roxbury Hall came into view across wide open uncultivated but overgrown fields—presumably what was left of a lawn.

"This is Roxbury Hall?" Connor asked as they paused at the edge of the tree line and stood in shadow.

"Yes."

Connor never expected a Blenheim Palace or a Castle Howard, but he envisioned something more than this, and he felt a pang of disappointment. Even the local squires in Cornwall lived in finer, more modern houses than this. And Connor could not see how it merited the name hall, as it appeared little more than an overgrown croft with multiple additions built onto it here and there. *Yes*, it was large, but nothing more than an old house, really. A hodgepodge of chimneys and gables, the three-storey house appeared at first glance to be all red brick, but those were just the additions jutting out from a timbered core with exposed studs in typical Tudor manner. Connor, however, suspected that original portion dated much earlier, perhaps even to the medieval period.

They approached from the east side of the house, and as they continued on, slowly walking toward the front, Connor hoped the house would improve on closer inspection. It didn't. Green moss covered the slate roof, and while there were a score of windows—some quite large—the house looked dreary, lonely, as if long abandoned. Blown, dead leaves piled against the walls. One section of the slate roof had broken off and lay in a heap on the ground below. Dying weeds filled the gardens, brown wheat-like grasses coming up between the flagstones.

"Good God, it *is* a wreck."

"Nonsense," Miss Woodbridge protested, "It's perfectly lovely."

Connor couldn't see what she saw, and for a moment, he thought she jested. "Do you really think so?"

"Yes." She was serious. "The house needs work, and the fields I've seen are fallow, but nothing a brilliant estate manager couldn't fix." She smiled at him.

"Brilliant? What makes you think I'm brilliant?"

"Well, I doubt His Grace the Duke of Rutland would have kept you on if you weren't."

"Does the house look better inside?"

"I've never been inside," she admitted.

"Then for all you know, it really could be a crumbling wreck."

"I suppose, but in that case, you can still fix it. Mr. Carter and his sons could use the work, and with the money...." She stopped, and Connor realized what she almost unintentionally implied. His throat tightened with the thought, and he wondered if she had made her decision—a decision to accept his proposal—but he didn't want to get his hopes up.

"Perhaps we should take a closer look before hiring workers," Connor suggested with a smile.

They reached the long drive to the hall, but as they approached the house, no signs of life could be seen. No groomsman scurried around the stable block. No gardener labored in the dead flowerbeds. No maid washed the windows. No line of laundry dried in the sun. No stray dog greeted them. No horse pranced in the paddock.

"Is the hall deserted?" Connor asked.

"No." Miss Woodbridge pointed to smoke rising from the chimney. "The housekeeper, Mrs. Morris, resides in the hall, as well as a couple of servants."

Reaching the door under the portico, Miss Woodbridge rang the bell.

"Wouldn't want to startle poor Mrs. Morris with the new Lord Roxbury just walking in, now would we?" Miss Woodbridge smiled, quickly raising her eyebrows.

The door opened, and there stood a plump, older woman, perhaps in her sixties. She wore an outdated dress and flowing white mobcap.

"Oh, Kitty. What a lovely surprise," the woman said, all smiles and sparkling eyes.

"Mrs. Morris," Miss Woodbridge said, "My apologies for the intrusion."

"It's no intrusion." Mrs. Morris stepped back and waved the pair in as she opened the door wider. "Come in, come in."

They entered the dark interior, Mrs. Morris closing the door behind them. It took Connor's eyes a moment to adjust after the bright sunlight. He soon realized they stood in the so-called hall of Roxbury Hall—no vestibule, no antechamber, just straight from outside into the hall. And it was nothing more than a long room with a slightly higher than average oak ceiling. Sunbeams rained down from mullioned windows. Cold fireplaces stood at both ends alongside doorways leading to other parts of the house. Wood-paneled wainscoting topped off by plastered walls completed the structure of the room, while a few antiquated chairs and a settee comprised the only furniture.

Miss Woodbridge leaned toward him and whispered with a smile, "You could hold a ball in here."

Connor couldn't understand what she saw in the house that he kept missing. All he saw was massive amounts of work needed to make the place habitable. Still, as he looked the room over, he realized she was right. Move the furniture and there was plenty of space for dancing. There was even an alcove where the musicians could sit. Granted, a ball here would never match the grandeur of a London ball, but Connor thought this would probably be more fun. With better company.

When Connor turned to greet Mrs. Morris, Miss Woodbridge stood waiting and said, "My lord, this is Mrs. Morris, your housekeeper."

"My lord?" Mrs. Morris asked, her eyes wide.

"The new Viscount Roxbury," Miss Woodbridge said. While it was not the most proper introduction of a servant to the master of the house, Connor suspected Miss Woodbridge knew he would feel more comfortable this way.

"Oh," Mrs. Morris stood gaping for a moment and then attempted a deep curtsey. "My lord. Welcome to Roxbury Hall."

"Thank you, Mrs. Morris. I'm happy to be here at last." To Connor's surprise, it wasn't a lie. He *was* happy to be there.

"We've been expecting you ever since Mr. Thornhurst told us of your existence. We had no idea his lordship even had a nephew."

"Mrs. Morris," Miss Woodbridge said, "could you get his lordship a brandy...?"

"That won't be necessary," Connor said, "I'm quite all right now."

"If you are sure, but I could use a cup of tea before we leave," Miss Woodbridge said.

"Leave?" Mrs. Morris sounded appalled by the idea. "You mean you aren't staying?"

"I hadn't planned on it," Connor said, "I'm staying at the inn. That is, until you're ready for me."

"Forgive me for speaking plain, my lord, but a man should sleep in his own house, and this *is* your house. We're ready for you now. I know it don't look like much—the west wing is closed off and quite the mess. His lordship... that is, his late lordship, wouldn't let us care for the house as we normally would. We've been cleaning since his death, and when we received word you would be coming.... Well, it's been hectic. But your rooms are aired and clean."

When Connor hesitated, Mrs. Morris continued, saying, "The boy can collect your belongings from the inn, and when you're ready, you can use the curricle to escort Kitty back to Lilac Cottage."

He owned a curricle... which meant he also owned horses. Connor wondered how many, and he suddenly found himself conceding to Mrs. Morris's suggestions.

"Now, you'll be wanting to explore the house," she said, "I'll bring some tea to the drawing room and then see about dinner." She pointed to a low doorway. "Just up the stairs and to the left." And then she hurried off, lifting her skirts a bit and nearly breaking into a run, as she disappeared through the doorway at one end of the hall. Connor heard her shouting as she went, "Mr. Baldwin? Mr. Baldwin? Oh, Mr. Baldwin!"

Connor almost laughed out loud.

"She's very excitable," Miss Woodbridge said with a smile and began removing her knit gloves, her coat, and finally her bonnet.

"I don't want her to go to any trouble," Connor said, also removing his coat.

"You pay her to go to the trouble. She is employed to see to the running of this house and to care for everyone under its roof—crumbling as it is."

"I hadn't considered that. Well, I just hope I pay her from the rents, otherwise, she might not get a penny from me." He did not say it, but he knew Miss Woodbridge was thinking it, too—*unless you marry me.*

They did not immediately do as Mrs. Morris suggested and go upstairs but, instead, investigated the rooms just off the hall—a gentleman's study and a library in want of more books. It was probably just as well, Connor thought; given the amount of work the house required he'd have little time to read, as much as he enjoyed the leisurely occupation.

Next, they quickly ascertained that the doorway through which Mrs. Morris had passed led to the dining room and a corridor connected to the kitchens and the servants' portion of the house.

When they finally did as Mrs. Morris suggested and passed through the low doorway to which she had directed them, they found an octagonal turret with a winding staircase, as if from a gothic castle. Connor led the way up, taking Miss Woodbridge's hand as they ascended. While the stairs continued up to the next storey, they emerged in an ante-room. But rather than going left as instructed, they instead explored the rooms to the right—the private apartments of the viscount and his viscountess, with the first room a sitting room with two doorways leading to separate chambers.

Miss Woodbridge declined to go any further and waited while Connor continued on into his own chamber before passing through to his future bride's chamber. He paused, finding the room bright and airy— freshly cleaned as had been all the rooms—and he tried not to let his mind wander as he stood too close to the bed. He tried not to think of the lady in the next room. He tried not to think of her here instead, in this room. Waiting. Waiting for him. And then welcoming him.

Connor hurried back to Miss Woodbridge before his imagination could get the better of him.

Katherine couldn't very well follow Lord Roxbury into his bedchamber. It embarrassed her just to stand outside the door. But she had to admit, if only to herself, she would like to see the future Lady Roxbury's bedchamber. She wanted to see if she could imagine herself there, with the full knowledge that he slept in the next room. And that he would often wish to join her. In her bed. As his wife, of course. The details of that thought frightened her to no end. And filled her with an excitement she hadn't expected to feel again this side of Heaven. So much so that when Lord Roxbury returned to the sitting room, Katherine was certain she blushed and quickly looked away.

They finally reached the drawing room—a large room that in many ways matched the private sitting room of the viscount and viscountess, with an ornate plaster-molding ceiling in a state of good repair making the room brighter than it might otherwise have been despite the large windows. And while much of the furniture in the rest of the house appeared to predate the Hanover kings, there were several newer pieces designed for comfort in this room. The fire was newly lit—though they had not seen anyone, and Katherine presumed a back stair led up from the kitchens. They quickly confirmed this assumption when they discovered a closed door leading off from the sitting room to an entirely separate portion of the house—the west wing, all dusty and long out of use, with a staircase descending below.

When they returned to the drawing room, Mrs. Morris waited there with tea. Something seemed amiss with her, and Katherine thought she looked worried, as if she had done something wrong and needed to confess all. Lord Roxbury looked at Katherine with uncertainty. Aware that he probably never dealt with domestic matters in his capacity as an estate manager, Katherine took Mrs. Morris aside and asked her what was wrong.

"Oh Kitty, I've made a terrible mistake. Only when Mr. Baldwin said something did I realize."

"What is it, Mrs. Morris?"

"We didn't know when his lordship was coming, so I haven't ordered any meat from the butcher. I can send the boy, but the household accounts.... We'd have to buy it on credit."

"No." Katherine knew Lord Roxbury would not approve of that. There was no point in even considering that option. "What did you plan for your supper before we came?"

"The boy caught a fish this morning. A fine specimen but modest. I was going to bake it with potatoes and carrots, but that's not enough fish for all five of us. And I don't want to serve the new master a fish pie."

Katherine suspected *the new master* was quite accustomed to eating fish pie but understood Mrs. Morris not wishing to serve such a dish on this, Lord Roxbury's first day in the house. So she quickly ascertained what they had on hand and then proceeded to instruct Mrs. Morris on the making of a simple fish stew cooked with potatoes, carrots, and dill, all simmered in milk—*his lordship will like that having come from Cornwall*—to be served with bread and butter, pears and cheese, with a dessert of apple pudding with cream, all served *á la française*—with everything at the same time—so as to appear as if there were more food than there really was. To Katherine's surprise, Mrs. Morris approved the menu, despite it being essentially the same ingredients as for the fish pie, as it allowed the housekeeper to use the formal soup tureen rather than common crockery from the kitchen.

"I can also see to his lordship's getting a good portion of fish this way," she said before hurrying off to the kitchens.

Katherine rejoined Lord Roxbury by the fireside, and he motioned for her to pour. Once she sat down, he sat down opposite her.

"So," he asked, "does *the boy* have a name?"

Thankfully, Katherine had only picked up an empty cup and saucer. Had it been the teapot, she probably would have dropped it from shock as the full realization dawned on her that he had overheard the entire conversation with Mrs. Morris. As it was, the cup and saucer rattled in her hand, but she managed to hold firm and keep them from falling.

"I'm sorry," he said, "but I have exceptional hearing."

"I'll keep that in mind." She reached for the teapot and poured a cup of tea. "And no, my lord, I don't know the boy's name. Sugar?"

He nodded and said, "Then that should be my first task—learn the boy's name. And while we're on the subject, could you do me a favor?" He accepted the cup she held out to him.

"What would that be, my lord?"

"Call me Connor."

"If you wish, Connor." Katherine said it evenly, as a matter of course, but she hardly felt relaxed. She poured herself a cup of tea. She really did need it. The air in the shade of the forest had been cold, and the warmth of the tea took away the lingering chill. But she needed the calming effects of it as well. She needed to soothe her nerves. She felt like she was trembling uncontrollably on the inside with her stomach all in a jumble.

"And may I call you Kitty?"

"Heavens, no!" That surprised her. And despite her feigned outrage, Katherine nearly laughed. "Kitty is a name I've always abhorred."

"Well, then. Katherine it is."

The deep resonance of his voice when he said her name eradicated any calming effect the tea might have had on her nerves. And then she immediately wished he'd say it again. *Oh, dear.* She suddenly realized she could easily lose her heart to this beautiful, ginger-haired boy.

Over tea, they talked of what repairs needed to be done first to the house, and Katherine explained to Connor the general make up of the estate; there was the home farm, a dairy, a lake full of fish, and numerous tenants. To his surprise, she didn't recommend redecorating the entire house. When he failed to inquire about the quality of the hunting, she quietly asked what he wished to know about it. His indifferent response— *let's leave such matters until a gamekeeper's hired*— appeared to perplex her.

Before they left to explore the house further, Connor watched as Katherine made particular note of a suite of rooms just off the drawing room. While the rooms needed additional furniture, they were bright and airy, and in Connor's experience, large enough to house a tenant family. Appearing deep in thought, Katherine lingered in the rooms, as if she planned some particular use for them, and Connor wondered what she had in mind.

Eventually, they made their way up to the second floor of the house—just a series of rooms for storage plus a few bedrooms, along with what had once been the nursery. Fortunately, before either had to comment on the sad state of long abandoned toys and dusty cots once belonging to Connor's now dead cousin, Mrs. Morris announced dinner from the stairs.

Over dinner, they continued the discussion of the house and the need to hire more servants to help; Mrs. Morris, Mr. Baldwin—the butler—and the boy were insufficient staff for the running and repair of the house. Katherine suggested a master builder be brought in to determine if the foundation were sound. Repairs to the roof should follow. The same should be done with the outbuildings and tenants' cottages, she recommended. As for the fields and land, she left that to Connor's care.

All the while, neither mentioned the money required for all this work nor the source for that money. But it was always there, in every thought, in every word, lurking between them, that unspoken answer to Connor's proposal.

Dusk came early these days, and Katherine said her aunt would worry. So Connor had the curricle with a mismatched pair brought around by the boy. Connor was too impressed by the quality of the vehicle to concern himself over the horses—*as long as they can do the job*. He assisted Katherine up, took the ribbons, and they drove away from the house.

They sat in silence for a while, the still evening air cold despite the sunny warmth of earlier, and Connor smelled wood smoke. It was the first awkward moment they'd had so far, with neither seeming to know what to say as the curricle gently bounced with the rhythm of the horses. Connor drove slowly. He'd never driven a curricle before and feared turning them over. But one day, when he'd learned the possibilities—and limits—of the vehicle and the horses, he planned to race it down the road. He wondered how Katherine would react— *with screams of delight, or would she scold and fuss?* He suspected—hoped—the former and looked forward to finding out.

Connor finally broke the silence.

"Thank you for ordering the dinner. It was nicely done."

"It was my pleasure."

"I'm not the sort of man who wants beef three times a day. I'm not my uncle. I've lived simply." Connor realized he sounded defensive, but he wanted her to understand he didn't need all the refinements that normally came with a title. He still wanted to live as quietly and as decently as he always had. And somehow, when Katherine ordered the meal, she seemed to instinctively grasp what he desired.

"Yes, I know."

But he still had his pride. "And while I am in debt, I am not impoverished, so I will make arrangements with the butcher."

"Perhaps you should leave that to me."

"You?" Connor feared he'd heard her incorrectly. If she took care of such a matter, it could only mean one thing... unless Connor were mistaken.

"I am acquainted with Mr. Stevens, and while he is not underhanded in his business dealings, he does need watching. He gets to talking and you return home to discover you've purchased mutton when you asked for beef. Give me a budget, and I will manage well enough. Of course, the pigs have yet to be slaughtered, so no need to purchase...."

Connor couldn't believe what he was hearing. "Am I to infer that you are willing to...?"

"Yes. I will marry you." She said it plainly, in a matter-of-fact way, without any hint of emotion. It should have given him pause—a lady should be elated when she accepts a gentleman's proposal of marriage—but he dismissed the note of caution and allowed his own emotions to run away.

"Thank you. Thank you, Miss Woodbridge... Katherine. You will not regret this. I promise." He wanted to stop the curricle right then and there in the middle of the lane and embrace her, kiss her even, where anyone might see, but he did not wish to frighten her or offend her with an excessive display of affection. That small word—*yes*—solved all his problems and opened up a world of infinite possibilities. "I think we will do well together. Will the reading of the banns be sufficient?"

"Yes. It'll give us time to repent at leisure."

He thought he heard laughter in her voice, but doubt crept in, and he couldn't be sure. Once more, he dismissed it, his heart pounding with the excitement of it all.

"We can marry around Christmas time, then," Connor suggested, "or perhaps just after the New Year."

"Yes. After the New Year."

And they lapsed into silence again as the lights of the village came into sight.

❖ ❖ ❖

Katherine had awakened that morning an old maid with laundry to hang out while the sun still shined and no other future before her. Now, just after sunset, under the starry sky, she was betrothed. She would be a bride soon. And a wife. Perhaps even a mother. *Oh, dear.* It was a daunting thought. The things this gentleman, Connor, would do to her, in the bed they would share. Old maid she might be but she knew perfectly well what went on between men and women in that regard. She couldn't help but imagine Connor over her, pressing against her, in her. And here he sat beside her, ignorant of her thoughts. She felt painfully embarrassed, thankful for the darkness of the night so he could not see her face.

And then they were arriving back at Lilac Cottage, and she was grateful for the chance to get away from him. But at the same time, she didn't want to part from him. As tumultuous as she felt inside, Katherine liked being near Connor.

He leapt down with ease from the curricle—*how did he do that?*—and then reached up, took her by the waist, and lifted her down. With her feet firmly on the ground, Katherine didn't want him to let her go. She wanted to move closer to him, to wrap her arms about him and press her cheek to his chest, to hear his heartbeat and feel his warmth against the cold night air as he enveloped her.

But she didn't move closer. Instead, she pulled away, allowing him only to take her gloved hand. He bowed over it, and to Katherine's surprised, he kissed her knuckles, before bidding her goodnight.

"Will you be able to find your way back?" she asked.

"The horses know their way home," he replied, and she could hear the laughter in his tone.

And then she felt him watching her as she hurried up the walk and into the cottage.

Once inside, with the door secured behind her, Katherine resisted the urge to look out the window and watch him drive away. She was a bundle of confused emotion, all fear and excitement at the same time. She was supposed to have outgrown all this years ago. Yet, in many ways, she felt eighteen all over again. And then it occurred to her; if she were eighteen, Connor would be ten. She couldn't help but feel this whole thing was ridiculous.

"Kitty? Is that you?" Aunt Catherine called from the sitting room.

"Yes, it's me." Katherine stepped into the sitting room to see Aunt Catherine sitting in her chair by the fire—exactly as Katherine had left her earlier in the day.

"I thought he was going to keep you for the night."

"I beg your pardon?" Shock and outrage rose up in Katherine. She couldn't believe Aunt Catherine would say such a thing.

"You've been gallivanting all over Roxbury Hall with the new viscount. The entire village is talking of it."

"What of it?" Some of Katherine's anger spilled out, her voice rising. "There was nothing untoward going on."

"It's shameful. A boy half your age."

That barb hit its mark, and it hurt. "He is not half my age." Katherine realized she spoke too loudly and tried to calm herself, succeeding to some degree. "Yes, he is younger than I am, but by only a few years." *If eight years could be called a few.* "And you will find out soon enough that Lord Roxbury has asked me to be his wife, and I have accepted him."

Rather than satisfying her, the explanation appeared to anger Aunt Catherine. She opened her mouth to respond but then labored for words. Katherine didn't know what to expect, but she had thought anger would be the last reaction from her aunt over the news of her forthcoming marriage and elevation to Viscountess Roxbury. If anything, Aunt Catherine should have been pleased. *A viscountess in the family!*

"Did he, now?" Aunt Catherine appeared to calm herself, and her eyes grew icy cold. "Well, what does someone like that want with someone like you?"

Katherine felt as if she had been struck, as if she had fallen and had the wind knocked out of her and then struggled to set herself right again. She could not respond. She wanted to say Connor wanted her as his companion at board and bed, he wanted a mother to his children—*God willing*—and a mistress for his house.

But she could not keep the truth from herself. Connor wanted her so he would be financially sound and out of debt. He wanted her for the money.

"And ginger-haired at that!" Aunt Catherine snorted in a most unladylike manner.

"I like his ginger hair," Katherine said quietly, "And I like him."

"My dear, at your age, you'd fancy any man who gave you the time of day, be he baker, butcher, or the Archbishop of Canterbury."

And with that, Katherine struck back. With a feigned light-hearted and amused tone, she related to Aunt Catherine the provisions of the late viscount's will, of how, in order to obtain the money, the new Lord Roxbury must marry one Katherine Woodbridge of Lilac Cottage—*Katherine with a K*—and the late viscount had intended Aunt Catherine as some kind of cruel joke but due to a happy mix-up, the new Lord Roxbury could marry Katherine in the full knowledge that he was following the dictates of the will.

Katherine immediately regretted saying anything at all about the will. That was a private matter between her and Connor. And Mr. Thornhurst, of course. Never mind that such secrets had a habit of seeping out in small villages, it was not her place to speak of it. And she had no right to hurt Aunt Catherine, despite her aunt's cruel words.

"What a lark," Aunt Catherine said calmly, not only without any hint of humor but as if void of feeling entirely. She stared unseeing past Katherine, her lips pressed tightly together. Katherine waited for her to say something, but she didn't, for a long while, until at last, she blinked away her stare, looked down at the floor, and said, "I think I'll retire early. Find Mary. She can put me to bed."

When Katherine moved to help her stand, Aunt Catherine waved her away with indifference, and Katherine went to find Mary as instructed. It took but a trice, and once Katherine found herself alone, she realized she was trembling uncontrollably. All the emotions of earlier—the excitement, the fear, the expectation, the pleasure of just being with Connor— were now replaced by anger and shame. She had behaved abominably. But then, the lady who had said such horrible things to her was not the Aunt Catherine she'd known and loved all her life.

Just after dawn, Katherine sat straight up in bed, her heart pounding as if with a sudden shock.

Lord in Heaven! What have I done?

It was her very first thought upon waking. She couldn't very well marry a man she'd only just met. He might be a viscount—a strong, virile, beautiful viscount at that—but he was practically a stranger. Furthermore, Connor was marrying her for money, to settle his debts and restore his home, but she was marrying him out of cowardice. And she thought, *no*, she couldn't do that to him. He deserved so much more. He deserved better.

Some other solution could be found, but marrying her simply wouldn't work. She would have to say something. The sooner the better.

The whole thing was ridiculous. The possibility of a man like that marrying an old maid like her was so preposterous no one would believe it. Even Mrs. Morris wasn't suspicious to find them alone together. After all, a young man, especially one so handsome and of his standing, would never deign to pursue a penniless spinster so far past her prime. It was unheard of.

Climbing out of bed, Katherine discovered, as she had expected the day before, the wind had shifted during the night, bringing cold with a grey, overcast sky that promised rain. With the warm idyll now over, the last vestiges of summer gone, and winter well on its way, she had work to do in the cottage, and she set about her normal morning routine seeing to the minor but necessary odds and ends of daily housekeeping.

Due to the previous day's excitement, Katherine had failed to finish the laundry. Thankfully, Mary had finished the job. But Katherine had wanted to wash the windows as well, while the sun still shined and before the cold set in. Despite the change in temperature, there was still time to do this cleaning. Once Aunt Catherine—silent in regard to last night's argument but still her now-normal curt self—was dressed and in her place by the fire, with her breakfast of coffee and toast, Katherine lugged a bucket of water outside and started on the task.

It was mid-morning and she was almost finished, when she looked up to see a man on horseback staring at her. Only when he tipped his hat in greeting did she realize who it was.

"Connor." Her heart leapt up at the sight of him, and all the elation and expectation she'd felt the day before returned in an instant, driving away all her doubt, at least for the moment. Approaching him, she noticed the magnificent horse upon which he sat, a great black hunter. And then she noticed the basket of apples Connor held out to her.

"Apparently, I have an orchard." Connor smiled, and Katherine couldn't help but smile also as she accepted the heavy basket. "I also have eight horses. Isn't he beautiful?"

"Yes," Katherine replied looking up at Connor, "Beautiful." He was freshly shaved and neatly dressed, all the nervousness and uncertainty of the previous day replaced with confidence and satisfaction.

"You'll be happy to know that when I returned to the house last night, several men were waiting at the kitchen door in hope of getting work." He told her the names of the men, and she recognized all of them and gave her opinion of each—who needed to be watched, who was sloppy, who was slow but worked well, who was vulgar but good-hearted. Katherine noticed one side of Connor's wide mouth turn upward, and it occurred to her she sounded like she was lecturing him, or worse, gossiping.

"I'm sorry," she said, "I forget my place."

"No, Katherine." He grew serious. "I value your opinion. And a wife is duty-bound to advise her husband, even when he lacks the good sense to listen." And he winked at her. "With that, I must take my leave."

"Oh?"

"I have to see Mr. Thornhurst about the rents paid at Michaelmas. And then I will see the vicar about the reading of the banns. If that is still acceptable to you."

This was her chance. She could stop it all right now. All she had to do was say something. But she couldn't. She couldn't ruin his happiness and his bright optimism. She didn't want to see that spark fade from his green eyes. She didn't want a return of all his difficulties. She couldn't be the cause of that, especially when she was the solution. So she remained silent and simply nodded her head.

"Oh, *the boy's* name is Samuel." And with that, Connor rode on into the village.

It was several hours before Katherine finished everything she *had* to do for the day. There were still plenty of things that eventually would need tending to, but for now, they would wait, or Mary and Cook could manage them. Aunt Catherine, as was her routine after luncheon, sat dozing in her chair by the fire. She seemed pleased by the gift of the apples, despite her complaints about the quantity—*they'll spoil before we can finish them all*—and she even intimated that perhaps Lord

Roxbury would remember her after the hogs had been slaughtered.

With the sky looking drearier than ever, Katherine grabbed her umbrella and headed down the lane toward Roxbury Hall. Connor, no doubt, would be occupied with his business affairs and estate matters, but with so much work to do, she knew Mrs. Morris would appreciate an extra pair of hands at the hall.

While she was still within sight of the village, rain began to come down, steady but gently, and Katherine was thankful she had her umbrella to protect her. Holding her skirt with one hand so as not to get the hem too wet, she hurried down the lane. She paid little attention to her surroundings but focused instead on the ground as she watched her footing. She soon noticed, despite the rain, a distinct, pungent smell which caused her nose to wrinkle up in distaste—*farmer's perfume*, her father had always called it. And as she looked up, she saw one of the fallow fields alongside the road. Only now, it was black with freshly spread manure and men were plowing it under. The man nearest her, in his shirtsleeves despite the rain, labored behind a team of oxen tilling the earth. Then she noticed his ginger hair.

It was Connor.

She walked along, slowly, keeping an even pace with him as he moved just ahead of her, and she caught herself smiling. His linen shirt clung to him, revealing the broad expanse of his back. Katherine had never realized how captivating a man's back could be—solid, well-defined, all muscle and strength. It tapered down to his narrow waist and hips with those long legs beneath. She couldn't help but imagine her hand lingering over those shoulders and feeling all that masculine vitality just under her fingers.

It occurred to Katherine that she didn't have to do anything. She didn't have to say a word but just let it happen, let all this happen, and he would be hers, to touch all she wanted. *Her* husband, perhaps even the father of her children, if she just ignored the nagging voice in her head mimicking Aunt Catherine—*what would someone like that want with someone like you? A boy, no less.* Katherine well knew the answer to that—money. But she feared she was beginning to feel something for Connor, something so very dangerous in an arrangement like theirs, and again, she heard Aunt Catherine's voice—*at your age, you'd fancy any man who gave you the time of day.*

As Connor came to the end of the row, he stopped the team of oxen. Another man took over for him, but instead of continuing the plowing, he began unharnessing the oxen. Connor turned around, ran his fingers through his wet hair, and saw Katherine watching him.

"Miss Woodbridge!" he called out with a boyish smile. He snatched up his thoroughly wet jacket from the ground and pulled it on over his wet shirt as he trotted over to her.

"You'll catch your death of cold," she said and lifted the umbrella up to protect him from the increasing downpour.

"We were trying to get it done before the rain started." He took the umbrella from her and held it over them as they walked toward Roxbury Hall.

"Get what done?"

"This field has lain fallow for years, and I want to get it and all the others ready for spring planting. Just needed some manure and a good plowing to work it all in." As he spoke, Katherine thought this probably wasn't the sort of conversation normally conducted in *polite society*. Aunt Catherine certainly wouldn't approve. And Katherine refrained from laughing. Then she heard Connor demand, "And what brings you out in this weather?"

"Mrs. Morris could use my help at the house." Katherine motioned toward the men in the field, now all bringing in their teams of oxen and plows. "I see you found some help."

"Finding men who want to work wasn't difficult," Connor said, "Paying them is. Fortunately, the rents were better than I expected, and if I count my pennies carefully, we'll manage well enough for the time being." Katherine heard the unspoken part of that—*until I marry you and receive the inheritance money; then I can fix everything up proper, pay the workers, and settle my father's debts.* Everything depended on her.

"Have you seen the tenant cottages yet?"

"First thing this morning." He grimaced and sounded disgusted by what he saw. "A dozen need repair, four of them in serious need, while two are unlivable in their current state. Given the deplorable conditions, I was surprised any rent money came in. How my uncle could have allowed them to fall into such decay... and to let all these fields sit empty when people depended on them. They depended on him."

When Katherine walked and talked with Connor like this, even with the cold rain coming down, everything seemed possible. All her doubts about marrying him disappeared. Aunt Catherine's voice faded, replaced by Connor's optimism. She could imagine a life with him. Together, they could rebuild Roxbury Hall, restore the cottages, and make these fields fertile and productive again. And while it all frightened her a little, she had no reservations. Not when she was with Connor.

"No one knows why the late Lord Roxbury let it all fall apart," Katherine commented, "but it was all perfectly within his rights. The land was his, to do with as he pleased. That doesn't make it right, though, does it? I'd say he has a lot to answer for when he stands before his maker. But then, we all have a lot to answer for." And she thought of the argument with Aunt Catherine last night.

Connor had grown silent, almost sullen, as if lost in dark thoughts. And then he said, quietly, as if it were nothing extraordinary, "I think he did it to spite me."

It filled Connor's heart to see Katherine. He hadn't expected to turn around and see her standing there protected from the shower by an umbrella, skirts splattered to the knees. But he could just imagine what she thought of him in his shirt-sleeves, drenched, and smelling of manure. He hoped the realization that her husband-to-be was a man who liked to get his hands dirty didn't frighten her away. He would never be one of those puffed-up dandies bemoaning the fashions of the day with quizzing glass in hand. Hard work, a good meal, and a good bed were what he wanted out of life. And someone to share it with him. He didn't require love. He'd seen his parents' love, and he knew love faded. And when it did, they had nothing left to stand on—not their families' support, not money, not shared beliefs, not even friendship.

All Connor wished for in a wife was that he liked the lady. And he liked Katherine.

He took the umbrella from her and held it over them both as they walked to Roxbury Hall. With the cessation of work, Connor quickly began to feel the cold, and they hurried along, talking of all the work that needed doing. At times, he couldn't believe a female would know so much about the practical maintenance of a house, but then, from everything he'd learned about Katherine in the last two days, Connor knew she'd spent much of her life being responsible for other people's homes. In that regard, they had much in common.

Reaching Roxbury Hall just as the downpour increased, Connor looked up at the roof and saw—much to his relief—a tarp covering the damaged portions where the slate had fallen off. Katherine's simple comment the day before—*Mr. Carter and his sons could use the work*—proved truer than Connor expected, as there were nine sons by Connor's count. And four of them had climbed up atop the house at daybreak to start work.

Once inside, Connor started toward the stairs, but Katherine stopped him by laying her hand gently on his arm.

"Boots off here." She pointed at the settle by the door and waited as Connor plopped down to pull off his muddy boots. Once they were off, Katherine took them and said, as she headed toward the kitchens, "Mr. Baldwin can take care of these. Now, find some dry clothes. I'll get you some brandy."

"I really do not like brandy," Connor confessed as he rose.

Katherine stopped and turned to face him with one fist on her hip. "A fine nobleman you'll make." And then she smiled. "Will tea do?"

"Perfect."

Connor returned from his chamber to the hall a short while later in dry clothes, fresh boots, and still-drenched hair. He found Katherine sitting before the fire with her skirts spread out before her in an effort to dry them. Unfortunately, he thought, her hair was dry;

otherwise, she might have been forced to pull some of those pins from the brown mass piled atop her head. He wondered how long it was and looked forward to the day when he'd finally find out.

On the table beside her, a teapot waited with all the usual accoutrements, plus plates of sandwiches and thick wedges of cake.

"I thought you needed something more substantial to tide you over until dinner." Katherine poured a cup of tea and held it out to him. "Mrs. Morris appears to be preparing beef for you tonight, but that will be some hours away from now. I take it you gave her some money?"

"Ah, yes." Connor accepted the tea and sat down opposite her within the warmth of the fire. "I tried to explain I prefer pork and mutton...."

"And fish."

"All very dull and boring and common, I suppose. I do enjoy beef," he continued, "but for Christmas or such."

"Oh, good." She handed him a serviette and held out the plate of sandwiches. "That will make planning the Christmas menus so much easier. I can never decide between goose or beef."

Connor heard the teasing tone of her voice and matched it. "What? No turkey?"

"I've never cooked a turkey before. Mrs. Morris might know more about it, though."

"It's two months away, but you and Miss Woodbridge will come here for Christmas, of course." He selected a sandwich—a bit of smoky gammon left over from breakfast, he suspected. "We'll make a grand occasion of it."

"Roast beef with all the trimmings?"

"Exactly. And afterwards, we can have dancing here in the hall."

"Dancing? So you expect a large party?"

"Just a small dinner—Mr. Thornhurst, perhaps, and his family, but we have plenty of time to decide—and then after, we could open the house up for the evening festivities. Both you and Miss Woodbridge can stay in the suite of rooms just off the drawing room."

"Oh?"

"You must stay the night." Then Connor saw the shocked expression on Katherine's face and quickly clarified. "Chaperoned, of course. You have already picked out those rooms for her, haven't you? For when we are married. Assuming she wants to leave Lilac Cottage, that is." Connor noticed the cheerfulness fade from Katherine's face. "She doesn't have to, if she doesn't want to. We could hire a companion, plus another maid, if need be."

Katherine fidgeted with her skirt and then rearranged the plates on the table before taking a piece of cake and settling back into her chair.

"In truth," she said staring off into the flames, "we haven't discussed it. She didn't take the news of our betrothal well."

"She didn't?"

"No. But then, she's been most peculiar for some time."

A chill unrelated to the weather seemed to fall over them, Connor noticed. He knew Katherine did not need her aunt's—or anyone else's—permission to marry, but he understood her blessing was desirable. Strange, though, that Miss Woodbridge would disapprove of her grandniece marrying the Viscount Roxbury. Connor had witnessed the managing mamas throwing their daughters in the pathway of the Duke of Rutland's family, all for the possibility of forging a family connection.

Still, he knew from painful experience that some family relations were unwanted. So perhaps the elder Miss Woodbridge felt as his uncle had, that some connections were less than desirable.

I think he did it to spite me. Connor had said it to Katherine earlier as they walked in the rain. That was Connor's explanation for the deplorable condition of the house and lands. He didn't mean to bring up the past when a future of such possibilities lay before him. And the look on Katherine's face made him instantly regret saying it.

"That sounded like such an arrogant thing to say," Connor suddenly said in the midst of the cold silence of the hall.

"What sounded arrogant?"

"That I thought my uncle allowed all this ruin just to spite me. I must have shocked you."

"No. Not at all. I just couldn't imagine why someone would do something like that. To their own flesh and blood."

Connor couldn't imagine it, either. He'd never understood it. All he knew was that his uncle had rejected both him and his mother and condemned his father for the choices he'd made.

"I met my uncle once when I was seven." Connor held out his cup for Katherine to refill and took an offered wedge of cake. "He used to take a house in London for the Season. We lived in Bath, and one day, my father decided we'd go to Town. I think he'd finally run through all his money and was trying to get back in his brother's good graces.

"The house was full of aunts and uncles and cousins I knew nothing about. I was excited—there was someone to play with, but…. Children can be cruel. I was *the Irish boy*, even though I'd never been to Ireland and knew none of my mother's family beyond their family names.

"My mother had this thick, wild, unruly hair. I remember my father teasing her and pulling pins, making it all tumble down around her. It was glorious.

And I matched her in color. But in my uncle's house, she powdered it. Even so, my cousins kept saying things, horrible things, about her, about me. And I felt ashamed.

"So I darkened my hair with bootblack. The look on my mother's face. Shock and pain. I hurt her deeply without ever meaning to. I just wanted to look like my father and his family. My uncle laughed. 'Even the boy knows.' I didn't understand what he meant. *Knew what?* Now, I know he meant not an Englishman, not a gentleman, but someone inferior. Someone from beyond the pale.

"I tried to wash it out, but the best I managed was a mottled blackened ginger, like a mongrel cat. I ended up taking a pair of scissors to it, which, of course, just made it worse. We left the next morning when it was still dark and returned home to Bath. And I never saw my uncle or any of the family again. Eventually, my father found work as an estate manager."

Katherine reached over to Connor's hand resting on the chair arm and covered it with her own. Connor turned his hand over and clasped hers. Looking her directly in the eye, he said, "The humiliation my mother suffered because of me...."

"No. You were a boy." Katherine's voice soothed the old pain. "Your uncle should have welcomed you and your mother into his house. Had he done that, the rest of the family would have followed his example. The fault was his, not yours."

Connor raised her hand to his lips and kissed her knuckles.

When Katherine finally withdrew her hand and settled back into her chair, she asked, "And your mother's family in Ireland? What of them?"

"Never met them. Never even been to Ireland. Probably never will. It seems the women in the family have a bad habit of marrying redcoats."

Katherine smiled. "As do mine."

Connor smiled back. "Perhaps that explains Miss Woodbridge's opposition. You're breaking a family tradition."

"Scandalous."

Lord, he enjoyed her quick humor.

They sat before the fire and talked, the rain coming down outside and pelting against the windows, and Connor felt a deep and unexpected contentment. He thought as he had before, *yes, we will do well together.*

The banns were read on Sunday. To Katherine's surprise—and great relief—Connor came in the carriage and escorted both her and Aunt Catherine to church that morning. It was the new Lord Roxbury's first appearance at a village event, albeit merely church, and many people only learned of their engagement as the Reverend Mr. Tipton read the banns. Mrs. Boyle, the squire's wife, turned red. Only moments before, she had gushed over Connor, undoubtedly as a potential husband to one of her three marriageable daughters.

And as Katherine expected, Mrs. Boyle made a particular point not to offer congratulations to her after services while once again fawning over Connor. Katherine imagined quite a few village mamas and their daughters felt likewise, having prettier young ladies passed over in favor of an old maid.

The banns were read again on the following Sunday and the Sunday after that. And on each occasion—as well as every Sunday after that—Connor came with the carriage to escort Katherine and Aunt Catherine, for which Katherine was very grateful. Even though the church was just a short walk up the lane and across the green, Aunt Catherine had difficulties moving, and it was easy enough for Connor to assist her into the carriage—complete with warm bricks and lap rugs in these ever-colder days—and gently lift her down at the church doors.

Despite her continual grumpiness, Aunt Catherine responded to Connor in a polite and even friendly manner, and she went so far as to invite him to dinner each Sunday—which was only proper, as Connor took to sending over pheasants from his woods or fish from his lake and then haunches of pork when the time came for slaughtering and curing. All of this on top of the eggs and milk and cheese sent around to them from the Roxbury dairy.

Connor even hired one of Mr. Carter's daughters— the seventeen-year-old Nancy, who could read and write—to help at Lilac Cottage and with Aunt Catherine, especially when Katherine was busy at Roxbury Hall.

Over the weeks as the days grew shorter and darker, Katherine found a heaviness in her life was lifted with Connor. Without a word from her, he recognized her burdens and endeavored to make life easier for her.

And then one evening, as he lifted her down from his curricle, she realized she loved him. Worse, she was *in love* with Connor. And it terrified her more than anything ever had.

In her experience—limited as it was to her infatuation with Thomas Cooper and observation of other couples—love was always a one-sided affair. She never believed her father loved her mother. For his part, it seemed a relationship built on an understanding of toleration. For her mother's part, it seemed an endless endeavor to please.

Likewise, her brother, whose unwavering devotion to his wife bordered on a contained madness, while his wife seemed, at best, indifferent to his attentions, as content to sit opposite him at table as she would have been at any other man's.

And with all this thinking, her mind recalled poor Queen Mary Tudor—Bloody Mary—so many centuries before, married to a handsome prince eleven years her junior, and how she adored him—an unrequited love— and she went mad for want of love.

Now Katherine was less than a month away from marrying her own handsome lord, eight years her junior, with the full realization that she was in love with him. She would share his table and share his bed, perhaps even bear a child, and while she would love Connor, she knew he would not feel the same about her. Oh, she knew his kindness towards her was genuine, but it was the same kindness he exhibited to Mr. Carter and Mr. Thornhurst and the Reverend Mr. Tipton and even to Mrs. Boyle and her blushing daughters. And then Katherine wondered what gave her the right to expect anything more when theirs was just a marriage of convenience.

Part Two

CONNOR DISCOVERED KATHERINE MADE his life easier. He still worked hard, and he still went to bed exhausted from his labors, but before he had arrived in Roxbury, he had expected to hire a housekeeper and oversee her duties, with daily reports on the running of the household and decisions needing his every attention. Katherine, however, took care of all that, leaving him to the things he felt more qualified to deal with—the repairs to the house, the butchering of the hogs, the maintenance of the tenant cottages, the drainage of the lower field, and the dredging of miller's pond. To his surprise, Connor owned the mill, it seemed; the miller, despite his success at his profession, merely rented it from him.

Katherine appeared to have no difficulties running the house or managing the servants. When Connor's meager possessions arrived from Cornwall, mostly in the form of books, she knew exactly where to place everything within the house, although she never entered the apartments belonging to the viscount and his viscountess. And still, Connor found, she instinctively knew when to defer a matter to him. Only once since she began seeing to the household had he seen her hesitate.

They had been in the hall, and Katherine had issued an order to Mrs. Morris about serving tea in the drawing room. Immediately after Mrs. Morris left, Connor had noticed a shadow of worry and doubt pass over Katherine's face, and she suddenly apologized for forgetting her place. So he merely reminded her that as far as he could tell, she had no difficulties remembering exactly what her place was at Roxbury Hall.

He liked her. She made his life better. And he looked forward to the time when they would be husband and wife.

As autumn turned to winter and the first smatterings of snow covered the county, Connor and Katherine spent most of their days busy with work. Other than an hour snatched here and there when they'd take tea in the hall or drawing room, they had little time to be alone together. And every time, Connor ended up telling her things he'd never told anyone— simple things, often, his thoughts on Pope's poetry or what flowers he'd like to see in the garden, but also important, personal things, such as his love for his imperfect father. Connor escorted Katherine and her aunt to church every Sunday, and so far, he had dined with them afterwards on each occasion, only returning to Roxbury Hall well after nightfall.

However, they had one other moment alone. Connor had worked in the fields surrounding the ancient stone circle on his land. It intrigued him, and he remembered Katherine mentioning it on the day they'd met. So on the morning of the 21st of December, by prearrangement, Connor collected Katherine in his curricle well before dawn, and together they had gone to the stone circle to see if the old tales were true. Connor felt as if they were doing something nefarious, or even as if they were eloping to Gretna Green. He smiled at the thought when he realized all they had to do was show up at the vicar's door before noon if they wished to marry sooner rather than later.

There was no snow that day, just a thick frost as the sky gradually went from black with stars to blue with stars and finally glowed pinkish orange in a streak across the horizon. Connor and Katherine sat huddled together in the curricle, with lap rugs and hot bricks. Connor threw a blanket around her, and while he kept his arm about her and she clung to his coat, he wanted to hold her even closer... but someplace warm. He tried not to think too much about that idea and instead focused his attention on the horizon.

And then, as Katherine had told him, Connor saw the sun break just there, directly in alignment with the key stone. Katherine abruptly pulled away from him, and with a great smile, began applauding, as if they sat in a theatre. He half expected her to shout *Bravo*, followed by *Encore!* And to his surprise, he realized he enjoyed watching her reaction to the sunrise more than he enjoyed the actual sunrise. Her face glowed in the morning light, and he couldn't resist her, his soon-to-be bride. He leaned in and kissed her cheek. Katherine turned, still all smiles, to face him, and kissed him. On the lips. Quickly.

And that was their first kiss. Over and done with in a blink of an eye. No fireworks. No dissolving into the throes of passion. Simple, strangely natural, and affectionate. Connor wanted to do it again. Longer. To see where it might lead. But it could wait. Until after the New Year, when he would have her all to himself and they could do as they wished. In their own home. In their own chambers. In their own beds.

They drove back to Lilac Cottage for a breakfast of hot coffee and fresh buns with butter and jam as they warmed themselves by the fire. Miss Woodbridge still slept, but Nancy joined them, and even Mary slipped in to hear the plans for the party on Christmas when the doors to Roxbury Hall would be opened to everyone. Realizing he did not want to take anyone away from their own merrymaking on Christmas Eve, Connor suggested to Katherine that they gather all the greenery for the party on the 23rd. Katherine concurred, and she suggested a simple dinner be provided after the labor of gathering greenery in this cold to those who helped. Someone mentioned dancing, and the next thing Connor knew, he seemed to be inviting half the village—mostly young people—to come and help decorate Roxbury Hall for Christmas on the 23rd, with a light dinner and dancing to follow. In essence, Connor now realized, he would be holding two Christmas parties—one for the decorating party and one on Christmas night—and for a moment, he worried about the expense. But then he glanced over at Katherine. His concern vanished. All would be well, he knew; she would see to that.

At first glance, Roxbury Hall appeared to be at sixes and sevens. But, from Katherine's perspective, it was a controlled chaos, with men moving furniture and rolling carpets in the hall, while Mrs. Morris, the newly hired Cook, and several girls from the village busied themselves in the kitchens in preparation for the dinner. Miss Alice Thornhurst, the solicitor's youngest daughter, practiced on the piano forte, now set in the hall alcove, while one of Mr. Carter's sons—Katherine couldn't keep all those boys straight—played his fiddle, filling the house with melody. To Katherine's relief, both performed well and would provide a lively variety of music for the dancing.

While she looked forward to the evening, in truth, Katherine was tired. Aunt Catherine had been even more obstinate that morning and refused to attend the festivities. Katherine suspected she'd even refuse the invitation from Connor himself. She had declared that the party was for young people and no one wanted her there. Katherine thought perhaps Aunt Catherine felt unwell and just didn't want to admit it, preferring to keep her aches and pains and physical difficulties private.

But it was something else, some deep-rooted melancholy that Aunt Catherine couldn't seem to shake off. And Katherine couldn't offer any words of comfort.

"And then one day," Aunt Catherine kept rambling on that morning, "you find you've grown old, and you can't remember when that happened. You feel twenty-five, maybe thirty, but the glass tells you otherwise. No one loves you then. It isn't merely that gentlemen stop asking for a dance. It's everything. It's everyone. At the milliners, trying on a hat... I looked in the glass and said, 'Oh, no. This won't do. It makes me look like an old woman.' And the silly chit showing me the hats said, 'but you are an old woman.' I was only forty-two!" Aunt Catherine pointed at Katherine and said, "Your turn will come, too. And sooner than you think."

Nancy, somehow, managed to calm her and brought a cup of chocolate to her with additional promises of honey cake.

Then, while Katherine had arrived early at Roxbury Hall to prepare for the dinner and dancing, she had seen little of Connor. She thought nothing of it, as he was busy on the estate. Even when he had so little time that he rushed through luncheon, Katherine knew he was trying to finish things early that day. He seemed to succeed in this effort, returning to the house with just enough time to bathe and dress before appearing in the hall to welcome his guests.

Yet as the guests began to spill into the house, Katherine's mood slowly changed, from a happy mixture of anticipation and anxiousness to... something else she couldn't understand, a strange unhappiness that made no sense. Everyone was all smiles, with rosy cheeks from the cold and bright flashing eyes, filled with elation and ready for merrymaking. Connor took her hand and welcomed the guests with her by his side as if she already presided as lady of the house. Still, she felt a gloom fall over her, as if she stood in a shadow in the midst of bright sunlight. She dismissed it as lingering remnants of Aunt Catherine's melancholy that morning; perhaps the malady was contagious and now infected Katherine.

The Misses Boyles arrived with their mama. Two of Mr. Carter's sons appeared in the hall. The vicar's marriageable daughter arrived with her four eligible brothers, plus a tall cousin from London who'd had her first season that year, all with Mrs. Tipton. Mr. Thornhurst's eldest grandson brought his sister, not yet out as she was, but still deemed old enough to participate in village festivities among family friends. Mr. Morgan, the village schoolmaster, was an unexpected but welcomed guest, but then, it was rumored he had a *tendre* for Miss Alice Thornhurst. The butcher's daughters came, as did the draper's children, including the ten-year-old boy. And within no time, Connor had them organized and led them out into the forests to gather greenery—evergreen boughs, branches of holly, and even mistletoe, if it could be managed. The ten-year-old insisted he knew where some could be found, and he volunteered to climb the tree as everyone else—according to him—was too heavy for the job.

Before they all departed, Connor asked Katherine if she were sure she didn't wish to join them—on a cold, dreary December afternoon that threatened snow. No, she assured him, she did not wish to accompany them on this expedition, but she told him to have fun. Then Connor hurried off, looking like he had every intention of obeying her. And a small, irrational part of her, somewhere deep inside, felt annoyed that he hadn't been just a bit more disappointed when she declined his invitation for a romp in the forest.

A little before sunset, small groups and pairs, all in high spirits and full of laughter, trickled back to the hall, many carrying canvas bundles of holly, branches of pine, and even some mistletoe. Returning with the Tipton brothers and their tall London cousin, Connor brought up the rear, and then proceeded to oversee the decorating of the house while Katherine finished seeing to the dinner.

When Mr. Baldwin announced dinner, Connor joined Katherine in the dining room. The table now stood against the wall while numerous chairs lined the walls. Several smaller tables stood in the middle of the room, each with four chairs, but there clearly was not enough room at the tables for everyone. But no one seemed to mind and quickly found spots here and there to form little groups. And the repast laid out before them more than made up for the informality of the occasion—roasted chickens and smoked hams, boiled potatoes and dishes of vegetables, wheels of cheese and walnuts, cakes and tarts, apples and pears, chestnuts and sweetmeats, biscuits and pastries, all accompanied by coffee, tea, and punch.

Katherine found herself doing what she always did on such occasions, rare as they were in her life. She ate little, and instead, hovered about making sure everything was as it should be and seeing that everyone enjoyed themselves. When she finally sat down, her companions were Mrs. Tipton and Mrs. Boyle. And when the dancing began, she ended up sitting with them again.

If gentlemen ever had dance cards, then Connor's would have been filled, as everyone wanted to dance with him. Even the young ladies and girls who had their caps set on someone else desired a dance, simply to say they had danced with the new Viscount Roxbury. Katherine did not dance. There weren't quite enough gentlemen to go around for all the girls—even the draper's ten-year-old son was pressed into service— and a few young ladies sat out each dance. No one thought to request a dance from the older ladies chatting quietly in the corner.

Trying to hide her strange melancholy in the midst of all this merriment, Katherine pasted on a smile. She watched Connor, her beautiful, ginger-haired boy, although, in this company, he was the eldest man in the room. But he seemed unusually boyish tonight dancing among all those other young, attractive people. He smiled and laughed as he swung through a lively country dance full of rhythm and accompanied by many a forgiven misstep by the dancers. His partner this time was the tall Tipton cousin from London—an elegant beauty wearing the height of fashion, Katherine noted.

And then Katherine realized what a lovely pair they made—the lord of the manor and the belle of the ball. It was not jealousy at play but a simple observation of reality. Connor belonged with someone like that. Not the Tipton cousin, but Connor could easily go to London and find an heiress for himself. He deserved someone young, someone docile, someone sure to give him plenty of children. Someone less opinionated. Someone of the *belle monde*. He didn't need a housekeeper. And Katherine knew when she married Connor, she'd always be little more than a housekeeper to him.

Until this moment, she'd thought she could bear that.

But now, she realized Connor would tire of her. Not today, perhaps, but eventually. *What would someone like that want with someone like you?* Aunt Catherine had asked. And her aunt was right. Connor didn't love her. Once he had the money, despite their friendship, despite his kindness, he'd find, in the manner of countless men before him, someone else. Or several someones. He'd go to London. He'd be discrete, perhaps out of deference to her, but he'd still take a lover. And perhaps he would truly love this nameless, faceless woman he would find one day. When he tired of Katherine.

She had been so very practical about it all, this arrangement of theirs, but she could not be practical about this. She could be his wife, she could run his house, she could care for him and love him and do all that was expected of her. And she knew she could be happy, even knowing he didn't love her and that he'd only married her for the money. It would be enough. But she could not bear knowing her husband, the man she loved, was with someone else. She could not share him like that.

And Katherine knew.

She couldn't marry Connor.

Connor found it hard to believe he'd promised this many dances to this many young ladies. True, they were short a few men, so all the men present had been conscripted for every dance. But the partner he wanted above all others sat out each dance. He hadn't even had the opportunity to ask her. Instead, Katherine remained ensconced in the corner with Mrs. Boyle and Mrs. Tipton, which surprised Connor. While both ladies were affable enough, neither matched Katherine for intelligence and both seemed prone to gossip.

He'd also noticed Katherine appeared out of sorts all day. He understood Aunt Catherine had been particularly difficult that morning, but Connor had been unable to discuss it further with Katherine as he wished to get things done early in order to participate in the gathering of greenery and the party afterwards. Even when it came time for dinner, when he thought at last he'd have a moment to sit down with her, his guests called him away from her.

Then when the dancing began, he kept expecting to cross paths with her in some of the more intricate dances, but he never did. After a particularly lively country dance, Connor planned to sit down with Katherine. But then someone called for a waltz, to the great delight of everyone, and Connor saw his chance.

"There is only one lady with whom I shall ever waltz," he proclaimed with a great smile and then looked over to the corner as everyone sought out their partners. But Katherine no longer sat with Mrs. Boyle and Mrs. Tipton. Connor quickly glanced around the room but didn't see her anywhere. Assuming Katherine was tending to some matter, Connor motioned to Miss Alice Thornhurst to play. No sense in making all the others wait while he searched for his bride-to-be. When he found her, he'd simply demand another waltz. It was his house, after all.

As the music began, Connor went into the dining room in the full expectation of seeing her there. But only a few of the village girls lingered by the desserts. So he continued on into the kitchens, where he encountered Mrs. Morris. She hadn't seen Katherine, but then *the boy*,

Samuel, came in and informed Connor he had seen Katherine walking toward the village some time ago.

For a moment, Connor was utterly confused and couldn't understand why Katherine would venture out in the cold and darkness. Even from here in the kitchen, Connor could see through the windows that a light snow fell. Nothing to impede travel, but still very worrying to him given that Katherine was on foot.

Then it occurred to Connor that something could be amiss with Aunt Catherine. Perhaps word came from Lilac Cottage while he indulged in merrymaking and Katherine simply didn't wish to disturb him. He needed to make it clear to Katherine that, in the future, if she needed anything, no matter how trivial she deemed it, she was to come to him. Her concerns were his concerns, and she had already demonstrated the reverse daily, to his great satisfaction and more.

He told Samuel to saddle his horse and then retrieved his coat. He paused only to tell Mr. Baldwin that the party should continue without him and if anyone inquired to say he was seeing to an estate matter. And then he rode off into the cold night. Imagining Katherine out in this, he was thankful for the lack of wind, as the still air, despite the gentle flurry of snow falling, made the cold more bearable.

Just outside the village, Connor saw Katherine walking along the road, her head bent against the snow as she hurried but otherwise safe and sound.

"Katherine!" he called out as he neared. He saw her hesitate mid-step, but then she continued on without even turning to look back. He even thought her pace increased. He called out again, and as the horse drew close to her, Connor leapt down. He rushed to her side, but when he realized she was not going to stop, he grabbed her arm and forced her to face him. They stood just a few steps from Lilac Cottage.

"What is it, Katherine? Is it your Aunt Catherine? Is something wrong?"

Instead of answering him, Katherine jerked her arm away and said, "Please, Connor, just leave me alone." She sounded like she had been crying, although he could not see her face in the darkness, even with the trace of white snow.

He had enough experience with women to know to proceed with caution. He expected he had done something wrong—at least in Katherine's mind—to which he was completely oblivious.

"Did I do something wrong?"

He thought over everything he'd done during the course of the day and tried to remember anything that might have offended his bride-to-be. He knew it could be something completely innocuous... and then he realized it must have been the dancing. He had danced with every girl in the village while Katherine had sat with Mrs. Tipton and Mrs. Boyle—whom Connor knew treated Katherine indifferently at best. Given everything Katherine had already done for him—and everything she was preparing to do—Connor knew he should have paid more attention to her, especially at such a public event. He could just imagine the snide things Mrs. Boyle might have said to her.

"No, you did nothing wrong. You're...." She seemed to choke on her words. "I'm sorry, Connor. I'm sorry. I just can't do it."

"Can't do what?"

"I can't marry you."

Connor felt as if he'd been struck. He never expected her to say that. He thought they got on quite well. He liked her and looked forward to the time when they would be husband and wife. So he couldn't fathom why....

"You needn't worry about the money," Katherine said, "Go to London for the Season and find some heiress. They'll flock to you. You'll find a bride in no time. Someone young. Someone you will love and who will give you children."

She had slowly moved away from him and stood at the gate, a wide gulf between them. He wanted to go to her and demand to know why she was speaking this way, but he was too stunned by this rejection to move. His mind just kept turning over and over—*how do I stop this?*—but without finding an answer. They would not be getting married.

She opened the gate and walked toward the door, only to turn back briefly.

"You *are* a brilliant estate manager," she said. "I've seen everything you've done in the last two months. You'll do well. I know it."

And she hurried inside, leaving Connor standing there with the snow falling about him. Confused. He felt injured, hurt. But a subtle anger accompanied the pain. That emotion perplexed Connor even more. Katherine had spoken of the money. And he realized why he felt angry.

He needed to review his account books.

Katherine tossed and turned all night, and when she caught brief wisps of sleep, dreams plagued her— Connor's pained expression when she told him she would not marry him, even though in reality the night had hidden his face.

These were the darkest days of the year. Dawn came late, but Katherine did not rise at her usual time. Even after daybreak, she remained in bed. She saw no reason to get up. Mary could see to Aunt Catherine, Cook would see to breakfast, and Nancy.... Katherine didn't want to face Nancy. She would have to go, and Katherine wasn't ready to tell the girl she'd lost her position. It would wait until after Christmas, she decided. Everything could wait.

And at some point, everyone would know. She would have to tell them. And she wasn't ready for that either. Dealing with her own emotions was difficult enough. In some moments, she teetered on the verge of bursting into tears. She hadn't wanted to hurt Connor, but it was the only way. She'd told him the truth, even if she had left out her reasons for crying off. He didn't need to know she loved him. It would probably only embarrass him. It was better this way.

Realizing it was Christmas Eve finally got her out of bed. Since they would not be dining with Connor—Lord Roxbury, as she had to think of him now—Katherine needed to arrange for their own dinner. She'd always loved Christmas Eve as a child—coming home after Midnight Mass to cups of chocolate and plates of cake. And then, if there were snow, they would light a lantern and play half the night away. The little snow they had now amounted to nothing, but when she was child, it would have sufficed for her. She thought she should remember that lesson now.

Seeing to odds and ends, she went about her business as usual in the cottage. Then, she paid a visit to the butcher to order a goose for the following day. Other than exchanging polite pleasantries, she spoke to no one else. She returned home and continued in the course of her normal daily routine, as if Lord Roxbury had never come into her life. Only, nothing was normal. She was sullen and silent, merely going through the motions while her mind struggled with what she had done. It felt like mourning.

Just after dinner, as the sun was setting, Katherine was upstairs sorting through the linens, when Mary came up and said Aunt Catherine wanted to speak with her.

She knows, Katherine thought, descending the stairs. She found her aunt sitting by the fire, her eyes fixated on the hearth.

"Lord Roxbury has sent us a goose." Aunt Catherine spoke without preamble, never turning her gaze from the flames. "For Christmas dinner." Only then did she focus her attention on Katherine. "I can't understand why he would do such a thing when he knows we are to dine with him tomorrow." Her icy blue eyes, more than her even tone, seemed to accuse Katherine of some wrongdoing.

"If you must know," Katherine responded nonchalantly, but inside, she felt sick, "I have broken it off with Lord Roxbury."

"Broken it off?" Her brow furrowed while her mouth gapped open.

"Yes. We're not getting married." Katherine realized she trembled but continued as if none of it matter. "I'm sure you're pleased to hear it."

"Pleased?" Aunt Catherine looked genuinely confused, as if she'd forgotten all her cruel words over the last two months since Lord Roxbury's proposal. Katherine felt anger rising in her, certain her aunt was being deliberately obtuse.

"You are always pointing out how old I am. You're the one who questioned why a man like that would want someone like me. Well, it was just for the money."

Aunt Catherine sat quietly for a long while, the only sound the flickering flames. Then she slowly exhaled, as if letting go of a vast amount of energy. Her voice was calmer, and she suddenly seemed more like her old self. "It doesn't matter *why* he wanted you. Simply that he *wanted* you. You would have someone. You wouldn't end up alone."

Shaking her head, Katherine imagined Connor dancing with the tall Tipton cousin. "But he would never love me," she said. "No. You were right. He needs someone younger. Someone better suited to be a viscountess."

"Fiddlesticks! The last thing that man needs is some doe-eyed debutant running up the bills. He needs a sensible wife with a strong character."

"Sensible and strong? You make me sound like a pair of shoes."

"Be serious," Aunt Catherine scolded with a stamp of her stick.

"I am being serious." And she was. Katherine doubted Connor needed someone sensible and strong. He could hire people for that, even better suited to run his house than she ever would be. Besides, what Connor *needed* was irrelevant. He might *need* a sensible and capable wife, but gentlemen never selected wives on those criteria. A pretty face, a fine figure, an acquiescing disposition, those were the common traits men used to choose their brides. And if the first two were particularly exceptional, the third could be dispensed with altogether.

"I know of what I speak." Aunt Catherine stamped her stick again, harder this time. "You do not know the ways of men. They do not love us as we love them. The least bit of hesitation, the least bit of doubt on our part, and...." Her voice faltered, and again, she turned her gaze to the flames. "They are not the heroes we deserve. They are not knights errant. They are mere mortals, flawed, and they will disappoint every time. They do not come for us. They do not fight for us."

Her aunt was rambling again, Katherine thought, like so many times in the past few months, and still making no sense. "What are you talking about?" Katherine asked.

But Aunt Catherine continued speaking as if she heard nothing. "They are not the noble creatures we wish them to be."

Then it occurred to Katherine that Aunt Catherine spoke of her own past. "You are not speaking of Lord Roxbury," she realized. "You're speaking of someone else."

"No, I'm not. I *am* speaking of Lord Roxbury." Aunt Catherine raised her head and stared directly and unflinchingly at Katherine. "I was betrothed once. When I was seventeen. To Lord Roxbury. The *late* viscount. He asked for me and was accepted. By me and my parents." She looked away, her face wistful and filled with sorrow. "Everything was as it should have been. But then my mother informed me of what was expected of me in the performance of certain wifely duties. I was horrified. My eldest sister was in a delicate condition at the time, and all I could think was *you did that?* So I cried off."

She pulled a handkerchief from her sleeve and wiped her nose. "But I immediately regretted it. Now I know I should have gone to him, but I didn't. I waited for him. *Surely he will come, he will fight for me*—that's what I thought, fool that I was. But he never did. And now, all this business with the will, that the new viscount had to marry 'one Katherine Woodbridge of Lilac Cottage....' His final stab at me. One final laugh at my expense.

"In time, I thought there would be another. I kept waiting, thinking one day, someone would come, but no one did. And then, one day, you find no one loves you, and you are just waiting for death. Who will lie beside me in the churchyard?" She let out a great sob and dabbed her eyes with the handkerchief. "It should have been John."

"And now you've done the same thing to your own Lord Roxbury. You wounded him. You injured his pride. Despite all your selfless reasons, he won't forgive you."

Aunt Catherine suddenly rose, and leaning on her stick, she said, "I need to rest before we attend church tonight." She walked toward the doorway and called for Mary to help her. But then, before she left the room, Aunt Catherine turned and said, "And if you think Lord

Roxbury only wanted you for the money, then you're not as clever as I always thought you were."

Katherine did not attend midnight mass that Christmas Eve. Pleading a headache, she made her excuses to Aunt Catherine—who did not question her but seemed to know it was a lie—and Mary and Nancy helped Aunt Catherine to church. In truth, Katherine felt unwell. She was emotionally drained, resulting in a general malaise. She just needed to rest, and she thought a good night sleep would set her right. Then she could think more clearly about all this.

But she could not sleep. Aunt Catherine's words haunted her mind. Not so much the account of her engagement to the previous Viscount Roxbury, which was surprising enough. It explained the strange conditions of the will, for one thing, although Katherine still found it bizarre for a man to hold a grudge for so long. It spoke to a deeply broken heart.

No, it was Aunt Catherine's last words that haunted Katherine's mind—her suggestion that Connor did not want Katherine merely for the money. *Suggestion*, though, was not the right word. Aunt Catherine spoke with an absolute certainty that left Katherine thoroughly confused. She couldn't understand what Aunt Catherine had seen that she had not noticed in all her time spent with Connor. There was an affinity, yes, but he was friendly and kind to everyone, even Mrs. Boyle and her daughters.

These thoughts kept turning over in her mind long into the night. She rose when Aunt Catherine returned from church, just to make sure everything was all right and the house was closed up for the night, then returned to bed. Still, sleep only came in stops and starts, until sometime before dawn, when, with all the worries plaguing her, Katherine found herself wide awake.

She needed fresh air, and she remembered that morning, just days ago, when she and Connor had gone to the stone circle to watch the sun rise. After looking outside and determining that the sky was clear and full of stars, Katherine quickly dressed. She lit a lantern and headed out into the cold darkness. She wanted to see the sun rise again, over the stone circle. This time, though, there'd be no hot bricks, no handsome companion with his arms about her. And as she walked down the lane, the sky no longer black but faintly blue, she realized that she did everything alone. She was always on her own. Even when she was with Aunt Catherine or her grandmother before that. And she wondered what the point of living was if there was no one to share it with.

At the stone circle, Katherine brushed the previous day's snow from one of the fallen stones and sat down to await the sun's arrival. It seemed a longer wait this time, alone as she was, in the still, cold air, although the lantern provided a dim reminder of warmth. But then, in that miraculous way it did every day, the sky slowly transformed from the black of night to pre-dawn blue-grey then purple-pink and then an orange glow, until, at last, the sun burst over the horizon and filled the world with light and warmth. This time, though, it did not appear in alignment with the keystone but just there, on the very edge of the stone.

Katherine had always heard that this day, the 25th of December, was the first day after the winter solstice when it was possible to see that the sun was moving south again. It was a day of promise and renewal, full of hope and possibility. Life continued. The darkness would not win. Winter would pass, and spring would come again, when all the world would be reborn anew.

It was Christmas morning, Katherine thought, sitting there watching the sun rise. *How wonderful!* She knew the claims that this day was chosen for the birth of Christ merely as a means to convert the pagans of Europe who already celebrated the sun's return on this day. She had also read of the ancient Christian belief that martyrs died on the anniversary of their conception and the early tradition that Christ had died on the 25th of March—Lady's Day—nine months before Christmas.

None of it, though, mattered to Katherine. It was simply a perfect day for the Son's arrival. In the deepest days of cold and darkness, love and light came into the world. And hope.

It had been so long since she'd hoped. To hope at this point in her life had seemed futile. This was her life, she had told herself, and to imagine something more, something better, amounted to nothing more than mere wishes.

And then, as the days grew dark and cold enveloped the world, Connor had called at Lilac Cottage.

Society might say she was past her prime and too old. Mrs. Boyle might snub her, and gossip might abound. But *this*, what had happened to her, was the kind of thing that happened to other women—beautiful, rich ladies—but it *had* happened to her. Some might call it a slip of a clerk's pen, but to her, it still seemed miraculous. All the things that had to happen to bring her here, at this moment, and to bring Connor here, at this moment as well.

And she asked herself—who was she to reject this miracle? She had but to accept it, and she would know joy and happiness. And sorrow. And anger.

With Connor.

Katherine had no idea how long she had been sitting there on the fallen rock, but the sun was well above the horizon, and she felt quite cold. So she picked up her still-lit lantern and began the walk back to the cottage, thoughts of chocolate and hot buns and jam urging her on. Once warm and fed, she would seek out Connor and ask his forgiveness. She loved him. And assuming Aunt Catherine was right, he had an affection for her. *That*, she decided, would be enough. She would rather be with him and have just his affection than be without him.

As she neared the village and was in sight of Lilac Cottage, Katherine saw a man on a horse riding down the lane. Despite not recognizing the horse, she recognized the rider immediately. Connor. Her beautiful ginger-haired boy.

He spotted her, and she smiled.

"Happy Christmas," she said as he dismounted a half-dozen feet from her. She waited for him to respond but he simply stood there, silent, and stared at her, those green eyes piercing deep. She began to feel uneasy, and then he took a step toward her. She fought an instinct to step back away from him, even when he took another step, and then another, until he was so very close to her. And then he cupped her face in his gloved hands and brought his mouth down on hers.

She dropped the lantern.

This was not some chaste first kiss but a raw passion heralding an unbridled hunger lurking beneath. Some coherent part of her brain thought she should be frightened, but she wasn't. Instead, she opened her mouth, allowing him greater access as she bent her body against his. Her hands clutched at him; she couldn't get close enough. But then, panic set in. With a gasp, she pulled her mouth away from his but still clung to him.

"I can't breathe," she panted.

He smiled and seemed to restrain a laugh. He, too, she noticed, was out of breath. For a moment, she thought he wished to say something, but he didn't. He just stared at her, as if examining her, his eyes searching hers.

"Good God, you must be freezing," he finally said and began opening his coat. "Whatever are you doing out here?"

Before she could answer, he pulled her to him and wrapped his coat around her so that she was nestled snug against him. Even with the layers of clothing between them, Katherine could feel his warmth and his heartbeat. And she thought, *was this a taste of what life with Connor would be like?*

"I wanted to see the sun rise again," she said, "and then I was coming to see you."

"I was coming to see you."

"I needed to ask you something."

"No. Let me speak first. What I have to say may change your view of things." He shifted slightly, kissed the top of her head, and then pressed his cheek against hers. Katherine could not remember ever being this close to anyone, except, maybe, perhaps when she was a very small child, and she thought, *yes, I can bear a lifetime of this, even if he never loves me.*

"You see," Connor continued, "I love you." Katherine felt her heart jump, and a small sigh escaped her mouth. She pulled away just enough to look up into his face. He stared down at her and said, "I think that's why you cried off. You didn't know I love you. You thought I wanted you only for the money. Maybe that was true in the first moment we met, but since that first walk together, I have liked you and grown to love you. So I've come to tell you I don't want the money."

Katherine felt a wave of relief flow over her, but that ever-practical part of her hesitated.

"Is that a tad hasty?" she asked.

"Probably," Connor replied with a bit of a laugh, "but I suspect we will be much happier without the money than with it. The thing is... I don't *need* the money. Through hard work and diligence, I can earn what I need. But more importantly, I *need* you. I still want you to be my wife.

"After we last spoke, I took out the estate account books and looked over the estimates for all the repairs, and I began calculating everything and comparing it with the amount of my father's debt.

"Yesterday, I informed Mr. Thornhurst to send the money to George Meynell as I am unable to comply with the terms of that particular part of the will. For one thing, it refers to your aunt. My uncle clearly meant Miss *Catherine* Woodbridge, not you. The land and the title are mine by birthright, but that money came from his wife. I have no right to it, regardless of what the law says. Given how my uncle wrote the will, I think he expected the money would go back to her family... that I'd never consent to marry an eighty-year-old woman."

"Aunt Catherine thinks he did it to spite her," Katherine quietly pointed out, imagining all the sorrow and pain of those events so long ago.

"To spite *her*?" Connor looked baffled.

Katherine realized too late that she had spoken out of turn. "I'm sorry," she said, "I have no right to speak of it. That particular tale is Aunt Catherine's to tell. But from what I have learned, it is possible."

Connor took her explanation without question and said, "Be that as it may, I am left with a financial difficulty, and I have devised a plan to solve it. The properties in the village, it seems, are not part of the entailment. My uncle purchased them over the years, but they are not part of the original estate. Did you know I own the mill?"

"Yes, I did."

"Of course you did. You know my holdings better than I do." Connor smirked playfully. "What you don't know is the miller...."

"Mr. Howard."

"...wants to purchase the mill outright, along with four adjoining acres."

"No, I didn't know that."

"And by my calculations, the money from that, plus the revenues from the estate should pay off my father's debts within two years. If we practice economy."

"I happen to be very good at practicing economy."

"I know you are." Connor grew serious. "I don't think I could do this with another wife. It's like God arranged it all."

"God's timing is perfect. It's us mere mortals that get in the way and ruin it all."

Connor was quiet for a moment, and then he smiled.

"I'll have to sell my horse, too."

Katherine glanced over at his horse, the one she didn't recognize, nuzzling through the snow for bits of grass.

"No. Not your black hunter?"

"I don't need a great horse. I need a good horse. Besides, we'll get a very pretty penny for him." Connor suddenly stepped back, away from Katherine, and held both her hands before him.

"Now then," he said, "the first time I proposed, I never actually asked the question. It was all just understood. But this time, I'd like to do it properly."

"If we were to do it properly, we'd need to be in a conservatory somewhere, surrounded by hot- house flowers. But I am too old for that illusion, and besides, I'd worry about your knees." She was smiling, but Connor was quite serious.

"Katherine, it would be my honor and privilege to be your husband."

But before he could continue, she interrupted him.

"But Connor," she said, "you do realize it is unlikely that I could give you an heir?"

"That doesn't mean impossible," he countered. "You are still young. And if you will forgive me for saying so, it simply means we will have to... make... an extra effort in that particular endeavor." He grinned like a mischievous boy up to no good.

"Oh," Katherine said, not at first fully grasping his meaning, but as she realized his intent, she felt her face burn hot. "Oh! Oh, I see. Yes." And she quickly looked away in embarrassment.

"Yes? Does that mean you're willing?" He pulled her back into his arms and whispered in her ear. "Share my life. Marry me?"

Katherine felt exhilarated and frightened all at the same time, all the possibilities, all the difficulties, the joy and pain she would experience spending her life with Connor, but her answer came without hesitation.

"Yes."

He broke out in a wide, happy smile, and lowered his mouth to hers again. Gently, this time, savoring the moment. When he pulled away, he stepped back and took Katherine's hand. She retrieved the dropped lantern. Then Connor took the reins of his *good* horse and led Katherine down the lane toward Lilac Cottage.

"Oh, Heaven help us," Connor suddenly laughed, "We're going to be poor for a while."

"No, we're not." She shook her head with smile. "Everything will be fine."

"You're right. And Happy Christmas!"

"Oh. I'd forgotten." Katherine stopped walking abruptly. "This means we'll have dinner at Roxbury Hall."

"You sound disappointed."

"No. It's just.... I have two dressed geese in the larder."

Connor burst out laughing and declared that all their problems should be this difficult. By the time they

116 Anna D. Allen

reached the door of Lilac Cottage, it had been decided to send the two geese home with Nancy—with such a large family, Mrs. Carter would appreciate them—while Mary and Cook could dine with the servants at Roxbury Hall on their own roast beef dinner with all the trimmings.

Once inside the cottage, Katherine found it warm but quiet, the enticing aroma of baking bread filling the air. They quickly removed their coats and gloves, and then together, she and Connor entered the sitting room to find Aunt Catherine sitting in her chair by the fire. Christmas greetings were exchanged, and then Connor informed Aunt Catherine that he and Katherine were to be married.

"And when is this to take place?" Aunt Catherine asked.

Connor glanced at Katherine warming herself by the fire, and with a smile, he said, directing his words to her, "I would prefer this morning, but I suspect the vicar has a previous engagement scheduled for today. So tomorrow shall have to suffice."

Katherine burst out in a broad smile, joy and happiness filling her. She could not believe it. They had spoken about marrying after the New Year, but tomorrow.... she would be his wife. He held out his hand to her, and she took a step toward him, but stopped as Aunt Catherine suddenly burst into tears.

Stunned, Katherine knelt down before the weeping old woman and asked, "What's wrong? What is it?" as she reached for the handkerchief Aunt Catherine always kept stuffed in her sleeve. It wasn't there. But a slight movement caught her eye, and she saw Connor held out a handkerchief to her.

"Please don't leave me here," Aunt Catherine sobbed out, "Please don't leave me alone."

"Oh, Aunt Catherine," Katherine said, dabbing the falling tears with Connor's handkerchief, "we won't leave you."

Connor now knelt beside her and held Aunt Catherine's hand.

"Miss Woodbridge," he said, "Aunt Catherine. Don't you know that Katherine has already selected a suite of rooms for you at Roxbury Hall?" Aunt Catherine choked back a sob and turned to look at Connor as he continued, "That is, if you wish to come."

"Oh yes," she said, taking the handkerchief and wiping away her tears. She looked at Katherine for a moment, new tears forming in her eyes. Then, much to the shock and amazement of Katherine, her aunt threw her arms around her and hugged her tight. "Thank you," she said, "Oh, thank you." When she pulled away and settled back into her chair, she was smiling. "A suite?"

"Yes." Katherine felt tears welling in her own eyes, but just then, Nancy entered the room. She carried a tray with three cups and a pot of chocolate on it. Both Katherine and Connor stood up.

"Happy Christmas, miss," she said and then looked at Connor. "Happy Christmas, my lord." Mary followed with plates of hot buns fresh from the oven and accompanied by butter and jam.

Katherine took her position on the threadbare settee opposite her aunt, and as she poured the chocolate, Connor explained the plans for the day— Nancy would get to spend the rest of the day with her family, with the gift of the two geese, while Mary and Cook would take Christmas dinner at the hall, and then, beginning tomorrow, if they so wished, they would be employed at the hall.

"Oh dear," Aunt Catherine said, "If we are to spend Christmas at the hall, I must dress. I can't very well go to Roxbury Hall looking like this. Mary, Nancy." And before either Katherine or Connor could lend a hand, the two girls had Aunt Catherine up and heading toward the stairs. As she ascended the stairs, all the while chatting with the two girls, she was distinctly heard to say, "I do hope that new cook at Roxbury Hall knows how to cook beef. I so dislike overcooked beef."

Katherine noticed Connor struggled to keep from laughing. He sat down beside her on the settee and took her hand.

"You said you were coming to see me."

"Yes. But you were right. Everything has changed now. There's only one other thing that needs to be said."

"What's that?"

"Simply that I love you, too."

He raised her hand to his lips and kissed her knuckles.

"Oh good," he said, "I feared this might be a one-sided love."

About Anna

Anna D. Allen lives deep in the woods with too many books and not enough dogs. She spends most winters snowed-in and trying to remember what "warm" was... something she vaguely recalls experiencing in the 20th Century.

She holds a Bachelor of Science and a Master of Arts in Language and Literature. Anna is a recipient of the Writers of the Future award and a member of Science Fiction and Fantasy Writers of America, but she also has a great passion for Regency Romances.

Her future plans include growing tomatoes and cleaning out the freezer. When not writing or reading, she can be found in the kitchen. In the virtual world, she can be found on Facebook at:
http://tinyurl.com/k4gmanr

She is currently writing a Regency Romance novel. Her other available works include two collections: *Mrs. Hewitt's Barbeque: Seven Eclectic Tales of Food, Humor, and Love*, and *Lake People and Other Speculative Tales*; the novel *Charles Waverly and the Deadly African Safari*; and the Regency Romance Novelette "A Christmas Wager," as well as some boring scholarly stuff.

The Lord of Misrule

by

Hannah Meredith

CHAPTER ONE

November 1828
Cranmore Hall, Surrey

MARTIN TATE, VISCOUNT HAYHURST, calmed his irritation by pressing his hand against the windowpane and letting the cold seep into his fingers. Outside, the naked branches of the big chestnuts lining the drive tossed in the freshening wind. They looked like skeletal fingers clawing the leaden sky. He'd forgotten how unappealing England could be in winter.

"But you must come. It's a tradition." Drew's voice pulled Martin's gaze away from the gray, wet day back to his comfortable study with its bright fire.

Even in the midst of an almost-argument, Andrew Dabney, Earl of Morrell, managed to look like a great, tawny cat languidly draped across a chair. Years before, Martin had tried to emulate that pose, but he'd quickly realized he more resembled a marionette with its strings cut than a reclining feline.

"It can hardly be a tradition when I've not spent Christmas with your family in years." Martin crossed the room to lean on the back of one of the chairs facing the hearth. He composed his face in an expression of earnestness. Languid might be beyond him, but Martin was very good at being earnest.

"That's because you've been out of the country, wandering about in warm climes and shouting 'Independence for the Greeks' or some other such nonsense."

With that pronouncement, Drew managed to succinctly reduce Martin's *raison d'être* for the past five years to an irrelevancy. Martin moved around to sit in the chair. He hoped his movements appeared nonchalant. He didn't want to find another subject about which he and his oldest friend could quarrel. Drew, who had never devoted himself to anything that didn't involve his own pleasure, seemed inherently unable to grasp how one could become involved in a greater cause.

Theirs was an unlikely friendship of long duration. They'd initially met as boys at Eton—the awkward, orphaned viscount and the golden heir to a marquessate. They were totally dissimilar, yet discovered they meshed, one's strength covering a corresponding weakness in the other. They'd progressed on to Oxford, where Martin had taken a First in Oriental Studies, and Drew had taken every available female in a three county radius.

And during all those years, it was true, Martin had spent every Christmas holiday with Drew's large and boisterous family.

Martin had come to think of the Marquess and Marchioness of Pennington as surrogate parents and enjoyed being with their brood of happy children, all of whom had managed to conquer their world without a single serious thought in their collective heads. At Pencroft, the Dabney's sprawling countryseat, he'd discovered the importance of understated but expensive clothes and the delight of the quick riposte. When there, he'd enjoyed shedding his normal serious mien and living only in the present.

It was from Pencroft he'd fled five years ago, however, when he'd discovered he no longer wanted to be like the people who lived there. Instead, he became intent on finding an elusive *more* to his own life.

"I need to continue working on getting the estate in order," Martin said with a vague gesture of his hands that included the house and the sprawling acreage beyond. It was an excuse to avoid the Christmas gathering, of course, but it was an honest one. "I've neglected my duties for far too long. I really can't get away now that I've just started."

Drew gave him a soft, beguiling smile, obviously confident that he could convince Martin to spend the holidays at Pencroft. "Come on, Weed. You know Mother would be hurt if you didn't attend."

Ah, so Drew had chosen to use guilt as his persuasive tool. *Well played*, Martin thought, especially since he'd just confessed to feeling guilty about neglecting his patrimony. But in their years apart, Martin had become adept at playing such games, so he leaped on a different part of the comment. "Weed? I haven't been Weed for years. Now I'm Hayhurst, and to a select few, Martin."

He chose to ignore the fact that perhaps that *few* hadn't been as select as they could have been. "Martin" had been sighed across too many soft sheets in too many warm rooms to be considered select, but it was true most people now called him Hayhurst. Greece had been a turning point and a learning experience. He was a different person than he'd been five years earlier. He would never be Weed again.

Weed was the gangly boy he'd been at Eton. An overly tall, overly thin, and overly serious youth who had sought acceptance by pretending to enjoy a derogatory nickname. Weed was a boy who had laughed when an upperclassman had commented that Hayhurst didn't work since he was obviously a weed rather than something anyone would cultivate. And so, he'd become Weedhurst for a short time before the name became familiarly shortened.

Had Drew ever wondered if Martin enjoyed being called Weed? No, that was not something Drew would ever consider.

"Well, then, would the right honorable Viscount Hayhurst kindly accept the invitation of the most honorable Marchioness of Pennington to attend her Christmas house party?" Drew gave a half-bow from his seated position. "Beth would also like to see you. Or perhaps I should say, the Lady Elizabeth Dabney has also requested your presence. Beth made her come out this past year, by the way, and was a great success. Father fielded a number of offers, but none of the potential suitors appealed to her. Maybe she's holding out for you."

Drew accented the last statement by arching one eyebrow. Martin had never been able to make his eyebrows work independently—although he had, of course, tried.

It was hard imagining Drew's youngest sister as a debutant. When Martin had last seen her, Beth had still been a fair-haired sprite prone to mischief, although she'd exhibited the beginnings of the golden beauty that graced the rest of her family, so he was unsurprised that she'd had proposals. He was equally certain that she was not waiting for him, although he must admit he was curious to see what changes time had wrought.

"And I need you there for support," Drew continued. "Lord and Lady Tholea will be at Pencroft along with Alice, and I'm finally asking her to marry me. Even have the ring." Drew reached in his pocket, withdrew a small box, and tossed it in Martin's direction.

Martin deftly caught the projectile. "How can you need support to do something that has been anticipated since both you and Alice were in leading strings?" He didn't ask why it had taken Drew so long to get around to asking for Alice's hand. He didn't want to hear whatever excuses Drew would offer.

Five years earlier, when Alice had completed her second season and no announcement was forthcoming, Martin had thought that perhaps he'd misunderstood the situation. Anyone with half an eye could see that Alice had a singular beauty. Anyone who wasn't deaf had to appreciate her quick wit and questing mind. Martin certainly had.

He'd built a multitude of fantasies from brief glances, from tentative touches on his hands, from quiet laughs. And so, before Twelfth Night ended the festivities, he'd sought her father out. Lord Tholea had been polite, but he'd made it plain that Alice would marry Drew and eventually become the next Marchioness of Pennington. The two mothers had planned it since their children were infants.

Martin had fled his disappointment and arrived in Greece, ready to lose himself in a larger cause. He'd spent the first few years expecting the arrival of a letter from Drew announcing his nuptials. When none came, time eroded the significance. Martin had convinced himself that he no longer cared.

This conviction dissolved, however, when the ring box came flying toward him and he snatched it out of the air. Then years of vague longing again became concrete. He didn't want to see the symbol that would tie Drew to a woman he would never appreciate. But Martin could hardly toss the damned thing back without looking at it.

He opened the box. Nestled in white satin was a large emerald surrounded by diamonds. It might have been garish had the quality not shown through. "Very nice," he said through a tight throat.

"I thought it matched her eyes."

"Drew, Alice's eyes are blue." Martin didn't add they were the clear blue of the Aegean Sea at sunrise, although he now knew this to be the case.

"Oh, thanks. I guess I shouldn't say that when I give her the ring, then." Drew gave him a self-deprecating smile, leaned forward, and held out his hand to retrieve the box. "Mother picked it out, and I thought she did a good job."

Alice Caruthers' bedroom looked like the drying yard in the aftermath of a strong squall. Clothing lay in chaotic profusion across her bed, smothered all the chairs, and even festooned her delicate desk. Her mother, Lady Tholea, marched between the richly colored fabrics like a general assembling her troops.

"I think you'll need a few new dresses," Lady Tholea said. "Some of these look more tired than festive."

Alice looked at the abundance and wondered what her mother could find wanting in any of the gowns.

"We'll only be there a fortnight. I really think more would be unnecessary. I doubt there will a ball every night."

Lady Tholea frowned at her daughter. "You don't sound very enthusiastic. Aren't you excited about visiting the Dabneys?"

"Of course I'm looking forward to spending the holidays at Pencroft." Alice worked to keep the exasperation from her voice. She adored her little, plump pigeon of a mother, but the woman would peck and peck until she got the response she wanted. At least from Alice. Her mother had been much less successful in getting the rest of the world to behave in the desired manner.

Twice a year, at mid-summer and at Christmas, the Dabneys invited Alice and her family to visit their countryseat. Each excursion would be filled with breathless anticipation on her parents' part, her father becoming more affable and her mother more nervous.

And each and every time, their expectations came to nothing.

Since she was old enough to understand, Alice had been told that she would marry the Pennington heir. She knew her mother and Lady Pennington had discussed the alliance even before Alice was born. Perhaps the two older women saw this as a way of cementing their decades-old friendship. More likely, they saw it as a way of balancing the scales. Both were the daughters of earls who had made their debut in the same year, but Lady Pennington had married up by capturing a marquess, while Alice's mother had only managed to snag a baron.

Over time, Alice had become convinced that her marriage to Andrew Dabney would never take place. She was now twenty-four, and if not firmly on the shelf, she was nudging the edge of spinsterhood. And over these same long years, she'd decided that the lack of a proposal was probably for the best.

Perhaps if Drew had offered for her when she was young and naive, they would have managed a fulfilling life. Then she had seen only his handsome face and beguiling manner. But as the years went by, she'd discovered that there was no substance behind the attractive facade.

Andrew Dabney, Earl of Morrell, and heir to the Pennington marquessate, was a beautifully presented blank page on which others painted their own expectations. Drew was, therefore, all things to all people—and none of these supposed traits actually illuminated the real man.

To her irritation, Alice had been unable to express her feelings to her parents. She didn't want to be a greater disappointment than she already was. And so, she would once again be subjected to the lowering charade of being paraded before a man who had no interest. She could only hope this would be the last time. At some point, it had to become clear to her parents that the longed-for alliance with the Dabneys wasn't going to happen.

"You need an emerald green satin gown for the Christmas Eve Ball," her mother said with authority. "Lucy said green would be most appropriate."

Alice doubted that Lady Pennington had made any comment about the choice of color for Alice's gown. Why would she? "I was thinking of the wine velvet I already have," Alice said. She usually avoided wearing green. If the shade of that color edged too close to yellow, she looked sallow.

"No, it must be emerald." Her mother pulled herself to the top of her diminutive height and glared assertively.

Alice could tell her mother was mentally starting to sharpen her beak so she could begin pecking. After years of these constant pricks, Alice knew her wisest move was to give in graciously. "If you think I should have something new, we can call at the dressmaker's tomorrow."

Lady Tholea smiled her victory. "Good. I know dear Drew is fond of bright green."

Was he? After all this time, Alice had no idea if Drew had a favorite color. He always complimented what she wore—always, regardless of what it was. Drew was complimentary, affable, charming. He habitually asked for the supper dance, which was frequently a waltz. He'd eat with her, solicitously choosing food he imagined she favored. Then he'd return her to her mother's side and drift away, as insubstantial and beautiful as a rainbow, leaving Alice to absorb her mother's disappointed look and wonder what she could have done to change the perpetual pattern.

She'd finally come to the conclusion that she was not appealing to men. Any men. She was too tall, too angular. Oh, she always had dancing partners; men would talk and laugh with her. When she was younger, the house had bloomed with bouquets after a ball and the drawing room was filled with gentlemen who had come to call. Some had seemed truly interested in knowing her better. But after weeks of attention, these potential suitors would inevitably drift away.

As the years went by, the flowers and callers declined. There was something about her that could attract gentlemen but could not make them stick.

Not that she was without friends. Those she had in abundance. She had made herself indispensable on various charitable committees. Alice had early on determined that one way to popularity was to do the jobs that no one else wanted—and for the most part, she enjoyed them since doing something, anything, was preferable to sitting around and trying to look decorative.

She suspected it was in the decorative area that men found her wanting. Fate had laughingly dictated that she take after her father, and she towered over most people. One of Drew's attractions was his height, since they met eye-to-eye. People called her willowy, probably because she'd never developed the curves that were popular. She had waited in vain for a bosom like her mother's to arrive. Her dressmaker was quite good at making *not-much* look like *something*, but no one would think her figure lush.

"Alice, I can tell you're not listening to me." Her mother interrupted her thoughts.

"I'm sorry mother. I was considering whether I should have the sleeves on the blue ball gown updated." Her meandering had taken her next to her favorite dress, so the excuse was believable. She ran her hand over the shimmering blue and watched hints of turquoise appear.

"I was saying that Lady Pennington wrote that as he approaches thirty, dear Drew seems to be settling down. I've alerted your father to expect an offer." Her mother suddenly hurried toward her and gave her a surprisingly vigorous hug around the waist. "Oh, darling, I think this is the moment we've waited for. I'm thinking a spring wedding just at the start of the Season. Wouldn't that be wonderful?"

What could she say in the face of her mother's desire? "Yes, spring would be a beautiful time for a wedding."

But she didn't expect it to happen. And if by some miracle it did—she didn't know what she'd do. She suspected she would say yes. Yes, she would fulfill her parents' fondest wishes. Yes, she'd make the glorious alliance that was expected of her. Yes, she'd be the gracious countess and eventually marchioness that she'd been raised to be.

Yes, if Andrew Dabney, Earl of Morrell asked for her hand, she'd say yes. And perhaps, in some way, this would make up for her not being the male heir her father so wanted or the reigning beauty that her mother had anticipated.

Marrying Drew was not what she now dreamed of, but that made no difference. Most women of her station knew better than to wish for a husband who would treasure them. But sometime during her long waiting period to become the Countess of Morrell, Alice had discovered she wanted to spend her life with a man who loved her to distraction, and for whom she felt the same.

If and when she married Drew, she would have prestige and wealth and comfort instead. In the end, she would follow the path her feet had been set upon at birth.

No, he would not ask her. Her mother's fondest hopes were for naught. But if it did happen... Alice felt a sudden sharp loss for a life that could never have been.

CHAPTER TWO

December 31, 1828 – January 1, 1829
Pencroft, Hampshire

MARTIN STRETCHED HIS LEGS out in front of him and leaned back against the half-wall of a stall. The wooden bench was not particularly comfortable, but at least it wasn't moving. The frozen roads had turned his carriage into a bouncing torture chamber, and he was glad to be out of it.

"Fitch, please stop fussing with my greatcoat," he said to his valet, who was frantically brushing at the sodden mess draped over an open stall door.

Fitch frowned at the soggy fabric. "If this silly tradition is as important to the marchioness as you say it is, you can't arrive at the door looking like a vagrant. And if you hadn't insisted on helping the coachman remove that downed limb in the drive, your coat would be in a much better state."

"If I hadn't helped, we would still be sitting at the end of the drive. I doubt you would have relished a half-mile walk in this sleet and rain." Martin tried to keep his voice level. Fitch had been complaining since the trip began—making it a very long journey, indeed.

It was no one's fault that the bad weather had turned to worse. Normally, the trip from Cranmore Hall to Pencroft took two easy days. This time, they'd arrived at the first day's posting inn well after dark—and the road conditions had become even more degraded the second day. If he hadn't promised to be here by midnight, they would have stopped, but they pressed on through the night.

The cold rain coated everything with ice once the sun had set, causing weak branches to fall. On the main roads, they'd carefully made their way around the obstructions. The lane leading to Pencroft wasn't wide enough to allow such maneuvering, however, especially when the limb that had landed in the middle of the drive was the size of a small tree.

Martin had joined the coachman and the lone groom who had accompanied them, but it had still been a struggle for the three of them to wrestle the big branch out of the way. Fitch had not stepped a foot out of the carriage. The man was an excellent valet, but at the moment, Martin was not feeling charitable and wondered how long he would keep the man in his employ.

"Why don't you join the staff at their New Year's celebration?" Martin asked. "The stableman said you'd be welcome." And this would leave Martin in peace for the next half hour until he made his appearance in the hall.

"I don't know, my lord. I suspect all the upper servants will be busy with the party upstairs, and I might feel out of place."

Martin tried not to roll his eyes. Lord, servants were stricter about hierarchy than the snobbiest of peers. "Unless things have changed drastically in the past few years, Lord and Lady Pennington use a skeleton staff for what the Marchioness still calls Hogmanay. This allows everyone to enjoy the evening. I suggest you at least visit the festivities. You might have a good time." Martin didn't mention that the three oldest Dabney daughters had married men with ranks higher than viscount. He felt a perverse satisfaction that quite a few people would outrank Fitch in the servants' hall.

To Martin's relief, after some waffling, Fitch finally slipped out the door and left Martin to enjoy the solitude of the stables. He again checked his pocket watch. Twenty minutes until midnight and the New Year.

Just a little over twenty minutes until he was face-to-face with Alice Caruthers and admiring the big emerald ring on her hand. At least he'd managed to delay his arrival until after Drew had given it to her. The idea of having to pretend enthusiasm during all the congratulatory toasts left him feeling slightly nauseous.

But Drew had surely given her the ring on Christmas Day. Boxing Day at the latest. The excitement over the announcement would have subsided. A polite smile and a "best wishes" would now suffice.

Of course, he hadn't expected to be here at all. He'd sent his regrets to the Marchioness, telling her he would be unable to attend the house party. And yet, here he was.

Drew had found the argument that had gotten him here. He'd sent a note asking Martin to be the First Foot, stressing how much it would mean to his mother for Martin to be the tall, dark man who brings luck for the coming year. Even though he'd come to dislike the artificiality of Pencroft gatherings, in the end, he couldn't disappoint the lady who had been so kind to him since he was a boy.

So his participation in the tradition the Marchioness had brought with her from her native Scotland had been confirmed.

He had to see Alice again sometime, and it might as well be now. Their paths would doubtlessly cross from now on anyway, since she would be the wife of his oldest friend. Martin needed to wish her happy. Regardless of how hard it was for him, he wanted Alice to be happy—truly.

Martin didn't have any doubts that she would be thrilled to marry Drew. He attracted females of all types and stations, and there was no reason to think Alice would be immune to his charm. The connection that Martin had felt to Alice all those years ago was obviously an aberration—and probably one-sided.

Alice had been nice to him simply because she *was* nice. When she looked at him, she undoubtedly saw Drew's friend and nothing more. He needed to accept that role and get on with his life. He had let her slide into memory while he'd been in Greece, and he could do it again. In a few years, he'd look back on his reluctance to see her this Christmastide and laugh at his foolishness.

He again looked at his pocket watch, surprised that only two minutes had passed since he'd last checked his timepiece. His need to arrive at the front door of Pencroft at an exact time, a minute after twelve, was the cause of his nervousness—nothing more.

He lifted his greatcoat from the stall door, only to find it still heavy, chilled, and damp. He shrugged into it anyway. A mix of icy rain and sleet continued to fall and the coat was necessary.

He ducked into the stall and retrieved the basket Drew had left for him. It was filled with the appropriate First Foot's gifts to the household. Martin had not expected it to be decorated with red bows and strips of silver paper, however. He smiled ruefully. Good Lord, he'd look like some fair maiden ready to go a-Maying.

He nonetheless picked up the gaudy offering and had just turned toward the stall door when he heard footsteps in the central alley of the stable. "You decided against staying at the servants' party?" he asked as he exited the stall.

An unknown young man stood there instead of the expected Fitch. He was of middle height with brown hair, a rather prominent nose, and the kind eyes of a spaniel. His face reflected surprise that quickly shifted to distrust. "What are you doing here?" he asked.

Martin shifted the basket from his right hand to hang on his left arm. "I'm Hayhurst," he said, holding out his right hand. "I've been hiding out here until it's time for me to enter as the First Foot."

The younger man shook his offered hand. "I'm David Taylor, the local vicar, and what is the problem with your foot?" He looked pointedly down at Martin's shoes.

Martin laughed. "No, my feet are fine. I'm acting as the First Foot. You know, in the Marchioness's Scottish tradition, the first person to enter the house after midnight on New Year's Eve determines the luck of the house for the coming year. A tall, dark man is considered the luckiest, so I was pressed into doing the honors." He held out the basket. "See, I've come equipped with the requisite gifts for the New Year. A piece of coal for a warm hearth, some bread and salt so all within are adequately fed, a coin for financial security, and a small bottle of whiskey to represent good cheer."

The Reverend Taylor continued to look perplexed. "Does this happen every year? I've only had this living since summer, so this is my first Christmas season here."

Martin hoped the vicar wasn't terribly conservative or he might have inadvertently supplied next Sunday's sermon against relying on luck instead of the Almighty. "Yes, I believe this is traditional."

He would have said more except the stable door opened to admit a burst of sleet and a cloaked lady. "You do realize I've ruined a new pair of slippers getting here to wish you a Happy New Year privately," she said in a laughing voice. She pushed back the cloak's hood to reveal typical Dabney beauty, only her features were more delicate and her hair more flaxen than gold.

"Beth?" Martin asked. The sound of his voice brought her shocked eyes up to his.

"Martin? Oh, it *is* you." She launched herself across the space between them and grasped both his hands. Realization and embarrassment chased across her face, which immediately flushed such a brilliant red that it was unmistakable even in the dim lantern light.

"I've been sent to make sure you're not late," she said, now dragging him toward the door.

Martin was impressed Beth could lie so convincingly. He was quite sure she hadn't known he was in the stables and had only ascertained his purpose when she'd seen the ridiculous basket swinging on his arm. It was obvious she couldn't quickly come up with a way to explain the vicar's presence, however, so she pretended he wasn't there. Martin felt he had no choice but to follow her lead. She pulled her hood back up and dragged him into the icy night.

"Be sure to knock three times," Beth said as they approached the front door.

Martin hoped the timing was right, since being interrupted by a lover's tryst had lost him the opportunity to again look at his watch.

Alice laughed at Lord Chesterton's wry comments about his wife's dancing. They stood at the side of the room as they caught their breath and drank wassail after their own vigorous bout on the floor.

"I told her all this Scottish bounding about was sure to ruin those horn things she has on her head, and it certainly has." Chesterton exhibited a smug delight. "They're both listing like leaky boats."

"They're Apollo Knots, not horns, and they're a popular style," Alice said, feeling rather smug herself that she'd convinced her maid to avoid the wired arrangement for tonight. Unconsciously, her hand went up to feel the curls that came forward from her temples. They now seemed totally limp. It was a good thing she didn't have a mirror handy, since it would probably show she now looked like Medusa. Hardly an improvement over a leaky boat. Sometimes it was better not to know.

Maybe that could become her new philosophy—*If I don't look, I will not know.* If she didn't look at her mother, she would not see her disappointment. If she didn't look at Lady Pennington, she would not see a strain of anger that flowed beneath her gaiety. If she did not look at Drew, she would not notice that he was on the far side of the room. He'd been careful to stay away from her for the whole of the holidays. Yes, not looking made things easier.

Of course, unless she closed her eyes, she had to see something, and in this case, it was Chesterton. From her vantage point standing next to him, she could see the portly earl was developing a natural tonsure that even the skill of his valet could not hide. She could also see the fond way he looked at his wife. His expression made a tendril of envy curl through her. Goodness, he and Harriet, the oldest Dabney daughter, must have been married for more than fifteen years, and his face still reflected a deep affection.

Hoping the spicy liquid would drown such ignoble feelings, Alice took another sip from the wassail cup. She just had to accept that it was unlikely any man would ever look at her with his heart in his eyes. Some things were not meant to be. She would accept them and move on.

At least her mother now seemed to realize that the longed for alliance with the Dabney family was not going to happen. This morning her mother had referred to her supposed suitor as Andrew instead of *dear* Drew, and on one occasion she'd heard her call him Morrell. The distance Drew kept from Alice must have been obvious to all.

Alice was not particularly disappointed that Drew had not come up to scratch. It was the idea of never having anyone to care for her that saddened her, not the idea of never marrying Drew. But she was more fortunate than most women in that she had options.

In the new year, she would turn twenty-five, and she would have control of a large legacy left to her by her grandmother. She could take possession of her grandmother's vacant house in town and live there with a suitable companion. A *congenial*, suitable companion, she amended. Perhaps one who would enjoy traveling. There was a large world waiting out there, and Alice would have the money to see as much of it as she desired. Yes, visiting distant places would be wonderful. She could try all sorts of new things. She could ride a camel through the sands of Egypt and see the pyramids by moonlight. Masked and mysterious, she could indulge in the bacchanal that was the carnival in Venice. Why, she might even take a lover.

She blushed at her own wayward thoughts. How had she gone from independence to bawdiness in the space of one heartbeat? She wondered if years of watching her contemporaries marry and then stray had rusted her moral compass. But taking a lover shouldn't be beyond the realm of possibility. She would never marry and it would be criminal to go to her grave never having experienced physical intimacy.

She unconsciously straightened her shoulders. Yes, she could toast the arrival of 1829 with confidence. This was the year when she would exert her independence.

Like a butterfly, she would break out of her cocoon and spread her wings.

She felt a light touch on her arm and realized the music had abruptly stopped. "It's nearly time," Lord Chesterton said. "I must be with my wife at the stroke of twelve or I will never hear the end of it." He gave her a lopsided grin that suggested he didn't live in fear of his spouse and hurried across the room as the big, tall case clock in the hall began to chime.

Alice wished some besotted man were rushing to be with her when the New Year was ushered in. She tried again to think of a butterfly emerging from its chrysalis but was not altogether successful.

Just as the twelfth gong echoed, before the general clamor of shouts to welcome in the New Year began, the knocker on the front door sounded with three measured, firm raps.

"The First Foot to cross our threshold," Lady Pennington called out into the momentary stillness. Her slightly Scottish accented voice seemed to herald a portentous occasion. She and her husband hurried down the stairs and into the entry hall, the rest of the throng following.

Lord Pennington threw open the door. The lanterns on the porch showed blowing sleet and a large, dark man. His hair rioted around his head in wind-tossed curls with bits of ice in them that caught the lantern light like flickers of foxfire in a nighttime wood.

"A Happy New Year and Good Tidings to you and yours," the dark man said. His voice was low-pitched, deep and appealing. He held out a girlishly decorated basket of gifts to the marquess, who escorted him into the house and called for drink and food for their guest.

A servant bustled forward to take the man's wet greatcoat. The removal of the coat revealed an exceptionally tall man in formalwear, slender but with shoulders that seemed to span the doorframe. He was greeted with laughter and slaps on the back by those who stood near.

As he walked further into the hall, Alice got a good look at the First Foot and her breath caught in her throat. She knew him. It was Viscount Hayhurst, Drew's oldest friend. Or at least it was a larger and more substantial version of Hayhurst. She recalled that when they were in school together, Drew had called him Weed. Well, he was a gangly weed no longer.

He'd always stood nearly a head taller than those around him, but he'd been so skinny his height had looked odd. While still slender, the viscount was now a powerful-looking man with a physique commensurate to his height. His complexion was darker than she remembered, making his teeth flash a brilliant white every time he smiled.

He was all-together one of the most handsome men she'd ever seen, and that was saying something since he was surrounded by all the golden Dabneys. By chance, his eyes caught hers where she stood at the rear of the crowd—and her stomach fell toward her feet.

It was just his luck that he should see Alice Caruthers before he even made it to the ballroom. Looking at her felt like a punch in the solar plexus. Her face was flushed and her hair in disarray. She looked surprisingly like he'd imaged she would after a tumble in bed. And there had been a time when he'd imaged that quite a lot.

His impulse was to push through those around him and make straight for where she stood. He had to remind himself that she was not his to claim—and never would be. He pulled his gaze away from hers and tried to give his attention to Lord and Lady Pennington, who seemed to want to hear everything about his time in Greece while he stood in the middle of the entry hall.

The arrival of a servant with a traditional, three-handled, pottery wassail cup seemed to remind them of their duties as hosts. "Here's what Lady Pennington calls a wee dram to take the chill away," Lord Pennington said as he handed Martin the cup. It wasn't wassail. Martin could smell the strong aroma of Scotch whiskey before he got the cup near his face. The first sip went down like liquid fire, but it was decidedly warming.

"Now come and get something to eat," Lady Pennington said taking his arm. "We certainly don't want our good luck leaving."

They proceeded up to the ballroom where an informal receiving line formed. Martin enjoyed it, since it gave him the opportunity to catch up on the entire family. Drew's older sisters and their husbands were doing an admirable job of increasing the size of the family. The two younger brothers were growing into copies of Drew, although the youngest, Paul, seemed to have ambition, an unusual quality for a Dabney. When Beth came by, she acted as if she had not met him in the stables. Martin burned to ask her about the new vicar but continued with the charade of just seeing her.

Oddly, the two people he most wanted to talk with remained on the opposite side of the room. Or, in Drew's case, he'd been there when Martin last looked. By the time Martin was released by his hosts to wander, Drew had disappeared.

Alice, however, was still there, in earnest conversation with Paul. Martin walked toward them, feeling more relaxed than he had in some time. The potent Scotch whiskey he'd been drinking undoubtedly supported this languor. Wassail cups were large and intended to hold the spicy, ale-based punch. Martin's cup had now been filled to the brim four or five times with the smoky Scottish brew.

"Miss Caruthers, may I wish you a prosperous New Year and say that you are in good looks." Martin gave her a bow.

Alice curtsied back. "And may I also wish you the best for 1829. It's wonderful to see you again after all this time." Her smile was genuine, but something around her eyes suggested strain. Was she happy with her betrothal? From just looking, there was no way to know.

"I hope I'm not interrupting an important conversation," Martin said.

"Oh, no," she said. "Paul was just telling me that he hopes to join an expedition to the Amazon. I've been thinking about traveling this year, but Paul's managed to convince me that South America would not be a destination to my liking." She smiled at Paul. "Too many crawly things."

Martin turned toward Paul. "An expedition? What type is it?"

Paul immediately launched into an excited discussion of a journey to study the entomology of the rain forest. Martin laughed as realization hit him. "Ah, the crawly things are insects. Is this your area of study?"

Paul's lengthy monologue in reply allowed Martin time to examine Alice. If she were to be married, why would she be contemplating traveling? She might be considering a wedding trip. Or perhaps she had said no and simply wanted to see distant locales on her own. His heartbeat sped up with hope. Foolish, foolish heart.

Martin looked closely at her gloved hands, but he was unable to tell if she wore the ring. He would need to hold her hands, both of them, and this was impossible while he held a drink. He upended his cup, quickly finishing the potent liquor. Then, still nodding as if he cared about Paul's description of jungle ants, he surreptitiously flipped the cup in the direction of a sofa. He braced himself for the sound of pottery hitting the floor and shattering. When this didn't happen, he breathed a sigh of relief.

He then placed a hand over his mouth and faked a jaw-cracking yawn. Unfortunately, in the middle of it, he discovered he truly was exhausted. "I'm sorry," he interrupted Paul, "I've discovered that I'm almost too tired to stand. The trip here was quite onerous, and then Lord Pennington has been plying me with his finest Scotch whiskey. I'm afraid you'll have to excuse me."

He bowed to Paul, but he grasped both of Alice's hands and gave them a brief squeeze. With a wide smile splitting his face, he departed, leaving both of his companions looking confused.

He would have to apologize tomorrow morning for his odd behavior, but for now, he'd learned what he needed to know—and was delighted. Alice wasn't wearing the big emerald ring! He would have felt it when he squeezed her hands. Drew hadn't given it to her. The fool must have decided he didn't want to marry Alice Caruthers. To Martin, the idea was incomprehensible.

He hoped Alice hadn't been hurt by this. But Martin couldn't regret it. There was hope.

CHAPTER THREE

January 1, 1829

BECAUSE OF THE EARLY HOUR, Alice wasn't surprised she was the only guest in the dining room. The party last night had ended very late, and no one at the house party had proved to be an early riser even when the festivities hadn't ended in the small hours of morning. She would have still been in bed herself, but the tapping of frozen branches on her bedroom window awakened her and she couldn't get back to sleep.

Her mind was a tumult of ideas that kept spinning over and around each other. She realized she'd simply existed for years. She'd been so afraid of disappointing her parents that she'd turned her life over to them. She'd let them make all the decisions that by rights should have been hers.

Weak. She'd been weak. And the acknowledgement ate at her.

But the beginning of the New Year was just that—a beginning. She was going to change, and today was the first day she would put her ideas into motion. She just wished she had more practice at being assertive.

One of the dozing footmen—the staff too must have had a late night—suddenly stood up straighter. She turned to see Lady Elizabeth Dabney enter the room. As Beth made her selections from the sideboard, the now animated footman rushed to pull out her chair. He watched Beth with shy adoration. Alice doubted she had ever affected the household help in such a way even when she was younger. A tendril of unwanted envy curled through her.

Once Beth was seated and had ordered chocolate, she smiled at Alice and raised one eyebrow. Alice had seen the same expression on Drew's face more times than she wished to remember. It must be a family trait. "You couldn't sleep either?" Beth asked.

"No, I was awakened by the sound of tree limbs scratching at my window and couldn't doze off again."

Beth took a sip of her chocolate and let out a contented sigh. "I heard the branches too. Normally they aren't that close to the windows. I think the weight of the ice must have pulled them lower. Last night, my father was concerned that a lot of the trees in the orchard might be damaged, but we won't know until the sun comes up."

In concert, they both turned to look at the windows. Because of the light in the room, the edges that showed around the draperies appeared black. "The sun won't be up until about eight," Beth said with authority.

"Are you always up before dawn in order to time the rising of the sun?" Alice couldn't keep the amusement out of her voice.

Beth laughed. "Actually, I am often up this early. I'm a country girl at heart and much prefer living here than in the city."

Well, that was a surprise. Lady Elizabeth had been a tremendous success this past Season, and for good reason. Even at this ridiculously early hour, she managed to look like a fairy princess with her pale, platinum hair and sharply chiseled, regular features. By comparison, Alice, with her height and plain, brown hair, felt like a drab giantess.

Beth must have noticed Alice's skeptical expression. "You must have realized that Paul and I are the aberrations in the family. Maybe because we're the youngest. I like the country and Paul actually thinks."

"I suspect you think as well," Alice said, "and this is something we have in common. I don't necessarily recommend it as a way to attract gentlemen of the ton, however."

"Alas, my secret has been discovered." Beth's face reflected an insincere horror. "And I too thought we might have traits in common. Honesty compels me to admit that one of the reasons I'm eating now is that I heard you leave your room. I have a few serious questions to ask you."

Alice felt Fate's hand swoop down and place her firmly on the shelf. Was she now to become the repository of ancient lore for the younger girls making their come out? "I'll answer what I can," she forced out between tight lips.

Beth leaned closer and said in a quiet voice, "What do you think of Viscount Hayhurst?"

Martin? The chit was interested in Martin? For some reason, the idea irked Alice. "He's certainly handsome," she said, "although he might be a bit old for you. He's of an age with your brother Drew, you know."

"Oh, I don't care about that." Beth lowered her voice further. "I need to know if you think he's trustworthy."

"I've never known him to be anything but kind and honest. Although, like everyone else, I've not seen him in years. He could have changed, but it's unlikely." Yes, kind and honest was an accurate description of Martin, although in the heady, early years when she'd been dazzled by Drew, these characteristics hadn't seemed important.

There had been a time during the Christmas season before he left the country that Alice had wondered if he were courting her. Would she have come to appreciate his inner qualities if this had been the case? The answer was unimportant since, as so often happened, Martin seemed to lose interest. He'd never led her to believe that he intended anything more than friendship, however. "I think he would be worthy of your trust," Alice concluded.

Beth seemed to visibly relax. "That's good to know. He found me doing something I would just as soon keep secret from my parents. I wondered if he would have told them and if I should expect a dressing down today."

"Unless he thought you were doing something that would injure you, I suspect Martin would keep his own counsel." Alice's curiosity was certainly piqued, and she suspected she would ask Martin what this was all about if she were given the chance.

"How do you know if you're in love?" Beth abruptly asked.

Alice glanced at the attendant footmen and quietly said, "I think this is a topic we should continue in my bedroom." And then she rose.

Beth followed her from the room with a dreamy expression on her face. Alice didn't have the heart to tell the girl that she didn't know the first thing about being in love. In this case, Alice would be the student rather than the teacher.

The first day of her new butterfly life was certainly starting out in an interesting manner.

An arrow of bright sunlight shot across room from a break in the curtains and pierced Martin in his left eye. He threw up a hand to deflect the painful glare and groaned. It had been years since he'd awakened to discover his head housed all the imps of hell armed with hammers—and the light excited them to pound mercilessly.

The cause had to be that damned whiskey Lady Pennington's family estates produced. That drink was undoubtedly intended as the Scot's revenge on the English.

He rolled to the side, quickly discovering that motion also caused the little devils to increase their hammering on his temples. With deliberate care, he swung his feet over the edge of the bed and sat there, taking stock.

He hoped he'd not made an ass of himself the night before. He distinctly remembered gulping down the contents of his last wassail cup of whiskey and pitching the empty vessel at a sofa. But it had been necessary so he could take both of Alice Caruthers' hands... and discover there was no ring. Exactly! There was no ring! But after he'd ascertained that fact, the edges of his memory became fuzzy.

He clearly recalled the tasks he'd set for himself for today, however. And they were important. Although movement seemed impossible, he lurched across the room and yanked the bell pull. Then he settled in a chair to allow his head to catch up with the rest of his body.

Fitch quickly poked his head in the room as if he'd been waiting below stairs for the summons. "I've brought you my special remedy for a sore head," he said, crossing the room and holding out a glass of murky liquid.

Martin wondered how Fitch had known he'd be in need of something, but he happily grabbed the glass and took a sip. He managed to gag down a mouthful. Fitch's remedy tasted like it had been brewed from the contents of a squirrel's nest. He shoved the glass back at his valet.

"No, you must drink it all." Fitch refused to take the glass. "It works. My previous employer swore by it."

Martin eyed the suspicious contents. "I suspect he swore *at* it, and then he sacked you, which is why you were available when I returned to England three months ago."

"Actually, he didn't sack me." Fitch looked extremely offended. "He died."

"This stuff killed him?" Martin thought it tasted like it could.

"Just drink it, milord, and consider it penance for overindulging." Fitch stalked across the room and flung open the curtains.

What had been an arrow in the eye became a volley.

"For God's sake, Fitch, close the curtains, and I promise to drink all of this vile stuff." Making good on his word, Martin slugged the nostrum down while trying to think of happy thoughts. The only thing that came to mind was a hazy memory of Fitch putting him to bed. That was more humiliating than happy, but definitely took his mind off the taste.

Thankfully, Fitch closed the curtains. He was laying out Martin's clothes when a train of servants arrived with a hipbath and hot water. The idea of a bath seemed wonderful, even if the effort of fitting into the one now sitting in his room turned a man of Martin's proportions into a contortionist. Other than the specially built one at his own home, baths were not designed for a man of his height.

Martin guessed his day was about to officially begin. "What time is it?" he asked, surprised that the hammer blows of the imps had somewhat subsided. "Is everyone already about?"

"It's nearing noon, milord, and most of the household is stirring but not necessarily present in the public rooms," Fitch said. "It snowed overnight, and the younger crowd has been out playing in it. The rest have stayed abed."

Martin grunted. At twenty-nine, he was evidently relegated to the older crowd. Odd, how that stung. "Let's get on with it," he said, levering himself off the chair.

Alice made her way down the hall to her parents' suite of rooms. Her discussion with Beth Dabney had been eye-opening. Not in the area of defining love, of course. That was impossible. It was also an area that was beyond Alice's understanding. She'd never felt the life-altering emotions that Beth described. Alice had wisely kept quiet and let Beth wander about the topic until she reached her own conclusions—which were that she loved the vicar and her parents would just have to understand.

What now motivated Alice was Beth's decision to convince her parents that they should be happy with her choice. How could Alice, who was seven years Beth's senior, be any less courageous? She would confront her mother and tell her this fantasy of Alice's marrying Drew was at an end. He didn't want her, and she certainly didn't want him.

She knew Mother would be upset, but it was only fair to let her know that Alice would be going her own way once she had the use of her grandmother's legacy. Secretly, she suspected her mother might feel relieved at this announcement. Perhaps Mother was tired of worrying about Alice's future and would see this as an acceptable solution.

Alice knocked on the door with authority. She would not let her mother peck her into submission.

Molly, her mother's maid, answered the door. "Good afternoon, Miss Caruthers," Molly said, somewhat blocking the opening. "Lady Tholea is still dressing. I'm sure she will be ready for visitors shortly."

"Is my mother stark naked?"

The maid turned red with embarrassment and shock. "Good heavens, no."

"Then I'll speak with her. Alone. You're dismissed until recalled." Alice pushed past the startled woman. She hadn't realized how good it felt to be assertive until the maid quietly exited.

Her mother was fully clothed, sitting at her dressing table, evidently waiting for Molly to finish her hair. One side had been put up; the other hung long and straight. "Oh, darling. I'm not decent yet. It will just be a few minutes until I'm downstairs."

"I want to talk with you in private," Alice said. Then she added forcefully, "Now."

Her mother swiveled on her bench so they faced one another. "What is it, Alice?" She looked alarmed. And then a huge smile split her face, and she held out her arms. "Dear Drew asked you to marry him, didn't he? Oh, my dear, I'm so pleased. Let me see this ring I've heard so much about."

Instead of walking into her mother's embrace, Alice backed into a chair and sat down. "No, Drew didn't ask for my hand. As a matter of fact, he's kept his distance the entire ten days we've been here. But this is what I want to talk about."

With her first sentence, Alice saw her mother deflate. With difficulty, Alice avoided immediately manufacturing excuses to make her mother feel better.

"Mother, I think we must face the fact that Andrew Dabney is never going to ask me to marry him. He obviously doesn't want me as his wife and, to be honest, I don't want him as a husband. I've gone along with this elusive hope for seven long years now, mostly to placate you and father, but now I'm finished with it. I want to move on with my own life. One that has nothing to do with Drew Dabney. One that may have nothing to do with anyone as a husband. I want a life that is completely my own."

Within the space of two heartbeats, her mother rallied. "Alice, you're being overemotional. I know your feelings have been hurt this Christmastide by Drew's apparent disinterest. But there could be a thousand reasons for his behavior. If you only—"

"No! There is no more 'if only.' I'm no longer sitting around waiting for something to happen to me. I'm going to do what I want. And to this end, as soon as Grandmother Elliot's legacy is available to me, I'm moving into her old house in London. With a suitable companion, of course, but I will live independently. I—"

Her mother stood so suddenly the bench toppled over with a bang. "You will cease these ridiculous pronouncements! You will stay with your father and me until you marry. And marry you will. I don't want people feeling sorry for me because my only child is a *spinster*. If you have developed an objection to Drew, then we will find you another title, although I doubt we can again look as high as a marchioness."

Alice also stood, towering over her diminutive mother. She would not stay to be pecked and pecked. "I love you, mother," she said. "But this is a new year and a new me, and you're just going to have to get used to the changes."

She then turned and marched from the room, head high and all banners flying.

She managed to maintain that attitude until she got a few doors away from her mother's, and then the tears came. She lowered her head and walked briskly toward her own room—until she crashed into a large, hard chest. She brought her head up to look ahead, and then up more, into the face of Martin Tate, Viscount Hayhurst.

"Alice, are you all right?" Martin gently touched one of her cheeks that was wet with tears.

Alice hoped lightning would strike and she'd disappear in a puff of smoke. She prided herself on being always in control, and here she was bawling like a baby in a corridor in the middle of the day. She didn't know if she wanted to run away or hide her face against his chest. She irrationally chose the latter, tucking her face against his crisp cravat. Her fingers, splayed across his broad chest, could feel the solid beat of his heart.

His arms gently curled around her and it felt good—warm and safe. He laid his cheek on the top of her head and made shushing sounds. When was the last time anyone had held her like this? Her nanny came to mind, and that was long, long ago. Drew certainly had never done so. The only time he held her was when they were dancing, and then it was never so comforting.

She sobbed like an infant until finally, the tears ran out, and the embarrassment came crashing in. Good Lord, Martin must think she was an idiot. She pushed back from him, and he let her go, his arms sliding away to drop straight down from his shoulders. She already missed their embrace.

"I'm sorry," she said to his chest, not wanting to look him in the eye.

"Did Drew offend you in some way? Did he hurt you?" His voice was a deep rumble above her head, like thunder from a distant storm.

She swung her head up to look at him. She knew her eyes were red and swollen and that she undoubtedly appeared to be an escapee from Bedlam. But she couldn't let Martin blame Drew for something he hadn't done. "This has nothing to do with Drew. I had a stupid argument with my mother. I suspect I overreacted. You know how irritating mothers can be."

And then she realized what she'd said. She was a blithering fool. Martin Tate didn't know anything about mothers since his had died when he was born. His father had died shortly thereafter. And she was asking him to understand the tenuous relationship that existed between parents and their children. Fool was too kind a word.

She fled in embarrassment, literally running down the hall and into her room. Her first attempt at independence had not gone well. More than anything, she wanted to again be enveloped in Martin Tate's arms.

Alice ran away from Martin, and he did nothing to stop her. Holding her and feeling her trust in him had been a heady experience. His body had readied itself to offer more than comfort, but he didn't think she'd noticed. His embarrassing physical response to her nearness was one of the reasons he didn't pursue her.

The person he most wanted to see right now was Drew. Actually, he wanted to punch him in the face, but first, he had to find the bastard. He'd already been to Drew's rooms and he wasn't there. Since Drew seemed to be in hiding, his being in any of the public rooms was unlikely, and Martin was sure Drew would not be in the library. Drew had never been one to find solace in books. The billiards room seemed his most likely hiding place. Martin had been heading in that direction when Alice had crashed into him.

He continued on his way, taking the stairs two at a time in his haste. He heard the click of balls before he reached the door. No game was in progress, however. Only Drew was within, dispiritedly rolling a cue ball down the table until it hit against one of the other two balls, bounced off the cushion, and returned. He looked up as Martin entered. His normal pose of lazy competence was missing. Instead of a languid feline, Drew resembled a fox brought to bay.

"I don't suppose I could interest you in a game?" Drew asked.

Martin shook his head. He leaned his elbows on the opposite end of the table and watched in silence as the ball made its circuit, back and forth. "You didn't ask Alice Caruthers to marry you," he said, a statement rather than a question.

"No." The cue ball crashed into the red ball with more velocity, nearly jumping the rail before returning.

Martin watched the ball's progress, not looking at Drew. "Is there a reason you haven't asked her?"

"The best of reasons. I didn't want to."

The next time the cue ball came toward him, Martin put out his hand and captured it. He looked across the green field of the table to stare at his friend. "You didn't want to? After years of an informal understanding, you didn't want to? I think you bloody well could come up with a better reason than that." Martin gripped the smooth ball so tightly his knuckles hurt. He realized he badly wanted to fling the ball at Drew's head.

Drew studied the middle of the table. "I like Alice. I admire her. Just like I like and admire Beth and Daphne and Harriet and—"

"And those are your sisters, you ass."

Drew's eyes came up to meet his. "Which is rather the point, isn't it? Alice has been shoved at me for as long as I can remember. She's a fine person. I didn't want to hurt her. I thought I could marry her. I thought I could pretend and everything would work out. And then, I met someone else who showed me the impossibility of a lifetime of pretense, and I just couldn't go through with the charade. I couldn't say the lines someone else had written for me."

"Where does that leave Miss Caruthers? You could have told her how you felt years ago." Anger roughed his voice. Anger at Alice's having been left hanging for all those years. Anger at the squelching of his own opportunities to pursue the one woman who attracted him.

Drew gave an unpleasant bark of a laugh. "You can say that, Martin, because you know nothing of how expectations can hedge you in and weigh you down. You have no idea how I've envied you for *not* having parents. That's a horrible thing to say, but it's true. You could go dashing off to play at war and no one could gainsay you. I, however, had no choice except to stay here and fulfill my role of being decorative and charming and marrying the right girl and lightly overseeing the Pennington holdings. Heaven forbid that I should have any ideas that would change the status quo. All I had to do was what was *expected* of me."

"And this is supposed to make me feel sorry for you? All it proves is that you're a selfish bastard." Martin's voice had dropped into a low growl. "You could have released Miss Caruthers to find her own happiness, but you pretended—to use your own word—an affection you didn't feel. You blame your actions on others' expectations, but the truth is that with the slightest effort, you could have made things different. But you hadn't the bollocks to face Alice—and I think more importantly, face your parents—with the truth."

"The truth? You want to know the truth?" Drew pushed away from the table and came striding toward Martin. No longer the cornered fox but one on the attack, teeth bared, ready to protect his den. "The truth is that I'm in love with Miss Sylvia Turnbull. The truth is I've asked her to marry me and she's done me the honor of saying yes. She's the one wearing that bloody great ring. And yes, it matches her eyes."

By this point, Drew had charged around the table and nearly mowed Martin down. He stopped just shy of doing so, breathing hard, as if he'd run miles instead of traversing the length of a billiard's table. He said more softly, "And you're right. The truth is I don't have the bollocks to inform either my family or the Caruthers."

He looked up at Martin, who could have sworn he saw tears gathered in his friend's eyes. Drew radiated sadness. Gone was the insouciant gentleman. Here was a man who truly cared, perhaps for the first time in his life.

"Who's Miss Sylvia Turnbull?" Martin asked. He had visions of some green-eyed tart, a dancer perhaps, and could imagine nothing but disaster.

"She's Charles Turnbull's daughter. One of the properties that is considered my responsibility is in Staffordshire, and I met her there at a local assembly."

Drew looked as though he was ready to rebut any objections Martin put forth. But Martin couldn't think of any. Compared to his imagined opera dancer, the daughter of one of England's premiere pottery manufacturers appeared eminently suitable. If someone made an inventory of the china closet here at Pencroft, Martin was sure the bulk of the fine bone china would carry the Turnbull mark.

While he was not of the aristocracy, Martin had no doubt that Charles Turnbull was very, very rich. He still carried the taint of trade, of course, and the man must have been thrilled when the Earl of Morrell and eventual Marquess of Pennington offered for his daughter.

"How long has this been going on?" Martin asked.

"Well, nothing has been 'going on' except a very proper courtship. I met her last March, and I see her whenever I'm in the area. I go there as often as I can. Father has been impressed by my diligence in managing the Staffordshire estate." Drew gave him a ghost of a smile. "She really is all that is wonderful. When I'm with her, I feel clever and competent, as if I can do anything that crosses my mind. But when I'm here at Pencroft, I feel like a useless appendage who must charm since he can't do."

"If you want to marry Miss Turnbull as badly as you say you do, then you are going to have to tell Alice that you're engaged. Then immediately inform your parents and Lord and Lady Tholea of the fact. It will not be pleasant, but it's better than hiding out in the billiards room, hoping that something magical will happen." Martin felt a bit sanctimonious about giving this advice. When Drew made his announcement, he would remove himself from any potential attachment to Alice, and Martin would have a clear field for his own courtship. He would be on hand to sooth her hurt. Lord, what an ignoble thought.

His fury with Drew dissipated when Martin realized he was culpable in Alice's coming distress. He'd known something was wrong with the relationship years ago. He would not have attempted to receive permission to court her if he hadn't had his misgivings. But when Lord Tholea had rebuffed him, he hadn't stayed to press Drew to follow through or retire from the field. Instead he'd taken his hurt feelings and run away.

Drew pushed his fingers through his hair. "Not pleasant is a gross understatement of what will transpire. Mother will cry. Father will shout. The Caruthers will damn me to all and sundry. And what this will do to Alice I can't imagine."

"Putting it off will only make it worse. But you're right. There will be crying and shouting and damning. But after that, there's nothing else they can do. You do realize that, don't you?"

Martin could only shake his head when Drew looked surprised. "Good God, man. You reached your majority years ago. You're the heir. Everything entailed will eventually be yours, and your parents aren't stupid enough to allow a permanent estrangement. All you have to do is weather a bout of storms. If Miss Turnbull is all you say she is, then she will be worth it. As for Alice..." Martin shrugged, "she might be relieved to have the situation come to some sort of conclusion. She can't have liked being left a perpetual lady in waiting."

Drew rocked back and forth on his feet, uncertainty clear on his face. Martin wondered when his friend's backbone had dissolved. Or had Drew never had one? Martin tried to think of a time when Drew had had to make a hard decision and nothing came to mind. Perhaps for Drew, this was uncharted territory.

"You're right," Drew said. "And if I'm going to do it, I'm going to do it now." He strode out of the room like a man on a mission.

The next few days at Pencroft were going to be anything but benign. Oddly, in all the years he'd spent Christmastide here, he couldn't remember there ever being any sort of disturbance. The golden Dabneys had always seemed too special for mundane matters to upset their perfect world. When he'd left here five year ago, he'd known he didn't want to be like this family and now he knew why. Overcoming obstacles built character, and character seemed to be in short supply at Pencroft.

CHAPTER FOUR

January 2, 1829

THE DAY AFTER HER DECLARATION of independence, Alice Caruthers dressed for dinner with extra care. She'd chosen her favorite blue gown because it gave her confidence. She wanted to appear calm and collected when she met her parents at dinner, even though this was hardly how she felt. But she'd hidden in her room for over twenty-four hours, feigning illness and having trays delivered, and enough was enough. To continue to isolate herself just made her look weak. If she were going to be truly independent, then she would have to grow accustomed to her parents' disdain.

And she was sure it was disdain that they would show. She'd failed in her one appointed task in life. She assumed they'd now learned that Drew would definitely not be marrying her.

If she'd known this was what he wanted to talk about, she would have made herself available when Drew came by her room earlier in the day. But she'd refused him entry. Perhaps she secretly feared that he had finally come up to scratch. If this were the case, it was too late. She'd unilaterally made her decision to live independently. She refused to acknowledge that her inability to confront Drew didn't do much to support her vision of the new, stronger Alice.

Since she wouldn't meet with him, she'd received a carefully worded note from Drew. He assured her that while he thought she was all that was admirable in a lady, his affection had become fixed elsewhere.

She should have been devastated. Or at least angry that Drew had pretended an interest for so long. But she couldn't conjure these emotions. What she primarily felt was relief, and this relief quickly evolved into a wild surge of joy. She was free. A life of her own choosing lay before her.

And now she needed to show all those present that this was the case.

She swept into the drawing room prior to the dinner bell, prepared to meet her parents eye-to-eye, and found the room curiously empty. Only the three oldest Dabney daughters and their spouses were present.

Lord Chesterton was the first to notice her arrival, and he came across the room to greet her with an engaging smile. This was not the reaction she'd anticipate. She'd steeled herself for pity and commiseration. To discover there was none confused her.

"Ah, here is one of our patients. I hope this means that whatever mysterious malady has stuck down half the household is short lived," Chesterton said.

"Excuse me?" Alice had no idea what Lord Chesterton was talking about.

Lady Chesterton, the former Lady Harriet Dabney, joined her husband. "Didn't you realize that you were not the only one to become ill? Your parents and my parents, as well as Beth, Drew, and you, of course, were all absent from dinner last night and have been recuperating in their rooms all of today. I'll admit that Chesterton and I feared something we ate on New Year's Eve was tainted. Mother insists on offering those odd-tasting, Hogmanay dishes, so it's impossible to tell if the food has gone bad. But since we all were served the same thing, that didn't seem likely."

"I was more indisposed than actually ill," Alice said, giving Lady Chesterton a significant look and hoping she assumed Alice had female problems. That explanation was more palatable than admitting she was upset because of an argument with her mother. "I have no idea what ails the others."

What had kept the others in their rooms? She wondered if Drew had spoken to both sets of parents before approaching her. That would have caused an acute upset. But from the behavior of those now awaiting dinner, the story of Drew's betrothal to someone else had evidently not made it to all the household. Alice felt no curiosity or pity coming from those assembled. Their only concern had been for her health—probably prompted in equal parts by concern for their own.

"You're in good looks tonight," Lord Chesterton said. "Anyone looking at you could tell that you hadn't been felled by something dreadful."

Alice took the portly earl's comment as a compliment. She was sure it was meant as one, although looking as if one were not on death's door didn't necessarily translate into looking attractive.

"Oh, good, Lord Hayhurst is here." Lady Chesterton said, immediately hurrying in the direction of the new arrival.

"Was he also at dinner last night?" Alice asked.

"Most definitely," Lord Chesterton said. "He kept us all well-entertained with his droll accounts of his activities in Greece."

Alice turned to look where Lady Chesterton and one of her sisters were in animated conversation with Martin. They both beamed up at him like debutants fascinated by a handsome man. Of course, it had been years since either of the Dabney sisters were debutants, but there was no doubt that Martin Tate was the most handsome man in the room. He would draw women of any age.

During that distant Christmastide, when Alice thought Martin might be paying her court, she'd found him attractive, but his allure was nothing like what he now possessed. He seemed to have finally grown into his bones and skin. It was not just that his physique had broadened. He was now more completely *there*. Before, there was something elusive and shadowy about him. He'd easily been eclipsed by Drew's bright sparkle. That certainly wouldn't happen anymore.

And then, he looked over the heads of the ladies surrounding him to stare straight into Alice's eyes. He flashed her a bright smile—and the room seemed to tilt in his direction. She placed her hand on the back of a chair to anchor her in place, to keep her from being drawn to him like iron filings to a magnet. It was the most extraordinary experience.

"I think we should go in to dinner," Lady Chesterton said. As the most senior lady there, she had evidently taken it upon herself to make the decision.

"We are small in number again," Lord Chesterton said, offering Alice his arm. "I can only hope we're not seeing the beginning of a contagion."

Martin tried to keep from staring at Alice during dinner. He'd wanted to sit next to her, but she'd been standing on the other side of the room when Harriet had decided it was time to eat. So he'd led in two of the former Dabney sisters, with the others trailing behind. Alice had ended up a few seats down, their diminished group occupying only one end of the table, but she sat on the opposite side where he could easily observe her.

Paul had come in at the last moment and was seated next to her. Lucky Paul, who was the recipient of her attention. Alice wore a blue dress that shimmered in the candlelight like the wings of a dragonfly. The color accented her sea-blue eyes and porcelain complexion. Her face was mobile, all quick smiles and arched brows. Were they discussing insects? It seemed unlikely. Perhaps she was plying Paul with more questions on foreign travel. Martin strained to hear snippets of the conversation.

"From a rather ungainly, coltish beginning, Alice Caruthers has grown into a most elegant lady," Harriet, Lady Chesterton said from his right. His attention in Alice's direction had obviously not been as surreptitious as he had hoped. "She will make a fine countess and eventual marchioness."

Martin hid his surprise and bit his lip to keep from saying, "That isn't going to happen." Those at the house party evidently had no idea that Drew's affections had pulled him elsewhere. At least those who were present. Martin suspected the missing members of the party were very conscious of the fact and that this was the cause of their malady.

From her behavior, he assumed that Alice too knew nothing about Drew's reneging on their tentative understanding. He was disgusted his friend—perhaps now former friend—hadn't had the backbone to tell Alice she would never be the Countess of Morrell. Martin hoped she would not be crushed by the news. But after all this time, she had to know something was wrong with Drew's relationship with her. Martin wanted her freed from the prospect of a sterile marriage, but he had never wanted her to be hurt.

"I find Miss Caruthers too lively, too elemental, to be categorized as elegant, but perhaps we each see what we are looking for," Martin replied.

Harriet gave him a baffled look, and switched the conversation to the cold weather and the difficulty in heating large rooms. Martin made a concerted effort not to look at Alice.

Dinner seemed to last forever.

Finally, they were released to wander back to the drawing room *en masse*. Martin pretended to misunderstand Lord Chesterton's suggestions that he join a whist table and sought Alice out instead. She was still in earnest conversation with Paul. Or rather, Paul was still talking and Alice was looking interested.

"Miss Caruthers," Martin unrepentantly interrupted Paul's monologue, "would you care to stroll a bit. I was thinking perhaps the long gallery would be nice. We can enjoy the moonlight on the snow from the windows."

"It will be cold in there," Paul said.

"I'll ring for a warm wrap then." Alice bestowed a brilliant smile on Paul and left to call her maid.

Paul raised one eyebrow. He obviously was another inheritor of that damned family trait. "You're not thinking of poaching on a private preserve, are you?"

"Not if it were truly private," Martin said. "I understand the area in question is now open to the public, and I plan to stake a claim before this becomes general knowledge." Paul puffed up like a disgruntled hedgehog. Martin hoped the younger man wasn't about to suggest pistols at dawn. "Perhaps you should talk to your brother," he hastily added.

And then, blessedly, Alice returned swathed in a heavy tan shawl. While it added nothing to her ensemble, it did look warm. She took his arm, and they hastily exited the room.

"Thank you for the rescue," she said, once they were in the hall. "Paul is a dear boy, but I'd quite exhausted all the enthusiasm I could muster about varieties of mantises. They sound like the most predatory of insects, but Paul is enamored of them, particularly some that resemble flowers."

Martin too had no interest in insects, but he was pleased to hear Alice refer to Paul as a "boy." Paul was just a few years Alice's junior, and she had seemed quite attentive during dinner. "I hope you don't think me improper, whisking you away without a chaperone, but I've found I desperately need some exercise after being indoors for the past two days."

Her laugh was soft and low and did strange things to the rhythm of his heartbeat. "If I thought you were a danger to my virtue, I would have insisted our resident entomologist accompany us."

Martin didn't know whether he was pleased with her trust or annoyed that Alice didn't imagine he could be a danger to her virtue. He certainly wanted to be the latter—and had for some time.

"I think both of us are pleased to be spared Paul's passion," he said, "although it is nice to see a Dabney with a more intellectual bent." And then he realized he may have offended her. She undoubtedly still thought she was marrying into the Dabney family. He could see no indication that Drew had spoken to her. It would be like his friend to avoid a confrontation. He'd been doing so for years.

"Yes, I do find the family to be passionless for the most part, at least in their outside interests. Paul is a delightful breath of fresh air in this area, and I suspect Beth also has a similar mindset."

Alice sounded more thoughtful than offended. That was encouraging. But he could still not think of a way to introduce the subject of Drew and his wandering affections. He continued to mull over a way to approach this topic as they entered the long gallery

As anticipated, it was cold, but the moon coming through the bank of windows was brilliant on the snow, giving the area an eerie, otherworldly light. They stopped to admire the view outside. It seemed as good a time as any to broach the subject of Drew's change of heart. He turned from the window to look directly at her.

"Did Drew—" he began just as she said, "Drew..."

They both stopped and chuckled. "Please go first," he said.

She was silent a moment, as if reconsidering. Taking a deep breath, she said, "Drew wrote me a note saying that his affections were fixed elsewhere. I was wondering, as his friend, what you knew about this."

The stupid ass! He'd written her a *note*? Disgust rolled through Martin. He could hardly make a comment to a lady about Drew's lack of bollocks, but that's all that immediately came to mind.

"I hope you weren't terrible disappointed." He steeled himself for tears.

"No, not disappointed. I was probably more relieved. But I am quite curious about the who and why. And judging from the dinner conversation, no one else knows about this."

Martin hadn't realized he'd been holding himself stiffly until her words caused his muscles to relax. Alice was *relieved* that Drew wasn't going to offer for her. His own relief was dizzying. "Drew spoke with me last night, and I can only apologize that he didn't accord you the same courtesy of a personal discussion."

"Don't think badly of Drew. He tried to talk with me. But I wasn't receiving at the time, and that was the reason for the note. It was decidedly a note, however, and not a letter, and his brevity has left me with a myriad of questions."

Honesty seemed the only approach. Well, perhaps honesty tempered with some less offensive phrasing. "Drew *imagines* himself in love with a girl named Sylvia Turnbull. She's the daughter of Charles Turnbull, the Staffordshire pottery manufacturer. I've never met her, so that's about all I can tell you." He certainly wasn't going to mention that Miss Turnbull was now wearing a ring that had been purchased for Alice.

Alice nodded as if she'd expected this. "I haven't met Miss Turnbull either, but in the past two years, her father has produced some limited edition figurines that are supposed to be modeled on his daughter. Shepherdesses, I think. But if they are truly representative of her appearance, she's a beautiful blond with fine features and a rather impressive, eh, upper portion." She then looked down and mumbled something that sounded like, "Young and beautiful. That's what I expected."

Martin put two fingers under her chin and turned her face up to look at his. "She couldn't be more beautiful than you."

She shook her head, but he cupped her chin with his hand and didn't release her. "You don't have to say that to make me feel better," she said. "I know men don't think of me in that way."

"Well, the man standing in front of you thinks you're beautiful, and he's thought that for many years. And you have character and wit and humor—all those characteristics that enhance the physical beauty you already possess. I said as much when I asked your father for your hand, and my opinion has not changed."

He leaned forward just slightly and kissed her. It was a whispered brush of lips, a promise more than a real kiss, but it shook him to the core. This was what he wanted. Alice was what he hoped to have.

Martin kissed her.

Alice had expected many things of this evening, but she had not imaged that Martin Tate would kiss her. It was a very unsatisfactory kiss, however, over before it really began. Drew had kissed her a few times, and while those kisses hadn't made her toes curl as this one did, they had certainly lasted longer.

Almost without conscious thought, she reached up to the nap of Martin's neck and pulled his mouth back to hers. This time he met her with more purpose. His lips molded to hers with teasing caresses. He nibbled lightly on her bottom lip and then soothed the same place with a sweep of a velvet tongue.

Her lungs seemed to seize in her chest. She relaxed her mouth to draw a breath and Martin's tongue slid in to stroke the inside of her cheeks, to bush her tongue, to tease her gums. Warmth like molten gold flowed through her veins. This was a kiss like she'd never had—and it was wondrous.

She leaned forward to place her body against his. She wanted to feel all of him. As if answering her unspoken desire, Martin's arms circled her and pulled her even closer. Her suddenly sensitive breasts pressed against his broad chest. One of his hands moved tantalizingly up and down her back until it settled on her buttocks and pulled tight against him there as well. The molten gold seemed to settle between her thighs, heavy and wet.

This is desire, she thought. Desire that she'd believed she would never feel. It pounded through her, making her want more. Martin made an odd, low growl and raised a hand to cup one of her breasts.

He thought her beautiful. She would not worry that she lacked the endowment to overflow the low neckline of her gown or that she was tall. Martin thought her beautiful. How amazing. And more importantly, he admired her inner qualities. He had for some time. Even before he'd asked her father for her hand.

The last reflection stilled everything within her. Martin had approached her father about marrying her? The shock brought her hands to his chest and she pushed back. He let her go, his arms loosening but still encircling her. He lowered his forehead to rest on hers. "I'm sorry," he said, his breaths coming in pants. "I should not have taken advantage."

She exerted a bit more pressure so she could look him in the face. His hands slid from her body, filling her with loss. "When? When did you talk to my father?" she asked.

"Five years ago. After he rejected my suit, I decided I needed a change of scene. I wanted to do something with my life and left for Greece. Didn't he tell you?"

The knowledge was corrosive, like being covered in icy water that somehow burned. Five years! That Christmas, when Martin had *seemed* to court her, he had actually been doing so. His kindness, his consideration, had been in earnest. The compliments he'd paid her had been real. He had wanted to marry her and she'd never been told. She'd thought he'd simply floated away like other potential suitors.

"No, he never told me." Alice was surprised her voice was steady. The anger surging through her left her feeling shaky. For all these years, she'd felt unattractive. She'd thought she had to buy friends through good works. She'd believed herself to be a failure.

And it had not been true.

Irritatingly, her eyes filled with tears. Martin ran a thumb over her cheek to catch an errant drop. "Oh, love, I didn't mean any disrespect. I know I should not have kissed you..."

She placed her fingers over his lips. "I liked your kisses very much. I liked all of it. I've just had a shock. I can but wonder how different things would have been had my father told me. I—" Her voice broke, and she shook her head. "I need to consider what you've told me. But I will see you tomorrow, and we will talk some more."

She captured his caressing hand and kissed it. Then she fled.

CHAPTER FIVE

January 3, 1829

MARTIN WAS SURE HE'D SLEPT. There were stretches of the night when his mind was not actively trying to decipher Alice's abrupt departure from the long gallery, and those missing minutes must have been sleep. These periods of mental inactivity came further and further apart as the night progressed, however. He finally gave up and got out of bed.

The room was frigid. He reached back to pull one of the covers over his shoulders and then padded to the hearth. He stirred the coals and placed the last of the logs onto the embers. It seemed an eternity before the wood caught and produced a flickering light and a miniscule amount of heat. God, his feet were freezing.

He rooted around in the wardrobe but couldn't find any slippers. Maybe Finch hadn't packed any. He settled for two pairs of his heaviest socks. Pulling a chair close to the fireplace, he stretched his feet toward the puny flame and tried to think of summer.

But all he could think about was Alice. More specifically, kissing Alice. He'd wanted to do that for so damned long, and it had certainly not been the disappointment that so many long held desires turned out to be. No, kissing Alice had been an altogether incredible experience. And having kissed quite a few women, he had a firm basis for comparison. War, and its aftermath of affirming one still lived, was conducive to a great deal of kissing—and a great deal of what kissing preceded.

Therein lay his conundrum. If Alice hadn't come to her senses and pushed him away, he was more than prepared to take what had started to its inevitable conclusion. If they'd not been in the gallery with nothing but a few, narrow, hard benches and the cold marble floor to provide a horizontal surface, he might have done so.

He was not pleased with what this said of his character. And he greatly feared that he had frightened Alice away. Even if she said she did not care about Drew's desertion, she had to be in a fragile emotional state. Knowing this, he'd still been unable to keep his hands from roaming her body. From cupping one of her breasts and marveling at how perfectly it fit in his palm. From pulling her tightly against his straining erection and reveling in the heat.

Good Lord, no wonder the woman had pushed him away.

She had said she would see him today and that they would talk. His concern was that he wasn't sure exactly what that meant. If he explained that he had fantasized about her even when he thought she would be marrying Drew, would she be appalled? Being with her in all ways was his fondest wish. It seemed so right. He was, unfortunately, unsure of how to convince Alice that this was the case.

A log shifted in the fire, making him start. He'd been mesmerized by the wavering flame. A very anemic flame. He was trying to decide if poking at the fire again would be worth the effort when there was a scratch on his door. Goodness, had Fitch developed mindreading capabilities? "Come," he said.

The figure that loomed out of the darkness was definitely not Fitch. A massive form stomped toward Martin, causing him to rise from the chair. Closer to the firelight, what had seemed to be a massive creature was revealed to be Drew wrapped in an overlarge greatcoat and a number of scarves.

"Good. You're awake," Drew said. "I've come to tell you I'm leaving." He then ponderously pivoted back toward the door, only to immediately reverse direction. "Oh, and I wanted to let you know that your interest in Alice Caruthers is fine with me." He again turned to leave.

"Drew, wait. What are you doing? It isn't even dawn yet. And what makes you think I'm interested in Alice?" All Martin could think of was that Drew had seen them in the long gallery. A terrible thought. Or perhaps Drew saw Martin's attraction to Alice as some form of betrayal and wanted to distance himself. But leaving in the frigid darkness made no sense.

"I've just spent the night talking with my brother Paul. He mentioned that you were like a dog on point all through dinner, just quivering to flush the covey."

Martin pulled the slipping cover back onto his shoulders. Bloody hell. Had he been so obvious? He was absolutely sure he had not been quivering.

"And I'm leaving because, well, because I've been kicked out." Drew seemed to shrug, but with all his clothing, it was difficult to tell. "Father is in a rage. Mother is hysterical. It seems that I am the least dutiful son on the face of the earth. You were right. My father can't take my title as Earl of Morrell. He can't keep me from being his heir. But he's informed me that anything that isn't specifically entailed will never be mine. He would appreciate it if I never again darkened his door. So to hell with them. I'm leaving. Paul is out in the stable right now saddling my horse and I'll be gone at first light."

Martin plopped back into his chair. "Drew, sit down and let's talk about this. I'm sure that things aren't as drastic as they seem at this moment. In a few days, everything will settle down. There's no need to go dashing off into the night—on horseback, no less. If you persist in the lunacy, at least take a carriage."

"I've been forbidden any of the Pennington conveyances." Drew paced, ignoring Martin's suggestion to sit. "I'll leave the horse at the first posting inn and get another. I'll tell the ostler to return the horse here. I'll be damned if I let my father think I've taken anything that's not rightfully mine."

"You'll freeze your bollocks off," Martin said, realizing that for the first time in memory, Drew was acting as if he had some. "At least take my carriage. There's no need for a grand gesture."

Drew gave a quick laugh and a dismissive wave of his hand. It suddenly dawned on Martin that perhaps Drew needed to make such a gesture of independence.

"I'll be fine," Drew said, "but if Paul has to go anywhere before the weather breaks, his may freeze. Half of this overabundance of clothing is his. And with frequent changes of mounts, I will make much better time than in a carriage in this weather. I need to get to Staffordshire as quickly as possible. I need to have all the details ironed out so Charles can announce my betrothal on Twelfth Night."

"Charles?"

"Turnbull. Sylvia's father. He'd warned me that my parents might be displeased and that their retaliation might take this form. We've even discussed tentative plans to cover this eventuality."

Something in Martin's face must have revealed his surprise, because Drew stopped his pacing and looked directly at him.

"Yes, I've made plans," Drew said. "Just because I don't plan very often doesn't mean that I can't. Sylvia is an only child and Charles would like me to learn the business, since at some point in the future, I'll be responsible for overseeing it." The old, slightly wicked smile flashed across his face. "And I can tell you that making plates and expensive knick-knacks is more profitable than the income from ducal estates. My parents, of course, will be horrified, but they won't be able to control me with purse strings."

Martin abruptly stood and walked toward his friend, his hand extended. "Then I wish you nothing but the best, Drew. May you and Miss Turnbull find great happiness."

Drew stepped forward to take his hand. "And I wish you well in your pursuit of Alice. I know you've quietly admired her since we were boys. I'm sorry that I didn't step out of the way before now. But I've never had such a sure path to follow—and follow my heart I will."

Drew's grip was strong and confident. Then in a flurry of capes, he turned and was gone.

Alice breakfasted in her room, as she impatiently watched the clock until the hands reached an hour when she could decently seek out her father. All the while, she felt her anger growing.

Martin's voice saying, *when I asked your father for your hand,* kept echoing in her head. He'd wanted to marry her years ago and she had never known. She'd liked him and would have enjoyed the opportunity to get to know him better. But she'd missed her chance, perhaps forever.

Had all the men who had shown interest in her over time been turned away? She realized she'd been robbed of ever having a choice. And now that Drew had removed himself from the field, did her parents think they could come up with another potential spouse that *they* would like and foist him off on Alice? If that were the case, they were greatly mistaken. She would make that very plain when she confronted her father.

The clock hands finally inched themselves to the right numbers. Alice smoothed her dress, left her room, and made her way down the corridor. When she knocked on her father's door, his valet answered.

"I'd like to speak with my father," she said.

"He's gone next door to be with your mother." The grizzled older man looked both ways down the hall before whispering, "She's had a bit of an upset this morning."

As far as Alice knew, her mother had been upset since they'd talked two days ago. She wasn't even sure her mother would let her in. Making a quick decision, she pushed past the valet and walked into her father's room. "I'll just use the connecting door," she said, heading straight to her target and through the doorway before the man could react.

Her mother was indeed upset, sobbing in a chair while her father stood behind her, patting her mother's shoulder and looking perplexed. "I'm sorry to intrude," Alice said, deciding she was not sorry in the least, "but I must ask Father a question immediately."

Alice's voice instantly stilled all other sound in the room and brought both sets of her parents' eyes to where she stood. "Did Lord Hayhurst offer for my hand five years ago?" she immediately continued.

Her father glanced at her mother and then looked at various places in the room that were *not* where Alice stood. "Did he?" Alice's voice was more strident.

"Yes." Her father now studied his feet.

"And why did you never consult me?"

"Your mother so wanted you to be a marchioness and we assumed the match was set. I didn't think it was necessary." Her father still would not look at her.

"And were there other offers from other gentlemen at other times?" Alice wanted to yell the question, but her throat was too tight.

Her father said, "yes" so quietly she had to strain to hear.

The heat of her anger again scalded her. "Look at me." She walked toward them. "Look at me! I'm a twenty-four-year-old spinster. I'm pitied by most of my peers. I've been made to doubt myself on the most elemental level, as a woman. I've been made to feel that there is nothing appealing about me while I wait and wait for my mother's fantasy to take place. Not mine, you'll notice, but my mother's."

She suddenly laughed, harsh and without humor. "And for what? To prove that I'm a dutiful daughter. To make up for the fact that I was neither the diamond of the first water that my mother wanted nor the heir coveted by my father. Well, I can't be these things—and I can't make up for them. I am Alice Caruthers and I am beautiful with character, wit, and humor, even if neither of you has ever acknowledged that."

Alice stopped her tirade, surprised that Martin's assessment had come out of her mouth.

"The Earl of Morrell has left," her mother shouted at her, sounding angry now rather than sad. "He's gone to marry some unacceptable tradesman's daughter. Because you couldn't hold him. We gave him to you wrapped up like a gift and you let him get on a horse and ride away."

"I *let* him?" Alice's voice also rose in volume. "How was I supposed to stop him? I guess I could have thrown myself naked into his bed and then scream I'd been compromised, but I think even you both will agree that not much happiness would have come from doing so. And I still hope that my happiness fits somewhere in your plans."

Her parents looked at her as if she'd grown a second head. Sighing in disgust, she said, "If I thought I could get on a horse and ride away, I'd do so as well."

As it was, all Alice could do was stride purposefully to the main door and thrust it open so hard it banged into the wall. With the sound of that thump behind her, she stormed down the corridor.

Before making the turn into the hallway to her own room, her feet froze on the hall runner. Through a half-open door, she spied Martin Tate. Martin Tate in close fitting trousers—and nothing else. He stood looking out the window, his thumbs tucked in the top of the pants that rode low on his slim hips, his unhooked braces hanging down the sides of his long legs.

His shoulders looked impossibly wide measured against the window frame. Muscles bunched over his shoulder blades, and his spine was a deep crevice bisecting his long back. Alice had never seen an unclothed man. His body was so different from hers, she stood transfixed.

She must have made an inadvertent sound. Perhaps a sigh or a gasp. Whatever it was, Martin heard it and turned in her direction. "You made good time in finding..." his voice trailed off.

They stood like statues, staring at each other. Alice discovered she liked looking at his front even more than she had his back. His wide shoulders supported a broad chest, the very top of which was dusted with dark hair. Below that was a flat abdomen that looked hard and ridged. More dark hair seemed to tumble from his navel to disappear into the waistband of his trousers.

Alice felt something odd and tingly run through her. She remembered leaning against Martin's chest. How warm and firm it had felt pressed against her breasts.

She wondered what it would feel like to be held there without their being separated by layers of material. The thought made breathing difficult.

"Excuse me, milady." The words to her right cause her to jump. Martin's valet stood there, holding a freshly ironed shirt in his hands.

"Oh, my heavens," she muttered and, for the second time in just a few minutes, fled toward the sanctuary of her room. Once there, she dashed in, closed the door, and leaned back against it.

Whatever was she doing? Standing there gawking at a partially naked man. And then laughter bubbled out. She knew exactly what she'd been doing. She was enjoying the view. She would never have guessed that an unclothed male, especially one who looked like Martin, could be so stimulating. Fascinating. Exhilarating. Maybe every "-ating" that existed in the English language.

She wondered what it would have been like if Martin's valet had gone to the laundry room to retrieve his trousers as well. Martin would have been standing there in his unmentionables. Or, heavens, maybe even less. He would look like the statues in the British Museum that she wasn't supposed to notice. Only, she suspected, better. All long, lean, and powerful.

Goodness, she'd lived twenty-four years and was only now discovering she was wanton. She wanted to see him like that. But not just any man. Only Martin.

She thought back to the good times that she'd enjoyed with Drew, and there had been some of them. But they all had one thing in common. Drew's close friend Martin Tate had always been with him. She couldn't recall who had made the witty comments or who had made her feel special, but she now suspected that person had been Martin.

She marveled that she'd not noticed Martin when Drew would bring him home for Christmas from Eton and later the university. Martin never put himself forward, however, and that might have been why it had been so easy to overlook him before. He'd always been a satellite to Drew's sun. Or he had been until five years ago, but he'd then disappeared before she really got to know him.

Alice had believed that her best hope for happiness lay in carving out an independent life for herself. She now suspected this to be an error. Her best hope for happiness might be standing in a room down the hall, putting on a newly ironed shirt.

Martin purposefully made sure he wasn't seated next to Alice at dinner. He didn't want to appear to be hungering for her more than the nicely done roast.

Staying away from her before dinner had been easy, since the ladies all congregated on one side of the room, offering Alice what seemed to be condolences. When she laughed, they all appeared confused. But disparaging comments about Drew could be heard from that quarter.

As if by agreement, the men had grouped on the far side of the drawing room. Surprisingly, the support for Drew's actions was universal among the male contingent. While most thought his handling of the situation was poorly done, they applauded his standing on his own feet and doing what he, and not his parents, wanted.

Lord Chesterton's thoughts were echoed by the others. "Good God, the man is nearly thirty," Chesterton said. "It's about time he showed some backbone. I don't condone how he treated the Caruthers' girl, however. His behavior to her was shabby."

A few wondered what would now become of Alice. Martin held his tongue and didn't offer his opinion. He knew what *he* wanted to become of Alice, and that was for her to be his wife. The difficulty might be in convincing her of this.

Or, perhaps not. He'd been surprised to see her in his doorway, ogling him. Yes, ogling was definitely the correct word. When he'd turned toward her, she'd looked shocked. And then her face had quickly registered appraisal and finally approval.

It had been on the tip of his tongue to ask, "Do you like what you see?" Fortunately, Fitch had appeared at her elbow before he had the opportunity to prove to her that he was a conceited ass. But he was quite sure that the last flickering emotion that crossed her face was approval. How shallow he was to want her to admire him. But he did. That last look had heated his blood to the extent that he'd had to send Fitch on an unnecessary errand and take himself in hand so he wouldn't be embarrassed in front of his valet.

The images he'd pulled into his mind while he took care of his problem were what now concerned him. They were too vivid, too real. And he wanted to *make* them real. *Alice, lying on a bed, her thick, brown hair tumbling around her firm, perfect breasts, her long, pale legs wrapping around his hips, her...* he tried to pay attention to the food on his plate. He tried to make himself wonder if the plate itself were ironically from the Turnbull factory. But his mind kept slipping back to his reverie.

Yes, it was much better that he keep his distance. He was going to be strong and not suggest he and Alice wander away on their own this evening. There would be safety in staying with the group.

His resolve was tested when the meal finished and everyone retired to the drawing room. Alice and Beth were in conversation near the fireplace. The men had gathered around the port bottles near the windows. He would join the men.

His feet took him unerringly to Alice and Beth. Alice gave him a dazzling smile. He stood there like a lump, trying to figure out how he had gotten there.

Beth gave him a knowing look and said, "I see Harriet motioning. I'd better see what she wants."

"No," Martin said, nearly reaching for her arm to physically restrain her. "I'd like to know how your parents are doing. Their reaction to Drew's announcement seemed a bit excessive and I'm worried about them."

Beth laughed. "Their reaction has been extreme, but this is the first time their wishes have been thwarted by one of their children. I think they don't know what to do, so are unreasonably hitting back like spoiled infants. I suspect their behavior will have moderated by tomorrow, however, since mother has to get ready for the Twelfth Night Ball, and she'd never let any of the neighbors have fodder for gossip. The Marquess and Marchioness of Pennington have to be the epitome of charm and grace, regardless of how they actually feel." She suddenly grinned, the imp she'd been as a child showing through. "And I'm planning on taking full advantage of this trait."

Then she quickly crossed the room to her sister Harriet, leaving Martin alone with Alice—a circumstance to be both cherished and feared.

"She's right," Alice said. "So much of what happens at Pencroft is show without substance. I'm embarrassed that for years I allowed my mother's ambition to push me into being part of this meaningless charade." She shook her head, frowning, and looked around. "Do you think anyone here is happy, or is it all pretense?"

Martin realized the question was seriously asked and that the answer was important. He looked around the room, at the three oldest Dabney daughters and their respective spouses, at Beth and Paul floating like satellites between the groups. "Yes," he said, "I think *everyone* here is happy. I think the married couples here have true affection for one another. I think Beth and Paul are each finding their way in the world and are happy with their places so far, although they are different from their siblings and perhaps seek more meaning to their lives."

"They might be fooling you. I thought my parents were happy, and I've now begun to doubt that. I believe my mother regrets she settled for a mere baron and this was the reason she was so adamant that I marry a man with a distinguished title." Her eyes suddenly seemed to fill with tears. "I hate that she thinks my father isn't good enough, not when he's spent his life trying to please her at every turn."

Martin took her hands in his and didn't care what the others in the room thought. "Alice, parents always have dreams for their children. When I was in Greece I met people who were poor beyond our imagining, but they all wanted something better for their children, and were willing to fight to make it happen. My parents died before I can even remember them, so I have no idea if they had dreams for me. I hope they did. I simply don't know what those dreams were. I have no idea if I would have wanted for myself what they envisioned."

He looked around again, finding it impossible to imagine the hungry look of the Greek children on any of the people in the room. "I think what we see here is more of a life made too easy than one of constant pretense. Most of the people here have never had to strive for anything. They, therefore, let the gentle current of their lives take them where it will. They are untested, but that doesn't make them unhappy."

"But my parents..."

"Don't seem unhappy to me. They too are willing to float through life, however, and you may have decided that this is not your way. I made that discovery five years ago and that is one of the things that propelled me to Greece. It took me a number of years of heat and flies to figure out that for all the years I visited here, I was happy, but that I wanted more than the Dabneys ever will. Oddly, I didn't find that elusive *more* until I returned."

He couldn't bring himself to admit that she was part of what he'd gone away to find—only to discover it was waiting for him when he returned. It made him wonder if the rest of what he desired was here as well.

"Tell me about Greece," she suddenly said. It seemed a change of subject, but in some ways, it was not. What he'd encountered in Greece had helped make him the person he now was, and he wanted her to know that person—to know if he was someone who could give her the happiness she obviously sought.

"Just so long as you don't want to know about Byron. That's what interests most people. Unfortunately, he died shortly after I arrived, so there's not much I can tell you. But if you want to know about my experiences, then we'd better sit down, for it's a long tale." He smiled as he gave her hand a gentle tug toward the closest settee.

"Nothing about Byron," she said. "Just about Hayhurst."

The look she gave him did something strange to his insides. The feeling wasn't sexual as much as it was the elusive *more* he wanted. She sat a respectable distance from him, but one of her hands stayed interlocked with his.

And he told her about his time in Greece. This wasn't the humorous account he gave to most people to obscure his real feelings. Instead, he told her of all his impressions and emotions. He described the stark and beautiful landscape, the fear that gripped him during an attack, the exhilaration when they were victorious, the disillusionment when the Greeks themselves divided into factions, and the soul-destroying sense of betrayal caused by the waffling of the British government and its allies.

"And this is why you returned home?" At some point during his long dissertation, they both seemed to have lost their gloves. Alice's bare fingers now gently stroked his own.

"Part of the reason. But the major impetus was the illness of my estate manager. He'd successfully run things since I was a boy and I was comfortable leaving my property in his hands, but when I got his letter, I knew it was time I came home and took up my patrimony."

"And now you're home to stay." She gave his hand a quick squeeze.

He wanted to hold her and kiss her and assure her he would be here from now on. But this was not the time or place. He glanced around the room and was surprised to see that only Paul and Beth remained, randomly pushing chess pieces around with no pretense of a game.

Paul met his eyes, probably noticing the cessation of sound. "Finally," he said. "I thought you'd never quit talking. Now if you would go to bed, Beth and I would be released from chaperone duty. The others retired hours ago."

Hours? No, it couldn't be. A quick glance at the clock proved that it was. Feeling embarrassed, Martin said, "There was no need for you to chaperone."

"Oh, yes, there was," Beth interjected. "If you insist on courting in the drawing room, then you're stuck with chaperones. It's one of the house rules."

Then Beth walked over to them, which brought both Martin and Alice to their feet. Beth slipped her arm through Alice's. "You and I need to get our beauty rest," Beth said. "And on the way to our rooms, I'll remind you of the location of the conservatory. The family never goes there since mother long ago proclaimed she had no talent with flowers, but the gardeners use it for the plants and flowers for the house, so it's always kept warm. Ever so much nicer than the stables." She winked at Martin as they left the room.

Martin worked hard not to laugh. Paul would undoubtedly ask the reason for his humor, and Martin didn't want to disclose Beth's secret rendezvous on New Year's Eve. He turned toward the decanter of brandy to hide a smile he was unable to keep from his face. "I'm having a nightcap," he said. "Would you care to join me?"

"Lord, no," Paul said behind him. "I've been waiting to go to my bed for the past hour. But I had to sit here while you talked on and on. Now that I've been released from my duty, I'll bid you goodnight."

A nightcap, his excuse for turning away, now seemed like a wonderful idea. Martin poured some of the amber liquor and crossed the room to sit in front of the waning fire, twirling the snifter in his hands. He was chagrinned to realize that he *had* done all the talking. Lord, he must have sounded like Paul when the man droned on and on about insects. Alice pretended an interest in Paul's monologue. Had she done the same with him? What a lowering thought. No, Alice had been more than an audience. She'd asked intelligent questions and made insightful comments. He felt as if she truly understood him. As if they had made a connection.

He took a sip of brandy and felt the smooth liquor slide down his throat. It had been years, maybe forever, since he'd felt so comfortable about revealing his innermost thoughts and feelings. It felt like a marvelous gift. Almost better than holding Alice in his arms and kissing her. He'd never thought mental closeness was as important as physical closeness, but this seemed to be the case. The physical side would be nice, however. He smiled into his glass. He should have remembered the seldom-used conservatory—but tomorrow he'd figure out the least conspicuous way to get there.

CHAPTER SIX

January 4, 1829

ALICE CAREFULLY CUT the individual cards from the large, mass-produced Twelfth Night Character Sheet and placed them in a growing stack. The pictures and descriptions that Lady Pennington had purchased from a stationer would give everyone a good idea of not only what their particular character should look like but also how that character should behave.

The family drawing room was filled with the low hum of activity. All the resident ladies had assembled to work on their assigned tasks for the Twelfth Night Revel. Amazingly, everyone's supposed illnesses had disappeared with the need to finish the preparations for the coming ball.

Alice wondered whom Lady Pennington would choose to receive each of the characters. Some of the depictions were far from flattering. She certainly hoped she wouldn't end up with a character like Leticia

Littlebrain and have to pretend to be a half-wit all evening.

The choices for the men were even worse. Samuel Strutt. Sir Oliver Ogle. Her lips curled into a smile. It was too bad there wasn't an Olivia Ogle. Then she would have an excuse to stand around and look at Martin all night. If she were doing the picking, Martin would be Hector Hero. To match the picture he would have to come garbed in something medieval, however, and she doubted any of the costumes available in the Pencroft attics would fit him.

She smiled as she continued her work. She could easily imagine Martin in a short tunic and hose, the material hugging those long, long legs. That was certainly a happier image than looking at the picture of Clarissa Clutterhair who seemed to have a bird's nest in her tresses. Alice already knew what Martin looked like without his shirt. She mentally replaced his trousers with the medieval hose. If he showed up like that, every woman at the ball would be agog.

How was it that for years she'd never really paid attention to him? That now seemed impossible. She'd become instantly alert to his presence when he'd walked into breakfast this morning. The idea of his arriving to sit at a breakfast table with her for every morning for the rest of her life held definite appeal. She wondered if he felt the same.

Martin had obviously enjoyed her company last night as much as she had enjoyed his. He was witty, wry, and honest—a delightful change from the participants in most of her recent conversations. She was embarrassed that they'd talked so late, but she would do it again. She felt they were in concert with their view of the world. This feeling of connection was a new sensation, and she hugged it to her.

"Oh good, you've gotten the first sheet done." Lady Pennington appeared at Alice's elbow and whisked away the cut out character cards. Lady Pennington was now all brisk efficiency and bonhomie, as if she'd not been sequestered for days in a fit of either anger or pique. Alice wasn't sure which it had been. But Beth had been correct in her assessment that her mother would come out of hiding to put on a good face when she needed to.

Alice's mother had also reappeared, although she stayed away from where Alice was working. Her mother's ability to pretend was evidently not as well-honed as Lady Pennington's. Alice doubted that most people would notice the estrangement, since her mother was addressing envelopes at another table rather than working nearby. People from the area around Pencroft had been invited to the Twelfth Night Revel, and Lady Pennington was anxious to get the characters they were supposed to represent into the hands of those coming. They would need a day to organize their costumes.

The house party guests would have their cards delivered to their rooms before dinner this evening. The exact role each was to play was supposed to be a secret, however, so everyone would be surreptitiously trying to locate the pieces of their costumes without others guessing where they were going and what they were doing. This would be a night when everyone was almost expected to camouflage his or her movements, a perfect time to skulk around.

Alice hoped Martin would be interested in sneaking in the direction of the conservatory. Of course, if others discovered them there, it would be difficult to convince anyone that they were looking for costumes. Unless...

Alice picked up a second pre-made sheet, this one from another stationer so the characters were different. She suddenly smiled. Yes, there was the character she wanted—Beatrice Bouquet. The brightly colored drawing showed a young woman in a dress broadened by the panniers of an earlier generation. She knew from past holidays that old clothing was easy to find in the attics. A large garland of flowers, the essential part of the costume for Alice's purpose, hung around the woman's neck. In midwinter, these would normally be made from paper, but there was no reason they could not be fresh flowers. Especially when there was a conservatory available.

Alice carefully cut the card from the sheet and pushed it toward where Beth sat. "This is who I want to be," she said.

"Mother will know if you switched your card," Beth whispered from across the table. Beth's job was to check the names against a list her mother had given her and then place the right cards in the appropriate envelopes. "She remembers who everyone is supposed to be every year. It's uncanny."

"But couldn't you have made a mistake?" Alice also kept her voice low.

Beth laughed. "Of course I could. But I'd already decided I was going to switch my card, and two mistakes would seem a bit excessive, wouldn't they?"

"Don't you think it's unfair that you should do this for yourself and not for me?" Alice was not above using Beth's intrinsic belief in fair play to her own advantage.

"If I make two mistakes, my purpose will be obvious," the younger woman said.

"What's so bad about the character you've been assigned?"

"I'm to be the Snow Queen." Beth's face registered disgust at being the most sought after lady's character.

"Good heavens. What could possibly be wrong with that? I thought you said your mother was irritated with you. It seems to me she's assigned you the most glamorous character."

Beth shook her head. "No. She's made me the most *obvious* character. Everyone always knows where the Snow Queen is and who she's with. It's like being a belled cat. Every movement is noted. I'd hoped I might, eh, disappear for at least a few moments. But Mother is trying to make that impossible. It's part of my punishment for being, what she calls, too independent in my thinking. She's given me this hideous chore for the same reason."

Alice hoped her face didn't reveal her skepticism. "What's so terrible about getting to know who everyone will be beforehand?"

"Well, first of all, I do know, and that takes some of the fun out of the evening. The worst part, however, is that people will ask me who others will be and I can't tell them, since if I break the vow of secrecy I've taken for one, then I'd have to do it for all. And when I won't tell those who ask, they'll be angry with me."

"Maybe no one will ask."

"You're not going to ask me who Lord Hayhurst will be?" It was Beth's turn to look skeptical.

Alice didn't know what to say. She actually had planned to ask Beth to reveal Martin's character. "What if I step on your gown and rip it so you have to go to the ladies' retiring room for an extended visit? That would allow you to disappear for a while. Would you then consider only changing mine?"

"Okay, let's see who you want to be." Beth extended her hand across the table and pulled Alice's chosen card toward her. When she looked at the card, she started to laugh. "I get it. Beatrice Bouquet would have to visit the conservatory."

"That she would."

Beth sat and flipped an edge of the card with her fingernail for what seemed like an eternity. "I'll do it," she said, "but you have to promise to make a big rip so I'm gone for a long time."

"I'll make so many rips you'll be lucky not to end up naked." Alice gave her a conspiratorial smile. But she said nothing more, even if she really did want to know which character would be Martin's.

Martin checked his reflection in the long pier glass placed between the windows in his room. He looked as elegant as Fitch could make him. He felt slightly ridiculous about his concern for the impression he would make. Perhaps his nervousness was just an echo of what he'd felt on a similar mission five years ago.

But he was a different person than he'd been then, and the circumstances were different. The outcome would also be very different. Of this he had no doubt. He gave his waistcoat a final, unnecessary tug and left for his meeting with Lord Tholea.

Martin had requested that they meet in Lord Pennington's study. It had been the scene of the last debacle, and it was important to him that they revisit the same venue. Martin suspected he silently wanted to make the point that everyone's life would have been happier if Lord Tholea had given him permission to court Alice all those years ago.

When he arrived, he saw that Lord Tholea had preceded him and had seated himself behind Pennington's desk. Martin inwardly grinned at the blatant attempt to appear more powerful. He wouldn't be placed in the position of supplicant. "I think we would both be more comfortable sitting by the fire," he said, promptly taking one of the facing chairs by the hearth.

Lord Tholea hesitated, but when it became apparent that Martin was not going to budge, he stood and crossed the room to take the chair opposite Martin's. Tholea was a tall man, but not as tall as Martin, who felt the advantage of his height even when they were both seated.

"I'm sure you've guessed the reason I asked to see you," Martin began without preamble. "I'm courting your daughter and have every intention of marrying her if she will have me."

"I believe last time you had the good grace to ask." Tholea's voice was peevish.

"Last time, Alice was underage. I felt I needed your permission. This is, of course, no longer the case. I am now doing you the kindness of informing you."

Martin stared at the other man. He maliciously enjoyed the way Tholea fidgeted in his chair. Did the man now realize that he'd harmed his daughter by holding out for her marriage to Drew? "How greatly are you in debt?" Lord Tholea suddenly asked.

"Excuse me?" Martin asked, confused by the odd change of topic.

"I'm asking how much you need Alice's dowry? I thought I might offer a loan so you did not have to marry my daughter." The older man looked at him expectantly. "You feckless boys always want her money more than you want her."

Cold anger surged through Martin. "Well, to begin with, I am hardly a boy. I believe I passed that plateau a number of years ago and am considered a man. Secondly, I am hardly feckless. That title is more appropriate for the man you had chosen for her husband. And finally, my estate is financially solid. I have no need for whatever dowry you've managed to scrape together for Alice."

"Scrape together?" It was Lord Tholea's turn to look offended. "Don't you know that Alice is a considerable heiress? My title and entailed properties will go to my nephew on my death, but everything not entailed will go to Alice, and that doesn't even take into consideration the money and property left to her by her grandmother."

"I'm pleased to hear that. When we get to the point of discussing the marriage settlement, those funds can be held in trust for the benefit of our children."

When Martin was a boy, a bee had stung one of his setter pups when the dog had stuck his nose in a flower. Lord Tholea's expression was very similar. "You mean... you want Alice for herself?"

Martin found himself more offended by this comment than he'd been when Lord Tholea had called him feckless. How dare the man denigrate his own daughter, who was one of the most delightful women to walk the earth. "Any man with half a brain would desire your daughter. Not only is she beautiful inside and out, she has charm and a mind as sharp as a newly stropped razor."

When Tholea sat there looking shocked, Martin realized he had no more time to waste with the ass. He stood and gave the older man a weak smile. "I wanted to put you on notice of my intentions," he said. He needed to leave before he told Tholea exactly what he thought of him. At some point, this man would be his father-in-law, and there was no need to cause more animosity.

As he crossed the room, Tholea called after him, "You know you're just a face-saving substitute for the man Alice really wanted."

Martin continued out of the room as if that well-placed barb had not found its mark. Alice's father might be an ass, but he was a clever one who seemed to be able to find others' weak points and exploit them. God, how difficult Alice's life must have been. Her parents must have diminished her for her entire life. He was surprised she'd managed to have any self-esteem at all. He was beginning to understand how people could think his being orphaned at an early age might have been advantageous.

He entered his room to discover Fitch in a state of agitation. "The note with your character assignment has arrived," Fitch said. He seemed to paw the earth like a horse anxious to begin a race.

"So give it here," Martin said, extending his hand. "Let's see what impossible costuming Lady Pennington expects us to come up with."

Fitch gave him the envelope and Martin immediately opened it. Inside he expected to find a character card obtained from stationers. Instead, there was a hand-written note. Martin pulled it out and read the contents.

Martin,

I thought you would be a First Foot who would bring this house luck. Instead, you have brought disaster. My eldest son has run off to marry the daughter of a potter. My second son is leaving on a hazardous journey. My youngest daughter has informed me she has developed a tendre *for the local vicar. My oldest friend is prostrate with grief that her daughter will never marry. So many problems in such a short time can only mean ill luck. Therefore, your character will be the Lord of Misrule, since that is certainly who you are.*

Lucy, Lady Pennington

Martin then threw back his head and laughed harder than he had for some time. What Lady Pennington saw as disaster, he saw as people finally coming to their senses and discovering what would make their lives happy. He saw growth rather than stagnation. He was personally not responsible for any of the perceived problems, although he planned to be the solution for the friend's unmarried daughter.

But if his hostess blamed him for what had been happening, then he would be the best—or the worst, depending on one's point of view—Lord of Misrule that could be imagined. That character was no longer included on the stationer's sheets because it was considered a relic of the past. In the enlightened nineteenth century, no one wanted the normal rules of conduct subverted. But for this one night, Lady Pennington had given Martin the power to do so. Did she realize how foolish she had been?

"Fitch, we have a lot of work ahead of us." he said. "Do you think you can make me appear a combination of a Tudor jester and a king?"

His valet gave him a broad smile. "With delight."

As Alice had anticipated, the company immediately dispersed after dinner to begin finding the pieces of their costumes. While everyone was careful to keep their character a secret and not disclose too much information, people asked for the loan of small, specific items. Harriet was seeking a garish scarf. Beth admitted she had one an aunt had given her tucked away somewhere in her room. Paul was looking for a monocle. Unfortunately, no one seemed to have one. Goodness, could he have been given Oliver Ogle? Poor Paul.

Amid a lot of teasing and laughter, most people made for the vacant bedrooms that now held the old costumes that had been stored in the attic. She didn't immediately leave the drawing room and was gratified to see that Martin also tarried.

"You already have your costume?" she asked him.

"I've sent my valet Fitch out to hunt things down. The man is truly in his element for the first time since he's been in my employ." Martin's eyes sparkled as if he knew a secret joke. Heavens, the man was handsome. "Don't you need to begin assembling yours? Perhaps I could be of some help."

"Actually, I cheated a bit. Since I was the one to cut the cards from the sheet, I've known my character since this afternoon and got an early start. I have nearly everything I require. I am in need of a flowered garland, however. The picture shows one made of paper, but I thought a garland of real flowers would be more interesting. I was considering going to the conservatory to see if anything was in bloom. Would you like to accompany me?" Alice hoped Martin wouldn't recognize what was a practiced speech.

She'd thought up different ways to suggest they visit the conservatory and had decided this approach made her seem less like a wanton than any of the others she'd considered. Of course, she was feeling decidedly wanton and racy making the suggestion. They both knew she'd be looking for more than flowers. Unexpectedly, she felt a blush stain her cheeks.

Martin gave her a wide smile. "I'd be happy to go with you. A lady shouldn't wander by herself. I think we would be wise to take an oil lamp to light the way. Let me get one."

He said something to one of the footmen, who disappeared and returned with a lamp so quickly it was almost as if it had been waiting just outside the door.

"Shall we go?" Martin took her arm and guided her into the hall. When she turned in the direction of the conservatory, he stopped her. "I think this other way will be quicker," he said, redirecting her steps.

The need for the lamp quickly became apparent as Martin took her through cold and unlit rooms that were not presently in use. Alice wasn't even sure where they were until she saw the glass doors at the end of the hall. And then disappointment filled her. Light glowed from the conservatory. Some of the staff must be working within. Beth's suggestion of a good place for an assignation and Alice's stratagem for the need to visit that location were all for naught.

Martin seemed undeterred, however, and blithely pushed open the door. Warm air and the smell of soil and growing things met them. Although the large glass room seemed empty of occupants, it was obviously a work place. Tables held flats of seedlings, and large pots with mature plants covered much of the floor. Strategically placed oil lamps gave the area a pale glow of light.

"I think what you're seeking is this way," Martin said, indicating a pathway between pots of ferns.

Alice wondered how Martin knew where things were. "Do you think the staff should have left lamps burning?" she asked, feeling something was odd here.

Martin's deep laugh echoed behind her. "I asked them to light the conservatory. I'm afraid we were two minds with a single thought. I'd been unable to come up with an excuse for coming here, so my suggestion would have been less elegant."

The realization that Martin had planned this sent a shaft of longing through her. She stopped and turned to find him close behind her. "What would you have suggested?"

"I would have whispered, 'Let's go to the conservatory so I can kiss you.'"

Before she could tell him she thought that was quite elegantly phrased, he took a step forward, pulled her into his arms, and did kiss her. What started as a tender touching of lips quickly escalated into one of desire. His tongue teased and she reciprocated. His hands roamed her back, pulling her tightly against him. She ran her hands over his shoulders and then up to toy with the hair at the back of his neck. She could feel the humidity had already turned his carefully arranged waves into springy curls. Unable to resist, she ruffled her fingers through his hair, enjoying the way each tendril seemed to vibrant with life.

She rubbed her aching breasts across his broad chest. Heavens, this felt wonderful. Her nipples tightened, increasing the sensation. As if recognizing her desire, Martin moved a hand to the front and palmed her left breast, finger and thumb plucking at the peak. A low groan rose in her throat. This changed into a gasp when Martin suddenly swung her up into her arms.

"Lord, Alice, you're making a wreck of my careful plans. I had a bench moved in here, and we were supposed to get there before we started kissing." He sounded out of breath. Well, of course, he did. She was hardly a dainty lady. She was about to tell him to put her down when she realized how easily he held her, how well she fit in his encircling arms. She snuggled against him and kissed the side of his neck that lay tantalizingly close to her mouth.

"If you don't stop that, I'll never get us to the bloody furniture," he said, sounding so delightfully like a grumpy little boy that she laughed.

He avoided some sort of potted tree and there, in an opening in the foliage, was a wrought iron bench like those situated around the outdoor gardens. Material had been draped over the frame, however, so when Martin gently set her down, it was surprisingly comfortable.

He smiled down at her. "Now you are where you're supposed to be. Well, almost."

He sat next to her and pulled her onto his lap. She found this even more comfortable, especially when he began kissing her again. This position also allowed more access. He rubbed her back, and she didn't realize he'd been undoing the hooks there until the front of her dress loosened. He then slipped a hand into the gaping neck of her dress, pushing the material down and freeing first one breast and then the other.

She, plain Alice Caruthers, was half-naked and being fondled by a man—and it was wonderful. Martin broke the kiss and leaned back, looking where his hands played. "You are so incredibly beautiful," he said. His voice was as thick as treacle.

And Alice knew that to Martin she *was* beautiful. He lowered his head and took one of her tight nipples into his mouth. A fizzing sensation ran through her body and she arched her back, offering him everything, wanting more. "Yes," she murmured, clasping his head tightly against her. She never wanted this to stop.

He rucked up her dress and caressed the length of her right leg starting at the calf and ending at the junction of her thighs, a place that throbbed with every beat of her heart. As if he understood her need, Martin pressed a hand against this private place. This action elicited a panting groan from her.

She could feel the hard ridge of his erection under her rear. She wanted to cup it in her hand as he was cupping her. She wiggled in her frustration. There were just too many clothes.

"I have no idea what all these lamps are doing here." Harriet, Lady Chesterton's voice reverberated between the glass walls.

"They shouldn't be left unattended," one of Harriet's sisters said.

With amazing speed, Martin lifted Alice off his lap to sit in the seat next to him. "Bloody hell" he muttered, as they both tried to pull her neckline into a semblance of order.

"Lady Chesterton," he called out to the unseen ladies, "I have just asked Alice Caruthers to marry me and she's said yes. I'm afraid you find us in a somewhat compromising position and it would probably be best if you immediately departed."

"Oh, my heavens!" The tone indicated shock, but the words were followed by the sound of giggling and footsteps rapidly retreating.

Alice and Martin looked at each other in consternation. And then they too were both laughing.

"I said yes?" Alice got out between chuckles.

"At this point, I would hope so, although I completely messed up my plan. I was supposed to bring you here, go down on one knee, and ask for the honor of your hand in marriage. But you got me so distracted..."

"It was a wonderful distraction." Alice hoped that it would continue, but Martin seemed to be intent on righting her clothes.

He stopped his fussing with the hooks on the back of her dress and looked deep into her eyes. "Do you say yes? I want to be the man you choose and not a substitute for Drew. I love you, Alice, and I have for years. But I don't want to be anyone's second choice."

Alice framed his beloved face with her hands and gently kissed him. How could he doubt that he was the man she wanted? She was irritated with her own stupidity in not seeing it earlier. "Of course the answer is yes. It dawned on me a few days ago that you're the person who makes me happy. I've loved you for years, also. I was just slow to realize it. I can think of nothing better than being married to you."

She pulled his lips back down to hers, but Martin resisted the pressure. "I've admitted to our being caught in a compromising position," he said, "but if we fail to appear shortly, we will be a scandal. And if I kissed you any more, I would not stop. So we will marry in unseemly haste in London as soon as I can get a special license. And then we will never have to stop again. Does that sound agreeable?"

At the moment, Alice thought being a scandal would be a wonderful idea, but she could see Martin's point. The idea of a small, quiet ceremony and then the rest of their lives did have appeal. A big, showy spring wedding would have been more for her mother than herself— and from now on she was going to satisfy herself. Well, herself and Martin.

"Yes, we can be married as soon as possible."

"Good. I should have everything arranged by the tenth. Does that sound agreeable?"

So soon. It seemed impossible. No, not impossible. That was a word her mother would use. From now on, everything was possible. She grinned up at the beautiful man who had asked her to be his wife. Between her hands and the humidity, his dark hair was a riot of curls. He would look like a sensual satyr if it weren't for the impish grin that danced on his face. "I'd like to marry you now, so there would be no more stopping," she said

Martin took her hand and placed a warm kiss on her palm. "We don't leave until the sixth, so there is still tomorrow night." He folded her hand over her palm to make a soft fist. She felt as if she were holding his kiss— a kiss that seemed to be a promise of nights to come.

CHAPTER SEVEN

January 5, 1829

WHEN MARTIN LOOKED OUT his bedroom window, the light from scattered torches, as well as the regular door lamps, reflected off the snow and made the forecourt at Pencroft as bright as day. Passengers hurried from their carriages and coaches to the front door. Their muted calls and laughter filtered through the glass like the sounds of remembered gaiety.

From the size of the crowd, Martin suspected that everyone with even the pretense of gentility in the village and surrounding countryside had been invited. This made for a festive and boisterous group, especially when each person was attempting to take on the persona of an assigned character. There was something very freeing about not being oneself.

He turned from the window to where Fitch dozed in an uncharacteristically relaxed sprawl in a chair by the fire. The man had earned his leisure. He may not have been willing to leave the carriage to move a downed limb, but Fitch could move mountains when it came to assembling a bizarre costume.

Martin took a few more steps into the room, then turned to survey his finery again in the pier glass. Only his flat-soled dancing shoes were his own. Everything else was remade from disparate pieces of other costumes. Fitch had somehow pressed a hoard of maids into service to do the sewing.

Martin wore bright red, knit stockings with a flower pattern crawling up the outside of each leg. They had evidently been abandoned by a very fat lady years before. Fitch had declared that since they were knit, what was wide could be made long. A day of soaking and stretching had proved him correct, but Martin found the contraption his valet had constructed to keep them in place deuced uncomfortable.

This mare's nest of straps and clips was concealed by puffy green breeches that tied at his knees. Again remade from remnants of a portly gentleman's breeches, they were stuffed with pieces of an old quilt to retain their rounded shape. This was topped by a large full shirt, which had been lengthened in the arms by the addition of a lace ruffle. Their attempt to create a doublet had been unsuccessful. Martin had become irritated with trying on potential tops and had announced that the Lord of Misrule was expected to flaunt all the rules and therefore, he'd appear in his shirtsleeves.

The *piece de resistance*, however, fit on his head. A paper-mâché crown was overtopped by a purple jester's hat, complete with bells. It added at least six inches to his already substantial height.

All in all, Martin thought he presented an impressive characterization of the Lord of Misrule that all should enjoy. It was what he planned to do at the Twelfth Night Revel, however, that would probably be the most memorable.

"Fitch. It's time."

His valet sat up, instantly alert. "Yes. Certainly. I'll warn the staff and then tell the orchestra to watch for your entrance."

Fitch straightened his jacket and left the room. As they'd previously planned, Fitch would tell one of the footmen that Martin would soon be arriving in the ballroom and that footman would then pass the word below stairs. Since so many of the staff had been involved in coming up with his costume, it only seemed fair that they should observe his grand entrance. The orchestra would give him a fanfare. Well, orchestra was a rather grand name for the local trio of pianoforte, violin, and flute who were playing, but they would nonetheless announce his arrival.

Martin grinned at his reflection. He would certainly change the rules for the evening. Did Lady Pennington imagine she could give him this role and he would not take advantage of it? He put his capped crown on his head and made his way downstairs.

He slipped into the servants' hallway that skirted the ballroom. It was already filling with maids and footmen. Cook was not there, but she'd released much of her staff, all of whom were distinguishable by their flushed, shiny faces. Martin even recognized some of the stablemen. Word that something was about to happen had certainly circulated.

The crowd parted for him with many grins and giggles until he was face-to-face with Pencroft's normally starchy butler. Tonight, however, the man was grinning and holding a tall staff that was topped with a huge cluster of ribbons and bells. "Your scepter," he said, holding the staff out to Martin.

Returning the butler's smile, Martin accepted what he now recognized as a ridiculously decorated shepherd's crook. Even with limited movement, the bells rang gaily. "I thank you for the symbol of my reign." Martin bowed to those around him.

Then he walked into the ballroom.

At his appearance, the music abruptly stopped, leaving those on the floor for a country-dance in a jumbled confusion. The trio immediately began to play a fairly decent impression of a trumpet volley. Marching to stand in front of the musicians, Martin banged his newly acquired staff on the floor, its jingling bells keeping time with his steps. By the time he'd reached his position and the musicians had completed the fanfare, the room was hushed and all eyes were on him.

Pitching his voice as if he were shouting instructions over gunfire, Martin began. "I am the Lord of Misrule. These revels are mine to command. Anyone breaking tonight's special laws will be summarily expelled into the cold, dark night."

There was some rustling about, but his pronouncement was mostly greeted with smiles. No one took his threat seriously, and the truth was that he probably wouldn't try to make anyone leave, but he was not above embarrassing those who flouted his rules.

"My first command is that the staff of Pencroft and those servants who arrived with guests are ordered to join these revels whenever their duties allow." A muted cheer came from the servant's hallway.

"My second command is that the card room will be closed. A revel is dancing and talking and eating and drinking. It is not playing cards." Martin heard some masculine groans, but the ladies present were all smiles.

"My third command is the most important, since it will change the accepted pattern of a ball. Instead of restricting the number of dances between couples, tonight every married couple and those who are courting *must* dance every third dance together."

Young people flashed each other quick grins. Parents and older couples frowned.

"What about those of us who are not up to a lot of dancing?" asked a gray-haired gentleman Martin didn't know.

"Then you may sit out the dance with the person who should have been your partner or you may stroll together, but then there should be conversation."

The unknown gentleman nodded. Martin was gratified that those in attendance seemed to be willing to change their normal patterns for this one night.

"For the two dances between those reserved for spouses and potential spouses, one will follow the normal pattern of the gentlemen asking the ladies to dance. But the other will be by ladies' invitation." Oddly, of all his pronouncements, this one seemed to cause the greatest shock.

Martin hoped the ladies would not be too embarrassed to ask the gentleman of their choice to dance. The Dabney sisters had often lamented that there were gentlemen in attendance at every ball whom they would have liked to partner, but who never signed their dance cards. He'd given the ladies a chance to rectify this situation, and he hoped they took advantage of it.

Martin had to raise his voice above a general murmur. "And lastly, I decree that certain guests will be considered couples for the duration of the evening. As the highest ranking lady now here, the Snow Queen will be paired with the character of lowest rank, Hubert Humble." Martin smiled at the obvious disapproval aimed at him by Lady Pennington. She'd undoubtedly assigned the vicar the character of Hubert Humble to remind him of his place. Martin was delighted he could reverse her intention. "And as Lord of Misrule, I will be paired with Beatrice Bouquet, since this beautiful, flowered lady and I will shortly be wed."

This announcement caused an even louder buzz of conversation. Martin turned to the violinist and said, "Start with a waltz." He then pounded his belled staff on the floor and called out, "Let the spousal dance begin."

He leaned the staff against the pianoforte and made his way to his flower lady. He felt quite pleased with himself, although he couldn't decide if he was pretending to be the Lord of Misrule or if that character had always been hidden inside him. When he gathered a smiling Alice into his arms and began to waltz, he decided it really made no difference.

Alice smiled as she watched Martin weave his way toward the refreshment room. He managed to impart nobility and confidence to his ridiculous costume. She was happy he'd suggested they sit out this dance and have some punch. She couldn't remember ever dancing this much, and sitting down was a treat. She suspected that the same could be said for most of the people here.

Surprisingly, everyone had complied with the new rules with good grace, and for the younger people, with enthusiasm. The first ladies' choice dance had begun with awkwardness, but when she and Beth and a couple of the more forward local misses had led the charge to choose their partners, others quickly followed suit. Even

Lady Pennington had chosen a partner, although in her case, the choice was one of her sons-in-law.

One of the footmen had gotten up the nerve to ask Alice to join him during the gentlemen's choice. Blessedly, that dance had been a reel, since the man's stomping feet might have been lethal during a more intimate figure. But the night seemed to be filled with a great deal of laughter and good humor. Lady Pennington's Twelfth Night Ball would be longed remembered.

She turned toward the sound of her mother's laughter as her parents waltzed by. Their behavior had certainly been a surprise. Alice didn't remember ever seeing them dance together. Usually when they attended a ball, her father immediately headed for the card room and her mother stayed to chaperone Alice and to gossip. They danced quite gracefully together.

She became aware of Martin standing next to her chair, punch cups in hand. He was watching her watch her parents. "Not what you expected is it?" he asked, sitting down next to her and handing her a drink.

"I must admit, my parents' behavior is not what I'd anticipated. I'd become convinced that my mother regretted her marriage to my father, but that certainly isn't how they're acting." Alice took a sip of punch and immediately coughed. "I think something strong has been added since I last had a cup."

Martin laughed, but he managed a large drink without reacting. "Yes. I think someone other than the

Lord of Misrule has been rearranging pieces of the evening. The punch now has a distinct flavor of Scotch whiskey. And since the private stock is from Lady Pennington's family's distillery, access would not be open to all. I, therefore, suspect the liquor has been added by either Paul or Lord Pennington himself."

"Lord Pennington?" the question came out louder than she'd intended, and Alice glanced around to see if anyone nearby had noticed. But the idea was absurd. Then her eyes drifted to where Lord and Lady Pennington were also resting during their dance. Lord Pennington leaned over the chair where his marchioness sat, toying with a lock of her hair. Good heavens! He was playing with her hair like a besotted swain. "Drunkenness would be a good explanation for some of the behavior I'm seeing," she muttered.

Martin also looked in toward where the Penningtons sat. "No, I don't think it's drunkenness. I think that many of the married couples have simply been reminded of why they married in the first place. It's easy to forget when the years and the responsibilities start adding up. The affection that seems evident between many of the couples was an unintended consequence of trying to come up with a way that Beth could spend a good deal of time with her vicar and that I could spend the same amount of time with you." He leaned over and ran a finger down the side of her face, sending a shiver throughout her entire body.

"Are you promoting a match between Beth and David Taylor?"

Martin shook his head. "Not necessarily, although it wouldn't be a bad match. Taylor is the third son of the Earl of Byerly, so he is not without connections. Of course, Beth would have to be willing to shoulder the unpaid duties that are expected of a vicar's wife, but if she goes in with her eyes open, there is no reason a marriage between the two of them could not be a good one. My intent was to give them some time together without their having to sneak around. I wanted them to have the opportunity to get to know each other without the added titillation of the forbidden. People often think what they've been denied is what they want, when in reality, the attraction is to the danger rather than the person."

Alice didn't care if they were in plain sight; she leaned forward and placed a soft kiss on Martin's cheek. "You're a good man, Martin Tate."

"And glad I am that you've discovered this." He gave her a playful tweak on the nose as the music for the waltz came to an end. "And now it's lady's choice, so you had better find a partner."

"What if I want that partner to be you?" Alice pretended to look sulky.

"Ah, love, you are the partner of my life, and I hope I will always be your choice. But we will dance again in two more dances. Even the Lord of the Evening must follow his own rules."

"At least we will have a waltz."

Martin laughed. "I guess the pattern I arranged was a bit obvious. But go now, before you're trampled by the hoard of females who all want to say they danced with the Lord of Misrule."

Alice made a wry face. "Before you get too conceited, remember that tomorrow you'll just be plain Martin." And then she flounced off, heading in the direction where she'd last seen Paul. The poor man had been beset by dance invitations and was beginning to look like a startled hare. He would probably appreciate the arrival of a friend.

She glanced back to where Martin had been claimed by the daughter of one the local squires. The girl was petite and blond, but Alice didn't feel in the least threatened. She knew in her heart that Martin was hers forever.

The longcase clock in the foyer struck three before the house settled into the quiet of exhausted sleep. The Twelfth Night Ball had been a resounding success, but Martin wished the revelers had been motivated to either leave or retire earlier. The busy day was catching up with him, but he wanted to see Alice alone one more time before he lost the persona of the Lord of Misrule. It was odd how the costume had made him feel more decisive, more powerful.

Dancing so many waltzes with Alice had been exquisite torture. Holding her in his arms, feeling the subtle shift of muscle and sinew, seeing her quick smiles, hearing her unaffected laugh—all of this had made him want to find the first available horizontal surface and make love to her for hours. The stricture of only two dances for courting couples now made sense. If not for society's rules, Martin doubted there would be a single couple who didn't anticipate their wedding night.

He crept down the silent halls, glad his dark blue banyan blended into the shadows. If he were discovered, however, his objective would be obvious. And so he had to make damned sure he was not discovered.

His desire to hold and kiss Alice burned through him like a flame in a strong wind. He promised himself that he would not be one of those who left nothing special for the wedding night, but there were a number of things he and Alice could share that didn't infringe on their later consummation. Their wedding date was now just four days hence, and he could wait to completely make her his. Tomorrow they would return to their respective London homes, so tonight was the last time any sort of intimacy would be possible, and he wasn't going to miss the opportunity.

A floorboard squeaked and he froze, but no one stirred to investigate the cause of the noise. He was just a few doors from his goal, so he padded on. When he reached Alice's door, he thankfully found it unlocked. It easily swung wide on well-oiled hinges. He quietly entered, softly closing the door again and setting the lock.

This room also faced the forecourt, only from the opposite side. Light from the torches that hadn't yet extinguished filtered through the cracks in the drapes and made the room look oddly striped. Alice lay on her back with one hand thrown above her head. She made endearing puffing sounds with every breath. Tenderness welled up in him and settled in his soul. He wanted to just stand there and watch her sleep and drink in the peace of the scene.

She must have sensed his presence, however, as she roused and pushed herself up on one elbow. "Is someone there?" she asked, her voice still more sleepy than frightened.

Martin certainly had no intention of scaring her, so he stepped into a strip of light and said, "It's me, Martin, the Lord of Misrule."

Her lips turned up in a ghost of a smile. "Oh, good. I was dreaming you were here." She held out her hand in his direction.

Martin certainly needed no other invitation. He crossed to the bed and gently sat down next to her prone form. Still groggy from sleep, she looked like an innocent little girl with her hair in a long night braid and the covers bunched around her. Without thinking, Martin leaned forward and placed a kiss on the tip of her nose.

"You can do better than that," Alice said in a smoky voice. Her hands snaked around the back of his neck, and she pulled his head down to hers. In the blink of an eye, she changed from a sweet child into a seductive temptress.

Martin immediately responded to Alice's allure. He molded his mouth to hers. When his tongue toyed with her bottom lip, she relaxed and let him in. Their tongues dueled as their hands roamed. Alice dropped one hand from his neck and slid it through the opening of his banyan. Her hand was cool against his naked back.

She pushed back from him slightly. "My lord, you seem to have forgotten your clothing." Laughter colored her voice.

"Not forgotten," he admitted. "Their lack was intentional. I've dreamed of your touching me with nothing between us but moonlight. It's selfish on my part, I know, but it seemed right tonight, while I'm still someone other than Martin Tate."

He leaned down to kiss her again, wanting her hands touching him everywhere, but afraid to ask for fear of frightening her away. His motion stopped when her laughter bubbled out. "You goose. I don't want someone other than Martin. I love you as you are. Lie next to me and let me explore the landscape that can only be Martin."

He stood up, uncertain if he should completely discard his robe. She swept back the covers, saying, "Come." Heaven help him, he nearly did with just the sound of her voice. He shrugged the banyan free and stretched out next to her, pulling the covers over them both, cocooning them in warmth.

Her long-fingered hands and soft mouth were on him without any direction on his part. She unashamedly explored the contours of his chest and licked his flat nipples until he moaned. As her hands slid further down to brush his throbbing arousal, he could not lie quiescent. He returned her caresses, shaping her breasts in his hands, suckling their tight tips through the lawn of her gown.

He kissed his way down her torso as he worked the hem of her gown upward until her flat stomach and dark thatch of hair were exposed. The scent of her arousal surrounded him. When he placed his mouth on her curls, she tightened her grip on his shoulders, and he feared she would stop him. Instead, she arched into him, her body seeking what she hadn't the words to ask for.

With hands and mouth he brought her to the peak and then pushed her over, delighting in her mewing sounds that ended in panting moans. Never had he felt more powerful and sure. And he knew he was no longer the Lord of Misrule—he was just Martin, and Martin was who she wanted.

He held her as she calmed and then slipped into sleep. His own arousal was almost painful, but his turn would come on their wedding night. Until then, he would revel in her uninhibited reactions. His heart overflowed with love for the sleeping woman. His woman. His Alice. The gift he had long wanted and thought never to receive.

He gently slid from the bed. The air in the room chilled his overheated body as he found his discarded robe and put it on. He silently left the room and made his way down the hall, secure in the knowledge that he would never have to leave her bed again.

His own room now seemed empty and cold. The red hose lay draped over a chair. The silly green beeches, still fat with cotton batting, squatted on the floor like a misshaped mushroom. Only the crown topped with a jester's cap, perched on the dresser, still retained some of the Lord of Misrule's glamor.

Martin wondered if he should take at least the capped crown with him when he left, but he decided the entire costume should join the others to be used by someone else in years to come. He'd arrived as the First Foot, but he would be leaving simply as Martin Tate rather than the Lord of Misrule. Martin was the man beloved by Alice Caruthers, and that was all the title he would ever need.

ABOUT HANNAH

Since the day she first realized that letters made words, and words expressed ideas, and these ideas could tell stories, Hannah Meredith has been a storyteller. When she was a child, these stories were called fibs and frowned upon. As an adult, she's learned to lie on a larger scale and to share these tales with others. Now her fibs are called short stories, novellas, and novels.

Under another name, Hannah has sold over a dozen short stories—primarily science fiction and fantasy—to many of the major genre magazines. More recently, she's switched to writing historical romance. Her love of English history and the romance genre made this a natural choice.

Two novels and two novellas are currently available as both e-books and paperbacks at most of the online booksellers. They are *Kestrel – A Regency Novella*, *A Dangerous Indiscretion*, *Indentured Hearts*, and *Kaleidoscope – A Regency Novella*. Probably more information than you want about these books can be found on Hannah Meredith's **website** http://www.hannahmeredith.com Also please visit http://www.facebook.com/HannahMeredithAuthor She enjoys hearing from—and interacting with—readers.

Hannah is a member SFWA, RWA, and Heart of Carolina Romance Writers. She lives with her husband in a small town with a big library in North Carolina.

God Rest Ye
Murdered Gentlemen

by

Kate Parker

Chapter One

24 December

"I WISH YOU WERE DEAD."

As those angry words echoed down the hall to her, Eugenia, Countess Hunter, stopped near the top of the staircase, out of sight of the young lady who spoke them. No doubt one of the husband-hunting debutantes who'd arrived for the Christmas festivities was having a tiff with another over a young gentleman.

"Ah, you've wounded me. But not as much as I can wound you."

Eugenia stayed where she was, poised on the second to the top step and gripping the banister as if her life depended on it. The oily sound of menace in the easily recognizable voice of Major Sebastian Ward had shaken her, leaving icicles to sled down her spine. She couldn't imagine why the duke had invited such an odious man to Ivey Manor. Whoever the young lady was, she and her reputation were no match for Major Ward.

No one was.

Making as much noise as possible, Eugenia hurried up the last steps and turned in the direction of the voices. Major Ward leaned over Miss Abigail Wilton, a sly smile across his handsome face as he stared down at the girl. His hands gripped her upper arms; her hands were balled up in fists against his chest. Miss Wilton looked toward Eugenia, horror at being caught alone with a rake written in large letters on her reddened expression and in her deep blue eyes.

"Miss Wilton, are you going to join us in decorating the ballroom?" *Drat.* Eugenia hadn't meant to get involved in hauling holly around the house. She had far too much to do with the house party in full cry, but if ever a young lady needed saving, it was Miss Wilton.

"Yes," the girl squeaked as she shoved against the major. She clipped him with her shoulder in her haste to escape as she raced toward Eugenia.

A sardonic smile made Major Ward's devilishly good-looking face even more attractive. "Ah, Lady Hunter. I'm finding your father-in-law's party full of delights. And your husband is most amusing."

There was nothing wrong with his words, but his tone made him sound like a cat playing with a mouse.

"I'm so glad you're enjoying yourself." Eugenia spoke in a tone that made it clear she was anything but glad. "Come along, Miss Wilton."

"I'll see you later, ladies," the major drawled and sauntered off in the opposite direction toward his room.

Once he disappeared around the corner, Eugenia looked the girl over and noted her ringlets remained intact despite the major's assault, but her neckline...

Miss Wilton looked down and quickly adjusted the material covering her bosom. "It wasn't what it looked like," she said, patting her dark hair as they descended the staircase. Her face started to crumple, but she bit her lip and then put on a refined air.

"It seldom is," Eugenia said drily as they descended the staircase. That awful Major Ward always brought trouble with him. She knew. What she didn't know was the source of the power he held over her beloved Adam, and that left her twisting her rings.

As they reached the front hall, Eugenia saw the butler was holding the door against the wind-blown snow as a bundled-up foursome surged into the house. Laughing, they shed their outerwear in the vestibule and the Dawsons emerged into the foyer.

Eugenia pasted on a smile and stepped forward to greet them. "Aunt Anna. Uncle Charles. You seem to have arrived in a blizzard," she said as she deposited pecks on their cold, fleshy cheeks. In the distance, she could hear the group decorating the ballroom begin another carol.

When she glanced back at Miss Wilton, it was to see the girl shyly greeting Eugenia's cousins, Robert and Henrietta. In particular, Robert. So, that was the way things were developing.

They deserved each other in Eugenia's estimation.

Abigail Wilton had foolishly put herself at the mercy of Major Ward, and Robert had neither brains nor common sense. Eugenia had landed in the Dawson household after the deaths of her parents and quickly discovered learning and sound judgment were neither prized nor existed in her uncle's home.

"I doubt too many more will make it through the snow drifts. With the thick clouds, it will soon be full dark outside," Uncle Charles said. "I've had our coachman pull around back to unload some luggage in case we're snowed in for weeks. I've also brought some holly for decorating. Can't descend on our favorite niece without bringing something for the Christmas festivities."

"How sweet of you, uncle. I'm glad you made it safely. Everyone else has already arrived, including the musicians." Resisting the urge to sigh, Eugenia gave the man a faint smile. The last time they visited, the Dawsons refused to leave for fear of flooding from the fall rains. Ivey Manor was much nicer than the Dawson's dreary homestead, and it cost her uncle much less to stay here.

"Well, if the musicians are here, we will have a marvelous Christmas celebration. Now, where is that husband of yours? I hope standing near a blazing fire." Uncle Charles wandered off in the direction of the singing.

Eugenia wondered how the duke would uproot the Dawson family from the house this time. She suspected it might take an early spring or a smallpox scare.

Aunt Anna gave her a hug and said, "When will we be in anticipation of some good news?"

"What sort of good news?" Eugenia's back stiffened. She knew full well her aunt wanted to know if she were *enceinte*. With the current style of high waistlines, it would be easy to hide all but the latter stages of breeding.

"The future Duke of Edenfalls, of course. Is he on the way?" Her aunt patted Eugenia's stomach.

Eugenia flinched at the touch. She had no intention of telling her aunt before everyone else, even if she were in a delicate condition. But regrettably, so far, she had yet to do her duty by Adam and his lineage. "No." She attempted to hide the disappointment and shame from her voice but feared she failed.

"Oh, well. I imagine you'll manage it someday. Most people do," her aunt said in the dismissive tone she often used on Eugenia and followed her husband toward the caroling.

Miss Wilton, appearing fully recovered from her encounter with Major Ward, led Robert and Henrietta toward the ballroom. The threesome chattered happily of nothing, and Eugenia slowly brought up the rear.

Where was Adam, Eugenia wondered. She'd not seen him since they came in from sledding at noon. He'd been called into his father's study, and she'd busied herself taking care of the last minute household details for the duchess.

The sledding party broke up when it began snowing heavily. She hoped Adam hadn't gone back outside on some mission for his father.

As they reached the doors to the ballroom, Eugenia heard Adam's baritone from behind her, causing her heart to flutter even after half a year of marriage. She was about to follow the other three into the ballroom when she heard Major Ward snap an angry reply from the direction where she'd heard Adam's voice come.

Instead of joining the guests, she turned away. The footman shut the ballroom doors after the others, cutting off the carol in mid-chorus. Eugenia headed toward her husband's voice. She followed the argument the length of the gallery, past marble busts and draped-off windows, into the main part of the house.

She turned down a hall to follow the voices of Adam and the odious major but had only gone a few steps when the duchess flew out of the study. She barreled right into Eugenia, nearly knocking them both over.

"Oh, I'm so sorry, my dear," Adam's mother sobbed, dabbing at her eyes with a wrinkled handkerchief mangled in one hand.

Eugenia had problems making a proper curtsy while holding up the older woman who was fanning herself. If the duchess decided to swoon, Eugenia knew she'd never be able to keep her from falling. "Duchess, what's wrong?"

"You know how badly my nerves are affected when people quarrel, particularly at Christmastime." She sniffed loudly before giving a moan. Her blonde curls bounced. Her full lips pouted. But even close up, her beautiful face had few lines.

Eugenia had the unsympathetic thought that the duchess would need to worry, or at least think, to develop wrinkles. Eugenia had suffered through any number of the duchess's emotional upsets since marrying Adam and moving to Ivey Manor. The duchess's nerves weren't affected so much by quarrels or holidays as they were at the prospect of having to make a decision or resolve a problem.

After their marriage, Eugenia had quickly decided to copy Adam's technique of sending the duchess to her room with her maid while dealing with the problem himself. Over the past six months, the staff had decided, without a word being spoken by anyone, to approach Eugenia rather than the duchess if a decision needed to be made.

But that had been Adam's voice she'd heard through the study door and the duchess had been inside. Something was very wrong. Adam never raised his voice in the presence of his mother. People quickly learned the cost of even a mild disagreement around the duchess. Her hysteria had a way of forcing everyone to drop their plans and care for her.

This time, Eugenia would have to pay the price for her husband's raised voice and deal with the overwrought duchess herself. "Come. Let's go into the green parlor. It's so beautiful and restful there. We'll ring for your maid to join us. Then I'll go and speak to Adam, shall I?"

Normally, the duchess would agree with anyone willing to handle the difficulty. This time, much to Eugenia's amazement, the duchess grabbed her hands and loudly insisted, "No! You mustn't. No one must know."

They had a houseful of guests and the duchess was on the brink of a loud, extended bout of hysteria. Anyone could come along the hallway and hear them at any moment. Still, trying to explain this to the duchess seemed pointless. Eugenia sighed and said, "Let's go into the green parlor."

Helping Adam's mother into the garland-clad parlor, she sat the duchess in a chair and yanked on the bell pull. The butler entered moments later.

"Please call for Her Grace's lady's maid and bring some smelling salts."

He nodded and departed, never showing the slightest trace of emotion. The duchess's lady's maid would be equally stoic, which was why she was now the highest paid servant at Ivey Manor. She also held the distinction of being the longest-lasting of the duchess' personal maids. The lady's maid had threatened to resign when the duchess became too much for even that placid woman to handle. The duke had intervened, culminating in a more amicable financial agreement. Eugenia understood the other servants thought it a fair arrangement as long as they didn't have to deal with the duchess's agitations.

This arrangement, sadly, did not apply to Eugenia as well, and at the moment she felt like an unpaid servant. But then, the Dawsons had used her as a maid and governess when she lived with them. She had endured much worse in their household, and it had only ended when they'd allowed her to attend a neighbor's ball. There, she'd met Adam. Dear, wonderful Adam.

It had been love at first sight for both of them. Her Uncle Charles had seen the social advantages of having a niece married to a duke's heir and had presented no challenge. The duchess had championed her, although Eugenia had never discovered a reason for her kindness. With everyone's blessing, Eugenia and Adam had a summer wedding.

"Oh, Eugenia, it's too dreadful," the duchess wailed.

Pulled away from her pleasant daydream, Eugenia heard the duchess's favorite saying. "I'll take care of smoothing any rough edges, shall I? Doesn't the greenery smell lovely? Take a deep breath and enjoy the fragrance of the boughs." All the woman needed was distraction and a deep breath.

As the duchess's maid hurried into the room, Eugenia turned and left, for once not waiting until Adam's mother gave her permission.

Eugenia paused outside the closed study door. She was worried about Adam's argument in front of his mother. His thoughtlessness was unprecedented. Clearly, things were amiss in the house.

The male voices were now too muted for her to make out who was speaking behind the study door. She scratched once and waited a moment before she walked in.

Adam, Earl Hunter, the heir to the Duke of Edenfalls, paced across the study's dull-colored carpets, his polished boots marking out his precise steps. His form-fitting trousers shifted with each movement of toned muscles. His curly dark hair caught the lamplight and showed glints of gold.

After half a year of marriage, Eugenia still didn't believe her good luck. She and Adam were perfectly matched in patience, gentle good humor, and in the marriage bed. But she'd been married long enough to notice the signs that said Adam was worried. He paced with his hands clasped behind his back. Frown lines etched his brow. And when he looked at her, his blue eyes didn't sparkle.

Major Ward, on the other hand, was negligently lounging, his long legs crossed at the knee and one arm along the back of the sofa, with a smirk on his face. He managed to look handsome and elegant while lounging. Somehow, his casual posture made him seem more trustworthy to many, but he'd never fooled Eugenia.

Adam stopped pacing as she entered. "Is Mother all right?" he asked her.

"Yes. Her maid will see to her. What's wrong?" Eugenia looked from her husband to Major Ward, wondering who would tell her about the newest household upset. No doubt Ward was behind the trouble.

"If you'll excuse us, Major," Adam said, coming to a stop and glaring at Ward.

"Of course. My lady." Ward rose, sauntered over to Eugenia, and took her hand. His boots were as shined as Adam's. His trousers fit as handsomely. His cravat was as expertly tied. His vest and jacket were as elegant and probably came from the same tailor. But he lacked something Adam had, besides a title. He lacked warmth.

Then he looked Eugenia in the eye and said, "No heir yet on the horizon, I see. I suppose I could speculate on the reason."

"How dare you, Ward. Get out!" Adam thundered.

Ward's lips curled up in a smile. "I wish you good luck, milady."

Eugenia had to school her face to hide her dismay and resist pulling her hand away. Did everyone in London know that she and Adam had lived so much of their married life apart that begetting an heir was difficult?

She hadn't meant for things to go on this way. Adam had his duties to the estate and to the country that frequently took him to London. She bore the responsibilities of a duchess along with the duty to care for her mother-in-law, the current duchess. When Adam was home and ready, something always demanded her immediate attention—usually the duchess at the top of her voice. How the woman enjoyed bedtime histrionics.

Someday they'd have time for each other and the peace and quiet to raise a family.

Adam had only returned from his latest trip to London yesterday, and last night his mother was particularly difficult. Nothing would do but that Eugenia would read to her until she fell asleep. Thank goodness Adam had come into her room early this morning before his mother and the early arriving guests awakened. A smile reached her lips at the memory. Or would have if Ward not held her hand.

He bowed and then left the room with fox-like grace. His smirk was unmistakable.

Eugenia swallowed the sour taste in her mouth and asked, "What is going on?"

"Oh, Genie, he has letters of Mother's. He wants a small fortune for them. Father has entrusted me to deal with it." Adam picked up the duke's ornate letter opener and looked as if he'd stab the desk before he set it down.

It was so typical of his father to saddle Adam with problems the duke himself should handle. She walked over and put a hand on his shoulder. "Did Ward bring the letters with him?"

"Yes."

Eugenia raised her eyebrows at him.

"He also brought his man with him who never leaves his room." He slid his arms around her waist.

When she sighed, Adam smiled for the first time. "See, Genie, I know what you're thinking."

"I suppose we couldn't put a sleeping draught in the

valet's food?"

"Ward warned me against it, since he would know and the letters are too well hidden to be found. He said if we tried anything, he'd double the price."

I wish you were dead. Abigail Wilton's declaration came to Eugenia's mind. "I imagine your mother isn't the only one Ward is blackmailing."

"It's my understanding that our Christmas party is providing Major Ward with the opportunity to put pressure on several of his victims. He'll leave here after Christmas with more gifts than the rest of us combined."

"How awful." Eugenia shivered. They'd gathered family and friends together like a nest of mice for that snake Ward to devour. Christmas would be ruined for everyone.

"I've upset you. Come here, dearest." Adam pulled her tight against his chest. She snuggled tighter to him. "I must find some mistletoe to catch you under," he said, his lazy grin belying his quick moves as he placed butterfly kisses down her neck.

A giggle escaped Eugenia's mouth. "I wish I had time to linger," she said, laying her forehead against the smooth wool of his jacket, "but my uncle and his family have just arrived, your mother must be seen to, and I have to patrol the halls to keep young maidens from suffering the unwanted attentions of Major Ward."

Adam burst out laughing at her dry tone as she'd hoped he would. "Until tonight, then."

"I look forward to it." Eugenia gave him a heated

kiss. Then she slipped out of the study and walked down the hall and along the gallery to reach the ballroom, regret dogging her steps.

Chapter Two

WHEN THE FOOTMAN OPENED the door, Eugenia saw the guests were hanging a grand overabundance of greenery in one part of the room and ignoring the rest of the space. One of the husband-hunting young ladies was playing "Hark! The Herald Angels Sing" on the piano while most of the guests sang along and one young dandy waved a bough like a conductor.

Something else was off. One quick glance told Eugenia who was missing from the gathering.

"Aunt Anna, do you think you could organize everyone so we can have garlands all around the room? I need to look after something," Eugenia asked.

"Of course, dear."

Eugenia hurried out of the ballroom, the carol snatching at her heels. Where could Caroline, Adam's much younger sister, be? And where was that lecherous Major Ward?

As Eugenia reached the great entrance hall, a chord from the music room set her in that direction. She swung open the door without knocking to find Major Ward taking up more than half the piano bench and

Caroline sitting next to him. Adam's sister was giggling like a school girl. Nothing wrong with that. She still had one more year in the schoolroom.

"Are you rehearsing carols?" Eugenia asked in a mild voice.

"Yes," Caroline said. "Major Ward knows the naughtiest lyrics to the tune of 'Greensleeves.'"

"Perhaps not the most appropriate thing for a young lady to hear." Eugenia shot the major a look.

"I can't have any fun at all," Caroline whined. She'd developed a talent for whining when Eugenia and Adam married. The duchess, in a rare moment of logic, said it came as a result of no longer being the only young woman in the house to be fussed over.

Ward rose and gave Caroline a bow. Eugenia studied his handsome face and thought she detected a heated glance aimed at the girl.

Another problem. Eugenia was growing tired of needing to solve them. She wished someone would fuss over her and remedy all her troubles. Pasting on a smile she didn't feel, she said, "And here I was counting on you to take charge of decorating the ballroom. As it is, the guests are putting greenery up just anywhere without a plan."

"They've started without me?" Caroline leaped up. "Are you coming with me, Major?"

"I'll come along after I speak to Miss Janvier." He nodded toward the far corner.

Eugenia craned her head around the door to see the

mousy, gray-gowned governess sitting there. Then she saw the thunderclouds in Caroline's expression. Eugenia guessed being used as a contrivance to talk to one's governess must be a comedown for a duke's daughter.

Caroline raced out of the music room.

"No. I think I'll go with the young lady, Major." Miss Janvier rose, curtsied to both Eugenia and Major Ward, and followed her charge.

Eugenia slipped out, shutting the major in. She'd reached the grand foyer when she saw Lord John Hunter, Adam's younger brother, limping down the staircase toward her.

"Captain Hunter, I didn't know you'd be joining us today. I thought you preferred to be solitary in your room." Ward's voice, booming down the hallway behind her, was full of mockery.

Eugenia wished for an instant she were a man so she could punch Major Ward in the nose. John carried the scars of his service against Napoleon on his body and in his soul. It took coaxing most days to get him to leave his room when it was only the family in residence. That he'd come downstairs to see guests without too much nudging was a vast improvement.

"Oh, John, I'm so glad to see you. We're all in the ballroom, unless you're looking for your brother. He's in the study." Ignoring the major, Eugenia walked up to John and gave him her arm. She was beginning to enjoy foiling Ward's games.

"I can't go in there." John came to a halt in the gallery. "I might frighten the ladies."

John was a taller, lighter haired version of Adam, which made him incredibly handsome in Eugenia's eyes. If only they could persuade him to eat so he'd lose his gaunt appearance. "And you might have them all hovering around you, wanting to meet the hero of Waterloo." Eugenia tried to tug him forward, but he was much stronger—and stubborn—and didn't move.

"Yes, the poor, scarred, crippled hero of Waterloo. I daresay you'd bring out the charitable instincts in all the old ladies," Ward said in a taunting voice.

John's face crumpled as if he were in pain.

"That shows what little Major Ward knows about women. Come on. Just sit and watch the hanging of the garlands for a few minutes. If you don't like the attention you get from the young ladies, you can join Adam in the study." Eugenia urged him forward.

"You can always run," Ward said from behind them. "What you should have done before."

John's face took on a menacing aspect, made more frightening by the scar down one cheek. He turned and faced the major. "I wish I'd killed you that day, Ward. I may still."

Eugenia had never heard that Major Ward was with John at Waterloo. But then, the family had tried to protect her from all unpleasantness as they protected the duchess, not realizing she didn't need it.

Eugenia waited for the footman to open the door to

the ballroom and then dragged John limping inside with her. "The Holly and the Ivy" rang out as family, friends, and servants put up the greenery. Caroline must have taken them in hand. Boughs were coming down and being put up again in a semblance of order. Two of the hired musicians playing the piano and a violin kept all the voices within some proximity of the tune.

They were three steps into the room when Eugenia heard the door open behind her. Smiles slipped from people's faces, and the carol stuttered to a halt. She felt John stiffen next to her, his body rigidly at attention as he faced all those frightened expressions.

"Well, well, well," Major Ward said from the doorway. "When does the party start?"

Major Ward was helping a young lady hang greens with too much familiarity when one of the two matronly friends of the duchess came up to Eugenia and said, "The duchess asks you to find the duke and send him to her room."

Eugenia felt a momentary pang of sympathy for the duke, took a deep breath, and nodded. As if her mother-in-law couldn't send a servant to find the duke. Meanwhile, the young chit would be safe enough in the crowded ballroom. Perhaps one of the matrons would remove the major's hand from the small of the young lady's back and separate them so there was no more whispering. The image of Major Ward being thwarted by one of the old dragons brought a smile to Eugenia's lips.

She found the duke in the study, deep in discussion with her Uncle Charles. The duke neatly peeled a seal off a missive with his letter opener as he said, "I'm sure this record will show..."

"Excuse me, Duke. Could I have a word?"

"Of course, Eugenia. Excuse me a moment, Dawson." The duke set down the lethally sharp letter opener bearing the ducal crest and a ruby on its hilt before he rose from behind his desk.

Uncle Charles nodded, gave Eugenia a big smile, and closed his eyes with a sigh from the chair closest to the fire.

The duke stepped out of the room, and Eugenia gave him the message. He leaned into the study. "Our talk will have to wait, Dawson."

Leaving the duke and his guest, Eugenia made her way to the card room where she found Adam in a game of whist with some of the younger gentlemen. They were laughing and the whisky bottle was close at hand. He was finally getting a chance to relax with his male friends. He didn't need his wife intruding on the fun.

Next, she checked with the housekeeper to make sure both dinner and all the rooms would be ready for that evening. Coming back up to the main floor, she saw Miss Wilton coming out of the duke's study.

How very odd. "Miss Wilton, is the duke inside?"

The girl jumped. "He asked not to be disturbed."

"Then we should follow his directions."

Miss Wilton nodded and hurried away.

Eugenia watched the odd way Abigail Wilton clasped her hands together. She appeared not to carry anything, but Eugenia couldn't be certain.

As soon as the younger woman was out of sight, Eugenia scratched and then opened the door. The room was empty.

What did Abigail Wilton want in the duke's study? Nothing appeared disturbed. The shelf of books in front of the safe was untouched. The desktop looked a little cluttered, but the duke kept it that way even when he wasn't working. Satisfied that the debutante hadn't stolen anything, Eugenia left.

Eugenia, paired with the bishop, walked into the dining room and felt a flush of satisfaction. The long table, set for their party of twenty-eight, gleamed with silver and crystal. A large china epergne held pride of place in the center, the red of the holly berries contrasting nicely with the trailing ivy and adding to the festive mood. Candlelight glowed in the reflection from the mirrors, brightening the room. The servants had followed her directions to the letter.

While Eugenia was pleased that Major Ward had seated himself away from the duchess and from John and Adam, she was alarmed to realize he'd paired up with Caroline to walk into the room and now sat next to her. At least they'd chosen seats within hearing distance of the duke and herself. That would keep his comments polite and innocuous. Well, relatively polite and innocuous.

However, Ward flirted outrageously with Caroline. He also flirted with the married lady on his other side so that to the casual observer, he was merely being a convivial guest. Eugenia found him slimy and dangerous. The duke must have heard Ward's mildly outrageous comments, but at first he seemed to ignore Ward's lecherous gleam and Caroline's simpering.

At the end of the meal, the duchess suggested they all move to the ballroom because she wanted to dance and hoped they did, too. Eugenia saw the duke's angry gaze fall on Ward when he brushed his hand against Caroline's as she rose. Ward whispered something and Caroline blushed, her eyes bright as she nodded. Both parties ignored the duke's thunderous expression.

Eugenia heard the duke growl, "I'd like a private word, Ward."

She lingered by the door after the rest of the company strolled off toward the ballroom, until only the duke and Major Ward remained.

"Do you want to discuss business in your study, Your Grace?" Ward asked, his tone friendly and respectful.

"No. I want to warn you away from my daughter. She's still in the schoolroom, Ward."

"She takes after her mother, Edenfalls. Beautiful girl."

"Leave both my wife and my daughter alone." The

thunderous venom in the duke's voice frightened Eugenia.

The major laughed. "I'm afraid I can't. At least not until I finish my business with your wife. And your daughter is such a delightful young lady. I'm sure you plan an illustrious marriage for her. Must be a worry, keeping her unsullied."

"Now see here, Ward..."

Eugenia slipped away to her other duties, glad the duke was dealing with that flirtation so she didn't have to.

By the time she reached the ballroom, the musicians had begun tuning their instruments and guests wandered in and out, chatting and pointing out their efforts on the garlands and arrangements as they viewed the finished decor.

Then Major Ward strode in and cornered one of the musicians. Eugenia hesitated, wondering what horror the major had planned in order to wreck the festivities. As she watched, the young, dark-haired violinist pulled his arm out of the major's grasp and stalked out of the room, his instrument and his bow in one hand. The other musicians watched him leave with startled expressions. She imagined they, like her, hoped he would return.

With too many of the guests missing from the ballroom, Eugenia realized she'd have to round them up. She marched from room to room on the main floor, constantly on guard for some unpleasant surprise she couldn't predict. Young people wandered in and out of parlors. John had disappeared. At least he'd sat through dinner. Caroline had been sent up to her school room under the care of her governess.

Eugenia returned to the ballroom in time to see the duke lead the duchess out for the first dance. Looking over at the musicians, she was relieved to see the young violinist had already returned to his post and now played in harmony with his fellows.

Then it was Adam's turn to guide his beautiful mother around the dance floor. Eugenia looked for the duke to take her hand for this dance as he normally did when Adam partnered the duchess. But this night, when her father-in-law came toward her, instead of presenting himself for the dance, he hurried past her without a glance in her direction. When Eugenia looked around in surprise at his snub, she realized that both Major Ward and Miss Wilton were missing.

Blast. She'd have to go find where the silly girl had wandered off to. And she hoped the duke had given the major some rules of behavior in Ivey Manor.

Before she could go anywhere, her Uncle Charles came up and claimed the dance. Good manners said she had to dance with him and risk her slippers and toes. They waltzed twice around the room, Eugenia constantly wishing she were dancing with her husband.

Suddenly, her uncle dropped into a chair by the door. "Oh, Eugenia, I'm afraid I'm not as young as I once was. There's no more dancing left in these feet."

"Are you unwell, Uncle?"

"No. Just a little tired. You go on and find a handsome young gentleman to twirl you around the floor."

"Very well, Uncle Charles. You rest up and then perhaps we can have another dance."

Eugenia escaped the ballroom in search of Abigail Wilton. She'd only reached the grand entrance when the housekeeper came to her with a question about setting up the midnight supper that ended the ball as Christmas Day began. The woman dragged her off to the dining room where a battle of wills flared between the butler and the housekeeper.

While Eugenia solved that problem, she also eliminated the dining room as the site of an assignation between Major Ward and anyone. She hurried down the hall, opening doors and checking rooms, embarrassing young ladies and annoying young bucks. Unfortunately, she wasn't getting the opportunity to annoy Major Ward. Where was he?

She found Miss Wilton alone in the music room sobbing.

"What's wrong?" Eugenia asked, wincing inwardly at the trifle she expected to hear.

"It's R—Robert D—Dawson. He's ig—ignoring me!" she wailed.

Drying the girl's tears, Eugenia said, "Return to the ballroom. There are plenty of other young gentlemen in attendance to flirt with. Make my Cousin Robert jealous."

Abigail Wilton took Eugenia's hands in hers and smiled determinedly. "Yes. I will go in there and flirt outrageously. Let me go upstairs and get a fresh handkerchief and I'll be back to break men's hearts." She waltzed off, leaving Eugenia shaking her head at the girl's silliness.

Continuing on her tour of the main floor, Eugenia partially opened the door to the red parlor and saw Uncle Charles standing in front of the crackling fire. "Is everything all right, Uncle?" Eugenia asked.

"Balls are more a young man's domain. I thought I'd find a little peace and quiet here for a moment."

Eugenia nodded and shut the door. Her uncle was usually the life and soul of the party. She hoped he wasn't falling ill.

A moment later, she was startled to find herself facing the duchess in the empty hallway. Dropping a curtsy, Eugenia said, "May I be of some assistance?"

"No. No. I was looking for the duke. You haven't seen him have you?" The duchess hurried her words as she peered down the hall in both directions.

Eugenia couldn't imagine why she would take on such a task herself. Ordinarily, the duchess would send a footman in search of whomever she wanted for whatever frivolous reason.

"Have you tried the ballroom?" Eugenia suggested.

"The ballroom. How silly of me. Of course." The duchess hurried away, and Eugenia went on her search for the trouble she knew was coming. If only she knew what form it would take.

She suspected the duchess had truly been looking for Major Ward, just as Miss Abigail probably was earlier when she went into the duke's study. And the duke? Where had he gone instead of dancing with her?

When she opened the door to the study, Eugenia found John alone, his eyes focused on the paperweight in his hands.

"John, could you do me the biggest favor? Miss Wilton is devastated that my cousin Robert is ignoring her. Would you be a dear and go dance with her? Just one dance to bolster her spirits?"

He raised his head and gave her a woeful smile. "Is that to be my role in life? Bolster the spirits of chits who're in love with unsuitable rips?"

"If you're not careful, those chits, as you so delicately call them, will fall for you instead." Eugenia gave him a teasing grin.

John set down the paperweight he was holding and twisted his lips ruefully. "I notice you didn't object to my use of the word rip. Most of the young men here are worthless, you have to admit."

Eugenia shook her head, but she silently agreed. She'd met most of them while on the marriage block and had prayed she wouldn't be stuck with any of them.

John rose stiffly and said, "Miss Wilton may not thank you for suggesting I dance with her."

"If she objects, dance with me. Your father stood me

up tonight."

"Where is Father? He usually attends these events." John took Eugenia's arm and walked her to the ballroom. Taking a deep breath, he escorted her inside.

John limped off to speak to a laughing Miss Wilton and Eugenia did a surreptitious head count. Everyone was present, including the duke who now headed toward her. She hoped he would claim his dance. When he'd marched past her before, she'd been afraid he was displeased with some of her plans for the party. Now he looked quite pleased.

She glanced around again. Everyone was there except Major Ward.

She was thinking how nice it was not to have to listen to his nasty innuendos and threatening double entendres when the door swung open, nearly hitting the footman on duty. Major Ward took two steps into the room and looked about in puzzlement. His face was pale and drawn. Then he fell face first onto the polished wooden floor.

Chapter Three

AS MAJOR WARD COLLAPSED onto the ballroom floor, Eugenia gasped. One of the female guests screamed.

Blood covered the back of his light blue uniform jacket of the British light cavalry, marring it with a glossy, unattractive brownish spot several inches across. The duke's large, decorated letter opener protruded from the stain.

The musicians stopped playing in a flurry of jumbled notes. Exclamations filled the air. Eugenia gaped at the major who lay crumpled a few feet away from her. She blinked away her first angry thought— *leave it to Major Ward to upset their Christmas festivities*—as she realized how uncharitable it was.

At least, she thought he was dead.

She glanced from the letter opener protruding from Ward's back to her father-in-law. Where had the duke been when he should have been dancing with her? He looked as surprised as the rest of the dancers.

"He needs a physician." Adam rushed to the major's aid and felt for a pulse. While the rest of the crowd stood staring in horror, John winced as he awkwardly knelt next to his brother and turned Ward on his side. They loosened his cravat and felt his neck. They examined his eyes. Then the brothers stared at each other.

"He's dead," John said in a voice filled with shock.

Eugenia saw a look pass between the brothers.

The duchess began to sob and sway on her feet. Two footmen came to her aid and half-carried her from the room followed by two older ladies. Her cries echoing in the hall assured Eugenia she hadn't swooned yet.

Ordinarily, Eugenia's role would have been to see to her husband's mother, aiding her long-suffering lady's maid to calm her. But this was murder, and she wouldn't see the wrong person accused. Especially since she knew the flighty duchess was one of those who could be blamed for Major Ward's death.

Had the duchess been on a search for the major a few minutes before and not on a hunt for the duke? Was she determined to retrieve her letters by forcing the major to listen to her hysterics?

In that case, he might have stabbed himself. Eugenia fought down her hysterical thought. He wouldn't have stabbed himself, and certainly not in the back.

The duke said to the remaining servants, "Move his body to the game larder and lay him out decently. John, talk to the coachmen and see how long they think it will be before we can send word to Sir Wilberham that he's needed as county magistrate. Adam, follow me."

Everyone rushed to do his bidding. As soon as the body and the duke had left the ballroom, Eugenia knew she needed to do something to keep the guests occupied so the ladies wouldn't all succumb to hysterics. "As it is Christmas, perhaps we can adjourn to the music room and the musicians can lead us in Christmas carols."

They left the ballroom, skirting the blood-soaked spot on the floor. Once they reached the music room, the violinists gathered around the piano and made quiet suggestions to each other. The guests encircled them, some of the women sniffling, the men offering support. The bishop led them in prayer and then used his commanding baritone to lead the first carol.

As she sang along to "On Christmas Night All Christians Sing," she watched Miss Wilton out of the corner of her eye. The young woman looked relieved. Then she glanced around the room. There were more hopeful looks, relaxed expressions, and unburdened aspects than she would have believed one murder could produce.

Major Ward was truly an unpopular man.

They were on "I saw three ships come sailing in" when Eugenia saw John enter the music room, brushing snow out of his hair. She sang as she walked over to him.

"It's still coming down and blowing to boot. Just reaching the stables took a great deal of effort, and it appears to be forming large drifts beyond the buildings.

It'll be days before we can summon the magistrate."

Eugenia heard the strain in his voice. "Is everything all right in the stables?"

"Yes. They're snug enough, and all the animals were safe in the barns before the storm increased. Dawson's coachman was the last one to arrive. He said he thought they should have turned back, but Sir Charles was determined. Said he'd be here for Christmas if they all had to walk."

"Well, he and Aunt Anna have always been adventurous." And not practical enough to leave early in the face of falling snow, Eugenia added to herself with a sigh.

"Apparently, for once your aunt was not feeling up to the challenge. The carriage skidded several times and nearly turned over. The horses kept shying at the snow in their faces and the ice underfoot. Your aunt and Miss Henrietta begged your uncle to turn back and Robert agreed, but your uncle was adamant. Said he had something to take care of that wouldn't wait. Speaking of which, Eugenia, rescue me."

She turned to see where John was looking and found Cousin Henrietta and Abigail Wilton descending on them. Truly, descending on John. "Next time, believe me when I say you're in demand with the ladies."

He gave her his lopsided, sorrowful grin. "Heaven help us all."

Eugenia left John in the capable, determined hands of the two young ladies and went to the duke's study.

Empty. Walking quickly, she wondered what her uncle had to take care of that wouldn't wait. Was Ward blackmailing him too? She found it hard to believe someone as traditional as her uncle could be blackmailed. Perhaps her aunt or Cousin Henrietta. Henrietta would be silly enough to commit indiscretions to paper, and that would ruin her chances for a good match.

When she reached the duchess's room, Eugenia found the two matrons and her lady's maid were giving the duchess equal measures of bad advice, unfounded rumors, and handkerchiefs.

Eugenia backed out before they could draw her into the drama. Once in the hall, she turned in the direction of raised male voices. Far down a corridor, she found the duke and Adam arguing through a closed door with a man's voice coming from the opposite side. Joining them, she raised an eyebrow to her husband.

Adam gave her a weak smile. "Ward's man doesn't believe us that Ward is dead. He's locked himself in and won't come out. His master's orders."

Eugenia looked in surprise at her husband. "Why?"

"Ward had warned his man that someone might try some trickery to get into the room and steal certain documents. His man thinks that's what is happening now."

"That poor man," Eugenia said. For her this was a social embarrassment and a balancing act between what was expected for Christmas by her guests and what was expected after a death. For the valet, this meant the loss of his position and wages. There was probably no one to write him a reference so he could get another position. And the major's orders left him unable to leave the room to get food. "What a miserable Christmas for him."

She scratched on the door. "I know you don't believe us, Mr?"

"Thomas."

"Mr. Thomas, but he truly is dead. Can I at least send up a tray to you?"

"That would be kind of you, ma'am."

Eugenia turned to the duke who was frowning at her. "John went out to the stables. The coachmen agree it will be days before we can summon the magistrate. We are snowed in."

"With a murderer," the duke replied.

"At Christmas," she added. She couldn't think of anything worse.

Eugenia hadn't considered being trapped in the manor house with a murderer until that moment. A murderer with no means to escape. She felt a sudden chill, as if the duke's words had thrown her into a snow drift. Everyone she loved was imprisoned there by the snow and in certain danger. Worse, someone she loved could be the murderer. "I'd better check on Caroline."

Leaving the two men behind, Eugenia strode to Caroline's room. By luck, Miss Janvier, her governess, sat with her, sharing a pot of chocolate. Caroline was still in her dinner finery, while Miss Janvier wore a practical day dress of gray wool.

"Ladies," Eugenia said, "there's been a death downstairs. Due to the circumstances, I'd like you two to stay together as much as possible."

"Why, Genie?" Caroline asked, interest suddenly appearing in her expression. "What's wrong?"

"We had a death at the ball. It was distressing. Your mother is distraught."

"She always is," Caroline said with a mischievous grin. Then she brightened as she rose. "I'll have to find Major Ward. He'll tell me what's happened."

"No, he won't," Eugenia said, nearly snapping out her reply.

"Why not? You can't stop him." Caroline made a challenge out of her words.

"Because he's dead," Eugenia said. "He was murdered and the murderer is unknown."

Caroline gasped.

Miss Janvier fainted, sliding to the floor from her chair.

Caroline and Eugenia struggled to lift Miss Janvier onto Caroline's bed. Once the unconscious woman appeared comfortable, Eugenia studied Caroline. The girl didn't appear moved by the murder. She had the clear-headed logic of her brothers, no doubt her father's influence.

Eugenia whispered, "Stay with her. Find out why she fainted. She's not the type to faint at a little blood.

She escaped the revolution as a child."

"And so you find her less than a lady?"

Eugenia could see the angry gleam in Caroline's eyes. "No. I don't faint, and I'm a countess. But I didn't faint. I need to know why she found the news of Major Ward's murder so distressing."

"Why you?" Caroline challenged, hands on hips. "It's none of your business."

Eugenia tried a soothing approach. "I know you like her. I'm not going to tell your parents what you learn. A lot of people here for Christmas are very happy the major is dead."

"So why are you picking on Miss Janvier, Genie?"

"We need to find the murderer, and if Miss Janvier didn't do it, we need to know her secret so we can keep her safe."

"She was with me all evening since just after dinner."

"She never left you once?" Eugenia let her tone show her skepticism.

"She couldn't. She was afraid I'd sneak down to the ball." Caroline looked pleased that her obstinacy had helped.

Eugenia smiled in reply. "That's good. Please find out why she fainted and then tell me, will you?"

Caroline smiled slyly.

Eugenia went downstairs, ordered a tray for Ward's man and tea for Miss Janvier, and went back to the music room. She could hear the music leaping and footsteps prancing through the closed door. *What?* The man was hardly cold. Her mouth tasted sour as the unseen dancing continued. Then she realized Major Ward must have been widely hated.

When she entered, she found the doors connecting to the blue drawing room flung open and the carpets rolled up. Her Uncle Charles led a group of the younger guests in a sedate reel. Walking over to where John sat, she raised her eyebrows.

"You should have seen the jig he entertained us with earlier," John told her.

That sounded more like her uncle. "What brought on these high spirits?" she asked.

"He told me many of us were happy that Ward was dead and there was no sense pretending otherwise. He included me in that, and I couldn't deny it." John's face twisted in a mask of pain.

"Did you kill him?" Eugenia asked, knowing her tone was brutal.

"How can you ask me that?" Fury simmered in his tone but he kept his voice lowered.

"Out of love. You know what I want to hear." She knew she wore her desire that John was innocent on her face.

John's eyes snapped with anger. "If you loved me, you'd know the answer without asking."

"My opinion isn't what matters. I want to hear you say the words. They are what matter." She was nearly whispering now.

He shook his head. "I wanted him dead. I could have strangled him easily face to face. But put a dagger through his back? Never. That's the act of a coward."

Then he shrugged. "And he never would have turned his back on me. He knew I hated him and that I'm capable of killing. I've done it often enough."

"Thank you, John." Eugenia patted his shoulder.

"Your uncle's right, though. There are many people here for Christmas who would gladly kill the major."

"Let's go into the study and compare lists," Eugenia suggested.

John's gaze flew to her face. "Does Adam know how bloodless you are?"

"It's for Adam that I'm deliberately staying brave." If Adam were even suspected of the murder, he'd probably hang. Once the magistrate decided on the identity of the killer, justice was swift. Her dear, sweet, kind, loving husband could be taken from her for the death of an evil man.

She couldn't let that happen. "Your family will suffer gossip and ridicule if no one is found to have committed this deed. They'll think someone in this family is a murderer. Then who will you marry?"

"No one. Look at me, Genie. Who would marry someone who looks like this?"

"I see nothing wrong with your looks."

John gave a small smile. "I see this scar down the side of my face every time I look in a mirror, and despite my best efforts, I still limp badly. I'm not one to win a girl's heart in the ballroom. I'm not the man I was when I left to go to war."

The smile she returned was genuine. "I didn't know you then, but I like the man you have become. You need to win someone who can see to your heart and soul and know your true worth. You'll make a much better marriage that way. But if you won't think of yourself, think of Caroline."

"A reputation as the relative of a murderer wouldn't do her any good." He looked up as the reel ended and Charles walked over to them.

"Uncle, how could you? Dancing immediately after—a murder." Eugenia asked him in a low voice.

"The young people needed distracting from the horror of it all. They don't wish to wander about, courting in pairs, while a murderer is loose. Dancing keeps them occupied and together while things are being seen to." He pulled out his handkerchief and mopped his face.

"Then, thank you, Uncle, for your consideration."

He smiled. "I knew you'd understand, Genie."

"Keep up the good work while Lord John and I see to more distasteful matters." Eugenia walked away, certain John rose and followed her out.

"What are you planning?" John asked once they were alone.

"I want to find where Major Ward was murdered. Maybe the site of the attack will tell us something." She began by looking over each unused room in turn. When they reached the red parlor, she found a chair drenched in a rust colored stain. "John?"

He examined the chair. "This is where the blow was struck. With Ward seated, the back of the chair would protect his killer from having any of the blood splash on him."

"Or her. He wouldn't have turned his back on you, but he would have done so to your mother or me. Still, how would the blow have been struck? Wouldn't the chair back be in the way?"

John considered for a moment, looking at the chair from various angles. "He must have been in the act of rising or sitting down, so there would be enough room to strike the blow. Or we could be wrong. He was stabbed and then collapsed into this chair. He lost a lot of blood here, but he still managed to walk to the ballroom to die in a pool of his blood on the ballroom floor."

Eugenia looked at the chair in horror. "At least we can guess the stabbing took place here. And it doesn't tell us anything. Anyone could have been in here with him."

Leading John back to the study, Eugenia sat on the settee and said, "Your mother couldn't kill a fly, but someone may have had reason to kill the major for her."

John looked at her for a moment from his father's chair behind the desk and then nodded. "You're right. He got hold of some embarrassingly gushy letters mother wrote a male friend many years ago. An unsuitable man she was foolishly enamored with. She was only a girl. She'd not even met father yet. She'd forgotten all about the letters until Ward began blackmailing her. It wasn't until she'd run through her allowance that any of us found out. Father, Adam, or I could have killed him for the blackmailing scum he was."

"He wouldn't have turned his back on any of you. Especially not the duke after he caught Major Ward and Caroline flirting."

John's eyebrows flew toward his hairline. "My sister's a little fool."

"Unfortunately, he wouldn't see your mother as a physical threat and he could easily turn his back on her. I found her alone in the hallway shortly before the major's grand entrance."

He sagged in his chair. "Did she give any reason for leaving the ball?"

"She said she was looking for the duke. I would believe it, except why not send a footman? She loves balls. She wouldn't leave one willingly."

"You have to help her, Genie. Help all of us. You're the most clear-headed of the gentle sex. People talk to you." There was a begging tone to John's voice. He looked so hurt, so vulnerable, Eugenia's heart went out to him. He was the brother she'd never had.

"I'll do what I can. He was also threatening Miss Wilton with something. I don't know what. I did hear her say she wished he were dead."

"He'd have turned his back on her," John said with a nod.

"He'd also have turned his back on his man. He might have a reason to want Major Ward dead that we don't know about."

"Knowing the major is reason enough," John grumbled. "I learned from Ward he held some paper of your uncle's. Ward threatened to call in the debt simply to torment Sir Charles. He was that type of person. He probably did that to a lot of people."

"I don't want to think it was Uncle Charles despite the gloomy, hardworking life I had under his roof. At least, he and Aunt Anna took me in after my parents died. My father's title and his money went to another relative who wanted nothing to do with me." Eugenia shook her head in sorrow. Uncle Charles saw her as his ticket into higher society.

Then she rose and paced the room. "Miss Janvier fainted when she heard the major had been murdered. She went through the revolution in France. She deals with your sister on a daily basis."

"A hardy soul," John said with a smile.

"Precisely. She's not the fainting sort. What could Ward have had on her?"

"He spent part of the war hunting down spies. Could Caroline's governess have been one of them?"

"If she was, it certainly wouldn't do anyone any good now. Napoleon is well and truly vanquished to St. Helena." She gave John a big smile. "Thanks to those who defend our nation."

John's response to her praise was a grimace.
Then he faced the ceiling and drew a deep breath.
"Why in blazes did Father invite that swine to our Christmas celebration?" John smacked the arms of his chair in anger or frustration.

Whichever it was, Eugenia sympathized with his feelings.

Chapter Four

"I'D LIKE TO KNOW THAT MYSELF."

Eugenia turned at the sound of the new voice and saw Adam standing in the doorway of the study. Her heart leaped and butterflies took wing in her stomach, much as they had when Adam was courting her. No one who made her feel so bright and alive could kill anyone. She was absolutely certain.

"By the way," Adam continued as he closed the door, "Father was threatening to starve that poor Mr. Thomas when you came along and said you'd order him a tray. That was kind of you, Genie."

He walked over and bent over to give her a hug. "You're not too upset by what's happened, are you?"

Eugenia tilted her head up and quickly kissed him. "No. I'm all right. But I'm sure I haven't made myself popular with your father. I'll have to make up for it by coaxing Mr. Thomas out of the room so your father can try to find your mother's letters."

"Good luck with that," John said, groaning as he straightened out his injured leg. "Ward knew how to hide things very well. As I said, he worked with spies."

"Did he work with Mr. Thomas during the war?" Adam asked his brother.

"I don't know. Let's ask him." John's grim tone told Eugenia what he'd thought of anyone associated with Ward, particularly spies.

The three left the study. When they reached the base of the stairs, Adam stopped and put his arms around Eugenia's shoulders. "Genie, you shouldn't come with us." His eyes and voice were full of concern.

"Why not? I promise not to get the vapors like your mother." She smiled back at him, thrilled he would be so worried for her.

"It might be unpleasant."

"Seeing a man drop dead in front of me with a knife in his back is unpleasant. Everything else is a search for justice."

"John and I may have to ask uncomfortable questions."

"You do realize John knew Major Ward during the war and will be considered a possible murderer. Your father left the ball for a while and could easily have killed the major over your sister's honor. Your mother, quite uncharacteristically, left the dancing and definitely had a reason to murder the man. We should be working together to find the killer and protect your family." She put a hand on his arm. "Please, Adam."

"Father isn't going to like this."

"Your father will dislike a member of his family being hanged for murder a great deal more. Even the simple accusation of murder could ruin us. Think of the hysterics your mother would have if someone accused the duke of being an assassin."

Adam cringed. "Right. Let's go."

They walked to the room assigned to Major Ward and scratched on the door. "Who's there?" a male voice called out.

"Earl Hunter, Countess Hunter, and Lord John Hunter. We'd like to come in," Adam announced.

"Lady Hunter? Is she the one who sent me the tray?"

"Yes, I am. Was it to your liking?" Eugenia said.

"It was very kind of your ladyship. You may come in. You and you alone."

Adam opened his mouth to object, but Eugenia shook her head. Mr. Thomas could be the murderer, but she'd have to face him.

"No, Genie," Adam whispered.

"It's all right."

"No, it's not. Please don't." He clutched her hand.

"Yes, Mr. Thomas. I'll come in alone," Eugenia said and waited for the sound of the key in the lock. Then she turned the knob and walked in, shutting the door behind her.

The valet locked the door again. The sound of the key clicking behind her nearly made her scream in fear, but she swallowed down her terror and walked forward toward the windows.

The room was immaculate. Mr. Thomas was

apparently a diligent valet. Eugenia sat down on the chair and indicated to Mr. Thomas to sit on the footstool.

"Where are you going to sleep tonight?" Eugenia asked.

"I'll stay up until my master returns."

Eugenia looked at him sadly and shook her head. "Major Ward is dead. He was involved with spies. You must have known his was a dangerous life."

"The war's over. He should be out of danger."

"Out of danger? He came to our Christmas house party while blackmailing the duchess and possibly Miss Wilton. Who knows who else lived in fear of him? That is a dangerous life."

His eyes widened slightly. "I didn't know he was blackmailing anyone. Truly."

"Not even his former spies? Yourself, for example."

Thomas leaped up and paced to the window. "He was not blackmailing me."

"He had some hold over you. When a delegation comes to tell a servant his master is dead, most servants will come out to view the body and make plans for their future. They worry about the lack of a reference. They don't stay at their post in the face of all logic unless they are very much afraid."

"If I admitted such a thing, I could be hanged."

"No one will hear it from me."

He laid his head against the cold glass. "It is true. I am afraid. Major Ward not only spied for England, he also spied for France. I was one of his French spies. But I am not the only one in this house."

"Miss Janvier, the governess?"

Thomas looked at her with wonder. Tears glistened in his eyes. "How do you know these things?"

"Miss Janvier fainted when she heard of his murder. A strange reaction to the death of someone she'd scarcely met, don't you think?" Eugenia replied.

"I went to get my dinner the day we arrived, and I saw her talking to the housekeeper. I was shocked to see her in an English household. She begged me not to tell the major she was here. She recognized me because she used to give me her reports to give to the major. And now you swear that Major Ward is dead?" He sounded hopeful.

"Yes. His body's in the game larder if you want to see for yourself."

He nodded. Then with slow steps he walked over and unlocked the door.

The valet and the three aristocrats made an odd, solemn procession through the halls. They picked up wraps by the back entrance and John lit a glass-shielded candle. They went outside on the recently shoved walk and entered the game storage cold room.

Hanging carcasses of mutton and beef were near the far wall, past dressed turkeys and geese, beyond baskets of eggs and quarts of cream and wheels of cheese. Near the door on a table was the sheet-covered body.

Adam twitched away the sheet so Mr. Thomas could see the face of his late master. In the cold, Ward's dead face had become bloodlessly white and predatory, even vulture-like.

Showing his true nature, Eugenia thought.

"Thank God," Thomas said. "I'm free." His body sagged in relief.

"I don't understand," Adam said.

"He treated me like a slave, not a servant."

"Will you go back to France?" Eugenia asked.

"No. I'm English. Not French. The major paid my father's debts and then made me collateral, like a watch or a house," he grimaced, "until such time as my father could repay him. He wasn't able to do this before he died, and with no hope of a salary of my own, I was locked into service with him forever."

"Then you're free. Do you have a bed in the servants' attic?" Eugenia asked. The poor man couldn't stay in Ward's room any longer. Not if they wanted to search it.

Thomas shook his head.

"Go to the housekeeper, and she'll find a place for you. No one is going anywhere for a few days. Soon, we'll talk about getting you a reference if you'd like another position as a valet." Eugenia gave him a dismissing nod.

"Thank you, my lady." Mr. Thomas bowed and then seemed to spring from the game locker in his haste to return to the house.

The other three shut the body away and walked indoors, hanging up wraps and moving as a group toward the grand entrance. Everyone was leaving the midnight supper in the dining room and milling about in the hall. Eugenia looked wistfully in the direction of the supper. Maybe they could get something later.

"We're all afraid to go to bed because of the murderer," Aunt Anna announced.

Oh, what a silly woman, Eugenia wanted to say. Aloud, she said calmly to her aunt, "Major Ward was a very unpopular man. Unless you're as devious as he was, you have nothing to worry about. Good night, Aunt Anna. Sleep well."

"Good night, my darling niece. Happy Christmas." Anna gave Eugenia a kiss on the cheek and went upstairs. The others followed her in a long procession, each saying good night and wishing all and sundry a happy Christmas until Adam, John, and Eugenia were left alone in the hall.

"Well, shall we examine Ward's luggage for his secrets?" Adam asked.

"I'd rather find other people's secrets so we can return their papers and relieve their minds," Eugenia said.

Adam took her hand. "I'd like to know his, too. He might have been murdered for something other than blackmailing our guests, but I have no idea what other reason someone might have. Yet."

They climbed the stairs and walked down the hall.

They went into Major Ward's room to find a candle burning on the bureau and Uncle Charles bent over Ward's trunk. Clothes were scattered on the floor.

"Uncle Charles! What are you doing?" Eugenia asked.

He ignored her as he continued to dig through the trunk. "Ward took something of mine. I hoped to retrieve it before anyone else looked through his belongings."

Adam and John crowded in behind her as she said, "What did he take?"

"The deed to my manor."

John whistled.

Eugenia stared, shocked by his words for a moment. "Isn't it entailed to you?" she asked when she finally found her voice. The estate was the only source of the Dawson family's wealth and position.

"No. It came through my mother's family."

Adam asked, "How did Ward get hold of it?"

Uncle Charles rose stiffly. Then he walked over to the window and pushed aside the draperies to look out into the winter darkness. Standing with his hands behind his back, his stomach protruded under his embroidered vest and both of his chins were evident above his cravat.

"Through stupidity on my part. I made a foolish investment and used the manor as security. It was an investment that couldn't fail!" He banged his fists on the windowsill. "It couldn't fail, and yet, it did. It was so

"How did Major Ward get involved in this investment?" Eugenia asked.

"Ward bought up the securities and took the deed to my manor. He was charging colossal amounts of interest on the debt. I was going broke, and without the manor, I'd have nothing for my family. We'd be ruined. And the major didn't care. He thought it was funny."

Eugenia watched him through narrowed eyes. "Aunt Anna doesn't know, does she?"

He hung his head. "No."

Adam said, "Let's see if we can't find it, along with everything else we're searching for."

John looked at his brother. "No sleep for any of us tonight."

Eugenia moved in front of her uncle. "But there will be for you. Goodnight, Uncle. Go see to my aunt. She must be as frightened as everyone else at being trapped in with a killer."

"But surely he escaped into the night after murdering Ward. Whoever he is," Sir Charles said.

"No one's gone anywhere in this weather," John said. "Best head to your bed and lock yourself in."

Sir Charles lingered in the door. "If you find my deed...?"

"We'll return it. Goodnight, Uncle." Eugenia gently shut him out of the room and then turned to the others. "Now, where do we start?"

"Happy Christmas," Adam grumbled. Then he

pulled Eugenia close and kissed her forehead. "I'm sorry. It's just so beastly to have a murder on Christmas."

John looked around the room. "And we're searching for blackmail material. What an odd way to begin Christmas day."

As the sun rose weakly over a glistening Christmas morn, a weary Eugenia looked around the room where they'd searched every inch, turned to her husband and his brother, and said, "Any other ideas?"

"None." John grumbled and rubbed his unshaven cheek above his scar.

"Then I suggest we lock the room and go down to breakfast. It's Christmas and I'm sure your parents and our guests would appreciate a little normality in our festivities today." Eugenia yawned and stretched. Walking over to her husband, now sleepily rubbing his eyes, she leaned in and gave him a Christmas kiss.

"It's a good thing Father invited the bishop. We'd never make it into the village for church," Adam said with a smile, returning the kiss. "And could I interest you in a before breakfast Christmas present?"

John tried to turn his laughter into a cough. "I think I'll go down to breakfast. Let me know when you want to try again to find Ward's purloined papers." He escaped the room, leaving a trail of chuckles in his wake.

Adam drew his wife to him and said "Happy

Christmas" before their lips joined. Eugenia relaxed into the kiss as it wiped away her fatigue, leaving her blissful and joyous.

They enjoyed only a minute of solitude before the duke's voice was heard. "Have you had any—oh, pardon me."

Adam and Eugenia jumped apart like guilty children.

"Don't look like that," he playfully scolded. "No one wants grandchildren more than I do. The line must continue. But perhaps today, we should put our minds toward Christmas and finding your mother's foolish letters." The duke's tone ended as dry as last summer's straw.

"We've had no luck finding anything so far, Father," Adam said, standing a little straighter as he answered.

"We were about to lock the room and go down to breakfast," Eugenia said, hoping no one heard her stomach rumble.

"Good plan."

Eugenia swallowed and then took a deep breath, knowing she was about to make herself unpopular with Adam's father by asking the question she felt she must raise. "But first, Duke, where did you go last night after your dance with the duchess at the ball?"

"Why do you ask?" His gaze turned icy.

Adam squeezed her hand.

Eugenia knew she had to continue. "Because you were supposed to dance with me, but you disappeared.

During that time, Major Ward was stabbed with your letter opener. There will be gossip that you are the killer."

"I am not a killer." He boomed ducal displeasure at her, but Eugenia stood firm.

"I'm sure you aren't. But where did you go?" Eugenia knew the question would come better from one of his sons. He was a duke. She was the orphaned child of a baron. But then, she knew neither Adam nor John would put the question to him.

"I found it necessary to step outside for a few minutes," the duke said stiffly.

In the snow? "Were you unwell?"

"Not really." He colored slightly, and Eugenia realized a call of nature had sent him from the ballroom.

"Oh." Her own face heating, Eugenia curtsied to the duke.

"Why outside, Father? Why not your own room?" Adam asked.

"I didn't think I'd make it. Not as young as I once was."

He had hurried out of the ballroom, Eugenia recalled. "Why did you invite Major Ward to the party?" she asked in a quiet voice.

"I needed to deal with him to get the duchess's letters back. Seemed like the season to negotiate in good faith. And then Sir Charles asked me to invite Ward and I discovered he also needed to bargain with the little swine."

Falling silent, they left the room. Adam locked the door, and the duke pocketed the key. "We'll reconsider possibilities after our Christmas service. The bishop is going to lead us in prayer in the ballroom, and the musicians are going to play Christmas hymns," the duke said.

"Will the servants be able to join us?" Eugenia asked.

"If their work is caught up, of course. It is Christmas," the duke replied, striding off toward his breakfast.

"I'll inform the butler and housekeeper and have them send word to the stable hands," Eugenia said.

"Appropriate, considering the Christmas story," Adam said, grinning at his wife.

It wasn't until after breakfast and the church service that Eugenia could find a moment to speak privately to Adam again. She pulled him into the blue drawing room and said, "I think we ought to ask Mr. Thomas if he has any idea where the papers might be located."

"He said he didn't." Adam kissed her soundly, letting her know he had other things on his mind than blackmail that Christmas morning.

After a few treasured moments, Eugenia broke away with regret and said, "We have to find those papers and discover the murderer if we're to lift the threat of a murder charge against someone in your family. Mr. Thomas might know something he didn't think would be helpful. And right now, anything would be helpful." Eugenia gave a weary sigh and led Adam to the servants' hall below stairs. She'd had no sleep and no private time with Adam. What a terrible first Christmas they were having as a married couple.

When the next duke and his wife entered, the servants all leaped to their feet. Eugenia was glad to see the servants had decorated their hall with greens from the estate and bits of colorful ribbon. It gave the cheerless room a bit of Christmas joy.

"Please. As you were." No one returned to their tasks. "We want to speak to Mr. Thomas, Major Ward's man," Adam said.

"He's not been down here since breakfast," the butler said from where he'd been polishing silver. "And he didn't join our church service. Thought he might be chapel. Or popish," was added with a sniff.

With a thanks and a "Happy Christmas," Adam and Eugenia went up to the attic rooms where most of the staff slept. No sign of Ward's man there, either. Eugenia could see her breath and knew no one would linger up there, even on a holiday.

As they exchanged a look, Eugenia knew Adam also wanted to check Major Ward's room next. They hurried downstairs to find the locked door ajar. They'd locked the door before breakfast and the duke held the key. Why would the duke come up without them? Then Eugenia blinked as it registered in her sleepy mind that the lock was broken and the doorframe splintered.

Adam put Eugenia behind him and pushed the door open fully.

She peeked over his shoulder and saw Thomas on the floor, an ornate knife handle protruding from his stomach. Gasping, her stomach reeling, she reached out for something to steady herself. She leaned against the hallway wall outside the room and gulped down cold air. He'd been a nice man, lost in the shadow of his master's evil. He was an innocent in this terrible business.

"This is wrong," she managed to say. "He didn't deserve this."

Adam looked at her, his eyes wide. Then he walked over and held her, taking away some of the horror. "Who would do this? On Christmas? Have we invited a madman to our feast?"

"Or madwoman?"

Chapter Five

EUGENIA POINTED TO THE broken lock and doorframe. "And did Mr. Thomas break into this room, or did someone else break in and he caught them in the act?"

"I recognize the design on the knife handle. It belonged to Major Ward. No one needed to bring a weapon with them." Adam's shoulders drooped.

"I saw it in here last night while we were searching the room. I didn't think it necessary to take it away with us. Oh, Adam, this is so wrong. That poor man." The cold outside the house filled her bones as if the walls had suddenly vanished.

Eugenia pressed herself against her husband to replace the sorrow with happier thoughts, but still, she needed to know. "Has he been dead long?"

"From what I know of game, he's been dead for more than just the few minutes we were hunting for him. We couldn't have prevented this, Genie."

Eugenia gave Adam a shivered glance as she pulled away and looked him in the eye. "Who was missing from the church service? Because he must have been murdered while the bishop was telling us the Christ child came into the world to bring love and harmony. While we sang 'Come thou long expected Jesus' and 'Angels from the Realms of Glory.' How terrifying and ironic."

"That leaves my parents out." Adam shook his head.

The vision of his mother clinging to the duke and having hysterics before the first hymn would stay with Eugenia for a very long time. She wished the duchess hadn't pointed out in a loud voice that they were spending Christmas with a murderer and were all liable to be killed in their beds. She'd nearly drowned out the musicians.

Eugenia huddled against her husband. "It also leaves out John, Caroline, Miss Janvier, and both of us. Everyone must have been watching John and the two of us nodding off during the sermon. Oh, why did we have to sit in the front where everyone could watch us but we couldn't watch the doors?"

Adam held his wife closer, kissing the top of her head. "Oh, Genie, I'm so glad you're as unlike my mother as a lady could be. Every day I thank God I met you."

His words brought a smile to her lips. "I didn't think you'd notice me. The orphaned ward of Sir Charles."

"Oh, I noticed you immediately. You were the most beautiful, cleverest girl in the room. Although, once or twice, I have wished you were someone's ward besides Sir Charles's."

"Well, this clever girl can't think how to learn who

slipped out during our Christmas service to kill Mr. Thomas. And I'm afraid that is our best hope of discovering the identity of Major Ward's murderer."

"We'll ask the butler. He should know who left the room."

"You ask him. I'll ask the housekeeper. Between the two of them, we should get some idea of what occurred behind our backs."

"And I'll have him send up footmen to move the body and guard the room until we can search it again. This will give Mother another fit."

Eugenia smiled as she knew he'd meant her to. "Then let's hope she doesn't find out for a long, long time."

They shut the door with the now broken lock and splintered frame and went their separate ways. Eugenia found the housekeeper inspecting the main rooms after the maids tidied up.

"I need a quick word," she said quietly.

The housekeeper nodded. "Would my sitting room do, your ladyship?"

"Yes. We'd better."

Once they were ensconced in the housekeeper's small, cozy sitting room, Eugenia said, "Tell me where everyone was sitting or standing in the ballroom for the service."

The housekeeper stopped in the act of picking up some sewing. "What happened during the service?"

"Another murder. Major Ward's man this time."

The housekeeper, who Eugenia suspected had become more taciturn after years of working for the duchess, merely raised her eyebrows. "Oh, dear. Well, the maids were lined up on my right. Behind them was the cook's staff. Cook was to my left, and then your lady's maid and then the duchess'. The stable hands were lined up behind the male house staff."

"Everyone was there for the entire service?"

"Oh, yes, milady. They wouldn't dare sneak out. Not by me."

"Did anyone leave at all?"

The housekeeper's needle paused in midair. "Sir Charles Dawson had a coughing fit and left. Miss Wilton left but she came back in just a few minutes later looking white as a sheet. I remember wondering if she was ill."

Eugenia nodded. "Did Sir Charles return?"

"I don't think so, but I saw him in the hallway after service ended."

"Did anyone else leave?"

"No. The bishop gave a good sermon, didn't he?"

"Yes, he did." At least it was short for the bishop. A benefit, Eugenia guessed, of asking him to lead a service at the last moment. "Did you notice Mr. Thomas, Major Ward's man, talking to anyone, servants or guests, at any time?"

"He seemed to know one of the musicians. They both jumped when they saw each other at breakfast, and later I noticed them whisper briefly in passing."

"Which musician?"

"The young, dark-haired violinist. The other musicians call him Jock." The housekeeper's needle moved swiftly through the muslin.

"This group of musicians has played here before, haven't they?"

"Yes, several times. This is only the second time Jock has played with them."

But Jock and the other musicians had been in the front of the room behind the bishop playing throughout the service. And none of the musicians had left. Eugenia knew she'd have to check with someone who'd been in the ballroom at the beginning of the previous night's festivities, but she suspected Jock was in the clear.

Eugenia left the housekeeper to her duties and returned to the main floor and searched among the guests. Finally, she found her Aunt Anna gossiping with other matrons.

"Where's Uncle Charles?" Eugenia asked.

"Charles? Probably standing in front of a warm fire. The cold does make his bones ache."

Eugenia checked the fires in the main rooms and then headed upstairs. She heard the argument before she turned the corner and saw the men who were raising their voices just outside Major Ward's room. Uncle Charles and the footman charged with guarding the door.

When she drew near, Sir Charles Dawson spotted her and said, "Ah, Eugenia. Tell this stubborn man that I may enter this room. That's a good niece."

He tried to shift past the man before Eugenia said, "No. You may not."

He turned on her, his face rigid with anger. "What?"

"Adam said no one is to enter. Unless the duke comes here and countermands him, you may not go in."

"Is this the thanks I get for raising you?"

"Adam is my husband and commands my loyalty now." Eugenia found she was standing toe to toe with her uncle. He'd grudgingly raised her, at least for a few years, but now with her marriage, she outranked him. He used her high station to impress others, but when dealing directly with Eugenia, he tried to ignore her rank. "Please, uncle. Rejoin the other guests."

As he huffed and turned away, she added, "Why did you leave the Christmas service this morning?"

"Who says I did?"

"A number of people. I see you're not coughing now."

"If you must know, the bishop was boring me. I went to take a nap."

"So you were in your room sleeping?" Her amazement seeped into her voice. "I'm surprised you're not wrinkled."

"Yes. I rose looking mussed, so I changed my shirt and vest. I didn't want to look out of sorts for the Christmas feast, which I believe should be starting soon." Uncle Charles held out his arm to escort her downstairs.

Blast. Christmas luncheon. And there was no way to refuse his arm without being rude. Eugenia nodded to the footman and said, "Please stay at your post until relieved. No one is to enter."

Eugenia gave her uncle her arm and they went downstairs to eat.

The meal was as sedate and cheerless an affair as a Christmas luncheon in a full room could be. The room itself was made brighter by the sunshine streaming in the windows and reflecting off the blinding snow. Eugenia noticed Miss Wilton was clinging to the company of Lord John while looking pale and nervous. A champagne cork pop nearly made her jump out of her chair. When Robert Dawson approached her, she huddled closer to John. Robert looked baffled. John, the hero of Waterloo, looked like he wanted to get up and run away from this skirmish.

Eugenia was also baffled. Abigail Wilton had been discretely chasing Cousin Robert all day yesterday. After the meal was over and the guests began to scatter, Eugenia pulled Miss Wilton aside. "What is wrong?"

"Wrong? I don't understand." She tried backing up and ran into a wall. She glanced around and then sighed. There was no one in sight to interrupt them.

"You're obviously frightened of something."

"We have a murderer loose among us. Aren't you frightened?" the girl pouted.

Pouted? Eugenia made a mental note to tell John to avoid entanglements with Miss Wilton and pushed on.

"That's a lovely gown. It brings out the vivid blue color of your eyes."

Abigail Wilton gave a deep sigh. "Thank you. I discovered half way through the sermon that I'd dropped a spot of jam on my dress. I couldn't have everyone seeing me like that. A soiled gown! So I went upstairs and changed into this." She gave a little satisfied cat smile. "I hope Captain Hunter likes it."

Oh, dear. The girl was sly and had bad judgment since she was involved with Major Ward and wandered off alone with a murderer on the loose. Eugenia's mental warning to John grew sharper. "You're avoiding Robert Dawson. Was he rude to you?"

"No. Mr. Dawson has been a gentleman."

"Did something unpleasant happen when you left to change your gown?"

"Nothing. I saw nothing." The girl's cat smile grew larger and more self-satisfied as she walked away with her head held high.

Saw nothing? What did she see? Eugenia was still scowling in the direction Abigail Wilton had gone when Adam came up to her. "What is it?"

"Miss Wilton left the Christmas service and obviously saw something, but she won't say what. And she changed her gown during the service."

He scowled. "No one else left."

"Uncle Charles did. And I found him before dinner trying to get into the major's room again."

Adam shut his eyes and shook his head. "Oh, Genie,

no. He's family."

"Get John. We're going through that room again. Now."

This time, they emptied Ward's trunks onto the floor. The brothers, with the help of a footman, pried at the tops and bottoms. Finally, they pried open a false bottom in one trunk and found papers neatly fitted in a thin layer.

Adam sat down and flipped through them. "Mother's letters. Good grief. I can't look at those."

"You'll have to," John said. "At least enough to make sure they are Mother's letters and not someone else's correspondence in her envelopes."

Adam glared at his brother and then looked at the next item in the pile. "Sir Charles' deed."

"He'll be so relieved you found it," Eugenia said, kissing the top of her husband's head.

"Letters from Miss Wilton to some man," John said, tossing the packet aside with a sound of disgust.

"Reports in French on British troop movements and ship movements from Miss Janvier and Mr. Thomas," Adam said, scanning the small, densely written messages.

"And Jock," Eugenia added, sorting through what her husband set aside. "His name is really Jacques. That explains the surprise when the musician encountered Mr. Thomas."

"Ward was a double spy," John said, sitting down

heavily and then glancing through the messages Adam handed him. "The swine. It's a good thing he's dead."

Eugenia stared at the carpet beneath where Thomas's body had lain and then took two steps backwards. "How will we ever get the blood out? It splattered all over. On the floor and everywhere."

"We'll have to sell the carpet to a second hand dealer," Adam said, not looking up from reading his mother's letters with raised eyebrows.

"But it's so odd. The blood shot to the sides but not in the middle."

John looked over. "That's because the killer stood right in front of him. Where you're standing now."

Eugenia's eyes widened as she jumped back. "So his vest—or her dress—was covered with blood."

"Probably." John scowled at her. "What are you thinking, Genie?"

"Uncle Charles changed his vest between breakfast and luncheon during the service. Come on, both of you. We need to find it. If that doesn't have blood on it, we'll have to find Miss Wilton's dress."

"Probably spilled something on it at breakfast. Your uncle certainly packs it away," John said.

"He said he wrinkled it taking a nap," Eugenia told them.

"Well, he's not going to admit to being a glutton," John murmured.

Carrying the papers with him, Adam led the way to the room shared by Sir Charles and Lady Dawson. After a quick rap on the door, the trio rushed into the room only to find a startled Sir Charles holding a blood-stained vest and shirt in front of the blazing hearth. Whirling around, Charles threw both incriminating items into the flames. Then he stumbled back, a relieved look on his face.

"No!" Eugenia cried and started toward the fire. But John was quicker, leaping forward and grabbing the poker. He fished both pieces of clothing, now smoldering, free from the inferno.

Sir Charles wasn't finished. With an angry roar, he rushed to stop John, but Adam pushed him back. Eugenia watched in terror as the two men grappled. John, with a few stomps of his boots, put out the burning clothes. Then he stepped into the shoving match to help his brother.

"Stop it! Stop it!" Eugenia cried out, tears running down her cheeks. Her aunt and cousins would be ruined by his actions. "Uncle, how could you?"

Charles gave up the fight and sank onto a chair. "You know all, don't you?"

Eugenia, now that she knew the worst, wanted answers. Something had to explain his uncle's rash behavior. "Yes. But why kill Mr. Thomas? He didn't want your deed."

"He caught me looking for it." He covered his face with his hands. "I couldn't have anyone spreading the rumor that I'd lost the manor, even for a short while. I'd be ruined. How could my children make advantageous marriages?"

"We need to take you to the duke," Eugenia said, clasping her arms over her chest. "He'll have to decide how to proceed."

"Oh, yes, you've come out of this all right. You're already married," Charles snapped at her. "And to think of the time and expense I used to make certain you'd secure an advantageous match."

"None of your plans made any difference," Adam said. "I would have chosen Eugenia no matter what."

Eugenia looked up into his eyes and saw such love her heart melted. She threw herself into his arms. "Thank you, dearest."

They clung together until John cleared his throat.

All four of them walked in a close group downstairs to the study, where they sent a footman with a note requesting the duke's presence. When he entered, he immediately asked, "Now, tell me. What has happened?"

While they explained everything, Adam and John produced the papers and the half-charred clothing. Sir Charles sat in silence, staring at the rug.

Only when his sons finished the sordid tale did the duke look at Sir Charles. "You killed two men. What do you say for yourself?" he asked.

Eugenia didn't think the duke had ever sounded as much like God on his throne as he did at that moment.

Sir Charles said, "Major Ward was a blackmailer, a thief, and an unprincipled scourge. He deserved to die, but I am sorry about his man. He surprised me, and I acted before I thought. The dagger was the first thing that came to hand."

"You used my letter opener to stab Ward, making me a suspect in his death," the duke said.

"I'm sorry. I saw it lying there and thought, *just the thing I need.* Anyone could have taken it," Sir Charles said in apologetic tones.

"Did Miss Wilton see you murder Mr. Thomas?" Eugenia asked.

"Who?"

"Major Ward's man." You've killed a man and don't even know his name, Eugenia thought with disgust.

"I ran into her as I was returning to my room to change my shirt and vest. I was blood-splattered. Her eyes grew wide and she ran into her room. Then I heard the lock click. She must have been frightened, poor little thing."

Eugenia studied her uncle as she pictured Miss Wilton keeping silent when Eugenia questioned her. The poor little thing was probably planning to blackmail Uncle Charles once everyone could leave snowbound Ivey Manor.

"There's something else, Father," John said with anger. "We also just learned Ward spied for the French against us in the wars with Napoleon."

"There. You see," Sir Charles added.

"You may have a case for his death as a traitor, Sir Charles, but none at all for his man." The duke examined the papers and the scorched clothing. "Here is the deed to your manor. Don't put it up as collateral again." The duke held out the paper. Sir Charles snatched it out of the duke's hand and pressed it to his chest.

"It will be days before the magistrate can come here, and it is Christmas. I will put it out that you have taken ill while you remain in your room with a footman outside. Your meals will be brought to you. As soon as the way is clear, you and your family will leave here and never return. We will not know you in society."

"Not even my dear niece?"

I'm dear only when I'm useful, Eugenia thought. Aloud she said, "Not even me."

Sir Charles looked beaten. "And the magistrate?"

"Will be told all. It will be up to him to decide how to proceed. Now, go. Get out of my sight."

Sir Charles rose and bowed to the duke. Then he walked up to Eugenia. "Try not to be too hard on your uncle."

Eugenia turned her face away, biting her lower lip.

Head down, shoulders slumped, Sir Charles walked out of the room, followed by two footmen.

"Eugenia, I'm sorry you had to witness this," the duke said.

"Better that I know the truth. But you needn't worry. I won't have a fit of the vapors."

The duke looked relieved. "Very well. How are we entertaining our guests today?"

No matter her feelings on discovering her uncle was a murderer, Eugenia knew she was in training to be a duchess and the well-being and entertainment of many people depended on her. Taking a deep breath, she said, "Charades this afternoon, and dancing after supper tonight. Tomorrow I thought we could have a musical evening featuring our guests."

"Excellent. I'll tell the duchess we've determined it's safe without mentioning names. Otherwise, she'll get hysterical every time anyone so much as mentions Dawson, and that is a worse punishment than any man should have to endure. Go on. I'll write up a report for the magistrate and keep it in my safe with the evidence, just in case."

"John, do you want to give Miss Wilton her letters?" Eugenia asked, curious to see how he'd respond.

"Knowing she could fall for a blackmailer like Ward," John said with a grimace, "I've gone off Miss Wilton even more than before. Would you mind returning them, Genie?"

"I'll take charge of the duchess's letters," the duke said, putting them in his inside coat pocket.

Eugenia smiled and took her husband's arm. "Come along. Before we return Miss Wilton's letters, I shall be looking for a handsome man and a sprig of mistletoe."

"Well, you're half way there already." Adam put his arm around his wife's waist and guided her out. "And since I missed my sleep last night, I believe I'll take a nap and skip charades. Care to join me?"

"Oh, yes. A nap sounds wonderful."

Once they departed the study, giggles could be

heard echoing down the hall.

About Kate

Kate Parker grew up reading her mother's collection of mystery books by Christie, Sayers, and others. Now she can't write a story without someone being murdered, and everyday items are studied for their lethal potential. It's taken her years to convince her husband that she hasn't poisoned dinner; that funny taste is because she just can't cook. Her children have grown up to be surprisingly normal, but two of them are developing their own love of literary mayhem, so the term "normal" may have to be revised.

Living in a nineteenth century town has inspired Kate's love of history. Her Victorian Bookshop Mystery series features a single woman in Late Victorian London who, besides running a bookshop, is part of an informal detective agency known as the Archivist Society. This society solves the cases that have baffled Scotland Yard. This allows the victims and their families to find closure. The first two books in the series, *The Vanishing Thief* and *The Counterfeit Lady*, are available now at all major physical and online bookstores. The third book in the series, *The Royal Assassin*, will debut in July, 2015.

Follow Kate and her deadly examination of history

at: www.KateParkerbooks.com
and www.Facebook.com/Author.Kate.Parker/.

A Perfectly
Dreadful Christmas

by

Louisa Cornell

Chapter One

Christmas Season, 1809

FOR THE LOVE of Christmas pudding, please let the carriage be standing outside that polished oak door. All Elizabeth Sterling needed to secure a Perfectly Ordinary Christmas was their carriage at the ready and no witnesses. And the continued silence of her mother. Preferably until the end of time, but long enough to make a clean escape would do. Was it bad form to shove one's mother into the family traveling coach and shout to the driver "Spring 'em!"?

"I wish we had managed to get you married off this year, Lizzie." One dramatic pause and a sigh gusty enough to send Nelson's fleet back to Trafalgar later, Mama did the one thing Elizabeth prayed she would not do. She kept talking. "What a complete waste of a Christmas house party. Days in a carriage and all the expense."

There it was. One Perfectly Ordinary Christmas sent straight into plain Ordinary in three brief sentences. A record for her mother. At least no one was standing in the front foyer of Leistonbury Hall to hear it. Yet. In the last fortnight, Elizabeth had been forced to simper at, listen in rapt attention to, make pleasant conversation and dance with—

"Twenty-seven eligible men. Twenty-seven, and you could not bring even one of them up to scratch."

Eligible? Save her cousin, her brother, and a few of his friends, those *eligible* men either tottered around the ballroom to the accompaniment of creaking bones and rattling corsets or, in the case of one heir to a particularly wealthy viscount, appeared too young to be looking for a mistress, let alone a wife. The viscount's heir, however, proved to be one of the better dancers and had far more conversation than his fourteen years allowed.

"You smell nice, Miss Sterling. You aren't too tall and you haven't pinched my arse."

Apparently the twenty-five-year-old American heiress with whom he'd been forced to dance earlier had no qualms about seducing spotty young heirs to a viscount, especially a very wealthy one. She and Mama would get along famously.

The Earl and Countess of Leistonbury's annual Christmas house party was finally over. Their party was always well attended as their two sons were popular bachelors and the countess was inordinately fond of Christmas. The only thing Mama was fond of was throwing her daughter at any unmarried gentleman between the ages of fourteen and eighty-four. Elizabeth was grateful it had not been worse. Thus she stood the day after Twelfth Night, ready to leave and praying God, in the spirit of the season and all, would strike her mother mute before she launched into the rest of her lament.

"Lizzie, are you listening to me?" God apparently had left on holiday the day after Christmas. Fortunate fellow. "Had you spent your days with the gentlemen—"

"Hunting them down like the last Christmas goose in Christendom," Elizabeth muttered.

"Rather than entertaining that invalid girl."

"Mama!" Thank God her mother chose to insult their hosts' youngest child to an empty foyer. Where was the carriage? She'd tramp through the snow to harness the horses herself if need be. Anything to end her mother's ode to Elizabeth's impending spinsterhood.

"With your brother determined to remain in the cavalry and fight that awful Corsican he is sure to get himself killed." The aforementioned brother chose this moment to stroll into view. Unfortunately a number of his friends accompanied him. Which only caused Mama to raise the tone of her tragic soliloquy from the level of thunder to that of cannon fire.

"We shall be thrown out into the streets without a penny to our names when your horrible cousin inherits the estate. The least you can do is find a husband to take care of us after your brother leaves us alone and destitute."

Help. Elizabeth sent a fervent plea toward the cherubs cavorting on Lord Leistonbury's ceiling. A bolt of lightning or a pirate determined to kidnap a young maiden would do.

"Did I hear mention of a horrible cousin?" Christian Delacroix, Elizabeth's cousin a few times removed and a notorious flirt, tapped her nose with his forefinger. When she batted it away, he shook it in mock pain.

"Not you," Elizabeth explained. "You're the reprobate cousin."

"Really? Am I old enough to be a reprobate, Lizzie?"

"How old does one have to be?" Her brother's question elicited a ripple of laughter from his comrades.

"Far older than my tender one-and-twenty years, I am certain," their cousin announced. He gave Mama a noisy kiss to the cheek. "Not to worry, Aunt Sterling. I'll keep your boy safe. With luck, it will be years before the horrible cousin throws you into the streets."

Mama drew a handkerchief out of her sleeve and began to wail in earnest.

"Delacroix!" Elizabeth punched him on one arm.

Her brother, Michael, punched him on the other.

"Oww! That was uncalled for." Delacroix rubbed both arms vigorously.

"You're not the one who has to ride in a carriage with her all the way back to Suffolk." Elizabeth elbowed him in the side for good measure. "Reprobate cousin."

Mama pressed her handkerchief to her bosom and

conjured up a particularly pathetic sob. "This may well have been your last chance, Lizzie."

Not the last chance speech. Elizabeth fought to keep her eyes from rolling. Ladies did not roll their eyes. Ladies didn't pray for their mothers to succumb to a sudden coughing fit either, but such was her current entreaty to the Almighty.

The handkerchief fluttered dramatically before Mama trotted out the drying of the tears affect and added the final flourish to the last chance speech. "And you squandered it away with wallflowers and invalids and hiding in the library."

So much for the prayers of an ungrateful daughter. "Mama, I danced with every man here."

"Major St. Gabriel danced with you twice." The avaricious gleam in Mama's eye was frightening beyond belief. "That alone constitutes a proposal."

"He was being kind." Elizabeth gave her brother her best *Do something!* look. He and Delacroix took two steps back and pretended to admire the ceiling. They were willing to fight Napoleon but turned craven at the idea of going into battle against Mama.

"Mr. Sterling, surely you can find her a husband before you go traipsing off with Wellington and Major St. Gabriel." Mama punctuated her final plea with a storm of tears certain to send the most seasoned sailors rowing for shore.

"It is Lieutenant Sterling now, Mama," Michael reminded her in his usual long-suffering tone. "Has been for months."

Mama's cries reached a screeching crescendo envied by opera singers all over Europe.

Elizabeth closed her eyes and barely suppressed a groan. Could this day get any worse? An Ordinary Christmas was about to be shoved into the realm of Dreadful Christmas. She wrestled her portmanteau from a startled footman and headed toward the door.

"Good Lord, Mama, Lizzie is only sixteen-years-old," Michael groused. "None of my friends will have her. She still plays with dolls for pity's sake."

Silence boomed from the sparkling polish of the marble floor to the exquisitely fanciful mural overhead. Elizabeth spied Georgiana's golden hair peeking out of her portmanteau only a second before Mama did. The elegant doll was the last gift her father had given her three Christmases ago, the Christmas before he died. Mama grabbed the doll by the hair and yanked her out of the bag before Elizabeth could protest. No one moved. Hortense Sterling was nothing if not determined to see her daughter wed. She marched to the table of charity boxes set to go to Leistonbury's tenants and dropped poor Georgiana into the largest one. Elizabeth forced herself to turn away, back toward a foyer now crowded with people.

She gripped the handles of her portmanteau. Every stitch in the leather burned into her palm. Her brother opened his mouth to speak. Elizabeth raised her chin and shook her head. Then she saw him. Major Nicholas

St. Gabriel, Lord and Lady Leistonbury's second son and her brother's closest friend, stood at the top of the stairs. His blue eyes met hers. She blinked and swallowed against the burning sensation in her throat. His smile was the sort to make a girl go weak at the knees. He wasn't smiling now.

Tall, dark-haired, and desperately handsome (at least handsome enough to make her desperate), he had indeed danced with her twice at the Christmas Ball. During the quadrille he'd made her laugh for the first time since her father died. By the end of their second dance, he'd stolen her heart. He'd stolen the hearts of ladies of far better standing than Elizabeth Sterling that night. But an earl's son, even a second son, was beyond the touch of the daughter of a mere mister. Especially one who'd left his son an impoverished estate and a ledger full of debts and his daughter not even a prayer of a dowry.

Major St. Gabriel had seen and heard Mama's entire performance. Elizabeth wanted to die. As there were no lightning bolts or pirates available and God had gone on holiday, she spun on her heel and walked past Michael, past Delacroix, past Mama, past Georgiana, and away from Major St. Gabriel and the most Perfectly Dreadful Christmas of her life.

Chapter Two

Christmas Eve, 1815

A LOUD CRASH followed by a sharp, masculine cry issued from somewhere down the corridor. Elizabeth dropped the garland of holly and evergreen she'd been trimming and turned, scissors in hand, with a gasp of her own.

"There goes another footman," her fiancé offered from behind his newspaper.

"Delacroix, really." She stalked across the rich blue Aubusson carpet and snatched open the drawing room door. He remained seated in his comfortable chair before the fire and continued to read.

Elizabeth glanced at his Great Aunt Merryweather, nodding off in the chair opposite him. A battalion of falling footmen wouldn't awaken their supposed chaperone. Not that it mattered.

"Yes, really, my dear. That's the third one this morning." He tilted the corner of the news-sheet down, blinked his green eyes at her for a moment, and rattled the dashed paper back into place. Elizabeth contemplated tossing the scissors at him. However, explaining the presence of several wounded footmen to their guests would prove difficult enough. A fiancé with scissors protruding from his forehead might dampen the festivities considerably. Even if he did deserve it.

"Aren't you coming? Someone might be injured." She tapped her foot and swung the door back and forth the tiniest bit.

He folded the sheets in half and placed them on the inlaid Sheraton table before he reluctantly left his chair to join her. "From the din out there someone is most definitely injured. Are you determined to sacrifice all of my footmen to this Christmas bacchanalia or only a chosen few?" Delacroix pried the door from her hand.

Elizabeth tugged her overlong green velvet skirts from beneath his spotless Hessians and pushed past him into the corridor. "It is not a bacchanalia. They are hanging mistletoe."

"They are falling off ladders and crashing into mantelpieces. Not much mistletoe being hung at all from what I can see."

"Do hurry, Delacroix," she called over her shoulder as she headed toward the staircase. "You'll have to send for the physician if someone is badly hurt."

"I'm not the one who commissioned the construction of this mistletoe forest."

"You're not the one who'd like to be kissed just once before she steps into the parson's noose," she mumbled.

Elizabeth paused along the green and gold Persian runner to set an arrangement of hothouse roses and freshly gathered holly on the pier table to rights. Were he here, Michael would quiz her mercilessly about the abundance of holly. She'd always demanded he climb up the front of Sterling Manor to cut the best bits for her. It was the first Christmas since Waterloo, the first Christmas without the brother she loved dearly, in spite of his flaws. She took a deep breath and blinked away the sting of tears. There. The table was perfect.

She'd created every Christmas flower arrangement in Ivy House, Delacroix's country home. She'd planned every menu and every entertainment. No one was going to call her Delacroix's charity bride. Once he finally got around to marrying her, that is.

"Did you say something, Lizzie?" He stopped and offered her his arm.

"Nothing of significance." She tucked her hand through his crooked elbow and dragged him toward the first floor landing.

He was rich, a dashing blond Adonis war hero, and not remotely in love with her, but they'd known each other all their lives. He'd come to Sterling Manor with Major St. Gabriel after her brother's death at Waterloo in June. A month later he'd come to Brighton where she and Mama were living with some distant relations. The horrible cousin hadn't thrown them into the streets, but a crowded townhouse with two squabbling elderly aunts was the next thing to it, at least in Mama's eyes.

Delacroix had taken two days to assess Elizabeth's situation, proposed on bended knee, and she'd accepted. After all, as Mama so kindly put it, he was more than good enough for the likes of her.

Elizabeth wasn't in love with him either, but after a five month betrothal she'd hoped to get at least one kiss without the aid of Christmas greenery and tumbling footmen. It was the outside of enough to have to—

"Good Lord!" Elizabeth rushed to the landing and clapped her hands over her mouth to keep herself from screaming. Delacroix's last uninjured footman dangled from the chandelier two stories above the black and white marble floor of the entrance hall.

Delacroix pulled her hands away from her mouth and patted them gently before glancing back at his terrified servant. "It's not as bad as all that, Lizzie," he assured her. "At least he hasn't fallen."

"Oooh!" Elizabeth tugged her hands free, picked up her skirts, and rushed down the stairs. Once she reached the bottom, she had to push past several gawking maids to get a clear view of the mistletoe's latest victim. Every servant in the house appeared to have crowded into the hall to see their future mistress's latest catastrophe. Lovely.

"What is the meaning of this?" Delacroix's butler, Shepherds' quiet rifle-shot of a voice cut through the crowd and sent the entire staff — save the most stalwart footmen — scattering for the safety of their assigned tasks. Elizabeth often thought had they let

Shepherds talk to Napoleon, he'd have trotted himself off to Elba and stayed there. Having grown up with Mama, Elizabeth was immune, but she did appreciate the butler's ability to clear a room.

"John's had a bit of an accident, Mr. Shepherds," a footman with a cut lip offered as he nodded toward the ceiling.

"It's only an accident if he falls." Delacroix tried to run his hand along the banister as he descended the stairs, but Elizabeth's precisely twined fir garland got in his way. "I hope no one needs the aid of this during their stay with us, my dear."

"We haven't invited anyone elderly or infirm, Delacroix. Shepherds, where is the ladder? We must get this poor man down."

"We are accumulating the infirm at a startling rate, are we not, Shepherds?"

The butler was wise enough not to answer his master's question. He did, however, point to a mangle of broken wood and gave Elizabeth a disapproving *harumpf* before he said, "I believe these are the remains of the last of the ladders, Miss Sterling."

With a curt nod, Shepherds moved to investigate a commotion at the door. Cold wind swept into the hall and swirled around Elizabeth's skirts. An ominous crack drew her attention to the endangered footman. The chandelier swayed slightly. Elizabeth stepped directly beneath it. She doubted her ability to catch the man if he fell, but she wanted to give the appearance of competence.

"Try to keep still, John." What a ridiculous thing for her to say. To be sure, ladies did not receive nearly enough instruction on how to deal with hanging footmen. The man who would one day (the Almighty only knew when) be her husband stood with his arms folded across his chest, and appeared to ponder the bottoms of the footman's shoes. "You are a seasoned cavalry officer, Delacroix. Do something."

"He could let go. The floor will break his fall."

This elicited an *eep* of dismay from the footman dangling from the chandelier.

"Sacrificing a footman to the Lord of Misrule, Delacroix?"

The voice, singular and rough, set Elizabeth's heart to a slow, steady thump. She turned to find Major Nicholas St. Gabriel, brow furrowed, assessing the beleaguered footman's situation. And then the major looked at her.

"Elizabeth."

One word and the world became a small, light place. December breathed icy air and eddies of snow from the open door, but for Elizabeth it was late June and Nicholas had come home. Foolish, foolish girl.

"You're looking well," he murmured.

She certainly hoped she did. Those eyes, the color of a summer sky, had fixed on her face and never moved. He had a way of sending her to a place where she was the most important person in the room. She had experienced the sensation a scant few times, and never, save in his presence.

"If you're going to hang the help, *Little General*," another familiar voice drawled, "it is customary to use a rope." Only one person dared use that ridiculous nickname in her presence. A brief pause to stamp his feet against the cold and Lord Alexander Chastleton, Marquess of Winterbourne, swept Elizabeth into a short spin. "Shall I bring Nero in and try to rescue the poor fellow before he suffers more of Delacroix's help?"

"You will not bring that behemoth of a horse into this house, Lord Winterbourne." She pushed him away and smiled in spite of herself. Thank God for Winterbourne's entrance. He'd saved her from making a cake of herself before the major and the man she was to marry. Not to mention the remaining servants.

Decisive. She would be the decisive future mistress of this house. "No thank you, my lord. This has gone on long enough." She stormed along the corridor to the downstairs dining room, well aware of three sets of bemused masculine eyes boring into her spine until she reached the dining room and stepped inside. In one fluid motion, she whisked the large silk tablecloth from the table and returned to the befuddled and quite useless men.

She slapped a corner of the cloth into Winterbourne's hand. "Your Astley's circus antics were only good when my late brother wished to escape a tryst in a certain widow's first floor parlor."

"How did she know about that?" Winterbourne looked from the corner of silk in his hand to each of his friends' equally astonished faces. "I didn't tell her. Did you?"

"I didn't tell her," Delacroix declared. He took the corner she handed him and backed up to stretch the cloth beneath the footman. "And Sterling would never."

She had not seen Nicholas smile since his father's death from consumption over a year ago. His elder brother was lost five months later to the same smallpox outbreak that took their sister, Estelle, Elizabeth's dearest friend. Nicholas had managed to make it home for his father's funeral, but not for his siblings'. He was now the Earl of Leistonbury. He had no cause to smile.

Yet when she placed the third corner of the tablecloth in his long, strong fingers, the left side of his mouth lifted briefly and for a moment he was the young cavalry officer with whom she had danced at sixteen. The whisper of his fingertips across her knuckles sent her stomach into an odd pirouette.

"I fear Sterling told her about more than the Astley's circus trick." Nicholas looked at Winterbourne and Delacroix meaningfully.

Elizabeth turned the final corner of the silk tablecloth over to the sturdiest of the footmen loitering about at the bottom of the stairs. She grabbed his elbow and backed him up until the large white square was suspended beneath the now moaning footman. "My brother might have mentioned the use of a tablecloth in abetting Lord Winterbourne's escape from a married lady's bedchamber." She checked their positions one last time. "You can let go now, John."

"Beg pardon, miss?" Overhead the footman's voice jumped at least an octave.

"Let go. It's perfectly safe. They'll catch you." She smothered a smirk. "Mr. Delacroix and his friends are more than adept at this. Let go. We have other guests arriving soon. I should hate for you to fall on one of them."

"Yes, miss," came the weak reply. "Letting go now."

In spite of her assurances, Elizabeth closed her eyes until she heard the bounce of the silk cloth and the shouts of "Huzzah!" which signaled a safe conclusion to this latest domestic crisis. When she dared to look, Delacroix and his friends were shaking hands and exchanging good natured back thumps whilst John Footman, surrounded by his fellows, submitted to Shepherds' admonitions as to the correct way to ascertain a ladder's sturdiness.

"Well done, John. Are you fit to continue your duties?" Elizabeth gathered the tablecloth into a ball and handed it off to one of the maids who'd peeked round the corner to see the goings on.

"Yes, miss. Thank you, miss." He gave her a bow and went off toward the back of the house with the rest of his fellow servants. "Dead clever is that Miss Sterling," he told Shepherds as they disappeared from view. "I'd have never thought of using table linens for such."

"Dead clever indeed," rumbled behind her.

Elizabeth started at Nicholas's nearness and the ripple of awareness his words tripped across her shoulders. She put on her best hostess's smile and turned to answer him. Halfway through her curtsy she noticed something alarming.

"Major St. Gabriel, you are covered in snow." She allowed her eyes to follow the white flakes sprinkled abundantly over his ebony hair, the shoulders of his greatcoat, and on his boots. When she looked at Lord Winterbourne the result was the same. And a great deal of white, melting, dirty matter covered the heretofore pristine floor. "Why are you both covered in snow?"

"He is Leistonbury now, Lizzie," Delacroix reminded her gently.

Nicholas's brow creased in a brief scowl. "She may call me whatever she pleases."

Elizabeth squeezed his arm. "I shall hold you to that, sir."

"Will you call me whatever you please, *General?*" Winterbourne asked with a wink.

"I frequently do, my lord," Elizabeth shot back. Bless him for realizing what Delacroix did not. Nicholas's title was too new. He didn't care to hear it nor dwell on it. It reminded him of all he'd lost. "And none of this changes the fact you two have all the appearance of a pair of Scots come down from the Highlands. Why is that, gentlemen?"

Before they could answer, she stamped to the front

door and opened it wide enough to see and feel the makings of an impressive snowstorm. She turned on the two new arrivals.

"How long has it been snowing?"

"Calm down, *General*. This is England. We've had snow before, frequently at Christmas." Winterbourne nudged Delacroix and soon they were both grinning at her like idiots.

"It never snows here at Christmas." Oh this was a disaster. Not as disastrous as Nicholas accepting the invitation to this house party, but nearly so. "This is impossible. I didn't plan for snow." She fished the little leather bound book from her pocket and plucked the gold pencil from between its pages.

A mistake, for in a thrice Winterbourne had it in his hand and was thumbing through its contents. "She's right, you know. There is not a word here about snow."

"Give me that, you fiend." Forgetting her dignity, she chased after him and tried to rescue her book.

"Perhaps you should have shown God your plans, my dear. I'm certain had He realized your plans for the weather, He would have changed His."

"Delacroix, do shut up and make this infant return my book."

"Infant?" Winterbourne held the book over her head. "One does not refer to a duke's only son and heir as an infant."

Nicholas (Why did her mind insist on calling him Nicholas?) limped up behind him and deftly removed the volume from a shocked Winterbourne. He then offered it to Elizabeth with a careful bow. "One does if the duke's heir is behaving like a schoolboy. Leave the lady alone."

She'd forgotten. In all of the falderal with the imperiled footman and the teasing about their adventures before the war, she'd forgotten the injuries that had nearly killed him at Waterloo. She saw neither the twisted leg nor the jagged scar etched from behind his left ear to the dimple in his chin. Perhaps because in all the years she'd known him, he'd never been less than perfect in her eyes. Somewhere inside the betrothed woman, the sixteen-year-old girl still dreamt of what never stood the slightest chance at all.

"Well, now that the *Little General* has her battle plan," Winterbourne said as he shook the last of the snow from his guinea gold hair, "pray tell us all about this Perfect Christmas we are to be treated to, Delacroix."

Chapter Three

NICHOLAS EXCHANGED A LOOK with Delacroix. Winterbourne had ever been the joker of their group. Not even the worst of war's ugliness dampened his spirits. A façade to be sure. The three of them had survived. Sterling had not. And each of them had traded swords for façades. Soldiers armed themselves for all of life's battles. The made-wise-by-life scrutiny of a slip of a woman of two-and-twenty who had known them all their lives was a definite call to arms.

Elizabeth gazed at the group's scoundrel with obvious exasperation before she turned to Nicholas. In the grey mists of her eyes he saw her brother, and the pain of what Sterling's death meant squeezed his chest without mercy.

"A Perfect Christmas? With you three in residence?" She stretched up to brush the snow from his shoulders. Her hair smelled of jasmine and roses. Nicholas drew it into his lungs and held it to keep himself from holding her. Elizabeth touched her hand to his chest and handed his great coat to the butler before she turned back to Winterbourne and Delacroix. "A Perfectly Ordinary

Christmas is what I said and I will settle for no less."

"She has a list," Delacroix said with his usual tone of comic solemnity.

"Does she, indeed?" Nicholas teased. He was rewarded with the militant tilt of Elizabeth's chin he so admired. Her eyes flashed silver-grey daggers, but the nearly imperceptible twitch of her lips gave her away. No man would ever get the best of her. Good.

"Christmases, gentlemen, in my two-and-twenty years, have fallen into five sorts—Perfect, Perfectly Ordinary, Ordinary, Dreadful, and Perfectly Dreadful," she informed them.

"What, pray tell us, constitutes a Perfectly Ordinary Christmas?" Winterbourne tossed his coat to a footman with a black eye.

"A few minor episodes with burnt or undercooked food, no more than three arguments between Mrs. Holly and Shepherds, and perhaps a smattering of snow." She ticked them off the fingers of her left hand and tucked her right beneath Nicholas's arm. Across the marble floor made slick by the snow he and Winterbourne had tracked in, Nicholas matched his uneven steps to her dainty ones, just as she intended. They followed the others up the stairs at neither more nor less than the right pace. Slow enough to accommodate his nearly useless leg, but not so slowly as to acknowledge anything had changed. Had the others even noticed? He did. He noticed everything about her. Five minutes back in her life and nothing had changed. For him.

"Sounds deadly dull to me. I like a bit more excitement with my Christmas goose." Winterbourne sauntered through the drawing room door held open by another footman, this one with a nasty gash on his forehead.

"You and your excitement turned an Ordinary Christmas into a Dreadful Christmas last year, my lord." Elizabeth lowered herself gracefully onto the plump sofa nearest the fire and patted the seat beside her. Nicholas's body obeyed. His mind refused to keep quiet. *She is not for you, Nicholas. She is not for you.*

"Me?" Winterbourne adopted an attitude of affronted martyrdom even as he plundered the ornate sideboard for a bottle of brandy and glasses.

"I think she means your little tryst in the conservatory." Delacroix waved off the man's offer of a drink. "You remember. Screaming? Pistols? A small fire?"

"These things are expected at house parties." Winterbourne didn't ask Nicholas, simply handed him a glass and splashed a generous dose of brandy in it. With one booted ankle crossed over the other, he propped an elbow on the mantel and raised his own glass to Elizabeth.

"She was the vicar's wife, Alex!" Use of one's given name indicated the *Little General* was in high dudgeon.

Winterbourne being Winterbourne ignored it. "Well, it *was* Christmas."

Elizabeth laughed softly—a rich, sultry sound so

very different from the petite, proper lady she presented to the world. Nicholas watched in silent amusement as she took Winterbourne to task for his cavalier exploits with women. She'd directed Nicholas to the seat closest to the fire. He was grateful, but not surprised. The warmth stole into his aching bones and dulled the constant reminder of all he'd lost at Waterloo.

Shepherds arrived bearing a large tea tray, which he placed on the low table next to Elizabeth. "Will there be anything else, miss?"

"This is lovely, Shepherds. Offer Cook my thanks." She lifted the teapot, but stopped before she poured. "I am concerned about the snow."

"Yes, miss. I am not certain it is within my power to stop it, but if you have a suggestion, I am more than willing to try." The man's face moved not a muscle.

Delacroix succumbed to a coughing fit. Winterbourne choked on his brandy. Nicholas only had eyes for Elizabeth. She tilted her head up and curled her lips into a smile of terrifying innocence.

"And here I thought you could do anything," she said sweetly. "No matter. Send one of the grooms to check the roads from the village. We should make certain they are clear for our other guests who will be arriving tomorrow."

Delacroix took the cup of tea Elizabeth offered him and raised it in salute as Shepherds closed the door behind him. He and Winterbourne fell on the cakes and tarts on the tea tray like starving infantrymen after a week's forced march.

"Well done, Miss Sterling." Nicholas accepted the dainty plate she offered him and again she laughed.

"Shepherds doesn't quite know what to do with me. There hasn't been a lady of the house since Delacroix's mother died. I've only been here a fortnight, but it has been a very trying fortnight for him, poor dear."

He broke off a piece of warm apple spice cake and glanced at the elderly lady huddled in the commodious chair across the room. "What about Aunt Merryweather?"

"What about her?" Elizabeth placed a lemon tart on his plate.

They watched Delacroix's only living relative for a moment or two. Or three. At least he thought she was living. Nothing. "She is well?" Nicholas asked. "Isn't she?"

The old dear startled awake and began to work furiously at the bundle of knitting in her lap. After half a row, she nodded off again and began to snore, none too softly. Nicholas turned in time to see Elizabeth smother another of those dusky, all too alluring laughs.

"She is exceedingly well, my lord. But no match for Shepherds."

"Don't." God, he hadn't meant to snap. *My lord.* The words pounded hour by hour against the battlements he'd built against his grief. Her voice gave those words power, made being the earl real. And the battlements threatened to crumble.

"You must accustom yourself to it sometime, Nicholas." Her soft voice, in words meant for his ears alone, chided and soothed. It was her gift, one of many.

"Not now. Not by you." Was it strength or weakness to beg the understanding of the one person who never failed to give it?

"I'm sorry." She covered his hand with hers. "It's been seven months since you lost your brother. I just thought..." Her eyes met his. He wrapped his fingers around hers and held tight. His world had been in an ever-increasing spin for over a year. The war had held it at bay until Waterloo, a macabre solace against wars he could not fight at home. And now the touch of his friend's betrothed proved the only power to stop the whirl in its tracks. He should not have come.

"How is your mother?" With her free hand, she'd prepared a cup of tea exactly as he preferred it.

He let go of her fingers one by one, took the cup, and let the flavor and heat of it remind him he was in England again. He was home. When he opened his eyes, Elizabeth was studying his face even as she smiled at Delacroix and Winterbourne's squabbles over the teacakes.

"Mama is well. She sends her regards." He took another sip of his tea. "She is in London with her sisters. With everyone gone, she isn't ready to spend Christmas at the Hall. Neither was I."

"Then I am pleased you have come to us for

Christmas." She spoke with her usual sparkling sincerity, but he did not miss the little catch in her voice nor a flash of uncertainty in her gaze.

Us. Elizabeth and Delacroix. His appetite for spice cake and lemon tarts fled.

"What about me, *General*?" Winterbourne reached for a lemon tart and earned a swat from the lady for his efforts. He scooped up the last gooseberry tart instead. "Are you happy I am come for Christmas?"

"I am." She handed him a plate to catch the crumbs he was scattering over Delacroix's expensive carpets. "I am amazed Major St. Gabriel was able to drag you away from the delights of London at this time of year."

Delacroix raised an eyebrow at her avoidance of Nicholas's title. Nicholas answered with a raised eyebrow of his own.

"The delights became a bit too delightful." Winterbourne stuffed the entire gooseberry tart in his mouth and returned to the sideboard for more brandy.

"His father was in town." Nicholas finished his tea and moved his bad leg closer to the fire.

"Ah." Elizabeth looked from Winterbourne to Nicholas expectantly.

"As were three ladies of his acquaintance."

"Three of my former mistresses." Winterbourne crossed the room to perch on the arm of the sofa next to Elizabeth.

"Don't speak of mistresses in front of Lizzie." Delacroix warned. "She is a lady."

"I learned the meaning of the word listening to you three and my brother playing at cards when I was twelve years old, Delacroix." She leaned forward to refill Nicholas's cup of tea. Three small chestnut curls caressed the back of her neck. Were they as soft as they appeared? "And I am a gentlewoman, not a lady."

"Is there a difference?" Nicholas asked.

"Yes. Gentlewomen have more fun." The mischievous young girl they'd caught hiding in the window seat of the billiards room all those years ago peered at him from the beautiful woman's face.

Winterbourne snorted. "I don't know about that, but avoiding a devil incarnate father and three women one has bid a not-so-fond adieu can be dashed trying on a man with a constitution as delicate as mine."

"Delicate constitution." Delacroix rolled his eyes. "Tell that to the French."

"You look none the worse for wear." Elizabeth observed.

She had taken all their measures years ago. *Dead clever is that Miss Sterling.* She was indeed.

"You are ever kindness itself, Fair Elizabeth," Winterbourne said with an overdramatic sigh.

"Then again, you have had that just-leapt-from-the-wrong-bed-in-the-nick-of-time look as long as I have known you."

Winterbourne chuckled. "Have you made no effort to dull that sharp tongue of hers, Delacroix?"

"I simply try to stay out of striking distance."

"How sharper than a serpent's tooth it is to wed a shrewish woman."

"Try not to mangle Shakespeare and insult my future wife in the same hour, Lieutenant."

"As you command, Captain." Winterbourne took possession of Elizabeth's hand and raised it to his lips. "My apologies, *General.*"

Elizabeth pulled her hand free and gave Winterbourne a shove.

Nicholas had accepted Delacroix's invitation for this. Less than one hour in her company and Elizabeth had drawn them back to a time before wars abroad and losses at home had left the three of them living hollow lives in dark places. She had a gift for reminding them of the young men they'd been, and now that gift would be Delacroix's forever. The comfort that had begun to seep into the cold room where Nicholas kept his heart retreated and something inside him shivered. It was time to put an end to this. Delacroix needed to marry Elizabeth. Soon.

"When are you to marry?"

Well that certainly had all the subtlety of a cavalry charge. Delacroix had the expression of the last fox of hunting season. Winterbourne merely raised an eyebrow and downed his drink. Even Aunt Merryweather bestirred herself long enough to knit a few rows. Elizabeth, however.... Elizabeth snuffed out the candle of her smile in an instant. Damn.

"Sir." Shepherds stood in the door as stone-faced as

ever. Something Nicholas had never seen in Delacroix's butler lurked in the man's eyes. Panic. Panicked or not, his entrance could not have come at a more fortuitous moment.

"Yes, Shepherds." Delacroix threw Nicholas a furious glare. "What is it?"

"There is a small situation in the kitchens, sir."

"Oh for pity's sake." Elizabeth flounced to her feet. "What is it now?"

"I really think the master would be better—"

"The master couldn't handle a footman dangling from the chandelier, and he has guests." She spared neither Nicholas, Winterbourne, nor Delacroix a backward glance. "I will take care of this, Shepherds." She motioned him into the corridor ahead of her. "The rumor is I will be the mistress of this house one day." She grasped the door. "Eventually," she fired back into the room before slamming the door shut behind her.

Nicholas and Delacroix shot to their feet.

"Why haven't you married her?"

"You don't have to do this, Leistonbury."

Their words clanged like crossed sabers. They stood breathing at each other.

Winterbourne strolled between them and gave them both a shove. "Give over." For a man who wanted nothing to do with his father's dukedom, he played the arrogant arse exceedingly well when it suited him. "Sit down. The both of you." He collapsed onto the sofa Elizabeth had vacated and took a noisy pull from the brandy bottle. "It's going to be a long damned Christmas."

Winterbourne was right. And a long Christmas with Elizabeth Sterling was the last thing Nicholas needed.

Chapter Four

ELIZABETH WOUND HER WAY through the corridors of Ivy House toward the kitchens with a slightly winded Shepherds close on her heels. Her Christmas house party not yet underway, and already she contemplated disposing of Delacroix, his high-in-the-instep butler, and the unfathomable Major Nicholas St. Gabriel, sometimes Earl of Leistonbury. The butler and Delacroix she might get away with, but when earls went missing, even reluctant ones, people generally looked for them. Prinny misplaced a great deal of money, but he hardly ever misplaced a peer.

"Miss Sterling, I really think—" the butler huffed as he caught up to her.

Christmas pudding! She turned so sharply the man nearly plowed her over. "What do you think, Shepherds?"

The lump in his throat bobbed like an India rubber ball. "It would be better if Mr. Delacroix saw to this particular problem." He adjusted his waistcoat and inclined his head.

"No." She spun on her heel and continued her

march to the back of the house.

What on earth had possessed her to agree to include Nicholas on the guest list? Winterbourne was bad enough. None of the female guests would be safe from his long, lean, devilish good looks and horrid reputation. It was all Delacroix's fault.

No, it wasn't his fault.

She started down the back staircase. The butler, dash him, continued to follow.

Elizabeth had deliberately invited the handsome major. Her plan was to prove to herself once and for all her silly girlhood crush was exactly that—childish, outgrown, and done. She would exorcise him from her mind and thus leave room to fall in love with the man she was to marry—a brilliant plan worthy of Wellington himself. It really was unconscionable of her heart to put up a white flag the minute Nicholas said her name.

She skidded to a stop at the door to the kitchens and took a deep breath. Whatever the problem, she'd dispatch it efficiently and worry about her cowardly heart later. Especially as Nicholas wanted nothing more than to see her married to his friend posthaste.

Shepherds stepped around and pushed the door open for her. Everything appeared to be in order. Cook and the kitchen maids busied themselves with dinner preparations. Delicious smells wafted toward her from the stove and the two ovens. The polished wood floor was spotless. In the pantry, a number of Christmas puddings rested under their cloth covers.

"Ahem." Mrs. Holly, Delacroix's cheery housekeeper, drew Elizabeth's attention to the fireplace stretched across one entire side of the kitchen. On the bench before the hearth, a snow-covered figure huddled beneath a long black hooded cape. At the figure's feet lay a huge, wooly creature—a large dog or a small horse. Elizabeth didn't dare guess.

"Hello," Elizabeth said and laid her hand on the visitor's shoulder. "Can I ask your name?"

"This person claims to be expected." If there was a school of elocution for superior sounding butlers, Shepherds had to have taken a first.

A pair of thin hands in threadbare gloves slowly came up to push the hood away. The woman, pale and obviously weary, peered up at Elizabeth, her face not young, but perhaps not yet forty. "As I told this stiff-rumped toad," she said, her voice barely a whisper, "my name is Miss Mary Tidings. I was supposed to wait at the inn for a gentleman visiting this house to meet me."

"Then why are you here, madam?"

Elizabeth and Mrs. Holly waved Shepherds to silence, a definite affront to his dignity judging from the *harumpf* they received in reply. The grey, wooly beast lurched to its feet and growled at the butler. Elizabeth resisted the urge to encourage the animal. Barely.

"A party of squabbling matrons, screeching debutantes, and drunken toffs arrived an hour before I did, and they have taken all of the rooms. The innkeeper gave me the loan of a sturdy donkey and cart. I had nowhere else to go." Miss Tidings's voice ebbed to a rasped breath. She struggled to her feet and swayed slightly. Her cape slid to the floor.

"Oh. Oh, I see." Elizabeth did indeed see. Beneath a serviceable blue wool gown *Miss* Tidings was, in keeping with the season, great with child. Very. Great. With child. She was also thin and none too steady on her feet. "Please sit, Miss Tidings." She took the woman's elbow and guided her back onto the bench.

"Thank you," she whispered. "I have been traveling for days. I'm very tired."

"Cook, might we have a cup of tea and some of your excellent fresh bread?"

Built like a barrel, with a round face and greyish red curls escaping her white cap in all directions, Cook muttered something no doubt rude and unrepeatable in Gaelic, but she did as Elizabeth asked. Mrs. Holly gave their bedraggled visitor a pitying look and sent one of the maids for a blanket.

"I did try to tell you, miss."

Elizabeth turned on the butler with a vengeance. "You said a small situation, Shepherds," she hissed softly. "This is not a small situation." She gestured in the direction of Miss Tidings. "There is nothing small about this. One of the gentlemen invited to my house party has left this poor woman in a family way. Do you have any idea what a catastrophe this is?"

He nearly smiled. Not even gentlewomen were allowed to smack a butler. "Shall I fetch Mr. Delacroix?"

She grabbed his arm. "You most certainly will not."
Oh dear Lord, what was she to do? A quick search of the
servants' faces offered no help at all. Being the almost
mistress of the house was not as she pictured it. Calm.
She would remain calm. And at some point she would
get even with the butler, but not now. She gathered the
servants away from the woman hungrily devouring a
large slice of hot buttered bread.

"Mrs. Holly, when Miss Tidings has finished her tea,
please make her comfortable in the rose bedchamber
across from mine."

"Yes, miss." The housekeeper gave Shepherds an
arch look.

"Miss Sterling," he started.

"Shepherds, you will send for a groom to take care
of the innkeeper's donkey and cart."

"I see." He sniffed and flicked a bit of flour from his
sleeve.

Elizabeth slowly met the eyes of each servant—Mrs.
Holly, Cook, the two maids, and finally Shepherds.
"None of you is to say a word about this to anyone,
understood? Not even Mr. Delacroix."

They all nodded in wide-eyed agreement. Save
Shepherds, who *harumpfed*. Again.

Elizabeth stepped in front of him, narrowed her
eyes, and planted her hands on her hips. "In addition to
a number of perfectly lovely people and Mr. Delacroix's
two closest friends, I have invited his Merryweather
cousins to this runaway carriage of a house party,

Shepherds. Do you know what that means?"

"Mrs. John Merryweather." His horrified tone sent a shiver through every servant in the room. Even Mrs. Holly pulled her shawl more tightly around her shoulders.

"Exactly. The worst gossip between here and Bombay is coming to this house with her three eligible—"

"Spoiled," Cook muttered.

"Snooty," whispered the scullery maid.

"Sneaky daughters," Elizabeth finished. "Is Miss Tidings' condition and the fact one of our gentlemen guests might be responsible something you want printed in every scandal rag in London and posted in every letter on every ship the East India Trading Company owns?"

Silence. Some things spoke for themselves— Napoleon's tyranny, Prinny's weight, Wellington's cleverness, and Mrs. John Merryweather's penchant for ruinous gossip.

A loud crash and a few shouts sounded from the room above them—the dining room.

"What now?" Elizabeth groaned. "I'll see to it. Remember, not a word. Now go."

They scattered to do as she asked, even Shepherds. She knew his obedience was temporary. God only knew what mischief he'd get up to once she was out of sight. She had enough worries.

An *enceinte* woman, a giant hairy dog, a notorious

rake, a reluctant bridegroom, falling footmen, a snowstorm, the eminent arrival of England's worst gossip, and a fortnight trapped in a house with a man she had to drive from her heart at all costs. A Perfectly Ordinary Christmas? What was she thinking? She picked up her skirts and ran toward the noises in the dining room.

"What the devil was that?" Winterbourne sat up on the sofa and shoved the now empty brandy bottle they'd shared onto the tea table.

"Probably another footman." Delacroix leaned back in his chair and propped one booted ankle on his knee. "Leistonbury, my marriage plans are not a matter for discussion."

"And mine are?" Nicholas had been arguing with these two mother hens since Elizabeth had routed the usually unflappable Shepherds from the room. If ever there was a lady capable of rolling a condescending butler up foot, horse, and guns, Michael Sterling's beautiful and wickedly intelligent sister was the lady to do so. He didn't care what she said. Elizabeth was every inch a lady. She simply wasn't his lady. Delacroix knew nothing of the treasure he'd won.

"Are you listening to me, Leistonbury?" Delacroix waved a lazy hand at him.

"I'm trying not to, actually." Nicholas moved slowly to the hearth and propped his bad leg to catch the heat.

"Doing a damned find job of it too," Winterbourne

pointed out.

"You're not helping, Winterbourne." Delacroix observed.

"Was I meant to?"

"I appreciate your concern, gentlemen." Nicholas used his best commanding officer voice. It hardly ever worked with these two, but there was always a chance it might. "We all know I must marry Miss Tidings, and why I must do it. There is nothing more to be said."

"Very well. There is nothing more to be said about when I intend to marry Lizzie. Agreed?"

The door opened quietly to reveal an oddly flustered Shepherds.

"What is it now, man? Has she taken out another footman?"

"No, sir. Miss Sterling is seeing to the matter in the dining room. There is another problem in the kitchen, sir." Something in his tone made the hair on the back of Nicholas's neck stand up.

"What is the nature of this problem?" he asked. Delacroix and Winterbourne must have heard it as well. They got to their feet and gave the butler their full attention.

"A Miss Mary Tidings has arrived, milords. And I am afraid she has fainted."

"Here?" Delacroix shouted. "Miss Tidings is here?"

The butler was wise enough to stand clear of the door as the three of them made a mad dash for the kitchen. In spite of his bad leg, Nicholas stumbled into the room first. The sight of three gentlemen in a state of panic incited Mrs. Holly to send Delacroix's cook and the maids scurrying around the corner into the scullery.

Crumpled on the floor lay the late Sergeant Tidings's only daughter. Nicholas stared at Miss Tidings's monumental belly in disbelief. The three men struggled to lift her onto a bench before the fire.

Winterbourne pulled the blanket from around her and began to rub her hands. "What happened, Mrs. Holly?"

"She fainted, my lord. She drove here through the storm from the village in the innkeeper's cart."

When Nicholas finally brought himself to look up, it was to see Delacroix's housekeeper looking daggers at the butler. Why were they upset? This catastrophe wasn't happening to them. Elizabeth could not find out about this.

"Winterbourne, what is she doing here?" Delacroix demanded.

"She needs to be resting in a bed." Mrs. Holly turned her daggered scowl on each of them in turn.

"Never mind that," Nicholas snapped. "What is she doing here like... like... that?"

"I told you she was in an interesting condition." Winterbourne tucked the blanket back around her. "Wasn't that the point of the little bargain you and Delacroix made?"

"Not that interesting," Nicholas snapped.

Mrs. Holly cleared her throat. "My lords, if I may."

Nicholas restrained the urge to strangle Delacroix's housekeeper. Barely. Why did the woman keep interrupting? Didn't she recognize a full-scale disaster when she saw one? This was Winterbourne's fault. "You told her to come *here*?"

"Of course not." Winterbourne had the nerve to sound affronted. "Told her to put up at the inn in the village. Said you'd meet her there in a few days."

Nicholas tucked one arm under the young woman's knees, wrapped the other around her back, and got to his feet. "Then why is she here?"

"There was no room at the inn?" Winterbourne quipped with an imbecilic grin.

"I'm going to kill you." Nicholas said through gritted teeth. His leg fairly screeched in protest. "Delacroix, I'm going to kill him." How he managed to survive the war with these two under his command defied belief.

"If Lizzie finds out she'll kill all of us." Delacroix leaned a hip against the nearest kitchen table and put his head in his hands.

"Is the fair Elizabeth not to know?" Winterbourne had a habit of asking the most ridiculous questions at the most inopportune moments.

"No!" Nicholas and Delacroix said at once.

Winterbourne cut himself a slice of bread and dragged it through a dish of butter. "I see."

Nicholas hefted his burden against his chest. "We have to get her out of sight before Elizabeth sees her."

"Actually, my lord—" The housekeeper raised her

forefinger.

"He's right, Mrs. Holly." Delacroix snatched the bread from Winterbourne's hand and steered him toward the back staircase. "We'll put her in the Chinese bedchamber. It's in the east wing, but at the opposite end from Lizzie's. She has no need to go down there. The other guests will be in the west wing."

"The Chinese bedchamber, sir?" Mrs. Holly glanced at the butler.

Shepherds shrugged. Nicholas had not thought the man knew how to shrug. It didn't matter. All he wanted to do was get Mary Tidings tucked away somewhere before Elizabeth saw her.

"Do you want me to take her?" Delacroix asked as they started up the stairs.

"No. Lead the way. Winterbourne, you bring up the rear. If I fall I want to be certain to take you with me."

Mary Tidings head lolled over his arm. She emitted a snort and began to snore.

"I don't envy you sleeping with that racket for the next forty years," Winterbourne mused.

"I didn't say I'd sleep with her. I said I'd marry her." Nicholas's muscles began to quiver from the effort, but he refused to ask for help.

"Isn't that rather like buying the cow and letting the milk go sour?"

"Delacroix, has he always been this thick?"

"Yes," Delacroix replied as they reached the door which opened onto the wide, thickly carpeted east wing corridor. "We were too drunk to notice when we were at school and too busy not getting killed to notice during the war."

Thank goodness the footmen had survived the latest decorating disaster with only a few scratches. Elizabeth made a note in her little book to check all fir garlands for vermin before they came into the house. Three young men and one small squirrel did not make for a happy combination in a dining room full of fine china. Delacroix wouldn't miss a soup tureen or three.

She hurried into the kitchen only to find it empty save for Mrs. Holly and Shepherds in the midst of a hushed argument. They fell into immediate silence. Elizabeth started to remark on it when she saw the now empty bench before the hearth.

"Where is Miss Tidings?"

"She—"

"They—"

Butler and housekeeper stopped and looked at each other. Guiltily. Before Elizabeth might question them further, one of the maids came down the back staircase. She carried an empty tray. Thank goodness.

"She is upstairs." Elizabeth allowed relief to sigh through her body. Finally something had gone right.

The maid bobbed a curtsey and nodded. "Yes, miss."

"Did she eat?"

"Yes, miss. She's sleeping now."

"Thank you for taking care of her, Mrs. Holly. We'll

sort this out once the house party is over and our guests have left."

The housekeeper gave her a weak smile and glanced at Shepherds. How odd. Elizabeth had encountered Delacroix, Winterbourne, and Nicholas on the front stairs and their behavior had been odd as well. Odd even for them.

She gave the servants a final nod and started out of the kitchen.

"Christmas 'ere is wondrous excitin'," the young maid exclaimed.

"You have no idea," Elizabeth muttered. "No idea at all."

Chapter Five

ELIZABETH GENTLY PULLED the door closed. Miss Tidings was tucked up for the night. More importantly, she had agreed to stay confined to her room for the duration of the house party. She'd agreed so readily, in fact, Elizabeth was certain the woman had more secrets than a badly timed *situation*, as Shepherds so delicately phrased it. She wasn't the only one.

As she padded up the corridor toward her own bedchamber, Elizabeth called the evening's somewhat subdued dinner to mind. She'd shared many meals with these three gentlemen. Their families' estates were less than half a day's ride from each other and not far from Sterling Manor. Winterbourne, Delacroix, and Nicholas had attended school with her brother, and they'd often dined at Sterling Manor during holidays from school. Suffice it to say, meals in the company of her brother and his three closest friends had been described in many ways. Quiet had not been one of them.

As it was Christmas Eve, tonight's menu was replete with each man's favorite dishes. Indeed, they'd eaten heartily. They'd complimented Elizabeth and Cook with exuberant sincerity. And said little else. The teasing and insults of the afternoon had disappeared. Even Winterbourne chose his words with care, to be sure one of the signs of the Apocalypse. And Elizabeth knew why.

Marriage. The one topic guaranteed to turn His Majesty's finest officers into mute, coughing ninnies had been broached before she fled the room to deal with Miss Tidings. Apparently the conversation after she left had been frightening enough to turn three of the bravest men she knew into wallflower debutantes, stammering their way through such scintillating subjects as the weather, the quality of the mince pies, and the relative warmth of coal versus wood fires. She'd almost wished a footman would crash through the ceiling to give them a more entertaining subject on which to converse. When she rose to leave them to their port, they'd nearly pushed her out of the room.

She mused on it for hours. They'd decided to manage her. Misplaced loyalty to her dead brother had them feuding over her like a stray dog they'd taken to feeding at some tavern. Her slippers slapped a brisk tattoo against the burgundy Aubusson carpet. Her hands folded into tight fists at her sides. "I'll be dashed if I need Lord Winterbourne and Major Nicholas St. Gabriel to drag Delacroix to the altar like a felled deer. I am perfectly capable of—*umpf*!"

Elizabeth had turned the corner and run into a solid wall of well-dressed muscle. A pair of strong arms came around her. She perused the black dinner jacket, black waistcoat, fine lawn shirt, and neatly tied neck cloth until she came to the dimpled chin and sharply angled face of the last man she needed to see whilst dressed in her nightdress and dressing gown.

"You are capable of a great many things, Miss Sterling." Nicholas stepped back and inclined his head. "Reading minds must be one of them. I was looking for you."

She executed a brief curtsey. "Were you looking for Miss Sterling or Elizabeth?"

"Are they not one and the same?" He didn't smile. Something very like amusement glinted in his eyes and softened the stark lines of a countenance redrawn by injury and loss.

"That depends. Are you Major St. Gabriel, my lord the Earl of Leistonbury, or just Nicholas?" All her worries about scandal and gossip and here she stood flirting with her betrothed's closest friend in her nightclothes, no less. And it was wonderful.

"Touché, Elizabeth." Her name rumbled from his lips in the dark baritone that had haunted her dreams for years. "For you I am Nicholas. Just Nicholas."

Snow spattered against the window at the end of the corridor. One floor below a door slammed. The house creaked in protest of the storm battering its walls. And Elizabeth marveled at the thrilling comfort of the sound of a man's unsteady breathing as he gazed into her eyes.

"Was there something you wanted? Nicholas?"

He swallowed and cleared his throat. "Yes. I wanted to talk to you about Estelle."

A familiar pang thrummed her heart at the memory of his invalid sister. "Come." She took his hand. "We can talk in the blue sitting room."

She led him to the sitting room adjacent to her bedchamber. She'd taken to spending an hour or two in this room every evening—reading or going over her lists and plans. The fire had been allowed to die, but it wasn't completely out. Nicholas stirred it to life and bent down awkwardly to add several logs from the wood box. Elizabeth sat in one of the high-backed armchairs on either side of the hearth. She tucked her feet beneath her, indicated the chair opposite hers, and waited for him to speak.

He worked with the fire a bit longer and finally settled into the chair. For a few moments she simply watched him. He stared into the flames as if in search of words or answers. She'd done the same many times after her brother died. Nicholas had lost his father to consumption over a year ago. Smallpox had taken his older brother and his sister a month before Waterloo. His sister, Estelle. Made an invalid by a virulent fever at age ten. Dead at nineteen. Elizabeth's dearest friend.

"You were her favorite person in the entire world, you know," she offered softly.

He turned away from the fire, his face sad and not yet at peace with fond memories. "And she was mine. They told me she did not suffer long. Mama said she just slipped away in her sleep."

"Yes. Your mother wrote me the same thing. I wish I had been there."

"I am glad you were not. I— We might have lost you as well."

Elizabeth fought the burn of tears. It wasn't fair to cry in front of him. Men weren't allowed to weep no matter how great the loss. "I miss her letters. She wrote to me at least twice a week."

"To me as well. She was an excellent correspondent even if she did scold me in every letter for not writing more often."

Elizabeth laughed. "She believed you to be perfect, but I will admit she addressed your parsimonious letter-writing skills to me on more than one occasion."

"I can imagine." He leaned forward and rested his elbows on his thighs. "Your letters and friendship meant a great deal to her, a very great deal."

"I am glad." Elizabeth drew in a breath to calm the tremor in her voice. "I loved her dearly."

"And she loved you." Nicholas reached into his jacket pocket. When he extended his hand, an exquisite gold locket and chain rested on his palm. "Estelle wanted you to have this."

"Oh." She blinked violently to no avail. She stared at Estelle's most prized possession through a watery veil. "Oh, Nicholas, I can't."

He tucked a handkerchief and the locket into her hand. "I'm afraid you must. It was her dying wish."

"Not fair, you horrible man. Not fair at all." Elizabeth hiccupped two sobs and swiped at her eyes with the handkerchief.

"Have you ever known my sister to play fair?" This time he did smile, a small one, but a smile nonetheless.

"Never." Elizabeth closed her fingers around the locket. "She cheated at whist unconscionably."

"She cheated at chess too. The little minx even cheated at snapdragon at Christmas."

Elizabeth gave a watery laugh. "She would deny your charges were she here."

"Your letters brightened her life, Elizabeth." He clasped his hands together and pinned her with a look of such torment and sweetness she nearly cried out from the turmoil it stirred inside her. "You will never know what those letters meant. Never."

If he said another word, she'd have no choice but to kiss him. And more. Which would only make a painful circumstance worse. He wanted her to marry Delacroix.

"It is fortunate we had each other to write to as her brother and my brother scarcely put pen to paper from the time they bought their commissions to the time..." Elizabeth blinked back more tears. Christmas pudding. Hoisted on her own petard.

"Sterling loved you dearly, Elizabeth." He moved to the oversized footstool in front of her chair and took her hand.

"He loved me and he even loved Mama, but not enough to stay out of the fight."

"He felt he had no choice."

"A man's logic. Papa left us with nothing, and joining the cavalry was the way Michael chose to provide for us."

"Unfortunately a man's logic and his pride tend to point him in the same direction."

"The voice of experience, *Major*?"

"More often than I care to remember."

"You were a second son. It was expected of you. Winterbourne had no reason, save his rage at this father. Dukes' heirs don't go to war." Anger fueled her words. They'd risked their lives for pride. Her free hand tightened into a fist beneath her dressing gown. "We needed my brother at home."

"He did it for you, Elizabeth, for you and your mother."

"I would have less trouble believing he did it for us if I didn't know the price of commissions in His Majesty's cavalry."

Nicholas released her hand and turned to look into the fire once more. He made her no answer.

Elizabeth suppressed a sigh. "It is over and done now. I know he didn't take the money from the estate because there was no money to take. He either gambled for it or someone gave it to him. I know he loved me, Nicholas, but I often wonder when he had that money in his hands if he gave a thought to using it at home."

"You did well with what he sent you from his pay. He said you did far better with it than he would have."

"I had little choice but to do well, did I?"

Nicholas flinched. What was she doing? He'd come to her to talk about his sister. She had not meant to lay her useless grievances at his feet. She touched his shoulder. He turned back to her and shook his head.

"The thing I regret most is I was never able to visit Estelle more than once a year." A less than graceful change of subject, but Elizabeth's grace tended to desert her when Nicholas was near. "Mama refused to permit it. She said she could not do without me." Elizabeth snorted at the ridiculousness of such a notion.

Nicholas offered a snort of his own. "I understand Delacroix has delayed her arrival here with a shopping expedition in London."

"A temporary reprieve, but a much-needed one, for me at least."

"But Delacroix has freed you from your mother. You are safe now." There was an unasked question in his voice. Elizabeth didn't understand.

"Yes, I suppose I am."

"You do not seem happy. Sterling would want you to be happy."

"You and I both know Delacroix only proposed to save me from Mama. Not even Napoleon deserves Mama."

Nicholas struggled to his feet. "You are wrong there, Elizabeth. Delacroix is very fond of you."

"Fond?" Elizabeth wanted to scream at the unromantic nature of men. It was a miracle the human race survived at all. "You are right, of course. He is fond of me. And that is more than most marriages have."

"Yes. It is." He took three steps toward the open sitting room door, but turned back to search her face almost desperately. "There is nothing wrong between you and Delacroix. Is there?"

Elizabeth unfurled herself from her chair and loosed her most brilliant, girlish laughter on him. The sort of laughter a woman practiced to assure a man all is right in her world. "Nothing a little moonlight and mistletoe wouldn't fix."

"Let us hope Delacroix doesn't recruit some poor footman to hang the moon now the mistletoe is done." He gave her a wicked wink.

"All the ladders are broken. No danger there, my lord."

He crossed the room in three strides. Somehow the locket was in his hand and then it was around her neck, pressed over her heart with the heat of his palm like a brand.

"Someone should hang the moon for you, Elizabeth. You deserve the moon. The moon, the stars, and more."

She stared at him—bubbling on the inside, frozen in place on the outside. No sound save their breathing and the music of the wind against the window panes. Then with a muttered curse he was gone.

Elizabeth's knees wobbled. She sat down, missed the chair, and landed in a heap on the sitting room floor. "Drat you, Nicholas St. Gabriel. What the devil just happened?"

Chapter Six

"HAPPY CHRISTMAS, Lord Leistonbury."

Nicholas glared at Mrs. Holly from bleary eyes and muttered what might have been an appropriate reply before he continued up the staircase to the east wing.

"You're in a cheerful mood this fine Christmas morning." Winterbourne had joined him for breakfast. A surprise in and of itself as the man seldom rose before midday. Now, as they left the dining room and climbed the stairs, he appeared determined to drive Nicholas mad before Christmas dinner.

"I sat up half the night getting foxed with two fools," Nicholas said.

"You didn't sleep well? I always sleep like the dead after getting foxed."

"No, I did not sleep well. I can do this on my own, Winterbourne."

"Bad dreams?"

"What?" It was far too early to endure the lieutenant's perambulating conversation.

"Did bad dreams keep you from sleeping?" Winterbourne asked. "You were far quicker of wit when the French were trying to kill us, you know."

Nicholas had no desire to be reminded of last night's dreams. After making a cake of himself with Elizabeth, and then getting drunk to try and forget it, his dreams had been plagued with deliciously inappropriate visions of the lady in his bed.

"My dreams are none of your affair."

"I see."

"I truly hate it when you say that."

"I know." Winterbourne had a gift for getting under his friends' skins. Very likely the reason he had so few friends.

They stopped to look up and down the corridor. Not a soul in sight. Nicholas headed for Miss Tidings's chamber.

"I'm certain the irony of all of this has not escaped you, Leistonbury, even if you are half seas over."

The footmen all had injuries. No one would notice if Winterbourne sported the black eye Nicholas very much wanted to give him. "What irony?"

They reached the door. Nicholas raised his hand to knock.

"An *enceinte* woman named Mary arrives on Christmas Eve by way of donkey accompanied by a fellow named Joseph? There is no room at the inn? Quite amusing if one thinks on it."

"Joseph?" Nicholas rapped his knuckles on the door to keep from strangling his pestiferous friend.

"That four-legged carpet she passes off as a dog is

named Joseph."

"The dog's name is Joseph?"

"Come in," a woman's voice beckoned over the soft *woofs* of the dog in question.

"You would know that if you actually conversed with the woman you intend to marry."

Nicholas elbowed Winterbourne in the ribs and pushed past him into the chamber. To his surprise, Delacroix was seated in a chair at Miss Tiding's bedside.

"Good morning, St. Gabriel." Their host sounded entirely too cheery. "Winterbourne, what are you doing about at this time of day?"

"Shame, Delacroix," Winterbourne chided. "You will have Miss Tidings think I am a person of low character." He dropped onto the blanket chest at the foot of the bed. The ridiculously large dog ambled over and set to sniffing his pockets.

"I know you are a person of low character, Lord Winterbourne," Miss Tidings replied as she made an effort to sit up against the abundance of pillows at her back. "But you are vastly entertaining in spite of your faults. And Joseph appears to like you. You neglected to tell me Michael's sister would be here."

She accused Winterbourne, but she looked squarely into Nicholas's face.

"I did not know you would be forced to come here, ma'am." Unable to move, Nicholas stood a few steps from the door. His leg ached like the devil. Miss Tidings had improved a great deal since yesterday afternoon.

No longer pale, she was wrapped in a dark blue wool dressing gown with her hair in one long braid over her shoulder. The remains of a tray of food on the dressing table and another on the bedside table indicated she had a hearty appetite. Then again, the dog had probably dispensed with half the contents himself.

"We agreed," Miss Tidings said. "Miss Sterling need not know of our little arrangement, Lord Leistonbury."

Nicholas flexed his hand against his leg. "And she will not so long as you keep to this room. I will make arrangements to move you to Leistonbury Hall as soon as the roads are safe to travel."

"She has traveled from London by mail coach and barely made it from the village in that travesty of a donkey cart," Delacroix started. "I don't think she needs to be moved again."

"What is she like?" the lady in question inquired.

"I beg your pardon?" Nicholas checked his friends' expressions. Miss Tidings had managed to catch them all off their guard.

She folded the coverlet over her pronounced belly and crossed her hands in a prim governess pose. "What is Miss Sterling like? Is she the sort of woman who would scorn me? Is she a fine lady?"

Neither Winterbourne nor Delacroix said a word. Her tone sent a little niggle of alarm across Nicholas's neck. Why had she asked such a question? Her expression was smug, almost as if she already knew the answer.

"She is the finest of ladies, but she would not scorn you." Nicholas's stomach clenched. The two women he'd wronged the most were under the same roof; and he was selfish bastard enough not to want them to know what he'd done. He had come to this house party to fulfill a promise to Captain Michael Sterling, to his friend now buried on a Belgian battlefield. He had no right to salvage his honor or his heart. To his shame, he was coward enough to try.

"It will be more comfortable for all of us if Elizabeth knows nothing of this business." Nicholas tried and failed to keep the rancor from his voice. "Perhaps, in time, you will meet her as my wife and the mother of my child and the two of you may become friends."

His friends continued to do fair imitations of mutes. When he wanted them to speak, they were quiet. When he wanted quiet, they prattled on like maiden aunts at Almack's.

"I see," Miss Tidings replied.

Nicholas ground his teeth at Winterbourne's delighted bark of laughter.

"You laugh, my lord, but I agree with his lordship. Miss Sterling may well be a kind lady, but we would not want to upset her frail sensibilities, especially in the midst of playing hostess at her first Christmas house party."

"Thank you, Miss Tidings." Nicholas inclined his head. "Your father was an excellent soldier and a fine man. He raised a fine daughter." His throat grew dry.

The slow thud of his heart made it difficult to breathe. She'd lost so much and now, for the sake of her child would agree to a loveless marriage with a scarred, crippled wreck. None of this was her fault and still he resented her. In this moment, he resented her, and Sterling, and Delacroix, and all of the necessary horrors of war and honor that kept him from the woman he needed more than his next breath. He had to leave this room.

"I'm certain we will be most comfortable together once we are married. Happy Christmas, Miss Tidings."

If she made a reply he didn't hear it. He was out the door and halfway down the corridor before Delacroix and Winterbourne caught up to him.

"Stubble it," he growled and forced his leg to lengthen his strides.

"Didn't say a word," Delacroix offered.

"Wouldn't dream of it," Winterbourne agreed.

Where was an interrupting housekeeper or a superior butler when one needed one?

"I must say that was the worst proposal of marriage I've ever heard." Apparently Winterbourne simply could not resist.

Nicholas stopped on the landing and turned on the duke's heir turned cavalry officer. "It wasn't intended as a proposal."

"Damned good thing too." Winterbourne shoved his hands in his pockets and grinned.

"Delacroix, would you mind terribly if I pushed him

down the stairs?"

"Wouldn't mind at all, Leistonbury, but if he dislodges the greenery or bleeds on the carpets, Lizzie will have our heads."

"Happy Christmas, gentlemen."

The three of them spun to face the landing and snapped to attention like recruits on review. God, she was a vision. In a gown of blue and gold velvet she stood at the bottom of the stairs smiling up at them. She had no inkling of the scheme they'd hatched. And none of them suspected the flames licking up every inch of Nicholas's body at the mere sight of her.

"Hmm," she mused, her grey eyes bright with unspoken laughter. "You three have the look of boys who have been into the Christmas pudding. What are you doing in this wing of the house?"

"Uhm."

"Err."

"Happy Christmas, Fair Lizzie." Winterbourne met her halfway down the stairs and kissed her cheek. The look he cast up at Nicholas and Delacroix said clearly *I've done my part. You two ninnies are on your own.*

"Just checking the preparations are all in place for our guests, my dear," Delacroix said, a bit too desperately.

"I thought we were guests," Nicholas muttered.

"Pestilence, not guests," Delacroix shot back.

"You didn't go into any of the rooms, did you?" She peered at each of their faces. For a moment she seemed almost frantic. Then Nicholas's gaze caught hers.

Questions, mysteries, unspoken desires—a world of things passed between them. On the most hopeful day of the year, they were all for naught.

"We didn't disturb a thing on your lists, Lizzie." Delacroix ambled down the stairs, took Elizabeth in his arms, and kissed her soundly on the mouth.

"Oh." She touched her fingers to her lips and glanced at the mistletoe overhead.

Nicholas's blood went cold. He curled his fingers into his palms tight and tighter still.

She looked up the stairs at him, stunned and more than a little wary.

"I've a surprise for you, Lizzie," Delacroix announced. "I sent for a special license. I thought we might marry on Twelfth Night."

Delacroix continued to talk as he and Winterbourne escorted her down the stairs, but Nicholas heard not a word. Elizabeth murmured responses of some sort. All the while, she peered over her shoulder at Nicholas, her lips tilted up the barest hint at the corners. He stood on the landing and watched his every Christmas wish for the rest of his life glide gracefully out of sight.

"Another tray for Miss Tidings?" Elizabeth marveled at the abundance of food traveling up and down the back stairs to her secret guest's chambers.

The startled maid stepped away from the servants' door, bumped it closed with her hip, and approached with the tray clutched in shaky hands. She bobbed a curtsey. "Yes, miss. Cook sent it up, miss." The poor girl looked about the corridor as if she expected an attack by hungry highwaymen. Perhaps she'd met Joseph.

"I thought Miss Tidings just finished her luncheon." Why was the girl so nervous?

"I don't know, miss. Cook said bring it up. Said she's fair knackered taking all these orders."

Mrs. Holly knew what she was about when she'd placed Miss Tidings in the Chinese bedchamber rather than the one Elizabeth had suggested. This room was closer to the servants' stairs, which led directly to the kitchen. Still, when Elizabeth had questioned her about the change, the housekeeper had behaved most peculiarly.

The maid edged past Elizabeth, brushed the latch up, stumbled into the chamber, and shut the door as if the devil himself were on her heels. It had to be the weather. The snow continued to fall, the rest of the guests were trapped in the village, and no one cared to venture out of doors for more than the time it took to care for the horses or bring in more firewood. Everyone had gone a little mad.

Delacroix stood first among madmen in Ivy House. For months he'd been silent as the grave about kisses, weddings, and marriage. He chose Christmas Day to deliver her first kiss, pull a special license out of his pocket, and suggest they marry in less than a fortnight. Worse, he and Winterbourne conversed at length as to the details of her wedding and no doubt fully expected her to toddle along and say her vows without the first question.

The arrival of his friends had everything to do with her betrothed's sudden urge to marry. Elizabeth had nothing to do with it at all. As much as she had resigned herself to a comfortable marriage, their high-handedness infuriated her no end.

She stared at Miss Tidings's closed door a moment more before she set off to retrieve her shawl from her own bedchamber. The mysterious Mary wasn't exactly mad, but she wasn't terribly forthcoming either. Elizabeth had spent the last hour in a pleasant visit with her, but she seemed distracted and secretive to say the least. Every polite inquiry Elizabeth put to her was met with an equally polite, but odd question.

How long have you known the master of Ivy House, Miss Sterling? How long have you been betrothed? Do you have any family, Miss Sterling? What sort of person is your mother, Miss Sterling? You lost your brother at Waterloo? What kind of man was he, Miss Sterling?

Her odd questions coupled with her restless demeanor had Elizabeth's curiosity piqued. The mystery of Miss Tidings would have to wait. Two gentlemen very dear to her had conspired to force Delacroix into marrying Elizabeth before he was ready. She wanted to know why. They wouldn't confess the theft of a single tart under dire torture. Which meant she had to stoop to those most unsavory of women's wiles—badgering and eavesdropping.

　　She marched into her bedchamber and rummaged through the clothes press for her blue paisley shawl. The pier glass caught her reflection as she draped it around her shoulders. Estelle's locket glittered against the blue of her gown. Nicholas. He'd stood on the landing while Delacroix kissed her and announced they would marry, but he'd spoken not a word. His face, however, spoke volumes—if only she knew how to read it. She wanted to think longing and anguish accounted for the hard line of his mouth and the fire in his eyes. Something of those feelings fairly shook from him when he'd placed his sister's locket around her neck. Or had she merely wished it so?

　　Elizabeth closed her hand around the locket. *What am I to do, Estelle?* The reflection of the gold links of the chain winked at her from the pier glass. Right, then. Time to take fate into her own hands. And she knew just where and how to do it.

Chapter Seven

THANKS TO THE CONTINUED snowfall, Elizabeth had elected to serve them an abbreviated Christmas dinner. She promised the full dinner when the entire compliment of guests arrived. It mattered little to her. For all the pleasure it gave her, the venison in brandy sauce, roasted beef, and pheasant might have been one of the emaciated chickens she and Mama dined on when their money ran short. The gentlemen praised each course, ate the syllabub and Brussels sprouts, and applauded when the Christmas pudding arrived alight with good French brandy. Even Aunt Merryweather managed to stay awake long enough to enjoy several dishes and a large portion of pudding before she returned to the bundle of pink knitting in her lap for a few rows before she dozed off.

At the foot of Delacroix's table, Elizabeth sat fully aware that Nicholas watched her every move. She laughed and traded jibes with them. She kissed each of them on the cheek under the mistletoe. The comfort and camaraderie of those first few hours after they'd arrived had nearly returned. Nearly. Her brother's friends—her friends—were keeping secrets. Once the meal was finished, she suggested they take their coffee in the library, ensconced Aunt Merryweather in the family parlor, and set her plan in motion.

By the time the men strolled into Ivy House's large bookroom, Elizabeth had crept from behind the hidden door onto the library's mezzanine and crouched at the rails beside a faded fainting couch to peer over and eavesdrop.

"What did she say precisely?" Winterbourne asked as he settled onto the horsehair sofa before one of the two fireplaces.

They'd obviously countermanded her order for coffee. Shepherds appeared with a bottle of Delacroix's finest French brandy. Each time they'd returned from the battlefields, Elizabeth had noticed they smiled less and drank more. Their arrogance with regards to planning her future annoyed her; their pain broke her heart.

Delacroix sat in the armchair on one side of the hearth while Nicholas took the other. Once Shepherds filled each of their glasses with brandy and left the room, Delacroix answered. "She said she did not care to marry at Twelfth Night and we should wait until summer when the weather is more suited to a wedding."

Elizabeth suppressed a laugh. The look on Delacroix's face when she'd said this was beyond price.

"I see," Winterbourne replied.

"Leistonbury, did we not promise him a good thrashing the next time he used that phrase?"

"We made a number of promises to each other, Delacroix," Nicholas snapped. He downed his brandy in one swallow and banged the glass onto a nearby chess table. "We promised Sterling one of us would marry his sister before her harridan mother delivered her to some rich old cit or someone like Winterbourne's father."

Elizabeth covered her mouth with her hands. Of all the.... She didn't know who infuriated her more—these three loobies or her poor, dead brother.

"I am betrothed to her, Leistonbury."

"Don't."

"Your brother has been dead for months. You are the Earl of Leistonbury whether you like it or not." Delacroix studied him over the rim of his glass.

"We're not talking about me. Elizabeth believes you are marrying her out of pity. She thinks you don't love her."

Did he have to make her sound so pathetic?

"I don't love her. I'm fond of her. Very."

Winterbourne threw up his hands. "No wonder she doesn't want to marry you. You've certainly made a muddle of this betrothal business."

"I had help." He pointed an accusing finger at the duke's heir lounging on the sofa.

"Me? What did I do?" Winterbourne sat up long enough to find the bottle of brandy Shepherds had left them.

"You were the one who suggested I bring up the special license and Twelfth Night this morning."

"You're taking courtship advice from the worst rake in England?" Nicholas stood and began to pace.

"If Delacroix doesn't want her perhaps I should court her," Winterbourne suggested.

"I will not have Elizabeth married to a man who changes women as often as he changes his neck cloth. Especially one who deliberately started a rumor he has the pox to keep the debutantes from chasing him."

Elizabeth's head began to throb.

"It worked. The debutantes flee from me in droves."

"How terrible for you and your delicate constitution." Delacroix rolled his eyes and held his glass out for Winterbourne to fill.

"Apparently, as desperate as they are to become a duchess one day, they aren't willing to die for it."

"What about an heir? You're the last of the line." Delacroix moved his feet as Nicholas continued to prowl a path in the Persian carpet.

"I know. My not marrying is my last shot across Father's bow. But if you don't want Elizabeth, I might be persuaded to reconsider."

Lovely. They were trading her like a horse at Tattersall's.

"I didn't say I don't want her."

"Silence!" Nicholas roared.

Something hot crawled over her skin. They sat there talking about Elizabeth as if she mattered not at all. But in Nicholas's voice—a catch, a tone made her think he might care more than he wanted anyone to know.

"Neither of you deserve her, damn you. How can you speak of her like this?"

They stared at him, imbecilic grins on both their faces.

"Hell," Delacroix drawled. "Perhaps you should marry her."

Elizabeth held her breath.

"I came to this farce of a house party to marry one woman only. Elizabeth Sterling is most definitely not that woman."

Each word slashed her heart like a knife. She rose from her hiding place and brushed out her skirts. "For which, my lord, I am eternally grateful." Three horrified faces tilted up to greet her.

Her words treacle sweet, her face alabaster rose perfection, she glided down the spiral staircase from the library mezzanine in a cloud of blue velvet and serene fury. *Nodcocks!* How long had she been listening? She shushed past Nicholas as if he didn't exist.

My God, she's magnificent.

"Lizzie." Delacroix ran two fingers under his cravat and swallowed hard. He tossed Nicholas a pleading look. The man was barking mad if he thought Nicholas had any intention of getting in the middle of this lightning storm.

"I won't be marrying you either, Christian Delacroix. As soon as this house party is over, I will return to Brighton, where only one person feels the need to list my faults." Elizabeth's frigid, even tone slid across the foot or so of carpet between her and her betrothed with the lethal quiet of a rapier. Nicholas wouldn't have been surprised to see a pool of blood at his friend's feet.

"No need to throw a man over for a few ill-chosen words now, Lizzie." Winterbourne had risen from his normal sprawl on the sofa the minute Elizabeth had appeared at the top of the stairs. When she turned her unnaturally calm gaze on him, the usually unflappable heir to a duke appeared ready to leap over the sofa to safety. A part of Nicholas wanted to laugh, but something in Elizabeth's eyes seared any bit of humor in the situation to ash.

"And no matter what ridiculous promise my brother extracted from the three of you, I wouldn't be your duchess, Lord Winterbourne, for all the jewels in Mayfair, pox or no pox."

Winterbourne mustered a weak shadow of his much-vaunted smile. "Uhm...thank you?" He glanced at Delacroix, who had reduced his cravat, appropriately enough, to a wrinkled noose around his neck. He looked at Nicholas. Elizabeth's eyes never blinked from her expectant study of the future duke's reddening face, until Delacroix spoke.

"Lizzie, darling, I..."

Mistake. Nicholas doubted Delacroix realized the best tactic when facing an angry lioness was to play dead. She whirled on the man and chased him back into his chair.

"I am not your darling, Christian Delacroix." She poked a dainty finger into the man's chest. "Once this house party is over, I will not be your anything."

"But—"

"If it were not for this damned snow, I would leave in the morning and send Mama to serve as your hostess. I would leave you to the tender mercies of the Merryweather cousins, Mrs. John Merryweather, and Mama for the rest of the Christmas holiday and for all of the holidays to come."

"Fair Lizzie, how could you be so cruel?" Winterbourne took one look at her face and backed away.

"Cruel. Cruel? I daresay you gentlemen scarcely know the meaning of the word." She stormed to the library doors and flung them open. This time when she faced them, she only had eyes for Nicholas. "It has been a most enlightening evening, Lord Leistonbury. Thank you."

Delacroix pushed out of his chair.

Winterbourne started forward.

Nicholas rounded on them both. "Do. Not. Move."

He strode out of the library in time to catch a flash of blue velvet in the direction of the front hall.

"Elizabeth, wait." He pushed himself to catch her at

the bottom of the stairs.

"Unhand me, my lord." She tried to free her arm, an arm he didn't remember grabbing. He only knew he had to stop her. He had to explain.

"You weren't meant to hear that nonsense."

Her eyes blazed, luminous with unshed tears. "Oh, but I am eternally grateful I did."

"Elizabeth, please." He gripped her shoulders and turned her to face him. In all her magnificence, he'd missed the pain now so evident in her gaze, in the very way her body shook beneath his hands.

"You can have nothing to say which I care to hear, my lord."

"Don't."

"And if you think I am going to return your sister's locket you have run mad. Estelle was a dear friend to me. Made more so because, in addition to an illness, she had to suffer a complete arse for a brother."

Tears tracked glistening streaks down her perfect face. Her plump bottom lip trembled in spite of the even white teeth clamped over it to hold it in place. He didn't know what to do to stop her weeping. So he did the only thing he wanted to do. Nicholas wrapped his arms around her and kissed her.

He kissed her and she tasted of joy and sunlight, of tea and Christmas pudding. He cradled her head in his hands and knew why he'd fought so hard to survive swords, rifles, cannons, mud, and mayhem. When he paused to press his lips to her temple and trail them down her cheek, she whispered "Nicholas," and he pulled her into his body close and closer still. Her hands slid up his arms and locked around his neck. A few gentle flicks and she opened to his softly seeking tongue. She gasped for the space of a breath and then sighed. He caressed and sipped, and all the while, his body burned for hers. His hands ran down her sides and pulled her hips into his. He wanted her to feel, to know how much he wanted her. His right hand moved to brush the side of her breast and then cup it, shape it, feel the perfection of it. She shivered and then nipped at his bottom lip. Nicholas groaned. Elizabeth opened her eyes. And suddenly the whole world turned cold. Such trust shone in those eyes. Trust he would never, ever deserve.

"Elizabeth, I—" He let her go, inch by agonizing inch, and stepped back. She touched her fingers to his lips. He took another step back. Her hand fell to her side. He shook his head. "I'm sorry. I can't. I made a promise." His throat closed. Her confusion and hurt nearly knocked him to his knees. "I can't." He walked away. His footsteps boomed like thunder on the marble floors. He didn't run for fear he'd fall, and if he fell, he'd never get up again.

Elizabeth watched Nicholas until he disappeared into the conservatory. Is this how he survived the war? Overran his enemies defenses, rendered them senseless, and then walked away? The entrance hall finally stopped spinning, and when it did, she spied Winterbourne and Delacroix peering at her from behind a garlanded banister.

"Go to him," she heard herself say.

"Lizzie, about what you heard—"

"Delacroix, please. You and Winterbourne go to him."

Winterbourne pushed Delacroix ahead of him in the direction of the conservatory. Once they were out of sight, Elizabeth walked to the front door, opened it, and stepped onto the portico. After a few minutes, she came back inside and leaned against the door, eyes closed and heart still pounding. The icy wind helped but a very little. She still burned. Everywhere he kissed, everywhere he touched, her skin simmered on the inside and on the outside glowed as if she'd fallen asleep too near the fire. What had he done to her? And why had he stopped?

The three not-so-wise gentlemen's *tête-à-tête* in the library had hurt, yes, but it had also stung her pride. She slowly circled the entrance hall, hands clasped behind her back as she remembered their conversation word for word. *Brother, dear, I miss you terribly, but if you were here, I'd black your eyes and kick your shins for holding your friends to such a ridiculous promise.* Nicholas owned much of the blame as well. He used his honor to make decisions for all of them. He deserved a kick or two of his own.

He cared for her. He wanted her. What promise

kept him from loving her?

I came to this farce of a house party to marry one woman only. Elizabeth Sterling is most definitely not that woman.

Mary Tidings was to meet a gentlemen at this house party.

"Christmas pudding," Elizabeth muttered. "Flaming Christmas pudding."

She picked up her skirts, and in a very unladylike manner, raced up two flights of stairs, past two injured footmen, a maid with a tray, and a shocked Mrs. Holly to knock once on Mary Tidings's chamber door. Elizabeth lifted the latch and burst into the room so suddenly the dog jumped from his place on the hearthrug and began to bark.

"Miss Tidings, is Nicholas St. Gabriel the father of your child?" Apparently being kissed senseless deprived one of all thought of good manners.

"Hush, Joseph. Down." Once the dog obeyed, Miss Tidings indicated the chair next to her bed. "Sit down, Miss Sterling. It is time I told you the truth."

Chapter Eight

NICHOLAS DIDN'T STOP until he stumbled out of the conservatory and stood gasping for breath under the obsidian December sky. Snow blew down on him from the barely discernible mists of the clouds that blocked even a hint of stars. He stared into the darkness and marveled at the deafening thud of his heart against his ribs. How could an organ beat and die in the same moment? Other parts of his body throbbed as well, but there was no marvel in that. Elizabeth could give the statue of Neptune frowning at him from across the way a cockstand with a single sigh or touch of her hand. Holding her in his arms was the nearest Nicholas would ever come to redemption. He'd never hold her again.

"We didn't freeze our arses enough in Spain, you have to drag us out here on the coldest Christmas night in ten years?" Delacroix stood in the open French windows and blinked against the snow. "Come inside."

"No." He didn't want company. He didn't want anything save the one thing he'd never deserve.

"Winterbourne is pleading his delicate constitution." Delacroix stepped beside him, hands shoved in his pockets against the cold. "He's stopped to admire the daffodils."

"He's a pain in the arse."

"So are you." He turned and headed back inside, leaving Nicholas no choice but to follow.

They meandered through Ivy House's considerable conservatory until they reached a grouping of old settees in the middle of a raised circular bed of daffodils in full bloom. Winterbourne shifted over, and Nicholas sat down next to him.

"You do realize, of course, she'll be 'my lording' us until Twelfth Night and we'll never know to whom she is speaking," Winterbourne groused.

"I'll know." Nicholas's friends considered him in the sort of silence they practiced when they had much to say and knew he had no desire to hear it.

"When did you acquire these?" He waved a hand at the brilliant yellow blooms all around them. Misdirection worked as a military tactic. Nicholas had no qualms about using it to stubble his two interfering friends.

"Spring after we came home from the siege at Rodrigo." Delacroix gave Winterbourne a pointed look, which the man promptly returned. In happier times, Nicholas might have laughed at their lack of subtlety. He'd walked away from laughter the day he told Elizabeth her brother was not coming home.

"Why are they blooming now?" Winterbourne reached back to run his fingers along one row of the bell-shaped flowers.

"I have a clever gardener," Delacroix replied. "I spent a great deal of time sitting here when I was home on leave."

Something small and quiet passed between the three of them. The sort of thing only men who have shared the same corner of hell understood. He trusted them with his life. He had no choice but to trust them with the one thing more precious to him than that.

"I'm leaving at first light. I need to return to Leistonbury Hall. Delacroix, you will convince Elizabeth to marry you and you will make her happy or you'll answer to me. I trust you to send Miss Tidings on when she is fit to travel. Hire a companion to travel with her, and I'll pay the cost."

"And Elizabeth? She has broken our engagement. I don't think she will change her mind."

"You will have to win her back. I suggest you forego further advice from the scourge of Almack's here."

"I'd beg your pardon," Winterbourne snapped, and much to Nicholas's amazement leapt up and began to pace. "But I'm too damned angry at you to care. Sterling is dead. There is nothing to be done that will bring him back. You love Elizabeth. You have for years. We all know it. Marry her."

"You both know why I cannot, no matter what my feelings for her. One of you will have to do it. We promised Sterling we would take care of Elizabeth and Miss Tidings. This is the best way to do so."

"Bollocks," Delacroix said. "You did nothing wrong. She doesn't know. She doesn't have to know. She doesn't want me. I proposed to get her away from her mother. I knew she'd never go through with it. Unlike Winterbourne, I have a few scruples. Marrying and bedding a friend's lady is one of them." Nicholas stared at him. "You invited me here for Christmas."

Delacroix made no answer.

Nicholas slung out an arm to stop Winterbourne's pacing. "You made damned certain I came."

"We are her friends as well as yours," he said as he pushed Nicholas's arm aside. "We want her happy. Sterling asked too little for her. You ask too much."

"Your little conspiracy changes nothing. I cannot marry Elizabeth with such a lie between us."

"Then tell her the truth and beg her forgiveness," Delacroix said.

"She'll hate me," Nicholas rasped. "How could she not?"

"You underestimate our Lizzie," Winterbourne said, his voice devoid of its usual cynical bite. "The survival of the human race depends on a woman's capacity to forgive. Always has. Always will."

Winterbourne had saved his life on countless occasions. Delacroix had as well. They did not intend to be cruel. Their honor was not in question. Their hearts were their own. They had everything. They were handsome, whole, and had no sins against Elizabeth plaguing their conscience night after night

Unbidden, her face as he put Estelle's locket around her neck came to him. Every good thing in life shone in her eyes in that moment. How different it would have been had she known the truth. He'd been shot, stabbed, and burned on battlefields all over Europe. The pain of those wounds paled in comparison to this.

He struggled to stand, every bone in his body screamed the truth. Broken, crippled, scarred, and guilty he had no right to Elizabeth Sterling. He had no right to her forgiveness.

"I ask that she marry a man who is worthy of her," he said as he walked away. "I am not that man."

Elizabeth didn't realize she'd begun to weep until two tears splashed onto the hands she clenched in her lap. She took the serviceable linen handkerchief Mary handed her and blotted her face. A heavy, trembling sigh eased through her body. When she looked up it was to find Mary wiping away tears as well.

"Mary, I am so very sorry."

"Don't be. I loved your brother and I believe he loved me."

"I am certain he did," Elizabeth assured her. "And he would have married you, if..." She fisted her hands in her lap.

"If not for Waterloo," Mary finished for her. "I followed the drum with my father for six years, loved your brother for a year, and lost them both in the space of an hour. Napoleon has much to answer for where you and I are concerned."

"He does indeed. Perhaps we should send Mama to him."

"If she is half as bad as Michael described her, I think it a fitting punishment." Mary crumpled her handkerchief and placed it on the bedside table. "But I am glad you know, Elizabeth. I am glad you will not shun me or this child."

"I am glad as well." She squeezed Mary's hand. "And I could knock those three fools' heads together for trying to keep you a secret."

Mary laughed and adjusted the pillows at her back. "You cannot imagine how difficult it has been to pretend you have not visited me every day. They obviously don't speak with each other either. The food trays have arrived nearly every hour. One of those poor maids told me each gentleman has issued orders to Cook who has been sworn to secrecy by them, you, Mrs. Holly, and that horrible butler."

"Joseph has obviously enjoyed them."

The wooly beast raised his head and *woofed* softly at Elizabeth's mention of his name.

"I wish I had been there when you dressed them down in the library."

"I think you would have enjoyed it. I know I did." She had not enjoyed all of it, but Mary did not need to know. She liked her. This steady, courageous woman would have made her brother a wonderful wife. And she would make Nicholas a dignified and capable countess. Joy and misery were so closely mixed in her heart all Elizabeth felt was cold and far away from the Christmas she'd planned.

"I would have stood up and applauded." Mary tilted her head and studied Elizabeth. "I cannot marry him now. You must know that."

Elizabeth started. Her heart set to racing so quickly she barely caught her breath. "Oh, but you must." The words worked round her mouth like day old porridge. She had to say them. Her future niece or nephew needed a father, and after all she'd suffered, Mary Tidings needed a husband.

"Just as you must marry Mr. Delacroix?"

"My situation is different. Delacroix can never love me, not the way a man should love his wife. I know that now. He sees me as quite the little sister." Elizabeth snorted and fell back in her chair.

"And you think the major, rather the earl, could ever love me?" Miss Mary Tidings had been a governess for a time before she decided to follow her father to war. If the scrutiny with which she pinned Elizabeth was any example, she had been a dashed good one.

"I have no doubt of it." Drat her shaky voice. "I think you are a fine, brave woman and he will be the most fortunate of men to have you."

"Good Lord, you are a lady, aren't you?" Mary rolled her eyes and shifted in the bed. "Delacroix and Winterbourne have crept in here to speak with me every day. Lord Leistonbury has visited exactly once, and in that one time, I was able to discern only one thing. He loves you to distraction."

"Apparently that is not enough to sway him from *doing his duty.*" The last three words Elizabeth uttered in her best imitation of the irritating, stubborn man she loved.

Mary began to giggle. Elizabeth tried her best to hold it in. Soon they were holding their sides and drying their eyes once more. Joseph left his place by the fire to make certain they were well.

"Elizabeth dear, men love us as much as they are able. So long as that love doesn't interfere with their love for the things they hold most dear."

"Such as?" She had to admit Mary had her curious.

"Their honor, their reputation, their horse."

"Well, Nicholas does have a very fine horse," Elizabeth conceded.

"They made these bargains—Michael and the major and the other two nodcocks. It doesn't mean *we* have to honor them."

Elizabeth's head had been muzzy from the moment Mary told her she'd had an affair of over a year's duration with Michael, in the middle of a war, and was carrying his child. She hadn't quite conceded to the idea Nicholas loved her, but she knew she loved him. She was also, however, quickly on the way to being furious at his confusing behavior and high-handedness.

"Why is it men believe us too stupid to make our own decisions and too delicate to encounter anything more distasteful than a summer rain?" she demanded.

"They need us to be stupid so they can think for us and they need us to be delicate so they can take care of us. Otherwise they might come to believe we don't really need them for a damned thing." Mary glanced down at her belly. "Well, save one."

"If you will not have Nicholas, what will you do?" Elizabeth knew she would do anything in her power to help Mary and her child. With her broken engagement to Delacroix and Nicholas determined not to have her, she had little to offer.

"I saw a great deal of the three of them during the campaigns, but I didn't get to know them very well. I spent most of my time tending the wounded when I wasn't with your brother. But Lord Winterbourne is criminally handsome," Mary mused, her lips pursed in a teasing smile. "I don't know why some woman hasn't snatched him up. I do fancy being a duchess one day."

"There is a rumor he has the pox. It is a complete and utter falsehood, of course. But no respectable woman will come near him, future duke or not."

"Oh dear. Who started the rumor?"

"He did. To thwart his father's matchmaking efforts."

Mary responded with a shriek of laughter. "It's brilliant in a rather frightening sort of way."

"He's brilliant in a rather frightening sort of way. I can't blame him. His father is a horror."

"Oh?"

"Winterbourne has no brothers, only five sisters. His father refused to stop until he had his spare. A few weeks after the youngest girl was born, his mother refused the duke. When he insisted, she threw herself down the stairs to her death."

"I'd have thrown him down the stairs."

"As would I."

"How old was Lord Winterbourne?"

"Seventeen. His father made his sisters' lives miserable. Sent them away to some awful school. Winterbourne joined the cavalry, hired a governess and a cottage in Suffolk, and has supported the girls there with his own money ever since."

"And the duke allows this?"

"He has no choice. If he interferes, Winterbourne has promised to shoot himself at five o' clock in the afternoon in the middle of Hyde Park."

"*Humpf!* I'd shoot the duke, rotten old bastard."

"You are quite a violent person to be a governess."

"Have you ever had your hair sewn to your pillow while you were sleeping?"

"I take your point."

"Traveling from battlefield to battlefield with my father was safer."

A sharp rap on the door startled them both. Masculine voices whispered in none too quiet argument. Mary raised one eyebrow in wordless inquiry. Oh yes, it was time the gentlemen received their comeuppance. Elizabeth nodded her assent and turned in her chair to face the door.

"Come in."

Delacroix and Winterbourne stood in the doorway, their expressions of surprise comical beyond belief.

"Good evening, gentlemen," Elizabeth purred. "Do come in. Mary and I have been expecting you."

"Expecting—"

"We—"

To their credit they executed belated bows and edged through the door with all the enthusiasm of two bachelors entering a room full of matchmaking mamas.

"How long have you two ladies been acquainted?" Winterbourne finally asked.

"Since her arrival," Elizabeth said. "Really, Delacroix, did you think the only kitchen crisis I could take care of was burnt lemon tarts?"

He and Delacroix looked at each other and shook their heads.

"Well done, ladies. Very well done," Delacroix conceded. "Is there a reason you let us think we had succeeded in ..."

"Maintaining this charade?" Elizabeth asked sweetly. "Duping me? Assuming I would be too much the proper lady to want to meet the woman my brother loved, the woman who is carrying my niece or nephew?"

"In my defense, I wanted to tell you the truth from the beginning, Lizzie." Oozing rakish sincerity, Winterbourne took a seat on the blanket chest.

"Lickspittle," Delacroix muttered.

"To what do we owe the honor of this visit, gentlemen?" Good. Mary was using her governess voice. Elizabeth put on her best politely attentive expression.

Delacroix adjusted his neck cloth. He cleared his throat. He looked everywhere save at Elizabeth and Mary.

"Oh for pity's sake," Winterbourne groaned. "Fair Elizabeth, you have to marry one of us. If you don't, Major St. Gabriel, the newly minted Earl of Leistonbury, is going to kill us or worse, never speak to us again." He beamed at them benevolently.

Delacroix threw up his hands.

Mary leaned toward Elizabeth, as best she could in her condition. "I thought you said he was charming."

"He's having a few bad days. They are all having a few bad days."

"You'll get no argument from me," Delacroix said as he none too gently smacked Winterbourne in the back of the head.

"And you'll get no betrothal from me." Elizabeth rose and straightened her skirts. "Either of you. In fact, Mary has decided she won't have any of you either. Please convey our regrets to his lordship the Earl of Leistonbury, who in spite of being no relation to either of us, insists on ordering not only our lives but yours as well. You two may be content to do his bidding, but we are not."

"Brava, Miss Sterling," Mary said softly.

"This is ridiculous," Delacroix sputtered. "You have to marry one of us."

"No." They said together.

"Good Lord, she's in anticipation of an interesting event and not even she wants us." Winterbourne was clearly enjoying himself. "My delicate constitution may never be the same."

"I chose you, Lizzie," Delacroix declared. "Major St. Gabriel, as he was at the time, chose Mary and I chose you. Winterbourne's reputation saved him."

Winterbourne groaned and covered his eyes. As well he should. They had not come up with this last hurrah on their own. Nicholas had kissed her as if his life depended on it, her first real kiss, and then he'd not walked but run away as swiftly as his injured leg allowed. Not because he didn't love her, but because he loved his benighted honor more. She'd had enough.

"Are you fond of kissing, Miss Tidings?" Elizabeth jabbed a shaky finger toward her recently rejected fiancé. "You can sacrifice a dozen footmen to the hanging of mistletoe, and this one still won't offer you more than a pat on the head."

Mary coughed in an obvious attempt to cover the slight twitch of her lips. Simple enough for her to be amused. Elizabeth's brother had done a great deal more than kiss her.

Delacroix opened his mouth a few times, only to fall into the safety of silence, thus proving wisdom could overcome a man in desperate circumstances. Occasionally.

Elizabeth turned her wrath on Winterbourne next. He, at least, gave her the satisfaction of flinching when she poked him in the arm. "This one, however, is all too willing to kiss any woman within ten miles of his lips. He'll kiss your mother, your sisters, your grandmother, your dearest friend, and your vicar's wife."

"There is more to marriage than kissing and romantic fantasies, Miss Sterling." Nicholas stood in the doorway. Even in anger, he drew her to that place where only she and he existed.

This time, he was the first to look away. She had power, something she'd never before suspected. She wanted to wield it, no matter the danger. She'd pay the cost, whatever it might be. At this point, she had little to lose.

"Yes, my lord. According to you, there is duty and blind obedience to the manipulations of those who decide to make decisions for you whether you ask them to or not."

"There is security and care. Something you both need, especially you, Miss Tidings."

"I appreciate your kind offer, my lord." Mary reached for Elizabeth's hand. "The price is simply too high—for me and for you."

"What will you do, Lizzie?" Delacroix asked softly.

"Mary will help me find a position as a governess. She has friends with whom she can stay until the baby is born. Mama may be more willing to accept a grandchild who is already here."

"Being a governess certainly worked out well for you, didn't it, Miss Tidings?" Nicholas's voice sent a cold chill down Elizabeth's spine. Mary paled and released her hand. Delacroix strode to the other side of the bed and bent to whisper in Mary's ear.

"That is unfair, St. Gabriel." Winterbourne rose from the blanket chest and gripped Nicholas's arm. "Don't do this."

"Delacroix and I are trying to make life fair for two women who have no idea how unkind it can be to women with no resources and no one to look out for them." When had he grown so hard-hearted and superior?

"Life is frequently unfair, Nicholas." Elizabeth took a step toward him. "What we are willing to do to make it fair—that is living. Settling for something less than wonderful is not living. My brother sacrificed his life to make life fair for others. Are you doing this to make life fair for us or for yourself?" She'd crossed the room and stood so close she detected the scent of his sandalwood cologne. Anguish flitted across his face so swiftly she might have imagined it.

"Your brother died because I paid for his commission."

Elizabeth's ears rang. Had he struck her? Surely not. "What did you say?" Her eyes burned. An unseen hand squeezed her throat.

"He had decided to return to Sterling Hall and work the estate. I paid for his lieutenant's commission so he could go off to war with the rest of us. And I paid for his captaincy as well. I killed Sterling, Elizabeth, as surely as if I'd cut him down myself."

Chapter Nine

THE EVENTS OF THE LAST HOUR flitted around Elizabeth's mind like snowflakes. Each time she caught and held one, it simply melted away. Nicholas's face as he betrayed her. Mary's gasp of shock and surprise. Delacroix's deathly stillness at Mary's bedside. Winterbourne dragging Nicholas into the corridor. The shouting and the noises of a fight. She recalled someone helping her to her chamber and sending for one of the maids. A kindness to be certain, for her eyes still refused to see past the blur of tears she stingily refused to shed. Nicholas's hateful confession—the harsh, merciless expression on his face, she remembered with excruciating clarity. Her ears fairly rang with his words, save when her mind's litany of *No, no, no!* blocked out everything else.

Her calves began to cramp. She looked down and saw she still sat with her legs tucked beneath her as she had after the maid braided her hair, helped her into her nightdress, and tried to put her to bed. Wincing, she unfolded her legs from beneath her and rose from the window seat. Smatterings of snow beat against the windowpanes. It had slowed considerably, which meant the roads might well be cleared tomorrow. Their guests would arrive from the inn. Delacroix's guests. She would not be mistress here. She would not be mistress anywhere. Not now.

From her place of honor amongst the delicately embroidered lavender, yellow, and green pillows on the bed, Georgiana stared at her from bottomless onyx eyes. A few weeks after that most Perfectly Dreadful Christmas, a parcel had arrived at Sterling Manor. Georgiana had been returned to her wrapped in sheets and sheets of tissue paper with a note tucked in her porcelain hand.

Hide her well. Mama would not understand. I do.

"Oh, Michael," Elizabeth sighed. She retrieved her old friend from the bed and padded into the sitting room. The maid no doubt had suspected she would not sleep. The fire had been built up, and a tray with cakes and a fresh pot of tea sat on the low table before it. Elizabeth fetched a quilt from a stand in the corner and wrapped it around her legs once she'd lowered herself into the rocking chair before the hearth.

She'd been so angry with Michael the day Mama had taken Georgiana. When he'd returned their father's last gift to her, all of the anger had burned away, for a time. She'd imagined his joining the cavalry to be a great adventure, another of his efforts to ignore his duties at home. Whilst her brother went off with his friends to play at war, Elizabeth had no choice but to run the estate, make do with what monies he sent them, and deal with Mama's constant efforts to marry her off and spend money they no longer had.

When Nicholas came to Sterling Manor to tell them Michael was dead, her guilt had been beyond belief. And Nicholas, unnaturally pale and badly wounded, had insisted on being the one to tell her. His grief had been as great as hers, and now she knew why. He'd sent Michael to his death. The money was nothing to him, everything to them, and he'd handed the guineas over for her brother's commission with no thought to the consequences.

Worse, he'd lied about it. A lie of omission, but a lie nonetheless. She forced herself to remember every moment of his pronouncement. His handsome face drawn in sharp edges, no softness to hide the carved cheeks and brow, the patrician nose, the lips she knew to be soft and demanding in the same moment, and his eyes—icy blue and bleak. He'd stood so tall and straight, an officer delivering bad news to his troops and daring them to flinch. His hands, those long, powerful hands he'd run over her body in such adoration, had clenched and unclenched at his sides until he finally closed them so tightly they'd gone white.

A sting of hurt lanced her heart. Hurt for him, who had made her think he cared for her and had proven it all a horrible prank in the space of only a few days. His face pale and tight, his hands furled to the point of injury—these things pricked at her memory. His eyes so hopeless and in such... what? Anguish? Elizabeth reached for the cup of tea she'd poured and forgotten.

No. He didn't care. He'd decided Michael must go with them, and he hadn't given her one thought. He felt no pain. He'd said it himself. He'd killed Michael. He'd said it in that cold, imperious, lifeless voice. She'd heard that voice, seen that face with the heat of a June morning rising off the cobblestone drive and the pale blue of a motionless sky behind him. He'd risen from his sickbed and made a dangerous journey to tell her his friend, her brother, was never coming home again.

"Oh, God," she murmured. "What am I to do?" She'd had little luck with the Almighty in Christmases past. One would think at this time of year, He'd listen a bit more closely. The evergreen and holly garland around the slab table across the room glistened beneath the candles burning in a pair of silver candlesticks over the manger scene she'd placed with such care. There was an answer there somewhere. Pity her heart was so mangled it couldn't make it out.

A rap or two at the door stirred her from her musings. "Come in." It really was annoying to sound like a frail heroine in a horrible novel, when one wanted nothing more than to plant the entire world a facer.

The latch clicked, and a hand crept round waving a large white handkerchief. Elizabeth fought the urge to laugh. "Come in, Lord Winterbourne."

He stepped inside, his tawny hair mussed, his jacket and waistcoat askew, and the handkerchief still clutched at half-mast. "Is it safe?"

"I daresay it is," Elizabeth said with a Drury Lane sigh. "I left my pistols in Brighton."

"Thank God for that." He sat in the armchair across from her and perused the cakes the maid had left her. "You have been provoked to violence and rumor has it you are a crack shot."

"Miss Tidings is far more violent than I and she has already threatened to shoot your father."

"Splendid. I shall have to gift her with a brace of Mantons for Christmas." He popped a little lemon cake into his mouth.

"Is she well? I mean, I fear our little Christmas pantomime unsettled her." She knew Mary was as surprised as she, yet it was Nicholas's face she saw. Nicholas standing in that doorway, alone in a room full of people.

"She sent me to look in on you. She is fine. Delacroix is with her."

And Nicholas was alone. Why did she care? He deserved it. He was not to be trusted, the great Major St. Gabriel ordering all of their lives.

Winterbourne had stopped eating, a rare occurrence, and he was studying her with the strangest expression on his face.

"You weren't the only one who needed to escape your mother, you know," he said softly. Winterbourne not eating was disconcerting. Winterbourne serious was... she didn't know what it was. She'd never seen it.

"Sterling was not as strong as you, Elizabeth. He'd been your mother's darling for so long he didn't know how to be anything else."

"He could have learned. Had he stayed at home and managed the estate, he could have put Mama in her place."

"Do you really believe that or is it what you hoped would happen?"

There was no need to answer when confronted with the truth. No matter how much it hurt.

"Serving Wellington was the making of him, Fair Lizzie. You saw him when he came home on leave. He'd changed. He had purpose."

"He paid a terrible price for it."

"It was his price to pay. He chose to pay it."

His words landed like a blow and nearly struck the air from her body. She'd lived with her brother for sixteen years and yet, perhaps she never knew him at all.

"Had he not gone to war he might never have met Mary. He might never have known love. You like her, I think. Would you have wanted him to miss the time he had with her?"

"No. Of course not." She hardly knew what to say. Everything turned over and over in her head. The manger scene caught her eye.

"Mary loved him," Winterbourne said with

uncharacteristic sincerity.

"I know. I'm glad he knew love. I see it in her eyes when she speaks of him. I hear it in her voice."

"I see it and hear it in you, Lizzie. Every time our reluctant *Lord* Leistonbury walks into a room."

"It doesn't matter now." Why was he saying these things? Her heart was broken. How could she forgive Nicholas after all he'd done?

"It's the only thing that does matter." Winterbourne left his chair and moved to the window.

Not even snow beat against it now, only darkness. What did he see?

"Love is like," he turned and looked at her, a boyish smile on his face. "Daffodils after a storm. The sky runs black ink over the blue, the thunder growls and the rain beats and beats them into the ground and you fear they will never be the same. But when the rain stops, they stand up, shake their heads, and even if they're battered and bruised, they know they will endure because that is what they do. They endure."

Somewhere in his recitation, Elizabeth stood up. The blanket fell from her legs, and Georgiana landed on it. "How did you....Where did you hear that?"

"Ask Lord Leistonbury."

"What are you talking about? I wrote that to Estelle. How did you hear it?"

He picked up Georgiana and placed her in the rocking chair. "I see the beautiful but silent Georgiana made it home."

"Georgiana? Michael sent her to me. After the house party. Tell me how you knew what I wrote?" She grabbed his arm and gave it a shake.

"Sterling didn't send Georgiana." He squeezed her hand and leaned in to kiss her cheek. "It was always you, Fair Lizzie. For Nicholas, it was you as long as any of us can remember." He walked to the door. "And if you want to know how I knew about the daffodils, ask him."

Rooted to the delicately patterned Aubusson carpet in the middle of the room, Elizabeth stared at the door he'd left open. In her head, words and thoughts and images clanged together like pots and pans tumbling from the kitchen ceiling. Her world made no sense, not a single thing in it stood still long enough to contemplate. But her heart, her battered heart stood up and shook its head. Impossible. Improbable. She might pay a terrible price for what she was about to do. But it was hers to pay. Forget the whole world. Elizabeth wanted to plant Major Nicholas St. Gabriel, the Earl of Leistonbury, a facer. And then she wanted to know exactly how he felt about her.

Elizabeth ran into the corridor. She looked right and then left. Sprawled in a chair at the end of the corridor, Winterbourne nodded toward the west wing. "Green bedchamber."

She walked calmly past him.

"Give no quarter, *General.*"

Nicholas shifted the pillows behind him and leaned

forward to rub his leg. A few of the letters he'd been reading threatened to slide off the coverlet onto the floor. He rescued them and tucked them back into the small wooden chest he'd dragged from Ciudad Rodrigo to Waterloo. Once he'd read each one for the last time, he'd leave them in the little sitting room for Elizabeth to find. He had no right to them, especially after this evening's events.

He picked up the page he'd been reading. The words blurred. He wanted to go to Elizabeth. Her revulsion and anger at his betrayal struck at him with the force and precision of a blacksmith's hammer. Every pulse of his heart brought her face to mind and shook his body to the core.

It had worked. He'd wanted to drive away whatever tender feelings she had for him and he'd done a bang-up-to-the-mark job. She was free and in time, she'd thank him. She'd make a life with Delacroix, and perhaps in time, she'd forgive him enough for Delacroix's sake to at least speak to him when they met. Ever selfish where Elizabeth was concerned, he would take it. A hello every now and then would be enough. Bollocks. He almost believed that. He stared at the unread page once more.

A light, insistent tap at the door interrupted his misery. Probably Winterbourne with a bottle of brandy and a plate of tarts. He'd had as much Christmas cheer as he wanted for this Christmas and any Christmases in the future, thank you very much.

"Happy damned Christmas, Winterbourne. Now go away." The door opened with a faint click. He set about opening another letter. "Meddlesome mother hen."

"Meddlesome? You have no idea. Mother hen? Not yet. And I'm not going away until I say what I have to say."

"Elizabeth." Nicholas stopped breathing. With her arms folded across her chest, she was a glorious figure in a sheer white nightdress and a furious expression on her face. An avenging angel in her bare feet—and she was in his bedchamber.

Wait. Elizabeth was in his bedchamber. He was lying in bed wearing nothing but a dressing gown and an instant cockstand.

His head tried to move in several directions at once. Letters, her letters to his sister, littered the coverlet. He needed to get the letters before she saw them. She needed to get out of this room. What the devil was she doing in his room?

"What are you reading?" She bent to pick one up from the floor. Which afforded him a lovely view of—

"Give me that." Nicholas leaned forward to take it from her. And promptly fell out of bed. "Damn!" Agonizing pain shot up his leg. Worse. Letters cascaded off the coverlet on top of him.

"Nicholas," she cried and knelt beside him. "Are you hurt?"

"No." He tried to cover his injured leg and keep her from retrieving any more letters. "What are you doing here? You can't be here."

She plucked one letter from his lap and then another. His body hummed with awareness. The scent of jasmine and roses drew him to the long braid hanging over her shoulder. A vision of chestnut hair draped over his pillow flashed before his eyes.

"You have no right to dictate my whereabouts, and these are my letters," she accused.

"What?" Did she have any idea how diaphanous the firelight made her nightdress? He couldn't think. She shouldn't be here. She shouldn't be speaking to him. He'd send her away. Now.

She sat down on the floor and began to collect the letters into little stacks. "These are my letters to Estelle. How did you get them?"

"She sent them to me." He hadn't meant to tell her. He hadn't meant to tell her about Sterling's commission either. He'd done it for her own good. His twisted leg began to throb. The angry red scar peeked out from his dressing gown. "You can have them back. I was going to leave them for you. Put them in that box and go." He clutched the side of the mattress and started to pull himself to his feet.

She huffed, rolled her eyes at him, gathered the letters, and put them on the bedside table.

"Idiot," she muttered as she moved behind him and shoved her hands under his arms. "Up," she grunted.

Once he was on his feet, he steadied himself and turned to face her.

"Sapskull." She hit him in the chest. "Liar." Another hit. "Arrogant." Another. "Manipulating" She shoved him and he stumbled to sit on the bed. "Overbearing." Her fist landed on his shoulder. "You made decisions for all of us and then decided how we would feel as well."

"I know, dammit!" He struggled to his feet and walked to grip the marble chimneypiece with both hands. He had to or risk throwing her on the bed and keeping her there until all the guilt and sorrow he knew was burned away in her arms. His forehead came to rest on the cool, carved marble of the mantel. "I know."

He heard her footsteps behind him. With a shush of muslin against leather, she seated herself in the fireside chair and tucked her feet beneath her. She waved a sheaf of worn pages at him.

"My letters?"

He didn't dare look at her. She was speaking to him. He'd decided in his soul she'd never speak to him again. And now he hoped.

"Estelle sent them to me." Her scent, the sound of her breathing—he was greedy for them. "She found them so beautiful and entertaining and witty, she thought I would as well."

"Did you?"

He needed to see her face. And when he did, his heart kicked into a clumsy gallop. "Those letters saved my life, Elizabeth. They saved all our lives."

Her eyes widened. She lowered her feet to the floor. Perfect, dainty toes peeked from beneath the hem of her gown. "I don't understand."

"My sister did." He lowered himself in slow stages to his knees in front of her chair. "Your letters kept us from running mad. You gave us England, Elizabeth, in little moments on every page. And you gave Estelle the world outside her sickroom. I made decisions for you, for everyone I hold dear. I told myself I was taking care of my responsibilities. You didn't talk. You simply did it. You took care of Estelle. And you took care of me. Because of those letters I lived. And because I lived so did my men."

"But not my brother," she said softly.

He bowed his head. He'd had such hope. "No. Not Sterling. I decided he would come to war with us, but I couldn't keep him safe."

Dainty fingers threaded through his hair in gentle caresses. He shivered at every stroke.

"One of the things I've always admired about you is your ability to command—a room, a group of ruffian bachelors, your temper." Her voice brushed over the top of his skin in waves of snowflakes and fiery embers.

He tilted his head to press his cheek into her palm. If the memory of her touch was all he took from this Christmas, he'd count himself the most fortunate of men.

"You've tried to control everything and everyone for so long because you don't know how to do anything else." She bent forward. Her breast brushed against his face. Her lips moved against his ear. "Life isn't safe and the mighty Major St. Gabriel can't make it safe no matter how many orders he gives."

Nicholas's eyes snapped open. His fierce *Little General* pinned him with pools of iron mists. Whatever made him think he could command this woman? Whatever made him think he could deserve her?

"You lied to me."

"I never wanted you to hate me, Elizabeth. It was selfish of me." He couldn't lie to her anymore. Not when she touched his scarred cheek and studied him like some elfish angel. "I took Sterling from you because of my own arrogance. I thought I knew what was best for him. And he died. You struggled to look after the estate and your mother, and it was all my fault."

"My brother didn't lose his life because you bought his commission. He lost his life because he decided to live it. Which makes him the braver man, my lord."

"What?" Nicholas's entire body thrummed. He'd sorted through her every expression. He'd committed each one to memory. Never had she looked at him like this.

She cupped his face in her sweet hands and touched her lips to his in the most tender of kisses. "Forgiveness is an act of bravery and hope, Nicholas. You made yourself responsible for Sterling's death and you decided how you would pay for it, but you decided for me as well. Can you forgive yourself, forgive yourself enough to love me?"

He kissed her with a hunger born of staring at a

feast forever out of reach. "I fell more in love with you with every letter you wrote," he gasped as he somehow managed to get them both on their feet. "I never thought I was good enough." He leaned his forehead against hers.

She slipped her arms around his neck and laughed. "You're an earl, for heaven's sake."

"I'm a man, Elizabeth, with flaws inside and out. You deserve better."

"I want you, Nicholas."

He nearly groaned at the sensation of her body pressed to his. "You deserve perfect. You're perfect."

"I'm perfectly ordinary and you know it. And you're perfectly dreadful. And I love you, Nicholas, flaws and all."

He didn't know what he should do. So he did what he wanted to do. He kissed her.

Elizabeth's body simmered with new sensations. Nicholas plundered her mouth with his lips. He tasted, he sipped, he tugged her bottom lip between his teeth, and when she squeaked in response, he laughed. It vibrated against her lips and rumbled over her breasts to burst into her heart like a Catherine wheel, all sparks and light. His tongue flicked along the seam of her lips. She opened to him, only a bit at first and then in a sharp gasp as his hands gripped her bottom and he pulled her snugly to his hips.

She memorized his every move and mimicked it in

kind. Every gasp she drew from him, every groan, thrilled her. She ran her hand under his dressing gown and explored every amazing sculpted line. His chest was broad and crafted of hot skin over hard muscle. She plucked at one nipple and he shuddered. For some reason she wanted to taste him. She pulled her lips from his, ran them down his neck, nipped his collarbone, and kissed a trail to the hard knot at the center of his nipple.

Suddenly she was being carried in uneven haste and deposited with great care onto his bed. Nicholas began to pull his dressing gown from his shoulders, but stopped and gazed into her eyes with such fierceness and love she forgot to breathe.

"I'm an arrogant, overbearing arse, Elizabeth. I am not the man who danced with you six years ago. I can't let you go. Not now. I'll fight anyone who tries to take you from me. I love you, but if you have any doubts—" Whatever he intended to say was lost.

His magnificent chest, scarred and marked with wounds of honor, heaved with desire. She knew it was desire. Her own body burned and panted it with every breath. She tugged the sash of his dressing gown free and pushed the heavy brocade fabric from his shoulders. Her fingers could not resist. She ran them over his arms, his chest, down his flanks. A long saber slash ran down his left thigh, across his knee to the top of his foot. He flinched when she touched the puckered line of it. When she allowed her perusal to travel back up, she barely stifled a gasp.

"Elizabeth?" he rasped.

She wrapped her fingers around him. Soft skin over stone hard muscle. Oh. My. She sat up on her knees, never letting go, and ran her lips lightly over his.

"No doubts, Nicholas," she murmured. "It's Christmas. I know exactly what I want."

"Thank God," he groaned.

Before she knew it, he had whipped her nightdress over her head and flung it across the room. Elizabeth knew she blushed from head to toe. Then she saw Nicholas's face.

"You're beautiful, Elizabeth." He caressed the underside of her breast with his knuckles. And when he bent his head to taste her there, she bit her bottom lip to keep from crying out. Nicholas pushed her onto her back. His mouth explored every inch of her body. She went from embarrassed confusion to a heavenly haze of warmth and shooting sparks of sensation everywhere he kissed, everywhere he touched, everything he licked or caressed.

She stroked his hair as he worshipped her breasts, and she could think of no other words to describe the nips and gentle suckling he applied until she had no sense of her body at all—only the things he did to her, the rising excitement he made her feel.

It felt odd when his hand moved to the spot between her legs. He stroked and soothed, all the while kissing her and whispering such wonderful things against her lips. And when he moved between her legs and pressed himself against her entrance, a primitive and heavenly instinct made her move against him.

"Elizabeth, my love," he murmured. Over and over he said her name. She dug her fingers into the sinews of his back. A little sting and they were suddenly hip to hip. His eyes locked with hers.

"Good?" he asked in a strained voice.

"Yes. Odd. But, oh. Oh my." He'd begun to move inside her, slowly at first and then a bit faster and then back to slow. And once she got over the strangeness, something else began to bloom inside her.

He grinned at her, actually grinned. He had hardly smiled at all since Waterloo. And now he was grinning and his eyes were alive as they hadn't been in such a long time. Elizabeth marveled at the power she had, at the unspeakable closeness between them. She caught the rhythm and moved with him, awkwardly at first and then they were one. His hands meshed with hers, their fingers intertwined, and every beat of his heart pulsed against her palms.

"Don't close your eyes, my love," he gasped. "Look at me. Tell me you forgive me. I will do anything. Anything."

She looked until blinding light burst inside her into every color imaginable. She flew into the summer sky of his eyes. He groaned her name and shuddered again and again. No bells rung on Christmas Day sounded as clearly and sweetly as the sound of her name on his lips.

Nicholas bowed his head onto her breasts.

"I never dreamed, Elizabeth," he whispered against her heart. "All those lonely nights on battlefields on foreign soil I hoped, but I never dreamed of this. I don't know how—"

"Hope, Nicholas." Elizabeth traced his scar as he raised his head to meet her eyes. "With all of my lists and preparations and tumbling footmen and all my anger about Michael's death, I forgot."

"Forgot what, darling?"

"Hope. Christmas is about hope and forgiveness and—"

"And love, Elizabeth. Against all odds, even when a man has no hope of deserving it, enduring love."

Chapter Ten

"ST. GABRIEL! LEISTONBURY, whoever you are, get up!"

"It is the day after Christmas, Winterbourne." Nicholas groaned over the pounding on the chamber door. "Can I kill him?"

Elizabeth ran her hand over his chest. If all their lovemaking was as wonderful and as frequent as this, they'd never get anything done. "I don't think Delacroix would care, but you might bring down the wrath of Mrs. Holly."

He leaned over the side of the bed and when he sat up, he pitched one of his Hessians at the door. "Go away, Winterbourne. Now." He pulled Elizabeth on top of him with a growl. "Precisely where were we, my lady?"

The door burst open to reveal a half-dressed Winterbourne hopping on one foot as he tried to jam the other into his boot. He stopped mid-hop when Elizabeth emitted a small screech and pulled the covers up to her chin.

"Well good morning," Winterbourne stopped hopping and gave the bed a thorough scrutiny. "I hope you proposed properly, Leistonbury. I should hate to have to call you out."

Elizabeth blushed to the roots of her hair.

"Ah. I see he did. Congratulations." Winterbourne tapped two fingers to his temple in salute. "A most successful campaign, *General.*"

"Is there a reason for your unwanted presence in my chamber?" Nicholas fished around on the floor and retrieved his dressing gown, which he handed to Elizabeth.

"We've sent for the vicar and the midwife," Winterbourne said blandly. "Delacroix is going to use the special license to marry Miss Tidings because it appears the baby is about to make an appearance."

"What?" Elizabeth wiggled into the dressing gown and leapt from the bed.

"How is he going to use the special license? Whose names are on it?" Nicholas caught the clothes Winterbourne pitched at him.

"His and Miss Tidings's. Sorry, Fair Lizzie. Apparently he actually threw you over before you jilted him. Who knew Delacroix was such a reprobate."

"I am not fooled in the least, Alexander Winterbourne." Elizabeth shoved him out of the way and started for the door.

"Your entire name," Nicholas warned his friend. "You are in trouble."

"Yes, you are." Elizabeth returned to give Winterbourne a resounding kiss on the cheek. "You and

Delacroix concocted this entire house party for us. Thank you."

"Anything for you, Countess." He cleared his throat. "Now come and help me with Delacroix. The man is a raving bedlamite, and Miss Tidings is threatening to kill someone."

Elizabeth glanced at Nicholas. The way he looked at her made her shiver and wrapped her in such comforting warmth it took her breath way. Then it struck her. "Does Delacroix love her, Alex?"

"No. Not everyone is so fortunate as you two. But he will care for her and that is a start." Winterbourne had spoken more sincere words in the past few days than she'd heard him speak in all the years she'd known him. "She'll lead him a merry chase," he said with a grin. "Might be worth staying here to watch." There was the Winterbourne he wanted the world to see.

A muffled shriek and a crash drew their attention back to the impending catastrophe in the Chinese bedroom down the way.

"Oh, for the love of Christmas pudding." Elizabeth pushed past Winterbourne and Nicholas and traveled down the corridor to the east floor landing with both gentlemen on her heels. "Oh no."

Standing at the top of the stairs, Mrs. John Merryweather resembled nothing so much as a landed fish. Her mouth gaped open and shut several times. Her three daughters huddled next to her in similar poses.

Huffing up the stairs behind them, the local vicar

waved his prayer book at Elizabeth with a congenial smile. Until he saw the way she was dressed and the two less-than-dressed gentlemen behind her.

"I understand someone is to be married this morning?" He took in the scene with wide eyes.

"Where the hell is the damned midwife?" Delacroix lurched out of the Chinese bedchamber. Inside the chamber, a distinctly feminine voice was swearing in tones sure to embarrass the most hardened cannon crew. "Hello, vicar. You're just in time. Get in here and marry us. Now."

The poor man scurried into the bedchamber in spite of the language issuing from within.

"I'll see what's keeping the midwife," Winterbourne attempted to sidle down the wall to the stairs.

"That's the one with the pox," one of the Merryweather cousins whispered behind her hand.

"I do not have the pox," Winterbourne declared.

A loud shriek followed by a thump issued from somewhere down the stairs.

"What was that?" Elizabeth started forward.

"The vicar's wife." Shepherds stepped between the Merryweather girls. "She fainted."

"I'll get her." Winterbourne strode toward Mrs. Merryweather, who immediately pulled her skirts aside and backed away.

Behind Elizabeth, Nicholas chuckled, a rusty wonderful sound.

"Winterbourne, do not go near the vicar's wife,"

Elizabeth commanded. "Shepherds, send a footman to take care of her and send another to see where the midwife is. Mrs. Merryweather, I'll have Mrs. Holly show you all to your rooms and we'll have a belated Christmas dinner at two o' clock."

"How is it Delacroix is getting married and you are not his bride, Elizabeth Sterling?" The gleam of triumph in Mrs. Merryweather's eye bespoke a scandal of Biblical proportions. "Exactly whose bed did you crawl from to be giving orders in this house?"

"You are addressing the future Countess of Leistonbury, madam. I would adjust my tone were I you."

Elizabeth did love it when Nicholas grew imperious. The look on the notorious gossip's face was a Christmas gift in and of itself.

The servants' inset door from the kitchens staircase burst open. A large grey blur raced by trailing roast beef, Christmas pudding, and table linens behind him.

"I'd rethink dinner, were I you, my dear." Nicholas said against her ear, which he also took the opportunity to nip.

The bedchamber door flew open. "For God's sake, where is the midwife?" Delacroix roared.

"Are you married?" Nicholas asked as he circled Elizabeth's waist with one strong arm and offered Delacroix his hand.

"Yes. Wish me happy." Delacroix gripped Nicholas hand in both of his and leaned in to kiss Elizabeth's cheek.

"Always," she replied.

Delacroix was smiling. There was a wild look in his eye, but he was smiling. "And Winterbourne informed me this morning you two have finally come to your senses."

"How did he...?" Elizabeth glanced up at Nicholas who had wrapped both his arms around her.

"Do you really want to know?" he asked.

Aunt Merryweather toddled out of the sitting room trailing her knitting behind her and looked around the corridor. Shepherds was chasing the dog in an attempt to rescue the tablecloth. Mrs. Holly stood in the servants' door and wailed about the ruined dinner. The vicar was attempting to get past the loudly complaining Merryweather cousins to rescue his wife.

Delacroix's aunt made her way into the Chinese bedchamber and within minutes the sound of a baby's cry rendered the entire chaotic scene silent. No one moved. Even Joseph the dog stopped and listened.

Aunt Merryweather appeared in the doorway. "Delacroix," she handed him a squalling bundle wrapped in a beautifully knitted pink baby blanket. "You have a daughter. See to her." She ambled toward the door to the kitchen. "Is there any breakfast?"

"This is without a doubt the most Perfectly Dreadful Christmas I have ever seen," Mrs. John Merryweather declared.

Winterbourne started to laugh. Delacroix, cradling

the crying baby against his chest, leaned against the wall and guffawed. Elizabeth gazed at each of them, her heart fit to burst with all these men had given her. She missed her brother terribly, but he'd sent these wonderful, wounded, slightly inept angels to watch over her. Her eyes pricked with tears. Nicholas's body shook with laughter, and for Elizabeth, wrapped in his arms, it was the most wonderful feeling in the world. "I love you," he whispered against her temple.

"I love you too, Nicholas, so very much."

A Perfectly Dreadful Christmas indeed—filled with love, laughter, tears, chaos, promises, and the birth of a child—all of the things that endure.

ABOUT LOUISA

Louisa Cornell read her first historical romance novel, Jane Austen's *Pride and Prejudice*, at the age of nine. This inspired her to spend the next three years of her young life writing the most horrible historical romance novel ever written. Fortunately it has yet to see the light of day. As Louisa spent those three years living in a little English village in Suffolk (thanks to her father's Air Force career). it is no surprise she developed a lifelong love of all things British, especially British history and Regency-set romance novels. (And Earl Grey tea!)

During those same three years, Louisa's vocal talent was discovered. Her study of music began at the London College of Music and continued once she returned to the States. After four music degrees and a year of study at the Mozarteum in Salzburg, Austria, Louisa was fortunate enough to embark on a singing career in opera houses in Germany, Austria, and most of Eastern Europe.

Now retired from an active career in opera, Louisa has returned to her first love—writing Regency-set historical romance. She has completed four books to date and *A PERFECTLY DREADFUL CHRISTMAS* is her publication debut.

Two time Golden Heart finalist, three time Daphne

du Maurier winner, and three time Royal Ascot winner, Louisa is a member of RWA, SMRWA, and the Beau Monde Chapter of RWA. She lives in LA (Lower Alabama) with a Chihuahua so grouchy he has been banned from six veterinary clinics, several perfectly amiable small dogs, and a cat who terminates vermin with extreme prejudice.

You can learn more about Louisa and her future publication plans at: http://www.louisacornell.com and https://www.facebook.com/RegencyWriterLouisaCornell

CPSIA information can be obtained
at www.ICGtesting.com
Printed in the USA
LVOW04s1310061215

465619LV00026B/3442/P